I0719901

IRON SCARS

IRON SCARS

A Novel of the Spartan Empire

HAMILTON BAKER

This is a work of fiction. Although certain historical elements are utilized, the characters, events, and organizations depicted in this novel are products of the author's imagination or are used fictitiously. Any similarities between persons living or dead are purely coincidental.

IRON SCARS

For inquiries, visit the author's website at https://authorhamiltonbaker.com

Cover Illustration by Lorenzo Vasek
Cover Design by Avery Greaves

ISBN 978-1-73896-431-4 (hardcover)
ISBN 978-1-73896-430-7 (paperback)
ISBN 978-1-73896-432-1 (ebook)

1   2   3   4   5   6   7   8   9   10

For Anabelle.
Without her, this novel wouldn't exist.
Love you always, pup.

Contents

Acknowledgements

I would like to thank my advance readers, Lorrie Mann and Richard Scott. Your encouragement kept me going, and your insights helped immensely. Without a doubt, you both helped me see this through to the end.

I would also like to thank everyone in the author groups I've had the privilege of leading over the past six years. I'm so very grateful for your support, whether it came in the form of advice, tips and tricks, sharing your knowledge and experiences, or words of encouragement. Thank you all so much for everything.

Lastly, I would like to thank my amazing wife, Avery. Without your wise words and incredibly helpful feedback, I never could have completed this book. Thank you for being my editor and designer. Thank you for your brilliant ideas. And, most importantly, thank you for your patience and for standing with me on this journey.

DANUBE RIVER
AQUINCUM
THE FOREVER FOREST
ILLYRICUM
SEGESTICA
SARMIZEGETUSA
DACIA
CHERSONESUS
SALONA
TYLIS
THRACE
ROMAN REPUBLIC
BYLAZORA
MAKEDONIA
BYZANTIUM
THESSALONIKI
CAPPADOCIA
GREECE
CILICIA
CORINTH
ATHENS
SPARTA
RHODES
CYPRUS
PHO
JERUSALEM
LEONIDA
EGYPT
NILE RIVER
THEBES

THE SPARTAN EMPIRE
ARMENIA
ARTAXATA
MESOPOTAMIA
EUPHRATES RIVER
TIGRIS RIVER
ICIA
CTESIPHON
SUSA
PERSIA

YAGAR LANDS
FROST OCEAN CLAN
THE NORTH LANDS
TWIN LAK
DARK STON
OCEAN LAKE CLAN
WESTERN WOODLANDS CLAN
WESTERN WATERFALLS CLAN
CLANLESS
THE FOREVER FOREST

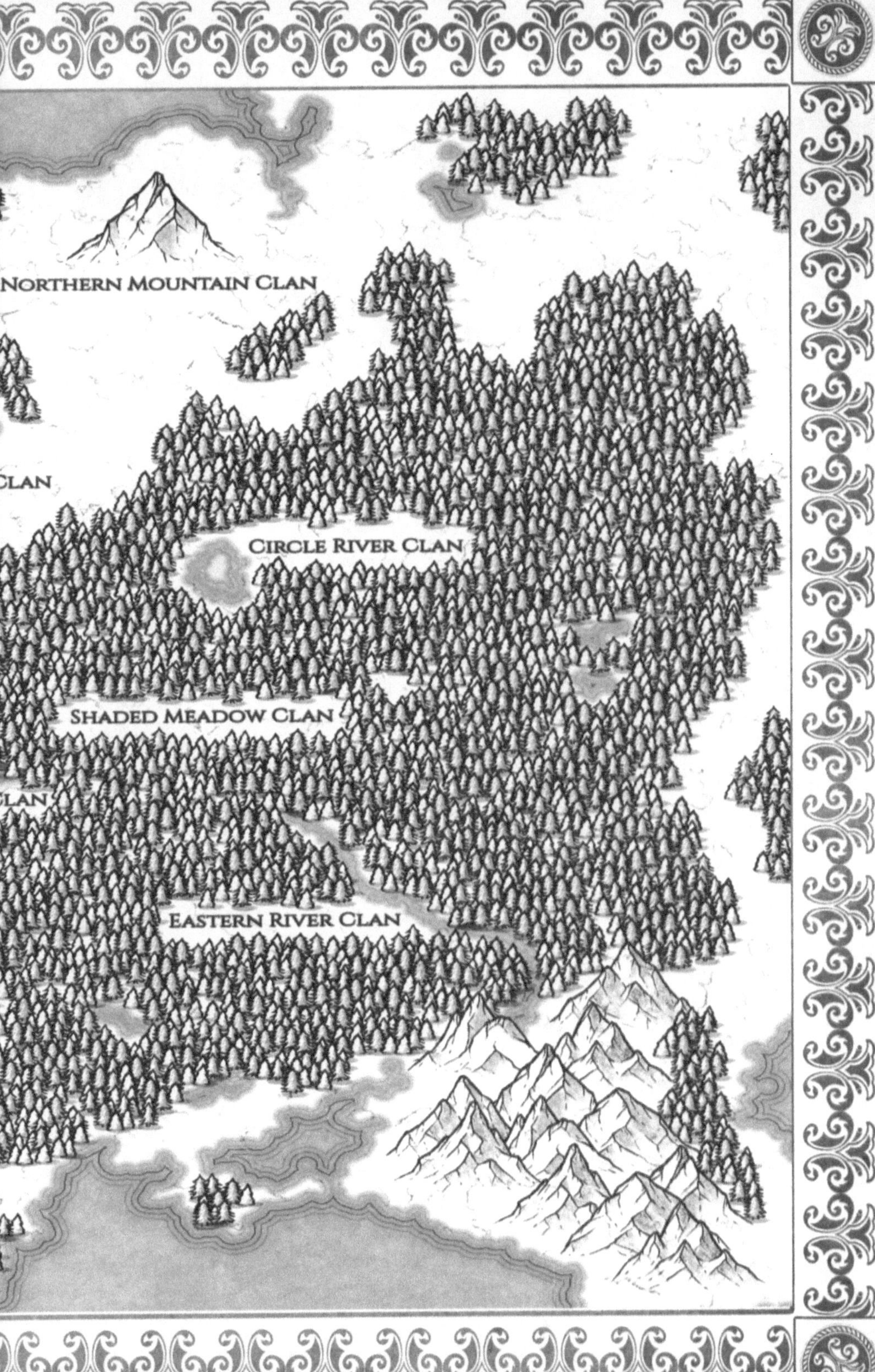

Northern Mountain Clan
Circle River Clan
Shaded Meadow Clan
Eastern River Clan
Clan
Clan

DRAMATIS PERSONAE

YAGAR

WESTERN WOODLANDS CLAN

Jarka	<u>jar</u>-kah	
Corthak	<u>core</u>-thack	Father of Jarka
Enoth	<u>ee</u>-noth	Mother of Jarka
Jazith	<u>jaa</u>-zith	Sister of Jarka
Warthux	<u>war</u>-thucks	Second Superior
Vawk	vawk	Son of Warthux
Traz	traz	Son of Warthux
Hirk	hurk	Friend of Warthux
Zonyx	<u>zon</u>-icks	Second Junior Superior
Kazog	<u>kaa</u>-zawg	Warrior/hunter
Mackurth	<u>maa</u>-kurth	Warrior/hunter
Essyx	<u>ess</u>-icks	One of the Superiors
Pix	picks	An adolescent female

DARK STONE CLAN

Alarix	<u>al</u>-ah-ricks	Warlord

NORTHERN MOUNTAIN CLAN

Tavyka	tah-<u>vike</u>-ah	Warlord
Jynx	jinx	Fourth Superior

WESTERN WATERFALLS CLAN

Bex	becks	Warlord

SHADED MEADOW CLAN

Pythax	<u>pie</u>-thacks	Warlord

CLANLESS / OTHER

Relyk	<u>rell</u>-ick	Clanless male
Imzen	<u>imm</u>-zen	Clanless Elder
Rox	rocks	Clanless female
Sola	<u>so</u>-lah	A yagar of Sparta
Kika	<u>kee</u>-kuh	Elder
Dynith	<u>die</u>-nith	A prisoner
Yathox	<u>yeah</u>-thocks	Warrior
Loriz	<u>lore</u>-iz	Elder
Anith	<u>ann</u>-ith	Warrior
Chalrog	<u>chal</u>-rog	Historical figure
Selka	<u>sell</u>-kah	Historical figure
Drofick	<u>dro</u>-fick	Warrior
Syvarx	<u>sigh</u>-varks	Warrior
Okanix	<u>oh</u>-kuh-nicks	Historical figure
Tarkoz	<u>tar</u>-kaws	Historical figure

HUMAN

SPARTAN EMPIRE

Kaletor	<u>kal</u>-ih-tore	
Vaseus	vuh-<u>say</u>-us	Kaletor's friend
Ockos	<u>ah</u>-kohss	Emperor of Sparta
Xanthos	<u>zan</u>-thoss	Father of Kaletor
Megara	meh-<u>gar</u>-ah	Mother of Kaletor
Hullis	<u>hull</u>-iss	Kaletor's friend
Belisar	<u>bell</u>-ih-sar	General/aristocrat
Doros	<u>dore</u>-ose	A famous hero
Ackadus	<u>ack</u>-uh-dus	Son of Ockos
Talos	<u>taa</u>-loss	Kaletor's slave
Zagris	<u>zag</u>-ris	A captain in the army
Heliodorus	heel-ee-o-<u>dore</u>-us	A captain in the army

REBELLION

Dacio	<u>day</u>-see-oh	Messenger
Masos	<u>maa</u>-sauce	War leader
Orzon	<u>or</u>-zawn	Soldier
Lagedin	<u>lag</u>-uh-din	Farmer / rebel
Thedin	<u>thay</u>-din	Farmer / rebel

LYCURGAN / OTHER

Antoninus	an-toh-<u>nine</u>-us	Farmer's son
Veera	<u>veer</u>-ah	Farmer's wife
Mammot	<u>mam</u>-utt	Farmer

Genrius	<u>gen</u>-ree-us	An old man
Isadoss	<u>ice</u>-ah-doss	A traveller
Rhea	<u>ray</u>-ah	A traveller
Charis	<u>char</u>-iss	Middle-class Spartan
Salagus	<u>sal</u>-ah-gus	Lycurgan

Glossary of Terms

HUMAN

Central Forum: the large, open area in the heart of Sparta

Elite: an elite soldier who is selected by the Spartan Emperor to form his personal guard

Hellespont: a narrow strait separating Europe from Asia near Byzantium

Hoplite: a heavily armed foot soldier primarily equipped with a large, circular shield and six-foot spear

Kohort: a smaller military unit within a Phalanx comprised of 110 foot soldiers

Lycurgan: a member of the Cult of Lycurgus

Peloponnese: a region comprising much of southern Greece

phalanx: a rectangular formation consisting of heavily armed foot soldiers that overlap their shields to create a shield wall

Phalanx: a military unit comprised of 4,400 foot soldiers

Spartiate: an elite soldier who is part of the Spartan aristocracy, some of whom form the personal guard of the army's Commander

Southern Laconia: a major road running north–south through the Peloponnese

YAGAR

Elder: honorific title given to all yagars over the age of 55

Home Village: the name of the largest, central village in a yagar Clan

Junior Superior: one of the Nine best adolescent warriors in a yagar Clan

Small Village: the name of any village in a yagar Clan that isn't Home Village

Superior: one of the Nine best warriors in a yagar Clan

Warrior Code: a set of norms, rules, and laws that govern life in yagar society

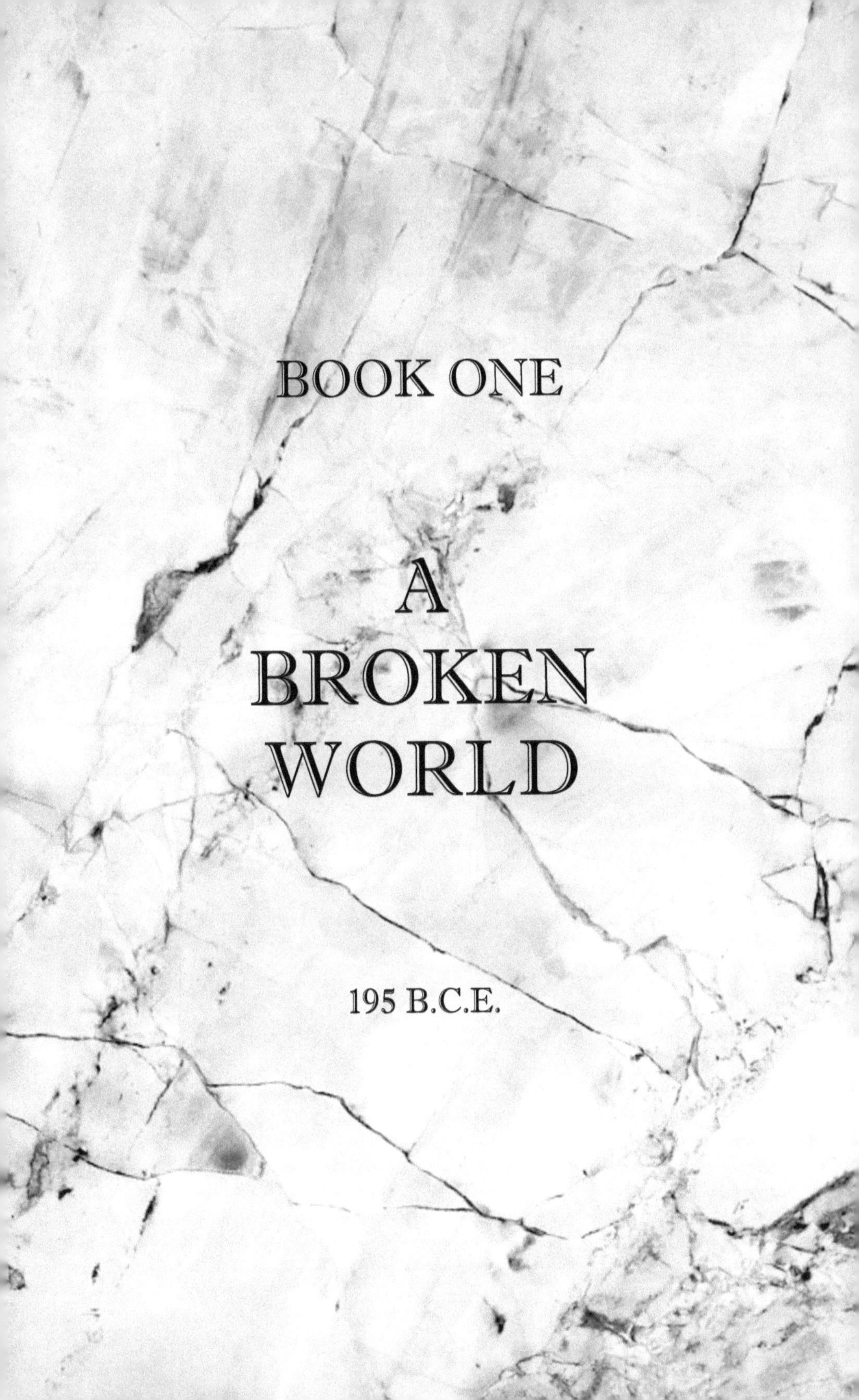
BOOK ONE

A
BROKEN
WORLD

195 B.C.E.

ONE

Every male born into the aristocracy was expected to join the army. Military service wasn't a choice for them; it was their duty.

Thrasilaus of Thebes

Spartan justice arrived as a cold, iron kiss, and no one in the Empire could escape it.

The executioner stepped forward, the axe held firm in his scarred hands. He stopped before the condemned man and raised it high. When he swung, wild cheers erupted from the crowd.

Kaletor, however, did not cheer. He looked down at the platform, his gaze steady on both executioner and criminal. He didn't feel much of anything, so it was easy to keep his gaze there.

When the noise died off, Kaletor looked left. Vaseus was sitting beside him, her fierce green eyes fixated on the crowd below. Her intensity reminded him that this was the first execution she had seen.

The impulse came to offer her words of comfort. But even as this crossed his mind, he knew that to utter such words would be a mistake. His father Xanthos, after all, would hear them.

"So dies every enemy of the Empire."

Kaletor glanced over, but his father's statement was directed at a nearby stranger. He allowed his gaze to linger, recalling the many times he had been told how much he resembled his father. They both had the same short, dark hair, the same sharp jawline, the same grey eyes.

It didn't take long before the crowd was getting restless. A few men called for the next fanatic to be dragged up to the chopping block. Others joined in, and their collective voices filled the packed square. From their position on the balcony above the masses, Kaletor took it all in.

"How many more are there?"

He looked back to Vaseus. She was staring at him intently, but he couldn't tell if it was excitement or fear in her eyes.

"Six," he told her.

"What did they do?"

"Conspired against the Empire," Xanthos said, his voice a commanding, deep boom. "Isn't that right, boy?"

Kaletor turned away to face forward once again. "Yes, sir."

But Vaseus wasn't satisfied. "What does that mean, conspired? What exactly did they do to deserve such an awful death?"

Kaletor glanced over to see his father's eyes darken as he glowered at Vaseus.

"Many things. Many dishonourable things. They may call themselves Lycurgans, but they do not deserve such a noble name. They are a cult of fanatics and dangerous criminals. That's all you need to know."

This final statement, Kaletor knew, meant the discussion was over.

But Vaseus still wasn't satisfied. Seeing that she was about to say more, he jabbed an elbow into her side.

When their eyes met, her face was screwed up in a snarl. "What are you—"

An eruption of cheers from the crowd cut her off.

Glad for the interruption, Kaletor saw that another Lycurgan was being forced onto the platform. He spared the bound, filth-stained man only a brief glance.

With the crowd still in full throat, he leaned close to Vaseus and said, "I'm sorry, but I had to. My father would have been furious if you had questioned him again."

Her small, round face scrunched up. "It's not your job to protect me. I'm a young Spartan woman, not some useless Athenian doll. I can take care of myself."

The intensity of the crowd's noise slackened, so he moved closer, his arm nestling against hers. "I know you can, but I like protecting you. It makes me feel like a real hero. Plus, I don't want you to cry."

"Please. I'm fourteen now, Kal. I haven't cried in years."

Unable to think of a response, he looked back to the platform.

The Lycurgan's entire body was shaking as the guards forced him to his knees. He collapsed and tried to squirm away, but the guards held the wretch in place. Despite his crying and flailing about, they draped him over the thick wooden block and kicked him in the ribs. He squealed and stopped trying to get away.

The guards held on to his arms and shoulders, and the executioner came forward with his massive axe in hand. The howls of the crowd became frenzied.

The words came to Kaletor then, and he turned back to Vaseus. "You might be fourteen, but I'm still going to protect you."

She too had been watching what was happening on the platform. Now she looked at him, her eyes wide. She gave a small nod but said nothing. He moved his hand to settle on top of hers.

The Lycurgan screamed then, a desperate cry that ended abruptly.

A roar punched out from the crowd, so loud it made Vaseus jump. The desire to hug her close swelled in Kaletor's chest.

But at the very moment he decided to act on the urge, a thought cropped up in his mind.

Father will see. I can't. Not here.

It was enough to hold him back.

Vaseus crossed her arms and faced forward again, her torso shaking. Everything inside him screamed, demanding that he do something. Instead, he did nothing, and his gut twisted into painful knots.

They watched in silence as the third man was executed. Then the fourth.

It was at this point, as the latest body was being taken away, that Xanthos said, "Do you enjoy watching men die?"

Still reeling from his failure to comfort Vaseus, Kaletor was slow to react. He pretended to be focused on something in the crowd until he gave his answer. "I enjoy seeing enemies of the Empire fall."

"That doesn't answer my question."

Hearing the hard edge in those words, Kaletor turned to his father and adopted a mask of neutrality. "My apologies, sir. No, I do not enjoy watching men die."

Xanthos loomed over him. "Why not? Are you a coward?"

Kaletor swallowed and tried not to shrink away. "Because death is only truly enjoyable when delivered by my hand."

Xanthos snorted. "Bold words for a child. Do you believe these men deserve to die?" As he finished, his eyes lifted and settled on Vaseus.

"Of course," Kaletor blurted, hoping to regain his attention.

It didn't work. Calculating focus still fixed on Vaseus, Xanthos said, "Don't lie to me, boy."

"I'm not lying. I never lie."

"You'd better not."

Slowly, Xanthos's gaze drifted back down to him. "Anyone who defies the Empire deserves to die. We Spartans, we *true* Spartans, are stronger than all other men. That is why those who oppose us always fail. Only those loyal to the Empire survive. Do you understand?"

"Yes, sir."

Xanthos fixed him with his unwavering glare. "Tell me, boy. What's the greatest city in the world?"

Kaletor straightened his back. "Sparta."

"Who do we fight for?"

"The emperor."

"What do we fight for?"

"The glory of Sparta."

"That's right," Xanthos said as he turned away. "Don't ever forget."

The test passed, Kaletor released a long, low exhale.

Suddenly, the chattering of the crowd died down. Seeing that everyone's attention had shifted left, he looked that way.

There, on the balcony that bounded the square on three sides, Emperor Ockos had appeared. He wore a blood-red tunic, the collar and short sleeves trimmed with gold. His head of short grey hair was ringed by a diadem of pure ivory. In places around the small, simple band, the ivory rose into the shape of delicate olive leaves, sporadic and unevenly spaced.

He raised a burly arm, palm facing the crowd. Nothing was said.

When he let it back down, the total silence was shattered as everyone boomed, "The glory of Sparta."

Ockos nodded in response and sat down. With his entrance thus acknowledged, conversations resumed, and everyone's attention fell away. Everyone's, that is, except Kaletor's. Something had caught his eye, something he had only ever heard about.

Standing behind the emperor, bound in chains and guarded closely by five of the Emperor's Elites, was a yagar. Kaletor stared, squinting hard to make out the details of its upper body, which was all he could see from his vantage point. Instead of skin, it had fur that was deep gold and covered with black spots. Its neck was thick and sloped forward.

Most striking of all, though, were its eyes. Those yellow orbs were fierce, fiercer than any eyes Kaletor had ever seen. Was it because the pupils were thin, vertical slits? Even from a distance, looking into them was almost frightening.

"What are you looking at?"

Kaletor blinked, licking his lips as he turned to Vaseus. "Don't you see it?"

"See what?"

"The yagar."

She whirled around, head jerking this way and that. "Where? I don't see it. Where is it?"

"Behind the emperor."

He knew the moment she saw it, for at that moment, she gasped.

"It's huge," she breathed. "Look how much bigger it is than the guards.

How much taller do you think it is?"

"I'm not sure," Kaletor said, careful to keep his volume lower than hers. "At least two feet."

"What's that wrapped around its shoulder?"

He hadn't noticed it before, but there was something small and white looped around its left shoulder. He squinted at it. "I think it's a band of bone. Or maybe teeth."

Vaseus looked back at him and frowned. "Why would it wear that?"

"I don't know," he said with a shrug.

"I bet your father knows. Ask him."

"No."

"Why not?"

"You know why not."

She blinked and tilted her head, her straight blonde hair dangling towards her shoulder. "Are you afraid?"

Kaletor shook his head.

"Then ask him."

"It's not my place."

"What a good little boy you are, Kal."

She gave him a smirk before looking over his head and saying, "Captain, I have a question."

Xanthos, who had been looking at the crowd in silence, turned and growled, "What question, girl?"

If she felt intimidated, she hid it well. "What's wrapped around the yagar's shoulder? What's it for?"

His glare lingered on her before he turned and looked towards the emperor's position.

As the seconds dragged, Kaletor could feel the tension crackle off his father. He was very still, and a vein throbbed along one side of his neck.

When at last he spoke, his tone was dangerously calm. "Curiosity about yagars is not something you need, girl. The only question you should be asking is why is it in chains."

"Very well," Vaseus said, apparently unaware of the tightrope she walked. "Why is it in chains?"

Kaletor could hardly believe her. How far was she going to go? Could she not see the simmering rage in his father that was moments from bursting out?

He shot her a quick look, trying to convey a warning. She ignored him.

Xanthos answered, venom dripping off each word. "It's chained because it's a mindless savage, just like every other yagar. They live in the wild like animals, always fighting and killing each other when they're not killing humans. They have no laws, no rights, no government, no leaders, and no love for anyone or anything. It's even said that they kill their own children when hunger gnaws their bellies. There is nothing to admire in them, girl. Nothing."

As he finished he looked over, and Kaletor could feel his father's rage like a wave of heat. The darkness in that glare could have silenced the great king Leonidas himself.

And yet, impossibly, Vaseus was undaunted. "I think it's pretty."

"Did you not hear what I just said?" Xanthos spat, chin jutting forth. "They're bloodthirsty savages that kill and kill and kill. That's all they know. They deserve to be wiped from the face of the earth."

It was incredible to Kaletor that his father had not shouted his loudest.

The silence that followed felt endless. The air between them all was harsh and stiff. Surely, he thought as he stared down at the crowd, Vaseus would say no more.

Slowly the seconds passed, and he relaxed. Down below, the fifth Lycurgan had been executed, and the body was being removed from the platform.

It was then, with his attention split, that Vaseus spoke again. "If they're so terrible, why did the emperor bring one with him?"

Kaletor growled a wordless snarl at her, but again she would not meet his eye. He shook his head and faced forward, not daring to look his father's way.

Several seconds passed before Xanthos replied. "The females amuse him. He taunts and teases them, and though I've never seen it, possibly tortures them. I hope he does. It's what they deserve.

"Sometimes he makes them fight each other," he went on, grim satisfaction in his voice. "If they displease him, they fight to the death. Other times he sets one loose in the arena to watch my Elites hunt it down. They are his playthings, his slaves to do with whatever he wants."

"That's horrible," Vaseus said. "How can he be so cruel? They are living—"

"Enough," Xanthos growled, leaning over Kaletor to glare down at her. "They deserve everything he gives them. Do not defend those savages, and do not speak ill of our emperor again. Understood, girl?"

"My name is Vaseus—"

"*Understood?*"

The half-shouted word finally did it. She gave a sharp nod, then rose and walked away.

Kaletor opened his mouth to call after her, but his father's presence stifled the words. Clenching his teeth, he watched her go until she disappeared from view.

"Women are foolish," Xanthos growled. "Remember that, boy."

His reply came automatically. "Yes, sir."

Silence fell between them, and Kaletor looked back to the platform. The last Lycurgan was babbling as the guards forced his neck over the block.

As he watched, there was a bad taste in his mouth. Usually, he considered everything his father said to be true and beyond any challenge. But were yagars really just savages? Did they really all deserve to die?

Something told him that Vaseus was right. Surely a being so powerful and elegant was more than just a mindless killer.

But then why does Father hate them so much?

It was a question he had no answer for.

Down below, the axe fell one last time.

TWO

When our ancestors first came to the Forever Forest, they were few in number. Legend says that they came from the south, from a great distance, and the journey was hard. Many perished at the hands of humans. It was perhaps our first lesson that humans are not peaceful, just, or tolerant.

The Spoken Tales

Jarka crouched and placed a hand on the forest floor, his extended claws brushing through the grass. In his other hand, he held his spear tipped with sharpened stone. Old, gnarled trees towered high above him, their wide leaves filtering the sunlight spilling through the canopy.

Jarka kept his focus straight ahead, peering through the tangled brush. He sniffed and knew his prey was close. Slowly, he scanned the forest, his body still, his muscles taut.

It was some time before he saw it—a lone deer, a female, moving gracefully between the trees. He stayed still as he watched and waited. She continued on her way, crossing from the left. One of her ears twitched, flashing the white spot against black. She mustn't have heard anything, because she did not stop.

Jarka waited for her to step into a small clearing, still motionless in his crouch. His breath quickened in anticipation. Long seconds passed at a crawl.

Finally, slowly, the deer stepped into the clearing.

In fluid silence, he rose, cocked his arm back, and threw. Without looking, the deer bolted, and his spear sailed wide of her flank.

"Impossible," he hollered, shaking his head as he turned around. "How did she know? How? I didn't make a sound."

Corthak rose from behind a tangled bush of red cherries. The dark antlers encasing his chest, shoulders, and neck rattled softly. "She sensed you."

Jarka growled even as a smile split his lips. "But how? I must have been too quiet. Maybe I was too still."

Corthak smiled back. "That's not why you missed."

"I didn't miss. She moved!"

"You missed because you were not calm. All living beings can feel tension. They can sense it."

"Even humans?"

The smile faded from Corthak's lips, and his eyes became stern. "We are not talking about them, Jarka. We are talking about the hunt. You must become one with the forest and one within yourself. Only then will you be a true hunter."

Jarka tilted his head, the tips of his whiskers grazing the fur of his shoulder. "So tell me how to become one within myself. Once I know, I'll do it."

"It's not something that can be taught. You must experience it yourself."

"Oh, come on, Father. You can tell me. Or is this another one of your tests?"

Corthak shook his head, but his eyes betrayed amusement. "Retrieve your spear. It's time to spar."

Jarka let loose a laugh as he bounded away, spotting his spear buried in the trunk of a tree. Grinning wide, he took hold of it, tugged it free, and hurried back. As he ran, he saw that Corthak was gone.

"Father?" he called, looking all around. No answer, and nothing but the green and brown of leaf and wood. He continued scanning his surroundings, rotating in place, alert and poised, sniffing the air and willing his ears to catch any sound.

A crunch of twigs at his back. He spun, spear level. He only caught a blur of blackened yellow before the kick took him in the chest. He flew back and hit the ground, allowing his momentum to take him through a backward roll all the way up to his feet.

Corthak closed with impossible speed, jabbing his spear high as he arrived. Growling against the fire in his chest, Jarka sidestepped and blocked in one motion. Their spears cracked off each other. Corthak had the step and so attacked again, a sweeping swing aimed for the neck. Jarka had to duck and slide away. The follow-up jab was at his gut. He saw a chance and gambled.

He stepped in, parried the jab aside, then swung out a low kick. Corthak didn't react, somehow knowing the kick would pass harmlessly through the space below his knee and above his foot.

The miss threw Jarka off balance. He could do nothing to stop his father's spear as it came down to slam onto his shoulder.

He snarled as he backpedalled. Corthak came on, not allowing any chance for recovery. He lanced two quick attacks high. Jarka ducked under the first and deflected the second. Another combo followed. Two left swings, a straight jab, then an overhead smash. Jarka survived it with parries and by giving more ground. He wasn't sure how, for his father's speed and overpowering size were too much. There was no time to think, only react.

Corthak came on harder, unrelenting, striking again and again. Jarka could only hang on, constantly blocking and moving. He parried another elaborate combo, then another.

Corthak went low, spear jutting at the thigh. Jarka leapt back and clear, but as his feet came down, his heel caught on a root. He went straight down, crashing hard to his back. He made to roll away, but Corthak's spear pressed against his throat before he could.

"Your surroundings are as important as your opponent," Corthak said. "You must remain aware of what's around you and where your body is."

In one fluid motion, he reversed his spear to offer the handle. Jarka took it and pulled himself up.

"Yes, Father," he said, and though he burned to add *'but such a victory is without honour,'* he managed not to. He knew better than to break the Warrior Code, which forbade the defeated to speak against the victor.

"There were four openings I left that you could have exploited," Corthak went on, looking down at him. "Did you see them?"

Jarka craned his head back, bones cracking along the left side of his neck. "Of course."

"Then why didn't you strike?"

"I didn't feel like it."

Corthak huffed a heavy breath. "How many times do I have to tell you that combat is not a joke?"

Jarka shrugged. "Another, it would seem."

"Yes. It would seem."

Corthak set the butt of his spear on the ground and fixed Jarka with an intent look. "Every aspect of your life, of every yagar's life, is governed by the Warrior Code, by combat and the Challenge. Only the strongest are permitted to lead. Through honour and skill, you can become the best. This is no laughing matter—"

"But I already am the best," Jarka burst in, unable to stop himself. "I'm the highest ranked in my age group. And I already know all about the Warrior Code."

"Yet still you do not take it seriously. Yes, your natural ability has served you well so far, but it won't be enough. Before long, those who train the hardest will surpass you. If you do not change your attitude, sooner or later you will lose."

Although it was subtle, Jarka detected his father's disappointment. It stung, even more than losing the fight had.

He swallowed hard, and with an effort, forced a nod. "I will never let that happen. No yagar my age, male or female, will ever beat me in the Challenge Ring."

Corthak grunted and returned the nod. "Well, if you're so good, why can't you beat me?"

"Come on. That's not fair."

Corthak tilted his head, a slight grin tugging the corner of his mouth. "It's not?"

Jarka swung his spear halfheartedly at his father's. "You know it's not."

"I do?"

Jarka darted close to land a playful jab to the ribs. He then tried to dance away, but Corthak wrapped an arm around his shoulders and pinned both his arms to his sides.

He looked up and said, "It's not just me, Father. You're our Warlord. No one can beat you."

A low chuckle rumbled in Corthak's chest as he looked down. "Oh yes. That's right."

THREE

The Lycurgans wanted a return to Sparta's so-called glory days of old. They wanted all of Lycurgus's original laws and institutions restored. While most citizens had embraced more modern ideas, these fanatics remained stuck in the past.

Podalinus of Sparta

"I thought today was supposed to be a celebration."

Kaletor looked over to Vaseus walking alongside him. "It is."

She pointed ahead. "Then why are there so many hoplites around?"

Instead of answering, he allowed his gaze to linger on her. Her white dress was snug to her toned body. One of the shoulder straps had slipped down, and the neckline plunged low.

A ragged breath rushed up his throat, and when she glanced back, he quickly looked away.

The street of uneven black stones they walked along was one of Sparta's main thoroughfares. Men, women, and children were everywhere, most clad in short-sleeved tunics. Lining both sides were the hoplites Vaseus was referring to. Each of them wore a polished gold helmet of iron, the high noon sun dancing rays of light off it. Crimson cloaks hung from their shoulders to whisper across the ground.

Looking on these impressive men brought a smile to Kaletor's lips. "They're here to keep the peace," he said as they continued along with the chattering crowd.

"I don't like it," Vaseus said, her tone acid. "I feel like we could be attacked at any moment."

"And if anyone did attack, these men would cut them down. The Lycurgans wouldn't dare strike with so many hoplites around. They wouldn't stand a chance against the soldiers of the Spartan army."

"But how am I supposed to have any fun when I'm so nervous?"

"Everyone else seems to be having a good time."

She scoffed at that with a clipped laugh. "Is that what you think? Everyone's on edge. Can't you feel it?"

"No. I think you're the only one who feels it."

She reached out and shoved his shoulder. "Shut up."

He laughed. "You just don't like it when I'm right."

"You're not. You're never right."

"Is that so?" he said, reaching out to poke her arm.

"Yes," she said, shrugging him off even as she smiled.

Kaletor laughed again and was about to say more, but a commotion up ahead cut him short. They both looked, but the reason for the hollering was concealed by the sea of bodies.

Then, moving against the flow of foot traffic, several young dancing girls emerged. They each had their long blonde, brunette, or black hair braided and tied back from their pretty faces.

Seduction was in their eyes as they passed through the crowd, dancing lithely, always moving, bare arms scything this way and that. Men on every side hooted and whooped their approval.

One dancer with black hair and pale skin weaved close to Kaletor. Her eyes flicked to his, and he stared without restraint.

As the pretty girl danced by, Vaseus said, "Do you like what you see?"

He turned so that he could take in the dancer's backside. "Yes," he said, grinning wolfishly. "Yes I do."

"Doesn't take much to steal your attention."

He turned back around. "Is that jealousy I hear?"

"Please," she said with an exaggerated frown. "I can shake my hips too."

His grin broadened. "I'd like to see that."

"Well too bad," she said, shoving him away. "You never will."

He shrugged, looking to another nearby dancer. "That's okay. There'll always be girls willing to dance for me."

She gasped and shoved him again. "You're the worst!"

He laughed at that. As he carried on, she joined him, and their peals rang out in unison.

They were nearing the heart of Sparta, and the crowd was becoming ever denser. The very air felt abuzz and alive. Kaletor felt it as if it crackled and sang.

He looked all around as they progressed. The city was awash in the colours of the Empire. Many homes and shops, normally just dull structures of grey stone, had red and gold banners hanging down from second-story windows. A tailor's shop had red and gold tunics hanging on racks out front. Next door, a small house had gold and red splashes of paint spiraling up onto its roof.

Cheering up ahead pulled his attention forward. He strained his neck to see what was going on.

"What is it?" Vaseus asked.

"There's a bunch of people gathered around something," Kaletor supplied. "Come on."

He took her hand and darted ahead. He expected some form of protest, but instead, she giggled and squeezed his hand back.

Grinning wide, he led her on, weaving this way and that. They cut through the plodding mob, a few people shouting after them. Their only response was laughter as they rushed away.

They were breathing hard when they came to the stationary crowd. He led her through the gaps between people until they came to a small ring in the center. There was a small, roped-off area, and within it, two men wrestled, both wearing only a loincloth. Their dirt-streaked bodies streamed sweat and their muscles bulged as they struggled to best each other.

"Oh," Vaseus said, her brow creasing. "I don't want to watch this."

"Just for a minute," Kaletor said, tugging her back to his side.

"No," she said, pulling her hand loose and rushing off.

At first, he resolved to stay and watch, but then reconsidered and moved to hurry after her. By the time he turned, she had already disappeared within the dense crowd.

"Vaseus," he called, darting through the cheering spectators. He didn't see her.

But just before he called out again, he came upon her stopped and facing towards him. He stuttered his steps and halted with only a few inches separating them. Standing so close, he noticed how soft her full lips appeared. In that instant, he wondered what it would be like to kiss her.

Before he could act, she took hold of his arm and spun him to her side.

"I thought you didn't—"

"Quiet," she hissed.

He glanced over. "Why?"

Her mouth tightened and she jerked her head to the left.

He looked that way, scanning for some obvious detail. He saw only strangers, everyone's attention fixed on the two wrestlers.

"I don't see anything—"

"Just shut up and listen."

He gave up and looked back to the wrestling. The bigger of the two men had his opponent on the ground, attempting to twist an arm up and around—

Suddenly, a nearby voice caught his attention, and he understood what Vaseus was up to. Resisting the urge to locate the two speakers, he too listened in.

". . . not heard the tales?" one man was saying, his voice reminding Kaletor of muddied water. "There seems to be hundreds, and many are about how much the yagars hate humans. The only reason they don't attack us is because they're too busy fighting each other. But what if that changes? What if they unite? The Empire would be their first target. It would be a war unlike any other."

"They're too stupid to organize themselves for war," the second man replied, his voice sounding strained and clipped. "And even if they did, they don't know how to fight a real battle. The Phalanxes would crush them. Like I said before, it's the Lycurgans we need to deal with. They're like an infection. If their treachery and antics are allowed to spread, the Empire could collapse."

"Ridiculous," the first speaker countered. "No one with any sense will join their insane revolution. Why should we go back to the old ways? Who needs two kings now? Or to beat boys from age seven to seventeen? Or to throw babies off cliffs? Such barbarity is of the old world, and that's where it should stay."

"But there is a case to be made that those old ways made Sparta great in the first place. Without such severity, would Leonidas and his three hundred have sacrificed themselves to save Sparta? Would we have defeated Athens in the Peloponnesian War? Would we have conquered the Persians and forged the greatest empire the world has ever seen? I doubt it.

"There's a certain appeal in their logic that could convince many people to support such notions," the second speaker continued. "I'm telling you, if something drastic isn't done, the Cult of Lycurgus will grow more and more numerous—"

"You're delusional, my friend. A few fanatics will never overthrow the emperor. But thousands of violent, angry savages that know nothing but killing just might. I'm telling you, the yagars are the biggest threat—"

A deafening roar from the crowd drowned the conversation out. Kaletor had been so intent on eavesdropping that he had no idea how the smaller wrestler won the fight.

As the crowd's adulation washed over the victor, Vaseus tugged his arm, and together they pushed through the jungle of bodies and limbs. He looked back to try and spot the men, but there was no way to know which two they were.

"Unbelievable," she hissed as they rejoined the crowd heading for the heart of the city.

"What's wrong?" he asked, sticking close to her side by matching her frenzied pace. "Was it something they said?"

She barked out a humourless, "Ha!"

"Well you shouldn't have stopped to listen."

"You know I can't help myself," she said, tossing her blonde hair as she shot him a fierce glance.

"I didn't think they were that bad. The yagars really could turn out to be dangerous, and the Lycurgans have somehow stuck around. Action against both seems like a good idea to me."

"That's because you think a spear and shield are always the answer."

"Not always."

She looked over at him, eyebrows raised in a silent challenge.

He stared back solemnly for a moment, but soon caved. "Okay, maybe I do. But you can't fault my motives."

"I can't?"

"Not this time," he said, smiling as they parted to get around an old man. As they came back together, he made sure to brush up against her bare arm and shoulder. "This time my motives are pure."

"I'm sure," she said, her biting tone at odds with the playfulness in her eyes.

"They are," he insisted. "By attacking the yagars, I'd be protecting the defenseless and innocent citizens all along the Empire's northern frontier. No one would be slaughtered by those savages ever again."

"But they haven't done anything to deserve to be wiped out. They only kill people that trespass on their lands."

"So?"

"So that means they're just defending themselves. If we leave them alone, they'll leave us alone."

He huffed out a snort, taking her hand to guide her through a cluster of small children running about. "Okay, but what about the Lycurgans then? Surely they need to be dealt a quick spear thrust to the belly."

Her only answer was to shake her head.

"Why not? They're nothing but trouble."

"They're not all bad. These attacks and executions only make them more extreme. It would be better if the emperor called a truce, sat down with their leaders, and reached some sort of compromise."

"That's no fun. Where's my chance to save people? Where's my chance for glory?"

"The Empire is full of unhappy people, Kal. You'll have plenty of chances for all that."

He let out a heavy sigh and slouched his shoulders. "But I want to fight someone *now*."

She laughed at that. "It's not always right to fight. Look at our history. It doesn't really solve anything, at least not for long."

"But sometimes you *have* to fight. It's the only way to protect those who can't protect themselves."

"It's not the only way. You'll be a man soon, Kal, and then a soldier, which means soon you'll have to kill. Just promise me you won't be like the rest of them."

"What do you mean?" he asked, trying to keep his tone light. "Spartan men are good, just, and free—"

"Kaletor," she cut in, hooking his arm to bring them to a halt. "I'm serious. One day you're going to have the power to either end a life or spare one. I want you to promise me that you'll never be cruel. Promise me you'll always do what you know is right."

As he held her intense stare, he felt heat rush into his loins. The thought *'she's so beautiful'* darted through his mind, followed closely by a strong urge to pull her close and kiss her perfect, rosy lips. Only the fierce sincerity in her green eyes kept him from doing so.

"Of course, Vaseus," he finally said, the words coming out thick. "I promise I will always be good. For you."

She tilted her head to one side, obviously studying him. Then she flashed a dazzling smile. "Good."

Together they turned and continued along with the crowd. Before long, they arrived at their destination. The Kolosaio was enormous, the largest building in all of Sparta. Colossal columns of gleaming white fronted the exterior, each one supporting slabs of arched marble that ran around the top. Beneath each arch stood statues of all kinds, including Spartan heroes and the gods of Olympus. The area immediately surrounding the arena was a wide expanse of smooth, white marble.

The mass of people was overwhelming as the crowd streamed towards the nearest entrance. Everyone packed tighter and tighter together, the pace became a crawl, and the voices of thousands battered the air.

After what seemed an eternity, they shuffled through the yawning black-iron gate. Clear of the chokepoint, they turned left and hurried along the shaded corridor.

They hadn't gone far when Kaletor spotted a familiar face. "Hullis!"

His pale, lanky friend pulled up, looking around until their eyes met.

"Well, hello there, you two," he said as they all came together. "I see you're still as fair as a siren, Vaseus. The question is, are you still as nasty as a gorgon?"

"Here we go again," she said, rolling her eyes. "You're always such a charmer, aren't you?"

Hullis blinked rapidly and gave her a bright smile. "Still a gorgon then."

"Alright," Kaletor stepped in, "don't start you two. Let's go find a seat before they're all taken."

Hullis chuckled. "Sounds good to me."

"Fine," Vaseus sighed before leading the way.

They soon climbed a steep flight of stone stairs and emerged in the seating area. Long slab benches circled an oval of white sand at the center, rank upon rank rising up and away, filled to capacity by thousands of citizens. Kaletor took it in for a moment, sweeping his gaze all around. The sight and sound of so many Spartans in one place spread a warm, pleasant feeling through his body.

He turned and followed the other two up and up, climbing almost to the highest row before they spotted a gap wide enough for all three of them to squeeze into.

"Impressive," Hullis stated as they settled in.

Kaletor leaned across Vaseus to ask, "What is?"

"Your friend here has more stamina than I thought. I'd like to put it to the test, if you know what I mean."

Vaseus laughed. "Hullis, you fool. I train more than you do. I'd wear you out."

Before he could reply, a great cheer erupted and drew their attention to the oval floor. A bare-chested man with a long, dark beard had appeared and was walking around the ring, arms raised to the roaring crowd.

Kaletor, along with everyone else in Sparta, knew who he was.

Doros of Rhodes.

Though he was quite a distance away, Kaletor could see that the muscled hero was laughing heartily as he cast his gaze all around the arena.

When at last the noise eased, Doros raised his arms higher and boomed, "Sparta! How are we today?"

Kaletor and Hullis added their voices to the answering explosion of wild cheering. It was so powerful that the stone floor shook beneath their feet.

At last, things calmed once more, and the grinning Doros, still walking around the ring, went on. "Welcome to the two hundred and eighty-fifth celebration of Leonidas Day!"

Another roar erupted in answer.

When it died down, Doros boomed, "Two hundred and eighty-five years ago, King Leonidas and his immortal three hundred held the pass of Thermopylae. For three days, they kept the Persians at bay, surviving wave after wave of attack, killing thousands upon thousands of the barbarian horde. It was the greatest stand the world will ever see. It was a stand that brought us victory over the disgusting Persians. It was a stand that set us on the path to empire. Today, we honour the sacrifice they made for the glory of Sparta!"

The answering call of thousands was the greatest yet. The crowd seemed to swell as everyone raised or waved their arms. Chills prickled across Kaletor's arms as he roared along with his fellow Spartans.

Doros grinned up at them all as he steadily circled the sands. When at last they settled, he continued.

"Yes. Without Leonidas and his three hundred, Sparta would have no empire—"

"Or without the bloody wars of conquest since."

"Not today, Vaseus," Kaletor growled.

This seemed to amuse her, for she gave him a teasing smile, turned her palms upward, and slowly raised her shoulders in a shrug. "Why not?"

"Just don't."

She chuckled but added nothing else.

Huffing a breath through his nose, Kaletor looked back down to Doros.

". . . stronger than ever," the heroic legend was saying. "The borders are secure, and all people of the Empire prosper. Gods know it hasn't been easy. We've fought many wars, and we'll have to fight many more in the years to come. But we will always prevail. If the Egyptian Wars taught me anything, they taught me that no matter the strength of an enemy, we are stronger. We have the blood of Leonidas and his mighty three hundred running through our veins. Just like them, we will never be defeated!"

Another eruption burst from the crowd. Kaletor hollered along with them until his lungs burned.

As things settled back down, Vaseus again lashed out with her tongue. "I don't know why you're all so impressed. The Empire spreads fear, pain, and death. The whole world hates us, and it's bloodthirsty men like Doros who are to blame—"

"What's wrong with you?" Hullis hissed, his voice hushed as if the emperor himself were sitting directly behind them. "You can't say that. People don't like it."

"I can say whatever I want—"

"No," Kaletor sliced in. "He's right. This isn't the time or place, Vaseus. We're celebrating the sacrifice our ancestors made to—"

"Wait," she interrupted with a sharp wave to silence him, looking back to Doros below.

Surprised by her sudden shift, Kaletor did the same.

". . . different this year. Fellow Spartans, the emperor gives you Xerxes and his barbarian horde of Persian slaves!"

As Doros finished, one of the gates leading into the ring opened, and from its dark depths emerged nine yagars. Golden fur with black spots covered their entire bodies, and yet the thickness of their necks, shoulders, and arms was plain to see. They moved with elegant ease, stalky heads turning as they surveyed the crowd all around them.

A rush of heat swept through Kaletor's chest as he watched the strange people, unsure if it was fear or fascination. The rest of the crowd seemed similarly affected. A confused, jumbled murmur was the only reaction.

"I've never seen so many," Hullis said, adding his voice to the swarm of others.

"I don't think anyone has," Kaletor managed.

Doros seemed to sense the unease of the crowd. "Opposing them," he hollered, the force in his voice quieting things, "are King Leonidas and his invincible three hundred!"

The gate opposite where the yagars had emerged was thrown open, and from its mouth rushed at least fifty hoplites. They formed into the phalanx formation, two long lines of overlapping shields, their golden-iron discs flashing in the sun. Thick, golden breastplates, helmets, and greaves protected their fronts in a blaze of iron.

"Those are Spartiates," Hullis shouted excitedly over the loud welcome of the crowd.

Upon looking more closely, Kaletor realized that he was right. Only Spartiates wore the iron breastplates of a sculpted torso that sheathed them from collarbone to waist.

Vaseus pointed at the yagars and said, "They don't have any weapons."

Kaletor hadn't noticed. He looked back and saw that the huge savages were indeed empty-handed. Despite this, they had spread out in a loose line and were advancing.

"Why don't they have weapons?" Vaseus asked.

"Who cares?" Hullis hooted. "Glory to Sparta!"

"It isn't fair," Vaseus countered. "Do Spartan men have no honour? This isn't what Leonidas and the three hundred stood for—"

Another blast of cheers and shouts drowned her out, and though Kaletor knew she was right, he said nothing. When he felt her eyes on him, he kept his attention on the ring below.

One Spartiate, who's helmet was pitch black to signify his role as Leonidas, raised his spear to where the emperor sat.

It was at that moment that the yagars charged.

Kaletor had never seen anything move so fast. The yagars closed the gap so rapidly that Leonidas had no time to rejoin the phalanx.

Standing alone, he levelled his spear, but the yagar nearest to him leapt high, cleared his weapon, and swung an overhand punch. The fist struck so hard it caved the iron helmet in, and Leonidas crumpled to the sand.

The cheers of the crowd died in their throats as the rest of the yagars slammed into the phalanx. Kaletor's eyes widened as he watched the impossible happen.

Most of the savages leapt over the shield wall, crashing down on the front line of Spartiates in a rush of yellow and black. They punched and kicked with incredible force, collapsing and crushing the men's helmets and armour. Spartiates were flung into each other in the frenzied melee. Screams rang out as the huge beasts wreaked havoc.

With the front line going down, the second line stepped in. Their shields remained interlocked, and from behind them, they thrust their spears at the preoccupied yagars. Screeches and howls mixed with the screams as the leaf heads plunged through fur and flesh.

Before long, as quickly as it had started, it was over.

Kaletor, like everyone else, looked on in silence. Seven men weren't moving. Several others were down, clutching at their wounds. Blood stained the sand. The survivors stood around, staring in shock at the dead yagars and their fallen companions.

As the long seconds stretched, Kaletor struggled to comprehend what he had just witnessed. It was Leonidas Day, a day that was all about celebrating Spartan glory and power.

What had just happened wasn't supposed to happen. Spartans weren't supposed to die.

A lone, shrill scream suddenly shattered everything. Distantly, Kaletor knew it came from close by. He looked left, at first seeing only the backs of people's heads. He looked a little further and saw something that froze his heart.

A woman had been dragged onto the stairs and was being stabbed by a young man. She screamed for help, and that desperate plea jolted people into action. Several men rushed her attacker from both sides. A kick connected with his ribs. As he toppled, the men closed in to rain blows down upon him.

As Kaletor watched, his mouth hanging open, a voice rang out to his right.

"Leonidas would be ashamed of what we have become! The Empire is corrupt and unjust. Join us! Join the Cult of Lycurgus, and together, we will overthrow the emperor!"

Kaletor turned and spotted a young man at the top of the stairs with fire in his eyes. He wore a black cloak and held a knife in each hand.

In that glance, Kaletor noticed that he wasn't alone. Many others wearing black cloaks had appeared at the top of most staircases, creating a nearly unbroken ring around the uppermost landing of the arena.

They were all shouting, and as if on cue, they charged down the stairs.

With cries of terror splitting the air, Kaletor grabbed Vaseus's hand and pulled her after him.

"Hullis, on me!"

They had descended only six stairs before the rushing mass of people blocked their way. Some leapt down the benches, falling over each other in the mad rush to get away.

Vaseus was squeezing his hand tight as they ran down the stairs, swept along with the rushing tide. Screams and shouts rang on all sides.

Kaletor was seized with the need to know where the nearest Lycurgan was. He looked back and glimpsed a black-cloaked man hurtling down after them, naked knives flashing and a wild grin splitting his face.

He faced forward and barked, "Run!"

Vaseus shrieked as he pulled her on at a faster pace. He skipped stairs, careening off bodies, barely keeping his balance. In his haste, he knocked a woman over, then a young boy.

He didn't care. He had to get Vaseus away.

"Stop knocking people over!" she yelled in his ear.

Kaletor tugged her on. "Shut up and run!"

A hurried step and his foot slipped off a stair. To keep from falling, he lurched his weight forward. He slammed into an old man, who tumbled over the benches.

Everyone was running, jumping, falling. Shrill screams split the air.

Through the chaos, Kaletor finally got them to the lower level. He turned sharply on the bottom step to sprint into the corridor—

Silver flashed in his vision. His reaction was instant, ducking under the Lycurgan's thrust. The blade whispered through his hair. He twisted as his momentum carried him straight into his attacker's chest. The collision was hard, but with a grunt, the Lycurgan absorbed the hit by taking one step back. He slashed again, high and fast. Kaletor weaved passed it and aimed a punch at the man's throat.

But the Lycurgan caught his wrist, redirected the punch wide, and stabbed his knife straight out. Kaletor pivoted aside, reversed the grip on his attacker's wrist, and pulled down. The Lycurgan was off balance, and he fell to his knees. Kaletor headbutted him, forcing him to let go and sink to the ground.

Freed, Kaletor kicked the man's throat. He felt a crunch, and he knew something collapsed. Growling, he kicked again, this time striking the sputtering man's chest—

"Kaletor!"

It was Vaseus, and the fear in her voice pulled him back from the burning need to attack. He gave the man a vicious snarl. Then, with teeth grit, he turned and ran after her, accompanied on all sides by panicked and frightened people.

Screams echoed off the hollow stone, and through the chaos, they fled.

FOUR

The strongest warrior is the strongest leader.
Only the strong may lead. The Warlord leads
the Superiors, and together, they lead the
Clan. All others, since they are not the strongest, must follow.

The Warrior Code

"**G**luck today, son."

Jarka glanced over his shoulder. Back down the road from where he had just come stood Mackurth, Sixth of the Nine Superiors. The distinctive white thigh bone of an elk was bound lengthwise across his shoulders.

Jarka threw up a wave. "I don't need luck. My skills have doubled since you last saw me fight."

Mackurth barked a laugh. "That pride is going to catch up with you some-day."

"Never," he hollered back.

Without waiting for a reply, he continued on. The morning was nearly gone, and the village was abuzz. Youngsters ran this way and that across the wide roadway of hardpack dirt, laughing and shouting as they went. Mothers and fathers watched from the doorways of their squat, mud-caked huts of stout logs and bound twigs.

Among the knee-high grasses between two such homes was a ring of five young females. At the center of the ring were two combatants, their short spears cracking as they fought.

Seeing this, Jarka grinned and called out, "Fight well."

A few of the spectators glanced his way, the vertical slits of their eyes narrowing.

He chuckled to himself. "Tough crowd."

As he continued, more familiar sights and sounds greeted him. A female flaking a spearhead, the clack of stone on stone sounding like a rhythmic drum. A male entangled in the weave of a basket, experienced fingers working with practiced precision. A pair of females cleaning a pile of bones, making them ready for use as ornamentation, cooking, or even toy spears.

The wind was whipping through the tops of the trees by the time he reached the edge of the village and approached the Challenge Ring.

A group of four hunting pairs had emerged from the forest. The scent of their kills, two adult boars that they carried on planks of wood, filled his nostrils as they hustled by.

He paused to inhale deeply. "Good hunting, warriors."

One of the group, a female with so many spots that her fur was more black than yellow, said, "Better get focused on the fight, Jarka. Distraction could see you defeated."

"You have it wrong, my friend," he replied. "Nothing, not even the delicious smell of fresh-caught boar, can slow my spear."

The group's laughter rolled easily.

"I guess we'll see about that," another said.

"Better hurry back. It's not going to last long."

With that, they were gone, and he continued to the Challenge Ring.

Though the space was used every day, it was a simple place. The ring itself was a one-foot-high stack of grey and black rocks, mixed with hunks of wood. It ran a circle around well-worn dirt and several smooth stones that were laid flush in the ground. Rising up and away, like one half of a shallow bowl, was a massive mound of earth, the top of which was nearly as high as the treetops beyond.

On this great hill of grass sat nearly every yagar of the village, about four hundred or so. Their chattering quieted considerably as Jarka stepped over the little wall and crossed the thirty-foot-wide circle. Disregarding the attention of the village, he continued to the foot of the slope, scanning those nearest the bottom as he went. Soon he found who he was looking for.

"Good morning, Jazith," he said, smiling wide. "You ready to watch me win another Challenge?"

She shook her head, her deep brown eyes revealing that she was nervous. "Will you never learn?"

He reached out to tug at her whiskers. "Learn what?"

She swatted his arm away. "What it's like to fear failure."

"No, I don't think so."

He glanced to those nearby to ensure they weren't listening in.

Satisfied, he sat down next to her and said, "But forget about all this. I need to talk to you."

"Now?"

"About Father."

Suddenly intent, she leaned forward at the hip, the bracelets of deer bone on her wrists clacking as she set her hands to her thighs. "Go on."

Jarka rubbed the back of his neck, feeling the fur flip through his fingers. "I don't know, Jaz. I don't know if I'll ever be able to please him."

"What happened this time?"

"It was during our last hunt together. I missed my kill, and even though it wasn't my fault, he was disappointed. Then we sparred. I couldn't best him, but I came closer than ever. I'm getting better, but he doesn't notice. He was just disappointed. I don't know what else I can do."

"Is this really about Father?" Jazith asked quietly, leaning a little closer. "Or is your wounded pride causing such thoughts?"

"Pride has nothing to do with it. He's impossible to please. His expectations are too high, and he never offers any encouragement—"

"Jarka, listen to yourself. Father may be demanding, but it's because he wants what's best for us. Imagine if he took it easy on you. Would you want to get better if he said 'you're the best' and that 'no one will ever beat you?'"

He shrugged and muttered a halfhearted, "I guess not."

She reached out to rest a hand on his forearm. "I know it isn't easy. You expect so much of yourself. But no matter how hard things get, you'll always have me to talk to."

"Yeah, I know," he said, giving her a brief smile. "Thanks, sis."

Suddenly, everyone stood. They both did the same in time to watch the Nine Superiors arrive. They were the best warriors in the entire Clan. Third, Fourth, Seventh, and Ninth were female, the rest male. Second was a huge male named Warthux. Though it hadn't happened yet, it was only a matter of time before he challenged Corthak for the right to become Warlord.

And, unlike the other Superiors, Jarka hated him. He glared at the brainless brute as the most powerful yagars of the Clan moved took their seats on the two long benches extending away from the foot of the hill.

The light poke of a finger drew Jarka's attention over to Jazith.

When their eyes met, she said, "Fight well, little brother. And good luck."

The words pulled him away from his fixation on Warthux, and he remembered that he was about to fight in a Challenge.

"How many times do I have to tell you, Jaz?" he said with a smile. "I don't need luck."

He turned away and stepped into the ring. His opponent, a female named Zonyx, emerged from within the crowd to join him. Both her upper arms were adorned with three small, yellowed rib bones. She was older than him, and much bigger.

"How was your night, Zonyx?" he asked when she stopped beside him. "Did you get much sleep?"

She glowered at him in silence.

Smirking, he added, "Why not—"

"Today's Challenge," Corthak called out loudly from the benches, cutting him short, "was issued honourably by Jarka and accepted with honour by Zonyx. Fight until your opponent yields or is forced from the ring. Understood?"

"Yes, sir," Jarka answered, his tone bright.

Zonyx only nodded.

Corthak's neutral expression remained unchanged as he motioned for the spears to be brought forward.

Jarka began bouncing on the balls of his feet, shaking his arms loose, and rolling his shoulders.

"Don't be too stubborn, Zonyx," he said as she moved to create the minimum ten-foot gap between them. "It'd be a shame to damage that pretty face of yours. Remember, there's no dishonour in losing to the Warlord's son."

The yellow fur at her throat and shoulders bristled as she glared him down. "Your arrogance is despicable. I will make you pay."

"So she *can* talk," he said to the young male who was handing him a spear. "I was beginning to worry she had lost all her charm."

This time she just snarled, revealing the tips of her top two fangs.

Jarka looked at the spear in his hands. He felt the tapered wood between his fingers, tightening and then loosening his grip a few times. He closed his eyes and breathed deep. A subtle smile tugged at the corners of his mouth.

"Begin."

The word came from Corthak, and it unleashed Zonyx. She charged with a roar, spear lancing high. Jarka spun left, whipping his spear around with him at chest level. The shafts cracked into each other. The power of the collision forced her back a step. He moved quick, jabbing for her hip. She batted the thrust aside. He followed with a three-strike combo, which ended with a heavy overhead chop. She parried the first two and rolled away to escape the finisher. He kept on, jabbing at her gut. His aim was slightly off, and the stone leaf head of his spear only nicked her side.

She ignored the inevitable sting and slammed a backhanded fist into his face. Stars burst down his nose. He loosed a growl as he staggered away.

He straightened out of it with his spear angled in front of him, but she had allowed a gap to open up between them.

"Terribly sorry about that," he said, tilting his head and pointing at her side with his spear. "I didn't mean to make you bleed—"

She roared as she leapt at him, spear arcing straight at his face. He ducked under it, braced at the knees, and launched himself forward. As he did, he brought his spear into both hands horizontally and rammed the shaft up into her throat. There was a loud crack, but he didn't let up.

He drove through with all his weight, lifting her from her feet. She landed hard on her back, a gasping groan escaping from her mouth. He went to the ground on top of her, pushing the middle of his spear down on her throat, feeling the wall sinking in.

Gasping and choking, she could only manage a feeble kick to his back before raising a clenched fist to yield.

"The victor is Jarka," Corthak declared, ending the subtle and brief applause. "He moves to Second Junior Superior. Zonyx takes his place as Ninth."

Corthak looked to the Superiors seated on the benches to his left and right. "Any who feel she did not fight well, let it be known."

Jarka stood beside Zonyx, who had regained her feet and was rubbing her throat.

This final part of the Challenge was critical. If five or more Superiors voted yes, Zonyx would be one step away from banishment.

Fortunately for her, only one Superior declared she had not fought well. Not surprisingly, it was Warthux.

When no one else raised their arm, Corthak said, "So be it. Well fought, warriors. May strength and honour be yours."

With the customary words officially concluding the Challenge, Jarka loosed a whooping cry, tossed his spear to the approaching male, and went to the hill. Many in the crowd began chatting and standing. Jarka made straight for Jazith.

"I told you," he called out as he neared.

She was standing now, a sly smile curling a corner of her black lips. "And what exactly did you tell me?"

He stopped directly in front of her and grinned. "That I always win."

*　　*　　*

Orange shafts of the rising sun poked through the canopy, bathing the leafy forest floor in warm light. Jarka wandered aimlessly, picking his way slowly between the tall oaks and dense vegetation. Red-and-purple-plumed birds sang their morning songs as they and other creatures awoke to a new day.

He barely noticed. Despite the light dancing around him, darkness swirled within.

It had started the night before. Initially, he had been overjoyed with his victory over Zonyx, and Jazith had allowed his celebratory mood. But their parents had not. It was during dinner that their disapproval revealed itself.

"That's enough about today's Challenge," his mother Enoth had said, sternness plain in her amber eyes.

Jarka's smile froze and fell away. "But why? I won again, Mother. Can't we celebrate—"

"When will you learn, Jarka?" Corthak cut in. "We do not celebrate victory. How many times do we have to tell you?"

"But this one was different. I just went from Ninth to Second. No one's ever done that before—"

"It doesn't matter. I didn't celebrate when I won my Challenge to become Warlord. Do you know why?"

Jarka glared at his father, the elation he had known evaporating like mist. "Yes," he managed through clenched teeth.

"Tell me why."

He glanced left to where Jazith sat. She was staring down at her slab of meat, steadfastly avoiding his eyes.

"Jarka—"

"We do not celebrate victory," he said before his mother could continue, "because that would suggest success and completion. But there is always room for improvement. So we must refrain, and in so doing, remember that we must continue striving to become greater warriors."

It was a part of the Warrior Code he knew well. And yet, even after hearing it so many times, it still felt wrong.

"That's right," Enoth said, her fierce gaze easing a bit. "We must never believe we are already good enough. Such acceptance would lead to complacency, weakness, and dishonour."

"But only if I let the celebration go on and on. But I don't. I just think it's fine for one night—"

Corthak's fist slamming to the table cut him short. "It isn't! To celebrate a victory dishonours your opponent, an opponent who fought well. Will you never accept our ways? Will you never grow up?"

It was this that had stung the most. Even removed from the argument by several hours, Jarka struggled to get beyond it.

He slapped a low branch aside that hung in his path, growling as the memory ran through his mind again.

They don't get it. I can have fun and still be the best. I haven't lost a single Challenge. Can't they see that? Why aren't they proud of me? Why are they so serious all the time? What's wrong with being happy when I win?

Such questions had plagued him many times before, yet he was no closer to any answers. It seemed like he would never truly understand the Warrior Code.

A twig snapped nearby. He stopped and looked towards the noise, ears rotating forward atop his head. Though he saw nothing but green undergrowth and hanging branches, he did hear a voice, distant but unmistakable.

Knowing he wasn't supposed to be out in the forest alone, he bounded to the nearest tree and began to climb. He moved fast, claws extending from his fingers and toes to grip the bark. He contorted his body as he ascended, snaking around the trunk as he moved from branch to branch. Twigs snapped and wide leaves rustled loose as he climbed higher and higher.

When at last he glanced down and saw that he was far enough from the ground, he stopped, draping his arms over a branch that was chest level. He felt the hot burn in his legs then, and with his heart hammering into his breastbone, he stayed still and waited.

It wasn't long before he picked up the voice again. Straining his ears, he could just make out the words.

". . . feel threatened once they know what we've done?"

"At first, yes. No one likes change. But once they realize we are not combining our strength to dominate or take over, that fear will fade."

Jarka's eyes widened as he listened, for the second speaker was his father. He peered down through the branches and leaves, trying to spot the pair. He caught glimpses of them, enough to see that the other yagar's fur was all black, but that was all he could determine.

"I'm glad you see the necessity of this," Corthak said, his voice now clear. "I thought I was the only one."

"Perhaps you were, but not anymore," the yagar Jarka could not place replied, his voice even deeper than Corthak's. "The world is changing. If we do not change with it, our people will be in grave danger."

"Yes. I believe all the battles we've fought against each other have prepared us for what is to come."

"But will the other Clans stop their infighting before it's too late?"

"I don't know," Corthak said. "We don't really have a choice. We have to try."

The unknown yagar grunted. "Hope. I hate relying on hope."

"You and I . . ."

The rest of Corthak's words were lost as the pair moved out of earshot.

Although his muscles no longer burned, Jarka's heart still hammered in his chest. With his father and the other yagar gone, his mind began to race.

Who was that? It seemed like a neighbouring Warlord. But why would they meet? And in such secrecy? They must be hiding something. But what?

These and other questions swarmed him like angry wasps. He sought to silence them by feeling the breath flow in and out of his lungs.

It was a long time before this soothed the buzzing, but eventually, his mind was quiet.

Certain words and phrases came back to him then. He realized that his father was preparing for something. Something was going to happen. But what? The War Season was fast approaching. As Warlord, that's all that Corthak needed to prepare for. Having a secret meeting with someone from another Clan did not serve that purpose.

So what was his father doing? What was he *really* preparing for?

He waited several minutes. When he was confident they were long gone, he clambered down and started back towards the village.

He didn't know how or where he was going to get answers, but he knew Jazith could help. As soon as the morning lesson and training were done, he would find her—

Something moving blurred to his right. He reacted instantly, jumping back and away, but something hard struck him in the throat. Choking, he staggered back. His foot caught on a root and he crashed to the ground. Before he could roll away, two males stepped on his arms and torso, pinning him in place.

"Well, well, well, what have we here?"

"Looks like we've caught an even better prey."

Jarka glared up at the twin sons of Warthux, Vawk and Traz, and tried to wriggle free. "Let me go, you cowards—"

Vawk cracked a kick into Jarka's side. "Don't you dare call me a coward."

"He called both of us cowards," Traz pointed out.

Vawk looked at his brother and snarled.

"You *are* cowards," Jarka spat, trying to break free. "Only cowards use ambush—"

This time they both kicked him, and more than once. Jarka tried to curl into a ball, but he couldn't with his arms pinned to the ground. He hissed and snarled as the hard blows hammered him.

"Shut your mouth," Traz barked through laboured breaths. "Keep your mouth shut, or we'll kill you."

"You are both . . . without honour," Jarka ground out.

Vawk kicked him again, though not as hard as before. "Didn't you hear him? Keep your mouth shut or we'll kill you, just like our father is going to kill yours."

Jarka bellowed and thrashed wildly. He managed to get one arm loose before they unleashed another barrage of kicks. Fire seared through his body. This time he couldn't stop himself from screaming.

When they finally relented, he could barely breath. He gasped for air, mouth opened wide, coughing and spewing like a wild beast.

Distantly, he noticed the pressure leave his arms and chest. Although he was free, he couldn't move. His body was numb. All he could manage was to drag in one shallow breath after another.

Vawk squatted down and leaned in close, his whiskers jabbing into Jarka's shoulder. "Corthak is a mad fool. Soon our father will challenge him, and when they fight, Corthak will lose. Enjoy being the son of the Warlord while it lasts."

Jarka tried to grab Vawk by the throat, but his arm wouldn't cooperate. All he could manage was to drag it slowly along the ground.

Vawk laughed in his face. Still laughing, he straightened, and alongside Traz, walked away.

Jarka drew in a shuddering breath, the throbbing waves unwilling to subside. He clenched his teeth and squeezed his eyes shut as hot tears trickled from the corners of his eyes.

FIVE

Leonidas and his three hundred were held up
as the ideal Spartans. Bravery beyond measure.
Stronger than ordinary men. Eternal glory and
fame. It was to these soaring heights that every
Spartan boy aspired to reach.

Thrasilaus of Thebes

"Supper's ready you two."

Kaletor continued his sequence of sword cuts, thrusts, and swings against the wooden post while his father gruffly called out, "Alright."

A moment later, he completed the set with an overhead strike to the post's right shoulder.

"Better," his father said, "but still not fast enough. You'll go again after we eat."

"Yes, sir."

Without another word, they left the courtyard, an open square of hardpack dirt and sand that was at the heart of the house. They proceeded through the atrium, a large room of red and black walls, which served as the main entrance. Straight benches lined the rear wall, upon which waited two of the household slaves. Facing the front doorway was a tall statue of Leonidas, the clean, white marble painted red and gold. The legendary King was depicted thrusting his spear straight out, his bearded chin jutting down, mouth open in a great roar.

Passing through the atrium, they came to the dining hall. A massive oak table, which sat thirty, dominated the sprawling space. By the light of blazing torches, Kaletor looked at the food laid out on its surface. Slabs of venison, steaming carrots and potatoes, and hunks of cheese and bread were heaped upon golden platters. As the delicious smells reached his nostrils, his stomach grumbled.

Xanthos assumed his spot at the head of the table, while Kaletor sat to his left. Four more of the house slaves moved forward from where they waited along the walls. Each took up a platter of food and brought it first to Xanthos, then to Kaletor.

They had nearly filled their plates when his mother strode in, her thin face set as hard as iron.

"Where were you?" Xanthos demanded.

Megara replied evenly, "There was a minor problem in the kitchen I had to deal with."

"Whose fault was it? I'll not have incompetence in my house."

"It had nothing to do with incompetence, dear. There was something—"

"Alright then."

Accepting the interruption without any sign of irritation, Megara sat directly across from Kaletor. She gave him a brief smile, then quickly looked away.

"Tell me, boy," Xanthos said, his grey eyes piercing. "What's the greatest city in the world?"

Looking directly at his father, Kaletor said, "Sparta."

"Who do we fight for?"

"The emperor."

"What do we fight for?"

"The glory of Sparta."

Xanthos nodded, and nothing more was said as they ate in silence.

When his plate was nearly finished and his ravenous hunger was sated, Kaletor's mind returned, as it had many times since, to Leonidas Day. The Lycurgan attack at the Kolosaio had left over twenty people dead and hundreds wounded. Never before had the fanatics struck on such a massive scale.

Tension pervaded the entire city. Hoplites and Spartiates were everywhere, searching and patrolling for any disturbance, no matter how small. The emperor had dispatched most of his Elites to join them, though Kaletor suspected they remained close to the palace. It was plain to everyone, right down to the smallest child, that the city was on high alert.

The militarized response was exactly what Sparta needed, or so Kaletor had been taught to think. Vaseus's words, however, had him questioning the aggressive approach, and now uncertainty plagued him.

Frustrated once more with his failure to dismiss the conflicting views within him, Kaletor couldn't hold back any longer. He needed the answers only his father could provide, even though asking for them would be dangerous.

And so, in the same way that water rushes forth from a burst dam, he blurted out, "Do you think it's wise to have so many hoplites and Spartiates patrolling the streets?"

Chewing what was already in his mouth, Xanthos leaned into the high back of his chair, eyes narrowed as he looked at Kaletor.

After a long silence, he swallowed and said, "What kind of question is that?"

"What if an armed response isn't the right way to deal with the Lycurgans?"

"Why wouldn't it be?"

"It's possible they'll feel threatened and go deeper underground, making it harder to defeat them. Or what if this is exactly what they wanted? By reacting with such force, the emperor has put the city on edge—"

"Force is the only way," Xanthos snapped, leaning forward to rest his forearms on the table. "That's what we do. That's how Sparta gained an empire. We don't talk things over with those who attack us. We fight and kill them until the bastards fall in line. That's the Spartan way. How can you not know that by now?"

Kaletor grit his teeth, barely managing to swallow down a scalding comeback.

"It isn't his fault, Husband," Megara said evenly into the charged silence. "It's that pretty girl he spends so much time with. She fills his head with nonsense such as this. He's still young and impressionable—"

"Do not speak of her like that—"

"Silence, boy," Xanthos barked. "Your mother's right. That girl is a bad influence."

"Her name is Vaseus—"

"I don't care what her name is!"

Despite the raging bellow, Kaletor glared back at his father. "She isn't to blame for anything—"

"She is," Megara interrupted. Unlike Xanthos, her expression was cold as ice. "Before her, you were a good, respectful son. She is teaching you defiance, and that is something no Spartan needs. Whatever the emperor decides is right. Always. You must not question him. You must not question anyone who outranks you. And you must not question your parents."

"I was just asking—"

"Enough," Xanthos snapped, a vein popping in his neck. "Listen to your mother, boy. You're spending too much time with that girl. From now on, you can only see her if I say you can."

Kaletor ground his teeth together so hard they hurt. His breathing was harsh as he glared at them both. He knew that to utter another word would result in a beating, and this knowledge alone made him hold his tongue.

As the seething silence stretched, one of the middle-aged Athenian slaves hurried into the dining hall. "Someone is here to see you, Master."

Xanthos kept his glare on Kaletor as he snarled, "Who?"

"General Belisar."

The name drew their attention. Without another word, his parents stood and strode from the room.

Once they were gone, Kaletor noticed a dull throb in his arms. Blinking as if waking up, he slowly released his clenched fists.

They don't know anything about us. Vaseus is the best part of my life. I don't care what they say. I will keep seeing her as much as I want to.

Before long, his mother returned, her hazel eyes and plain face set in the same, neutral mask. Close behind her followed Xanthos and General Belisar, a man also in his thirties. Though he was a bit shorter than Kaletor's father, his limbs were thick, and he was barrel-chested. Silver gauntlets, greaves, and breastplate encased the wealthy aristocrat.

"Join us," Xanthos said, indicating the chair next to Kaletor with an extended arm.

The famous general accepted without a word. As he passed by, the salty scent of his sweat invaded Kaletor's nose.

"You remember my son—"

"Kaletor," Belisar finished as he sat. "Of course. What have you been feeding him, Xanthos? He must be twice as big as the last time I saw him."

"He takes after his father," Megara supplied.

Belisar chuckled softly. "Yes, I can see that."

A plate was brought by one of the slaves and heaped with food. Kaletor eyed Belisar with brief, furtive glances. His long, black hair hung in greasy clumps, and his nose was large and crooked. It was hard to believe that this was the famous general who had yet to lose a battle.

Once Belisar had taken a few bites and gulped down some wine, Xanthos asked, "So does this mean you've crushed the Thracian rebellion?"

Belisar finished chewing and wiped a hand across his beard. "Nearly. The emperor recalled me to deal with these damned Lycurgans before I could deliver the final blow. I've been in the saddle for over a week."

"Will you return to Thrace once the fanatics are dealt with?"

"No need." Belisar paused for a noisy gulp of wine. "The few still alive are holed up in Tylis, which is surrounded by my army sixteen thousand strong."

"How many Spartiates?"

The question had escaped before Kaletor could contain it. He kept his gaze on Belisar, feeling the burning disapproval coming from his parents.

"Excuse our son, General," Megara said, her tone strained. "He is young and still learning his place."

Belisar ignored her. "I admire your courage to ask, boy. Seven hundred Spartiates remained there. Two hundred returned with me."

The reply was all the permission Kaletor needed. "Did you fight the Thracians in open battle?"

Chuckling softly, Belisar nodded. "Twice. They outnumbered us three to one the first time."

Kaletor's breath quickened as he imagined heroic Spartans battling a vast horde of barbarians. "And you defeated them anyway, didn't you?"

The famous general nodded again. "Would you like to know how?"

Dismissing his parents, Kaletor said, "Yes, sir."

"The Thracians had lined up atop a series of low hills," Belisar answered, the smile still playing on his lips. "They had the numbers and the superior position, but that didn't matter. It had taken us five months to get the cowards to fight in the open, so I wasn't going to let anything get in the way. I ordered all four Phalanxes to advance up the hills and crush the spineless traitors."

He paused to eat and drink. As the seconds passed, Kaletor felt his jaw clench.

Eventually, he couldn't take it any longer. "What happened then? Did the Phalanxes smash through their line?"

Belisar swished the wine around in his mouth, then swallowed it down. "The Thracians charged down the hill at full speed and slammed into us. Blood flowed and dying men howled as the killing began. That initial impact hit us hard, and three of the Phalanxes staggered. Savage fighting ensued. My men managed to hold on and reformed, keeping the mad horde at bay. While the glorious carnage raged, I led the cavalry around behind the Thracian line and we took them in the flank. Within minutes, the cowards ran in panic. We pursued, cutting them down with sword and spear."

Kaletor could feel a tingling sensation spreading through his body. In his mind's eye, he saw the scene of victorious Spartans cutting down fleeing Thracians, every spear thrust hitting home with perfect precision. His muscles flexed and his hands itched as he imagined himself there, among their ranks, striking down the enemies of the Empire.

"Your skill in the conduct of war serves us all well, General," Megara said, bringing Kaletor back to the table.

Again, Belisar seemed to ignore her. His gaze was fixed on Kaletor as he scratched at his beard.

Abruptly, Xanthos declared, "Glory to Sparta. May the Phalanxes always prevail."

Belisar held Kaletor's eye for a long moment, as if searching for something.

Eventually, he looked away and raised his cup to the statement. As Xanthos and Megara did the same, the general said, "To Sparta."

They all drank, and as they did, a wretched possibility invaded Kaletor's mind. Feeling like he had the general's approval, he decided to voice it.

"Forgive me, sir, but I fear your success could rob me of a chance for similar glory."

Setting his cup back down, Belisar looked over and asked, "What do you mean?"

"With all of our enemies defeated, what if there's no one left to fight? Surely such a day will arrive soon."

The confusion on Belisar's face cleared. "Eager for battle, aren't you? I like that. Don't you worry, my boy. Emperor Ockos is a conqueror. You'll have plenty of chances to fight for the Empire."

Kaletor grinned. "I can't wait."

SIX

In the early days, when yagars first came to the Forever Forest, humans occasionally travelled into, or even lived within, the forest. To be rid of them, our ancestors decided to sow fear in their hearts. They hunted the humans in the dark, not killing them, but terrifying them with a sudden roar, or by running right by them. These humans then told others of a dark beast in the woods, terrible and fierce. Gradually, the fear spread, and for a hundred years or more, not one human was seen in the Forever Forest.

The Spoken Tales

Jarka sat just within the forest's edge, back pressed against a wide tree trunk, arms limp at his sides. It felt like stone shards were cutting through his ribcage, though not as intensely as it had while he had walked.

He peered through the tall grass at Home Village. Most of the structures were beyond his field of vision, but one of the few he could see was his home.

The Warlord's Hall was the largest building in the village. It stood two stories high and had nine rooms. The walls and flat roof were made of thick wood and dried mud. From what he could tell, his mother and sister were still inside. His father could be anywhere.

A surge of fire coursed through his ribcage and his body seized up. He wrapped his arms around his middle and squeezed his eyes shut to ride it out.

Eventually, the pain eased, and he relaxed. He kept his eyes closed and cast his mind back to what he had overheard, going over it again. But he couldn't piece it together. Whatever his father had been discussing with that black-furred male, he couldn't fill in the blanks.

All he knew for sure was that his father was discussing something in secret with an outsider, which didn't make any sense. The Warrior Code forbid secrecy of any kind.

As he wrestled with this, the pain in his sides pushed other thoughts into his mind.

The twins defeated me. They had me at their mercy. How could I let that happen? I'm supposed to be unbeatable. I need to be better. That can never happen again—

"You don't look so good."

The words acted on him like a slap to the face. He snapped his eyes open, muscles tensing.

But when he saw it was Jazith, he let his arms back down. "Lovely morning, isn't it?"

She moved gracefully to sit cross-legged directly in front of him. "It is. But not for you."

"What do you mean? I'm doing great."

"It's just us, Jarka."

He slumped down, sucking in a sharp breath. "It's like you can see right through me."

She gave him a warm smile, revealing the tips of her fangs. "That's because I can. Now, tell me what happened."

Her expression was especially tender. Jarka swallowed and looked away, his face starting to burn. For some time they sat there, Jazith remaining silent as she waited.

Eventually, he forced the words out. "The twins. They, uh, they got in a few lucky shots."

"What do you mean? They attacked you?"

Jarka nodded.

She scowled and shook her head. "The little bastards. Where?"

"In the forest."

"An ambush?"

"Yes."

"Were they armed?"

"No."

"Still. Cowards. They're dishonourable, worthless cowards."

"That's what I said."

The fierceness in her eyes faded as she shuffled over to his side and reached out to place a hand on his arm. "Are you all right?"

He was about to play it off as nothing, but then stopped himself. After all, there was no one else around.

The words came out in a torrent. "It hurt so much, Jaz. They kept kicking me, over and over again. I tried to fight back, but I couldn't get up, no matter how hard I tried. Then they insulted Father. I got so mad I wanted to kill them. But even then, I couldn't get up. I felt so helpless and weak—"

"I know," she cooed, leaning close to wrap her arms around his head and neck. "You did all you could."

He broke down then, burying his face in the warmth of her fur as the sobs raked through him. As he let it out, she held him close.

When at last exhaustion forced him to stop, her voice drifted gently into his ear. "It's okay, little brother. I know it hurts. I know it hurts far worse on the inside. Strength and honour demand victory. That's why it hurts so much."

He focused on her voice as she spoke. Gradually, the harshness of his breathing subsided.

"But know this, dear brother," she went on quietly. "What they did was shameful and without honour. They are weak. Only the weak attack someone that's unarmed and unsuspecting. It's their honour that's been stained, not yours. They are cowards, not you. You didn't back down, did you?"

He shook his head, his breath even.

"Exactly. You did well, Jarka. You have nothing to feel bad about. I'm proud—"

"Wait," he cut in to silence her, for he had heard something rustle nearby. He sat up, scanning the thick brush of the forest and rotating his ears forward.

Before long, he picked up movement to their right. He narrowed his eyes, catching a glimpse of black and yellow moving within the hanging greenery. He kept tracking whoever it was as they moved silently toward the village.

Eventually, through a gap in the foliage, he saw who it was, and in that moment of recognition, he made a decision.

Wiping at the tears on his cheeks, he said, "Help me up."

"Who is that?"

"Father."

Jazith made no move. "It's probably best that he doesn't hear about this."

"He won't," Jarka insisted. "Just help me up."

She hesitated a moment, eyes locked on his. Then, without a word, she stood, took his hands, and pulled him up.

Again, it felt like stone sliced across his ribs, only more intensely. He grit his teeth to stifle a snarl.

"Thanks, sis," he managed, placing a hand on her shoulder.

She nodded once and, smiling, set an open palm to his chest. "Remember, it's you and me, Jarka. It's you and me."

He smiled back and set off, limping clear of the tree line before turning right. As he did, Corthak also emerged, making a direct line for the Warlord's Hall.

At that moment, he hesitated, and he thought to abandon his plan.

But his need to know was overpowering, so he pushed his caution aside.

"Father!"

Corthak pulled up and looked over, but the distance was too great to read his reaction. They both moved to close the gap, Jarka doing his best not to limp.

"What are you doing out here?" Corthak said as they neared each other.

"I could ask you the same thing."

They stopped with a few feet separating them, and Corthak waved a hand toward the village. "I don't have time for this. Come, the day's combat is about to begin—"

"I saw you in the forest. Who were you with? What were you talking about?"

Corthak let his arm back down, his dark brown eyes wide and his face completely still. It was a long moment of silence before he spoke again.

"I knew someone would find out one of these days. I just didn't think it would be you."

Jarka didn't know what to say to that.

Before he could think of anything, his father turned and moved towards the forest. "Come. I don't want anyone else to hear this."

It was not at all what he was expecting. His mouth felt dry as they walked into the forest. Strong sabres of sunlight stabbed down through the canopy all around them.

After several minutes, Corthak stopped within a thinned-out range of pines and said, "I'm glad it's you, son. I'm glad it's you I'm telling first."

Several questions rushed through Jarka's mind all at once. He chose the most pressing. "Who was that male you were with?"

"Alarix, Warlord of the Dark Stone Clan."

Without waiting for a reply, he walked on. Jarka kept pace, and after a few heartbeats, glanced over. His father moved as if floating, yet every step was powerful. The dark antlers fastened about his broad chest and shoulders gleamed in the filtered sun.

It wasn't until they entered a denser stretch of tangled brush and hanging tree limbs that Corthak spoke again. "I imagine that you're quite confused. Why was I meeting with one of our most bitter rivals? It's not something I'm supposed to do, is it?"

Jarka ducked under a low branch, and as he straightened, said, "No. I've never heard of two Warlords doing anything but battling each other."

"That's because that's what all Warlords have ever done. For as long as we've lived in these lands, a thousand years or more, we've always fought each other.

It's part of the Warrior Code, a tradition of honour and strength that has made our people into the greatest warriors in the world. But life is water, not stone. Things flow and change."

Question after question struck Jarka as his father spoke. He was so caught up that he forgot to move in such a way that prevented pain, and as he twisted through a cluster of thin branches, it felt like sharp stone was splitting down his left side. He ground his teeth in a snarl, barely managing to keep it quiet.

Hoping to keep him talking, Jarka said, "I don't understand. What's changed? Why did you speak to a rival Warlord?"

"I've come to believe that we can no longer afford to fight each other. I was speaking to Alarix about forming an alliance."

Jarka stumbled and nearly fell. "An alliance? What do you mean? We must fight other Clans during the War Season, not become friends with them. You've always told me that that's what keeps us strong."

"I know," Corthak said. "Many things must change now."

"But cooperation is for the weak. How can we maintain our strength and honour if we do not war with the other Clans? This is wrong. If the rest of our Clan finds out what you're doing . . ."

He allowed his voice to trail off, unwilling to finish that sentence.

They had come to a small, winding river. Standing on its stony bank, Corthak stooped down, cupped the flowing water in both hands, and splashed it to his face. He remained crouched, drips falling from his whiskers, his eyes steady on the river.

"I know, son. I know the dangers I'm stepping into. But I must do what I believe is right."

Jarka had never known his father to be so open. He swallowed down the tightness in his throat. "But why? What has happened to make you go against one of our oldest traditions?"

Corthak wiped at his face as he straightened to his full height. He looked directly at Jarka and said, "It's the humans. They have grown far more numerous, aggressive, and hungry for war. One Clan in particular has become very large and powerful. They are called Spartans. Their Warlord rules over many, many human villages. They have massive armies of ironclad men that conquer and kill wherever they go. I believe that one day soon, these Spartans will come north, into our lands, and attack us."

"That's impossible," Jarka said, his tone harsher than he had intended. "The humans are afraid of us. They think we're just mindless beasts that know nothing but senseless violence, and they fear what they don't understand."

Corthak shook his head. "That was true once. But not anymore. These Spartans aren't like the others. The aura of fear our ancestors sowed among the humans will no longer protect us."

This time, Jarka had no reply. He glanced away and extended his claws to scratch into the back of his neck.

Images of humans came to him, thousands of them moving through the Forever Forest, flashing swords and blazing torches in their hands. Some cut and hacked a path through the tangled branches, causing a shower of leaves to fall like rain. The rest set the flames of their torches to the trees, laughing as everything burned.

"That is why I'm doing this. I will not allow our people to be destroyed."

Corthak's words shattered his vision. Jarka licked his lips and looked back to his father. "How? How could we survive if thousands of humans come here?"

"By uniting," Corthak answered. "All yagars must join together and fight as one. We too are numerous, and if we stand together, as one force, we can defeat the Spartans when they come."

Jarka's breath caught as he stared at his father. "What? But that's impossible. Every Clan hates every other Clan. We've fought hundreds, if not thousands of times with our neighbours. It's all we know. You are Warlord because you're the greatest warrior in the Clan. Combat is what keeps us strong and honourable—"

"I know," Corthak cut in. "I know it better than most. But none of it changes the fact that if we remain divided, if we do not unite, everything we hold dear will perish!"

His sharp bark echoed through the still pines. Jarka's throat was dry, and though the urge to look away was great, he held his father's fierce glare.

After a short moment, Corthak released a heavy sigh. "Forgive my frustration. What you say is correct. But I already know that what I'm proposing is radical, perhaps even insane. But it's the only way, son. If we do not adapt, we will be destroyed. The Spartans will not stop until every yagar is captured or killed."

Once again, Jarka did not know what to say.

Corthak stepped close and brought a hand up to rest on his shoulder. "This path I'm on will be difficult, and I don't know if it will work. Most yagars will oppose, including those in our own Clan. But I must do what I know is right. I must follow my heart. You understand?"

Jarka wasn't sure if he did, but he nodded all the same. "Yes, Father."

With a soft smile, Corthak thumped a fist gently to Jarka's chest. "That's my son."

He smiled back, and with the tightness releasing in his throat, they turned and began walking back to the village.

As they proceeded in silence, Jarka's thoughts swirled. How could this plan possibly work? All the Clans knew was war with their neighbours. It had been going on for a thousand years. How could that change? What Warlord would choose peace? Surely any who did would be called weak, and the Challenges would come one after another. Even if they kept winning and held onto their power, this would disrupt any attempts to form alliances with other Clans.

His thoughts went on and on in this vein, and before long, he was convinced his father's plan could never work.

And yet, what if the humans really did invade? If the Clans were still fighting each other, defeat would surely come swiftly. Everyone knew that the humans had spread across all the lands south of the Forever Forest. Should these so-called Spartans send an army, it could very well number in the thousands.

Jarka swallowed around a lump in his throat.

When they finally stepped clear of the forest and Home Village came into view, his thoughts fell away. Jazith was running towards them, and beyond her, at the village's edge, was a rushing flow of activity.

Both he and Corthak ran to meet her.

"What is it?" Corthak called as they closed.

Jazith pulled up and drew in a deep breath, her chest heaving. "Someone has killed a human."

SEVEN

Lycurgus, the legendary lawmaker who turned Sparta into a militarized state, was held aloft by the cult as the founder of Spartan strength, power, and success. They believed his past reforms were not only good and right, but necessary. They believed that any deviation from Lycurgus's laws was dangerous and would lead to disaster. In short, they were conservative to the point of resisting all change.

Podalinus of Sparta

"I don't know about this, Kaletor."

From where they stood in a mostly empty side street of Sparta, the soft light of the fading sun painted Vaseus's face in hues of orange and yellow. It made her golden hair, which spilled onto her shoulders, shimmer.

As Kaletor looked at her, the tightness that had been in his chest melted away.

"It's fine," he assured her for the second time. "They think I'm with Hullis."

She crossed her arms and shifted her weight onto one leg, causing her hip to stick out. "They better. I don't want to face your father's wrath for going behind his back."

"I'd be more afraid of my mother."

She giggled at that and looked around. "So what are we going to do?"

The street was quiet, lined on both sides by small peasant houses and closed shops. The city was settling in for the approaching night, and few people remained on the streets. Still, there was a low hum of voices coming from the main road two blocks away.

"Come on," he said, taking her hand and setting off in that direction. "I'll show you."

The warmth of her palm sent a flutter through his stomach. As they walked, he shot darting side glances at her, and she did the same. When their eyes met, they laughed.

They reached the main road. A few dozen people were flowing by, and the smell of wine rode the air. On one corner of the intersection stood eight hoplites, their spears pointed skyward as they watched the passersby.

He tugged her over to the opposite corner and stopped. "Now we wait."

"For?"

"Someone that looks like a Lycurgan."

"What?" she said, her green eyes widening. "How? It's not like spotting a yagar."

"Just trust me. If we watch closely enough, we'll know."

"No, we won't. And even if we did, what would be the point? What would we do then?"

A smile crept onto his lips as he scratched just above his ear. "We'd follow him."

Her reaction was not what he had expected. She seemed to think it over for a moment, eyes narrowing. Then, slowly, a smile of her own tugged at the corner of her full lips.

"You're not like the other boys, Kaletor. Not at all."

At first, he didn't know what to say, and all he could do was stare at her as if mesmerized.

It was a moment before he grunted and managed, "You're welcome."

Another of her intoxicating laughs escaped her. "So what heroic deed are we going to accomplish by following this Lycurgan?"

His smile broadened. "You know me all too well, my lady. First, I'll rough him up a bit, you know, a little payback for what they did at the Kolosaio. Then I'll make him tell us who their leader is—"

"Is that really necessary?"

Her interruption drove the smile from his face.

"Yes, Vaseus. It is. "Don't you remember what they did? They killed innocent people. They tried to kill you. I won't let them get away with that."

"I know what they did was horrible," she said, her flirtatious air evaporated, "and they shouldn't get away with it. But maybe attacking them isn't the right way. All that will do is cause them to fight back, and then we fight back again, and on and on it goes. Violence breeds more violence, which makes everyone afraid. When does it end?"

The answer came to him instantly. "It ends when they surrender or when they're all dead, and there's only one way to achieve either."

She sighed and shook her head. "Yes, you're right about that. There's only one *Spartan* way."

"What's that supposed to mean?"

Despite his harsh tone, she held his gaze with softness in her eyes.

Eventually, she turned her attention to the meandering crowd. "Nothing. Let's find us a Lycurgan."

He knew she was holding something back, but what more could he do? Besides, he didn't want to fight.

So, with silence reigning, he let it go and started studying everyone he could lay eyes on. The passing faces were unfamiliar. Many were too intent on where they were going to even notice that they were being watched. They saw all sorts as they stood there. Children, old women, young men, even a few dark-skinned Persians or Egyptians, and a heavily bearded, blonde-haired Dacian.

The sunlight was fading fast, and Kaletor was growing more and more frustrated. He was considering giving up when Vaseus leaned close and breathed one word in his ear.

"There."

He glanced at her and tried to follow her gaze, but he couldn't tell who she meant. "Where?"

Her hand intertwined with his. "He's getting away," she said, pulling him after her.

As they set off, he still didn't know who they were following. He scanned everyone ahead of them, but looking at the backs of people's heads didn't help.

"I don't see him," he rasped out of the corner of his mouth. "How do you know he's Lycurgan?"

"I just know."

He could tell she was determined, and that was good enough. Hand in hand, they passed through the sparse foot traffic at a brisk walk.

He continued eyeing the backs of people's heads as they went. Most had black or brown hair, each the same as the next. They wore simple, short sleeve tunics of red, white, or black. No one stood out. But Vaseus seemed to know where she was going, so he let her direct their path.

Eventually, however, he needed to know.

"Vaseus, I don't see—"

"There," she cut in. "Him."

All at once, he knew who she meant. A short, scrawny man wearing a ratty, black tunic had veered down a side street. He vanished around the corner.

"I see him," Kaletor said, breaking into a faster stride.

Before long, they gained the side street and turned. Within the deepening gloom of evening, the Lycurgan was hurrying away.

"Come on," he growled, pulling her along with him.

Without a word, she matched his speed. The Lycurgan was moving fast, almost running.

"Has he seen us?" he demanded.

"I don't think so."

"Then why is he going so fast?"

"I don't know. Maybe all the hoplites standing on every corner made him nervous."

Kaletor grunted but said no more as he picked up the pace.

Gradually, the gap shrunk between them. The Lycurgan continued on, turning several times down ever-darkening side streets and narrow alleys.

It was a long time before finally, with darkness shading everything in deep gloom, he stopped at the mouth of an alley. He stayed within the shadows, peering out at a main street where torches now blazed and only the occasional person walked by.

Kaletor pulled Vaseus over to the doorway of a dark shop. "Wait here," he said in a whisper.

He released her hand and moved towards the Lycurgan—

"Wait," Vaseus hissed, grabbing hold of his arm and dragging him close.

With just inches separating them, he saw the worry in her eyes. He brought a hand up and rested his thumb against her cheek, the tips of his fingers in her hair.

"It's alright," he said quietly. "I know what I'm doing."

"You don't have to," she whispered back. "You don't."

He brushed his thumb down the side of her nose. "I'll be fine. You'll see."

For a moment, she stared straight at him, her eyes wide. Then, all of a sudden, she stepped close and pressed her lips to his. The soft warmth of her mouth and body sent a thrill through his chest and spine.

She broke off the kiss and stepped back. "Be careful," she said, her voice so low he barely heard.

He grinned, for no words came. After a long look into her eyes, he turned away.

His grin vanished when he spotted the flash of a dagger in the Lycurgan's hand.

Everything seemed to happen all at once then. Someone screamed. Loud bellows and shouting followed. The Lycurgan sprang into action, sprinting from the gloom of the alley into the light. The clash of iron rang within the shouting.

Kaletor ran ahead. The moment he emerged from the alley, he saw it all. At least ten Lycurgans were attacking a handful of Elites, one of whom was already down. The others had formed a tight circle, spears levelled at their oncoming assailants. The Lycurgans came on from all sides, wielding swords and knives as they rushed the defensive circle.

One fell as a spear was rammed into his chest. But before the Elite could pull his weapon back, another Lycurgan arrived to cut him down.

Kaletor charged into the fray. He released a roar as he slammed into the back of an unsuspecting Lycurgan. The man fell hard, the collision with the cobblestones jarring his short sword from his hand. Kaletor snatched it up and swung it across the man's back. Barely hearing the scream, he stepped close and swung again. The scream ended abruptly.

Breathing hard, he looked to the defensive circle of the Elites. Only three remained upright, dead and dying men at their feet. Through the gaps between them, Kaletor spotted a finely dressed man sheltering within the circle. In that glance, he saw that it was Ockos, and a clear truth struck him.

They were going to kill the emperor.

A Lycurgan slipped between the preoccupied Elites and made straight for Ockos. Kaletor knew he was too far away, so he raised his sword over his head and threw. The blade spun end over end to punch through the middle of the Lycurgan's back.

As the man crashed to the ground, Ockos's eyes found Kaletor's. In that brief, frozen moment, he saw that disbelief filled the emperor.

A tall, dark Lycurgan turned and rushed Kaletor with a yell. As he arrived, he slashed his knife on a downward arc. Kaletor met the attack with a sharp jab to the wrist, and the knife skittered across the cobbles. The Lycurgan followed with a sweeping left hook. Kaletor ducked under and jabbed stiff fingers into the man's kidneys, causing him to groan and crumple. Kaletor straightened in one, swift motion, and slammed a rising fist into the Lycurgan's chin. Something cracked and his eyes rolled up as he collapsed.

Snarling, Kaletor ran towards the emperor. He could only watch as the second-last Elite went down from a thrown knife to the chest. Two Lycurgans converged on the last one still standing, leaving a third free to go for the emperor.

Kaletor sprinted harder, running so fast he felt as if he were flying.

As the Lycurgan arrived, sword raised to cut Ockos down, Kaletor slammed full tilt into his side. The impact jarred bones and they both went down.

Kaletor hit the ground flat on his back so fast he barely realized what had happened. The moment he hit, he felt something crack. An obliterating fire exploded down his left side.

Loosing a wild howl, he pitched his body around so that he could see the Lycurgan. The man was on his stomach, pushing himself up with both hands.

Kaletor surged up, roaring as he leapt on the man's back. The Lycurgan flattened beneath his weight and tried to squirm away. Kaletor took a fistful of hair, yanked the man's head back, and rammed it straight down to the cobblestones. The Lycurgan went limp.

A hideous scream demanded his attention. It was the last Elite's death cry as he went down. His killer pulled the knife from the Elite's back and turned to Ockos, who had backed away from the circle of his dead bodyguards.

Gasping for air, Kaletor willed strength to come as he pushed himself up. He staggered forward, the shooting fire in his side threatening to pull him back down.

He roared and loped into a run. At the same instant, the Lycurgan, his focus fixed on the emperor, rushed ahead. Ockos stood ready, but he was unarmed and unprotected.

The Lycurgan drew his knife back, screaming as he closed, poised to deliver the killing blow—

Kaletor dove in between the two, taking the thrusting blade in the gut while he grabbed the Lycurgan's upper arm with both hands. He gasped as he tumbled, his grip on the man's arm sliding off. He hit the ground and rolled, ending up flat on his back.

He was still then, staring up at the dark, blank sky. He could feel the searing rip of the blade in his belly.

He brought his hands to it and felt hot blood spilling out around the handle. He tried to crane his neck to see, but the moment he did, everything went black.

EIGHT

The Challenge has been around since before
yagars came to the Forever Forest. It's so
much a part of who we are that we have no
memory, stories, or even legends to explain
how it started or where it came from.

The Spoken Tales

"Kazog, is it true that you've killed a human?"

"It is."

Nearly everyone in the village was gathered at the Challenge Ring. They were all looking down to Corthak and the Superiors sitting on their benches, as well as Kazog, a lean male who stood alone in the center of the ring.

Jarka, having arrived late with Jazith, looked on from the top of the hill. Everything was still beneath the morning sun.

"Were there any witnesses?" Corthak asked.

"No, Warlord."

"I see. In that case, tell us what happened, every detail, and we will judge if the deed was necessary."

Jarka leaned close to Jazith and whispered, "When's the last time someone did this? Wasn't it Aksorg? That must have been over a year ago—"

"Quiet," she cut in, bringing a finger up to her lips.

He looked back down, gaze travelling over the heads of all those on the hill to Kazog. For the first time, he noticed that some blood speckled the sleek, yellowed bone that ran the length of the male's left forearm.

". . . to hunt," Kazog was saying, his tone steady, "when I came upon the trail of a boar. I tracked her, but I was careless. She heard me approach and took off through the forest. I pursued—"

"Why were you alone?" Warthux interrupted, rising from the bench.

"I awoke early and felt it was unnecessary to wake my son to join me," Kazog replied smoothly.

Warthux grunted but said nothing more as he sat back down.

"Go on," Corthak prompted.

The tall warrior with thick bands of black in his fur resumed his account in the same steady voice as before. "It took me some time to run the boar down, but eventually I made the kill. By then I was far to the south, deep in the forest. Within moments of pulling my spear free, I heard voices. The trees and undergrowth were sparse, and before I could do anything, they spotted me."

"How many?" one of the female Superiors asked.

"Five."

The answer caused a murmur to ripple through the crowd, and Jarka knew why. Humans were rarely seen in their region of the Forever Forest, and almost never more than one or two at a time.

Once the hushed voices calmed, Corthak said, "Go on."

"They were all Spartan warriors," Kazog said, "and they attacked me without hesitation. It happened so fast I had no choice but to engage—"

"Wrong," Warthux barked. "You could have run and lost them in the forest. Don't you know our ways? We cannot kill humans. They are vengeful, spiteful, and aggressive. They attack whenever they feel threatened. Why would you invite their wrath by killing—"

"Warthux," Corthak snapped, standing to glare at the brainless oaf. "Enough. Let him finish."

"But you know our ways, Corthak. You know we cannot let this pass."

"We will allow him to finish before passing judgment. That is our way."

Even from his distant position, Jarka could feel Warthux's rage as he glared back. It was clear that only Corthak's rank as Warlord silenced the brute.

Jarka's breath came harsh through his nose as he looked on.

The long silence that followed was broken when Kazog picked up where he left off.

"I met the Spartans at full sprint. My aim was to injure, not kill. At first, I succeeded. Two fell to my spear with wounds in their thighs. But then the others surrounded me and pressed their advantage, attacking on all sides. In that moment, I knew the terror of imminent death. The desperate need to live guided my spear higher, and I struck down the closest one. As I rushed by the fallen Spartan to get clear of the trap, one of them shouted something, and the four survivors fled. I considered giving chase to cut them all down, but decided that would only make things worse. Once they were gone, I returned to the village and reported what I had done."

When Kazog finished, silence followed. Jarka strained his ears forward as he and everyone else looked to the Superiors.

Corthak stood, his attention on the tall warrior alone in the ring. "Thank you for your account, Kazog. Based on the circumstances you just described, I am of the opinion that you acted honourably. The human you killed was neither innocent nor helpless. He attacked you with aggression and with numbers, and so left you no choice but to do as you did."

Corthak shifted his gaze to the crowd on the hill. "I propose that Kazog be found innocent and allowed to remain with us as an honourable warrior without change to his rank." He looked to the Superiors on either side of him. "All those in favour?"

The reaction was swift. All but two stood. One was Warthux, who had his arms crossed as he shook his head. The other was Hirk, his close friend and Eighth Superior.

Nothing more was necessary. With the majority vote aligned with the Warlord's will, Kazog was declared innocent. He nodded to the Superiors and exited the ring.

Jarka heard Jazith release a sigh. He twisted over to nudge her shoulder with an elbow. "You weren't worried, were you?"

The look she gave him was unreadable. "Weren't you?"

"Nah," he said, flashing her a wide smile. "Kazog would never go against the Warrior Code. He's always fought and behaved honourably. I knew there had to be a good reason for him to ki—"

"I can't!"

The shout silenced the general din that had arisen. Along with everyone else, Jarka looked down to see that Warthux was standing and glaring at Corthak, his chest heaving and his arms stiff at his sides.

"I will tolerate your weakness no more, Corthak. You step on our traditions at every turn. I won't accept it any longer!"

"What are you going on about?" the Fifth Superior demanded.

"Our Warlord is not who he pretends to be," Warthux boomed, moving away from the bench to address the crowd from the center of the ring. "He plans to destroy all that we value. If he has his way, our way of life will vanish, our sons and daughters will become weak and cowardly, and we will lose all respect and honour among the Clans."

"This is outrageous," Third called out. "The Warlord has done nothing to warrant such slander."

"Agreed," Ninth echoed. "Enough of this nonsense, Warthux. Just because you dislike the Warlord is no reason to drag us all into your baseless accusations."

Many in the crowd voiced their agreement, and as the noise built, Jarka shouted, "Sit down, you fool!"

"None of that," Jazith scolded.

They were words he would have expected their mother to say. The thought caused him to cast his gaze about to search for her.

Before he could find her among the crowd, the noise died down, and he returned his attention to the scene below.

Corthak had raised both arms for quiet. Now that he had it, he said, "Let Warthux speak. Do not forget that he is Second. We will afford him the honour and respect that rank deserves."

The thick brute grunted and continued to call out in the same angry tone as before. "Corthak is no longer fit to lead us. He plans to stop the wars with our neighbours, the wars that have kept our warriors strong for a thousand years. Even worse, he seeks to make alliances with them. I wouldn't be surprised if he's planning to bring back the disgraced Clanless!"

This time no one countered. Instead, stunned silence was the only answer. What Warthux spoke of was unthinkable. It was too insane to be true.

This, Jarka knew, was surely going through everyone else's mind. He would have thought the same if his father hadn't told him that this was exactly his plan.

How had Warthux found out? With his entire body tensed, Jarka couldn't even begin to guess.

As the silence stretched, Warthux turned, looked directly at Corthak, and said, "Warlord, I challenge you."

It felt as if the air itself became still. The silence became even heavier. No one moved. It seemed like time ceased to pass.

The Warlord was challenged. There was no greater thing.

Corthak stood, straightened to his full height, and said, "I accept your challenge."

His words were followed by total silence. Jarka looked from his father to Warthux and back again.

He felt Jazith's hand brush against his. He took hold and squeezed.

NINE

Be like Achilles—a fearless, powerful, skilled
warrior—and Sparta will love you.

Eurydemos of Corinth

The morning air was still cool as the sun rose over Sparta. Despite this, Kaletor felt warm in his dark red, short-sleeved tunic.

His body had felt hot ever since the Lycurgan's blade pierced his stomach. Six days on and it still hurt with every shift and movement.

"Are you sure you're alright?"

Kaletor looked over to Vaseus walking beside him. He forced a smile and let his hand fall away from his bandaged midsection. "Of course. It's practically healed already."

Her frown made it clear that she knew the lie for what it was. "Maybe this was a bad idea. We should go back—"

"No," he cut in, stopping and taking her hand. "I need this. I can't take another day of lying in bed. I need to be with someone other than my parents."

The creases on her brow melted away, and she smiled warmly. "Well in that case, let's keep going."

He squeezed her hand a little tighter before letting go. "Thanks."

They continued on, walking aimlessly through the quiet streets. One and two-story homes and shops remained closed, dark, and silent. The few people they came across were much like the buildings, their heads down as they hurried on their way. At almost every street corner, two or more hoplites were posted, their presence more obvious than ever.

The sight of their iron helmets, red cloaks, and long spears was comforting.

If the Lycurgans made another attack, he would not have to fight.

As they came upon a bakery that was pumping out the aroma of freshly baked bread, Vaseus blurted, "So do you want to talk about it?"

He had known this was coming, and having prepared his answer, the words came easily. "There's not much to talk about. I had to fight to save the emperor, so I did. Luckily it worked out."

He hoped this simple response would spare her the experience of that night.

"Come on, Kaletor," she said, her tone betraying her excitement. "Tell me everything."

He released a heavy sigh. *I should have known it wouldn't be that easy.*

His hand returned to the heavy bandages covering the ragged gash in his belly. "It was all a blur. I moved without really thinking, almost as if I had no control. It was different than training. I was faster and stronger. It felt like I couldn't be stopped."

He paused as fragmented memories of that night flashed in his mind. He heard the screams and moans of dying men, and tasted the iron of blood on his tongue.

An urge to share details seized him, but he grit his teeth and pushed it back down. Vaseus knew almost nothing of violence. She wouldn't understand.

Once they were past a trio of hoplites, she asked, "Were you scared?"

"No. There wasn't time to be scared. There was only aggression and anger."

"Well, I was scared. I thought you were . . . dead."

"You saw?" he said, looking over.

She met his gaze briefly, but quickly looked away. "Some."

Not knowing what to say, he reached over and took her hand. "I had to, Vaseus. I had to save the emperor."

With her free hand, she wiped at her face but didn't respond. They walked on in silence.

Before long, his mind turned to what he desperately wanted to tell her. Yet even as he burned to speak of it, he hesitated. She might think he was a monster. Maybe it would be best if he never told anyone.

Minutes passed, as did the buildings, the streets, and the hoplites. He grappled with the choice, going back and forth all the time.

Eventually, the need to get it out was too great.

"There's a darkness in me, Vaseus. It's hard to describe, but I know it's there. Sometimes it takes me over. When it does, I can't stop it."

As soon as he finished, she pulled up. "What are you talking about?" she asked, eyes boring into his.

He felt sweat prickle to life on his face and neck. "It happened when I saw the Lycurgans attacking the Emperor's Elites. Rage and hate exploded in me like an erupting volcano. All I wanted to do was kill them, and not because it was good or right. I thought protecting and saving people would be noble. I thought it would feel good and heroic. But it didn't. All I felt was this darkness, this hatred, this need to kill."

As he spoke, her eyes had widened, and her breath had visibly quickened.

But now that he had started, he felt a desperate need to get it all out.

"I had hoped that once I finally killed someone that it would go away. But it didn't. I don't feel bad about what I did. There's no guilt or pity. I can still hear their screams, but it doesn't bother me. I don't really feel anything. Do you think that's normal?"

"No," she said, stepping close and taking his other hand. "But it's not your fault. Our parents, our people, and this city are to blame. They've taught you to be violent and brutal your whole life. That's why you feel the way you feel.

"But you are good, Kaletor. I know you are. You want to protect those who cannot protect themselves. You want to save those who need saving. You want to become a great hero."

As Kaletor looked deep into her eyes, her brilliant, green eyes, something stirred within him. Gradually, the black darkness that had been there fell away, and as it did, a brief smile came to his lips.

"I don't know what I'd do without you, Vaseus. You shine brighter than anyone else I know."

For some reason, the statement did not please her. She seemed to shrink back a little, and after a moment, she turned away, saying, "Follow me," over a shoulder.

Before he could react, she set off, her pace quick and determined.

His long strides brought him alongside her. He opened his mouth to ask what was going on, but when he saw the rigid look on her face, he stopped himself. There were times, he had learned, when asking her questions was a bad idea. This was one of them. Clamping his mouth shut, he stayed at her side, walking silently where she led.

The city was waking up for yet another day. More people were on the streets, a few chatting here and there, but most moving in silence. There was also an increase in hoplites and the addition of Spartiates. Their numbers swelled to eight or more men per corner. The threat of a Lycurgan attack seemed distant.

The rising sun had turned the morning air hot, and Kaletor's wound was starting to throb when Vaseus turned down a winding back alley. The polished, smooth cobbles of the main streets gave way to cracked and worn ones. The walls crowding in on either side were made of cheap, flimsy wood.

For several minutes, they continued along more alleys, slanting sunlight lancing down in thin strips. The air remained cool in the shadows, though it stank of musty mold. More than a few rats scurried back into the sewers as they proceeded.

Alarm horns sounded in Kaletor's mind, but he remained silent.

At last, they emerged onto a proper street. Small, cramped houses crowded each side, their doors and windows crude and crooked. They were all squat and dark and packed tight together. The skinny channel running alongside the cobbles was overflowing with piss and shit. The rank stench of it crawled into his nostrils and down his throat.

"Where are we?" he asked, bringing a hand up to cover his nose.

"The real Sparta," Vaseus answered.

At that moment, he realized there were no hoplites or Spartiates in sight. A little further down the street, four people were hunched over and huddled by the front door of one of the shabby houses. They were casting quick, darting glances this way and that as they spoke amongst themselves.

As he gave the group a long look, Kaletor asked, "What are we doing here?"

Several seconds passed before Vaseus answered. When she finally did, her voice was somehow soft and strained all at once.

"The Empire is not the good, virtuous, or glorious place we've been told it is. We've been shielded from the truth because of the families we were born into. They told us the Empire is just and fair. They told us that people are happy and prosperous. But it's all lies. Many are poor, homeless, or starving. Taxes are so high they cripple almost everyone. People aren't happy, but to speak out is to invite slavery or death. The Empire is cruel and oppressive. Only fear of the Phalanxes prevents more people from rising up in rebellion. It's wrong, Kaletor. All of it is wrong."

While she spoke, he had kept an eye on the huddled group of men and women down the street. The alarms sounding inside him had become much louder.

"We should leave. It's not safe here—"

"Did you hear a word I just said?"

"Of course—"

"Look at me, Kaletor. Don't worry about them and look at me."

Reluctantly, he did as she asked. As his gaze met hers, he saw tears in her eyes.

"What's wrong?" he said, moving close to place both hands on her shoulders.

She wiped at her face and released a rattling breath. "I'm scared."

"Why? Because of what happened to me?"

She shook her head. "No. Because of who you're turning into." She brought her hands up to his face. "I don't want to see you become like them."

"Like who?"

"Like all the other violent and merciless Spartans. Promise me you'll always be good. Promise me you'll always do what you know is right, no matter what happens."

He had never seen so much fear in her eyes. He had to help. He had to do something. So even though he didn't understand why she was so upset, he knew what he had to say.

"I promise, Vaseus. I promise."

For a long moment, she looked at him, as if making sure he meant it.

Eventually, a sad smile came, and she wrapped her arms around him. He hugged back, holding her tight, his chin resting on top of her head. Her golden hair smelled of lavender.

They held each other for some time. His breath was calm and even. At some point, there was only the soft warmth of her body pressed against his.

It felt good. It felt right.

He didn't know why she was so upset, but that didn't matter. He knew, without a shadow of a doubt, that he would always protect her.

"I want to run away."

As they held each other, he had closed his eyes. Now he opened them, and without letting her go, he looked down, their faces inches apart. "Run away? Why?"

Her expression had changed to one he was much more familiar with—fierce determination.

"The Empire is broken and corrupt. It's cold and cruel and brings nothing but desperation and death. I don't want that to be my life. I don't want to be afraid all the time. I want to be free of all this violence. I want to be happy."

Several objections came into his mind like a rising phalanx wall.

But as he looked at her, his perfectly beautiful best friend, he realized that he wanted her more than anything else. In the face of everything she had said, all the objections in his mind rang hollow and false.

So, pushing them away, he said, "Would you like me to come with you?"

Her eyes went wide and her mouth fell open. "Are you serious?"

He smiled as he nodded.

"You would leave Sparta? Just for me?"

"I would do anything for you, Vaseus."

She seemed to hesitate, as if doubting his sincerity. But then she laughed and set her hands to his face. "Thank you, Kaletor. Thank you, thank you, thank you."

His smile became so wide it felt like all his teeth were showing. For a moment he held her eyes, her amazing green eyes. Then he moved a hand to the side of her head and kissed her. She kissed back, warm and full, her lips soft and eager.

When they pulled back to look at each other, she was beaming. He brought his hand over to brush a strand of hair away from her face, then slid his fingers through her golden locks.

Releasing a heavy exhale, he said, "So where should we go?"

"Somewhere warm and pretty," she said, somehow beaming even brighter.

"What about Rome? They say it's become the richest city outside of the Empire."

"I like that, and it's right by the sea."

"There's Sicily too, if you'd prefer an island."

She giggled, the most perfect of all sounds. "Islands are fun."

"Or maybe the lands to the East," Kaletor went on, smiling wide as he imagined their travels. "They say there are exotic lands beyond the former Persian Empire, beyond Babylon, where animals roam that you've never heard of—"

"Get away from my son!"

The bellow flipped Kaletor's gut. In that instant, he was frozen, unable to move.

Then he stepped out of Vaseus's arms and turned. His father had emerged from the alley and was coming straight for them.

"Father, wait—"

"Go!" Xanthos shouted as he arrived, waving an arm at Vaseus. "Get out of here, you traitor—"

"That's enough," Kaletor barked, stepping directly into his father's path.

"Save it, boy," Xanthos fired, spittle flying, veins standing out on his forehead and neck. "I heard what she said. My son will not betray the Empire. Not while I still draw breath."

"She didn't mean it. She was just talking—"

"No! I know who she is now. She has turned on her own people. She's our enemy. I wouldn't be surprised if she's a Lycurgan. I'm taking her to the emperor—"

"No!" Kaletor roared, shoving him back as he reached out for Vaseus. "Leave her alone."

Xanthos's glare had been fixed on Vaseus. Now it fell to him. "You dare defy me, boy? For her?"

Kaletor stared him down. "You'll have to kill me if you want to get to her."

His father was practically foaming at the mouth, but Kaletor didn't care. He stood his ground, jaw set as they faced each other down.

In a sudden burst of movement, Xanthos attacked, left fist lashing out faster than Kaletor expected. The punch slammed into his face. Sensing more than seeing the follow-up, Kaletor brought both arms up to block. Sharpness shot through his forearms as they absorbed the second punch. As another came, he sidestepped clear and countered with a jab aimed at his father's throat. Xanthos batted this aside and countered quickly. Kaletor ducked, but the right cross still connected with his cheek.

The blow spun him round. For a brief instant, he glimpsed Vaseus. Tears were on her cheeks, and anguish marred her face.

"Run, Vaseus. Run—"

Something heavy struck him between the shoulder blades. He seized up and fell to his hands and knees.

Through watery eyes, he saw Vaseus hesitate, giving him one final, ravaged look. Then she turned to run.

When Xanthos moved to pursue, Kaletor lunged and wrapped both arms around his father's leg. Xanthos roared and rained his fists down on Kaletor's head and neck. The pounding was terrible, but Kaletor grit his teeth and snarled spit as he held on.

"Run, Vaseus!" he called out again. "*Run!*"

His yell died, and all he knew were the blows smashing into him as he held on with everything he had. "

The iron tang of blood filled his mouth. Black dots blotched his vision. Still, he held on.

Another heavy blow struck the back of his skull, and he knew no more.

TEN

Become a Superior. Join their ranks, and all
will know your prowess, your strength, and
your skill. This is how you become great.

The Spoken Tales

"Good morning, family," Jarka said as he strolled into the dining hall,
the scent of fresh boar intensifying. He sniffed deep and smiled. His
mother, father, and sister looked over from where they sat around
the oaken table.

When no one replied, he added, "Fine day for a Challenge, wouldn't you
say?"

"Jarka," Enoth said. "Not today."

"Oh come on, Mother," he said, sitting next to Jazith. "It's going to be fun.
This is a Warlord Challenge. Even some from the Small Villages will be here!"

"Listen to your mother."

He looked to Corthak, who sat at the opposite end of the table across from
Enoth. He had already donned his antler bindings that encased his neck,
shoulders, and chest. His eyes were intent as he chewed a red hunk of the
boar's flank.

Despite the somber mood surrounding him, Jarka said, "How fast do you
think you'll win? Ten seconds? Five? If you wanted, you could play with him a
bit, make him believe he's got a chance. That way, when he loses, he'll be even
more devastated."

"That is not honourable," Enoth scolded. "And you know it."

"Yes, Mother," he said dutifully. "But it *is* Warthux. You must admit it's going to be great to watch him lose. I wonder how Vawk and Traz will handle being Clanless. My guess is they'll cry for weeks."

As he fell silent, no one responded. He grabbed a chunk of meat from the platter and took a hefty bite. Juice dripped down his chin as he chewed. He wiped his mouth with the back of a hand, his whiskers giving way, then bouncing back out.

Once he swallowed, he looked sidelong at Jazith. "You're rather quiet. You feeling alright?"

"I'm fine," she said, meeting his eye with a neutral look. "Just not as good as you, obviously."

"What's not to feel good about? The sun's shining—"

"It isn't, actually," she cut in. "It looks like it's going to rain."

He glanced out the nearest window and saw how grey it was outside.

"Oh. Still, Father is going to beat Warthux in front of everyone. He won't be a Superior anymore, and with any luck, he'll fight dishonourably and be one step away from banishment. Everyone's life will be better with him and the twins gone. What's not to like?"

"I'm just a little nervous," Jazith said quietly, crossing her arms atop the table. "No Challenge is guaranteed."

"Yes, but Father never loses—"

"Enough," Enoth said. "I don't want to hear anymore. Let your father eat in peace."

This time there was a sharp edge in her voice, so Jarka knew he had reached the end of his spear. He turned his attention to his food, and the four of them ate in silence.

Before long, Corthak stood. "It's time."

"Fight well, Husband," Enoth said.

"Fight well, Father," Jazith echoed.

Jarka dismissed the formal words. "Crush him."

Corthak nodded once then turned and strode from the room. Jarka wasn't sure, but he thought his father had let slip a smile.

"Oh, Jarka," Enoth said once there came the thud of the front door shutting. "What am I going to do with you?"

He looked her way with an exaggerated frown. "Whatever do you mean?"

On his left, Jazith chuckled, but nothing more was said.

Jarka blinked and smiled as he looked from one to the other. They both shook their heads.

*　　*　　*

Steady rain pattered down, dripping through the canopy overhead to drench everything beneath it. But the grey, wet day was not enough to keep the Clan from witnessing a Warlord Challenge.

From where he stood at the very front and base of the hill, Jarka turned to look around. Hundreds were jammed together, covering every inch of the slope. All of Home Village and many from the Small Villages were present, young and old standing shoulder to shoulder, silent sentinels awaiting the momentous fight. Despite the numbers, the only sound was the constant thrum of the heavy downpour, steadily soaking the mass of yellow-and-black-furred bodies.

"This is incredible. I've never seen so many of us on the hill."

Jazith, who was standing on his left, quietly said, "Me neither."

"Oh come on, Jaz. You're not still worried, are you?"

She didn't answer, studiously keeping her gaze fixed on the ring.

He couldn't remember the last time she had been wound up so tight. "It's pointless to worry," he pressed on. "It won't help, and—"

"Jarka," Enoth cut in. "No more."

Looking past Jazith to their mother, he narrowed his eyes and opened his mouth to speak—

But then stopped. Corthak had appeared and was walking into the ring.

Jarka wiped the wetness from his forehead and looked on. Striding in from the opposite side came Warthux. Three bands of bone were wrapped around his left forearm, and four long femur bones encased his shoulders and upper back.

Both looked grim as they faced each other within the ring. The rain grew heavier and louder. Neither Corthak nor Warthux spoke. The crowd was still and silent.

One of the Nine Superiors, a female named Essyx, rose from the bench. "Today's Challenge," she hollered through the pounding rain, "was issued honourably by Warthux and accepted honourably by Corthak. Fight until your opponent surrenders or is forced from the ring. Understood?"

Though it was difficult to tell through the constant downpour, Jarka thought he saw a grin tugging at Warthux's lips as he nodded.

"Smile while you can, filth," he muttered under his breath. "Soon you and your cowardly sons will be disgraced."

"Very well," Essyx called out. "Arm the warriors."

Two spears with stone leaf heads were brought forth. Corthak rolled his head, shook his arms loose, and rotated his torso back and forth. Warthux remained motionless, maintaining rigid focus on Corthak even as he was handed his spear.

No one made a sound as the entire Clan waited. It was as if everyone was holding their breath.

Soon the spear bearers were clear of the ring, leaving Corthak and Warthux alone, poised and ready to fight. There was only one thing left.

A moment stretched that seemed to last forever.

But then, over the pounding rain, there came the lone word from Essyx that everyone was waiting for.

"Begin."

Corthak rushed in with incredible speed, so fast he was almost a blur. As he came upon Warthux, he jabbed his spear high. The bulky brute had stayed stationary and blocked the strike by thrusting his spear up horizontally in two hands.

As the spears smashed into each other, Corthak used his forward momentum to deliver a two-footed kick to Warthux's chest. The impact sent him staggering back. Corthak hit the ground, water splashing. He quickly bounced up and closed the gap, the speed of his movements uncanny. Warthux leapt aside to avoid Corthak's slashing spear. The move put him at the very edge of the ring.

Warthux roared as he swept his spear out wildly to keep Corthak at bay. Jarka watched his father angle his spear to deflect the blow over his head. He then stepped in close and swung a left hook that struck Warthux in the cheek. The brute snarled as the blow forced his head to one side. Corthak followed up quick with a rising knee to the gut. As Warthux folded forward, Corthak swung the butt of his spear in a rising uppercut into Warthux's chin. The combination lifted Warthux from his feet, laying him flat out to fall straight on his back.

The instant he landed and settled, Corthak put the tip of his spear to the base of Warthux's throat.

It all happened so fast that Jarka had barely followed the action. In no more than ten heartbeats, it was over. Corthak had won.

Elation bloomed in Jarka's chest, and he was about to cheer aloud. But knowing the wrath he would face from his mother if he did, he managed to hold it in.

Smiling wide, he watched as his father straightened, reversed his spear, and offered it to Warthux. The defeated Superior took hold and Corthak pulled him up. The pair looked at each other and seemed to exchange a few words, but the heavy rain was too loud to hear what was said.

The exchange ended, Corthak turned away from Warthux to face the crowd. In the corner of his eye, Jarka saw Essyx rise from the bench, but he paid the Superior no heed. He watched as Warthux, now directly behind Corthak, stooped low and sprang up in one fluid movement—

"Father!"

Corthak's eyes locked with Jarka's. In that instant, Warthux drove the spear through his back. The stone head punched out through his chest. His body went slack, and his eyes went blank.

Enoth and Jazith screamed and wailed. Jarka's throat seized up, and his heart lurched as he watched his father fall to the ground.

Nausea swarmed his belly. His knees buckled. He couldn't move or breathe as he stared at his father lying far too still in the mud.

"What have you done!?"

"Dishonour on you, Warthux! Dishonour on your entire family!"

"Kill him! Somebody kill that coward!"

Shouts of this kind exploded forth from all across the crowd. It sounded like everyone was yelling. The power of the roar shook the very ground, vibrating through Jarka's seized-up chest.

As the outrage seethed all around him, he felt his jaw clench. His breath gusted hot through his clenched teeth. His hands balled into fists as he looked from his father to Warthux.

Despite the fury of the crowd raining down upon him, Warthux was shouting back, the flesh from his nose to his forehead ridged in a permanent snarl, his arms gesticulating wildly. In the face of this, the crowd noise slackened, and Warthux's words could be heard.

". . . the only way. He had lost his mind and would have dragged us all down with him. We would have become weak and been destroyed. This was the only way to save you all!"

The noise had almost entirely died off. Warthux moved closer to the hill, leaving Corthak's body in the center of the ring. "The Warlord is dead, slain during an honourable Challenge—"

"The fight was over," someone shouted. "Corthak won—"

"And yet *he is dead*," Warthux bellowed. "Slain by my hand. According to the Warrior Code, that makes me Warlord—"

Shouting exploded from the crowd to drown him out. Jarka felt his claws extend and dig into his hands. His jaw bunched up even more. Each breath came out harsher than the last.

Once again, Warthux shouted back at the crowd, this time demanding silence. It took a while, but eventually, the bellowing and yelling trailed off.

The coward bared his fangs as he called out, "I don't care if you like it or not. You will all accept me as your Warlord—"

Shouts of, "No!" and "Never!" erupted.

"You *will*," Warthux bellowed. "Because if you don't, I will destroy or banish you and your family—"

The answering roar that cut him off was the loudest yet, and it seemed that a rush of raging yagars would surge with Jarka to attack the mad murderer.

But at that moment, Warthux raised a fist into the pouring rain, a signal that brought all the Superiors rushing into the ring, each brandishing a spear. As they arrayed themselves at Warthux's back, at least twenty warriors appeared, bursting forth from within the forest to sprint towards the hill.

But it was the backing of the Superiors that discouraged any notion of an attack. They had declared for Warthux. The Warrior Code demanded that the lower ranks accept their decision.

Jarka released a roar that ripped through his throat as he charged. But before he took a third step, someone leapt onto his back and dragged him down.

He barely noticed the impact of hitting the ground. With another roar, he rolled and threw his attacker off. He whirled around, snarling as he lashed out with a fist—

But stopped short. It was Jazith. She was on her side, arms raised to protect her face. In the instant their eyes locked, he saw that terror consumed her.

Before he could do anything else, he heard his mother call out, "Jarka—"

A piercing wail sliced the air. He looked up to see his mother with a knife in her back, stabbed from behind by Traz. She screamed again as she fell to her knees.

"*No*," Jarka howled, surging to his feet to run towards her. Traz ripped the knife out and drove it in again. Enoth cried out, her face twisted in agony.

He was nearly there, about to ram into Traz—

But out of nowhere, Vawk launched into his path from within the crowd. They slammed into each other, bones jarring. The collision sent Jarka spinning. He hit the ground on his side, water splashing as he bounced and rolled.

Eventually, he ended up flat on his back. His left shoulder screamed, his chest and gut were seized up, and he couldn't breathe.

He ground his teeth as he struggled to rise. When he rolled onto his side and propped himself up on an elbow, he saw that Vawk was closing fast.

Jarka snarled, spittle spraying as he willed his body to cooperate. But his screaming shoulder and frozen lungs slowed him down.

He could only watch as Vawk arrived, teeth bared in a triumphant smile as he drew an arm back, knife in hand, poised to drive it home—

Someone came flying in from the side with a two-footed kick to Vawk's middle. The blindside attack sent him sprawling.

Jarka looked to his saviour and locked eyes with Zonyx, the female he had beaten in his last Challenge.

"Get out of here," she snapped, "before it's too late. Go, now!"

With that, she turned to face Vawk.

Jarka pushed his hands into the sopping mud, snarling from the effort it took to get to his knees. Air finally flowed into his lungs again. He sucked it in as rattling growls.

Everyone around him was running. As he struggled to his feet, Jazith was there, emerging through the rain and chaos.

"They're going to kill us," she cried, clutching at his chest. "We have to run!"

He gasped for air, taking hold of her forearms to keep from falling.

"I'm going to . . . kill them," he rasped, peering over her shoulder to search for the twins, squinting from the water streaming into his eyes. "They can't get away with this. I won't let them—"

"It's too late for that," she cut in, pulling at his shoulders to drag him away. "There's too many. We have to run."

"But Jaz. Mother and Father . . ."

"I know, Jarka, I know. But they would want us to live. We can only do that if we run."

A few other yagars had joined Zonyx in fighting off the twins. But just beyond the melee, Jarka noticed the armed warriors crossing the ring and making straight for them. He looked to their father, still lying where he had fallen. A heaviness crushed down on him, and it felt like his chest was collapsing. With tears in his eyes, he looked for their mother, but she was lost in the chaos.

"We have to go *now*."

The desperation in his sister's plea gave him a push, and he allowed her to drag him away. Together they ran, making for the trees, the shouts and cries of combat sounding behind them.

He gasped for air as every part of him screamed and demanded that he turn back to fight. Somehow he kept running, even as it tore and slashed and rent him apart.

Alongside Jazith he plunged into the forest, releasing a roar that ripped straight through him.

ELEVEN

Every Spartan boy was told the stories of Achilles, Leonidas, Menelaus, Herakles, Lysander, and all the rest of the great heroes. Their strength, glory, and power were idolized. This was one way that generation after generation was indoctrinated into the cult that is the Spartan Empire.

Eurydemos of Corinth

After ascending the streets to the very apex of the city, Kaletor stopped before the high wall of grey stone. He looked up to the rampart, squinting against the blazing sun. Six Elites were staring down at him, faces shrouded within their golden helmets. Unsure of how it worked, he waited in silence.

Eventually, one of them called down, "State your name and purpose."

"Kaletor, son of Captain Xanthos. I'm here to see the emperor. He summoned me."

There was no response. Kaletor brought a hand up to his brow to shield his eyes as he peered up at them. Two appeared to be in quiet conversation.

Assuming this meant he would be denied entry, possible excuses for his parents began to crop up in his mind.

But then, without a word, the huge wooden gate started to open, creaking and complaining as the doors were winched out.

Four other Elites came out to meet him. One stepped away from the others and growled, "Arms up."

Kaletor lifted his arms, and the man patted him down.

The search done, he said, "Come with us."

With two in front and two behind, they escorted him into the emperor's fortress. Three buildings sat side by side, each one made of the same stone as the huge wall that encircled the grounds. The two on the flanks were identical, both large, three-story barracks that housed the Elites, the personal guards of the emperor. The middle structure was a massive palace that rose five stories high and sprawled out to either side. A towering set of three hundred marble stairs rose straight up to the ceremonial front entrance. The entire exterior of stone was adorned in red and gold banners.

But Kaletor had seen the palace before, and so only spared the impressive building a fleeting glance.

As they progressed along the path that cut through the training grounds and led to the main side entrance, familiar flashes and sensations from a week earlier came flooding back. The harsh shouts of his father as he went for Vaseus. The fury that had consumed him as he fought to defend her. The numbing pain as Xanthos rained down blow after blow. But worse than all of this was the sight of Vaseus's face as she watched, tears streaming down her cheeks.

He released a heavy exhale and shook his head, but there was no escape. It was the last image he had of her, for she had not returned home that night. Once two days had passed and she still hadn't turned up, the wretched truth had struck him like a hammer blow—she was gone, and she wasn't coming back. He didn't know how, but somehow he knew. Her family was still looking for her, but it seemed pointless.

The purple bruises on his face and neck throbbed as his gut swirled and his head pounded. How could she leave without him? How could she do that? He needed her now more than ever. Didn't she love him the way he loved her? Were they not best friends that would always be together?

As usual, these questions triggered swift answers in his mind. *She ran because I could not protect her. I am weak and useless and unworthy to have her. If only I could have stopped my father, we would still be together. It's my fault that she's gone.*

He grit his teeth and dug his fingernails into the flesh of his palms.

They were inside the palace, walking along the winding corridors, passing empty rooms, and ascending flights of stairs. He barely noticed. The swirling in his gut had worsened. He wanted to scream or hit something. But he couldn't, not here at least.

His escort stopped before a set of towering double doors. Eight Elites stood guard, each fully girded for war. They regarded Kaletor in silence.

One of those that had escorted him announced his name and purpose. One of the eight, a man with long, black hair and dark eyes, nodded to the speaker.

"He is expected," the man said, looking to Kaletor. "Have you been summoned by the emperor before?"

"No, sir."

The Elite grinned. "Good."

He turned, pushed the doors in, and proceeded into the room beyond. Uncaring of the hard looks the other Elites gave him as they made a narrow lane in their ranks, Kaletor followed the leader in.

The huge, high-ceilinged throne room was familiar to him. Eight-foot columns ran evenly spaced all around, bordering a vast open area in the center. Paintings depicting epic battles, burning cities, legendary Spartans, and the mighty gods adorned the walls. Marble busts and statues of past emperors stood on the inner side of the columns. Their hair and beards were either chestnut brown or charcoal black. Their dark eyes were piercing and stern.

He walked between these lifelike sculptures of dead emperors, footsteps clicking on the stone floor.

At the far end of the room towered the very seat of the Empire, the emperor's throne. Eighteen white stairs led straight up to a wide, flat dais. Centered atop the rising spire of marble was a molten seat of gold, high-backed with straight, sharp edges, a solid, heavy mass. It was said that the shields of Leonidas and his brave three hundred had been melted down to forge the throne of ultimate power.

Perched on the seat atop the tall spire of marble was Ockos himself. He wore a gold-trimmed, blood-red robe that hung loose on his body.

Kaletor stopped before the bottom step, took a knee, and bowed his head.

Once his gaze was on the floor, his escort announced, "Emperor, I present Kaletor, son of Captain Xanthos."

Ockos's voice cut through the huge, empty hall like a knife. "Of course it is. Don't you think I recognize the one who saved my life?"

"Yes, sir."

"Rise, Spartan."

Kaletor did as instructed, his gaze lifting. Ockos was descending the stairs, a slight smile tugging at his thin lips.

When he was halfway down, he said, "Thank you, Captain. Dismissed."

As his escort saluted and left, Kaletor swallowed. He had never been alone with the emperor before. Suddenly, his mouth was dry and his palms were sweaty.

Ockos stopped on the bottom step. "How are you feeling?"

"Better, sir."

"Healing up alright?"

"Yes, sir."

The emperor's smile widened as he stepped down and moved closer. "I'm glad to hear it. I need brave men like you protecting the Empire. What you did that night was the most selfless and loyal act I've ever witnessed. You sacrificed yourself to save me. I want you to know that I am deeply grateful."

Unsure how to respond, Kaletor could only manage, "Thank you, sir."

Ockos reached out and clapped a hand on his shoulder. "You did well, Spartan. I am in your debt. So, tell me what you want in return. If it is within my power to make it so, I will."

The image of Vaseus fleeing while his father beat him flashed in Kaletor's mind.

A ragged breath came out, and ignoring his first instinct to decline the offer, he rasped, "There's a girl I care for. A friend. She's been missing for a week. No one knows where she is. I would very much like her found."

The warm smile left Ockos's face and he withdrew his hand. "I see. Do you know what happened?"

"You dare defy me, boy?"

His father's shout rang loud in his mind.

He swallowed and glanced away from the emperor. "Yes. My parents disapproved of our friendship. When my father saw us together, he moved to attack her. I couldn't allow that, so I stopped him. I held him back so she could get away."

Without realizing it, his hands had curled into fists. He forced them to relax as he looked back to Ockos, bracing for him to side with Xanthos.

The emperor's response was level. "So those welts on your face aren't from when you saved me?"

Kaletor shook his head. "No, sir."

Ockos chuckled and gave him a light tap on the shoulder. "You are not what I expected, my boy. You do not disguise your true feelings from me, as so many others do. And what's even more impressive is that you fight for what you believe in, even in the face of death. These are qualities I value highly."

Praise was not at all what Kaletor was expecting. Taken aback once more, he repeated the automatic response. "Thank you, sir."

Ockos laughed heartily. "Your wish is granted. I will send out search parties to look for your friend."

The emperor paused, his expression one of someone searching for a decision. Before long, he must have reached it.

"I feel a bond with you, Kaletor. It was forged in that instant when I thought I was going to die. When I saw you take the knife meant for me, I felt it then and there. First, you saved my life, then, when you were on the ground, I saved yours. Such deeds are how unbreakable trust and loyalty are gained and earned between men. And now, hearing what kind of Spartan you are, I feel it as strong as I felt it that night. Do you feel it too, son?"

The naked vulnerability of the emperor's statements brought sweat to Kaletor's brow. Although he didn't really know what Ockos was talking about, he knew what answer to give.

"Yes, sir. I feel it too."

Ockos smiled warmly. "I'm glad. Trust in others is something an emperor cannot afford to misplace. But I can already feel that you are someone I can trust."

As he finished, he turned and started walking toward the back of the room. "Come with me, son. There's someone I want you to meet."

Kaletor hurried to keep up, his thoughts awhirl. This was not how he had imagined their meeting playing out. The emperor had always seemed detached and distant. On the rare occasion Kaletor had been in his company, he barely spoke to anyone. But this was normal. Many highborn Spartans did the same.

Yet now he was lively, cheerful, and talkative. What was the reason for the change? Was it because he could open up with someone he trusted? Or was there something else going on?

He didn't have any answers. Girding himself, he followed the emperor through an open doorway into a wide, winding hall. A dark purple rug with silver trim ran down the middle of the stone floor. Huge tapestries depicting battle scenes adorned the walls.

When the hall split in two, Ockos went right. After a gradual bend, the hall straightened and ended at a single wooden door. Black bands of iron stretched a rectangle across its surface.

As they approached the door, Kaletor noticed his mouth was dry. He let out a shaky breath as Ockos opened the door and proceeded inside.

In the instant of entering, he was hit by a strange smell, something pungent yet sweet. The room was dimly lit and shrouded in shadow. He could sense it was spacious but could hardly see anything. One small window at the back wall was thirty paces or more away, and the light spilling in was a veiled, deep orange.

Ockos shut the door behind them, and the darkness deepened.

"Do not worry," he said, "your eyes will adjust in a moment."

Kaletor felt sweat prickle to life on his neck and back. His muscles tensed as he stood at the emperor's side in silence. It was uncomfortable not being able to see his surroundings. He felt too vulnerable.

He was about to ask where they were when he heard something. It was so soft and faint that he wasn't sure if he had heard anything at all. He closed his eyes and listened. There it was again, a gentle swish of something passing through the air. It came from straight ahead.

He opened his eyes and bent at the knee, ready to act—

The emperor's hand settled on his shoulder. "It's alright, son. She won't hurt you."

"Who won't?"

As his question died, something huge stepped up to them. Kaletor braced, but nothing happened. Through the dark, he glimpsed hints of yellow as he tilted his head back.

There, at least four heads taller than himself, he met the gaze of whoever it was. She was looking straight at him, her eyes bright and piercing.

"This," Ockos said softly, "is Sola."

Kaletor swallowed. His sight was adjusting, and suddenly he could make out the yagar's round ears and the black-and-yellow fur of her face. But it was her gleaming, golden eyes that captured his focus. The pupils were vertical slits, and the full weight of her attention made it feel like ice was jabbing into his heart.

Several seconds passed in total silence.

It was finally broken when the emperor chuckled and moved off. "Sola, meet Kaletor."

"The boy who saved you?" she asked, her voice both youthful and full of power.

"A boy no longer, my dear."

Blue sparks spat in the dark as the clack of metal broke apart the still quiet. The next moment, a small flame bloomed in a torch. By its light, Kaletor watched Ockos lay down a knife and piece of flint on a small desk.

"Must you make it so bright in here?"

The emperor chuckled again as he moved to rejoin them. "We must accommodate our guest."

Kaletor looked back to the yagar. She stood tall and straight, towering at least seven feet high. She wore nothing, revealing the deep, yellow fur with black spots that covered her, save for a plume of white at her chest. She was sleek yet solid, her limbs and neck thick with muscle.

He couldn't help but stare.

Her eyes narrowed as she looked down at him, the long, silver whiskers at her cheeks bristling. "Does he not know it's impolite to gawk?"

Kaletor's face burned as he looked away.

"Think of it as a compliment, my dear," Ockos said, coming to a stop beside her and looking at Kaletor. "Have you ever seen a yagar?"

"Only from a distance," he answered, the words coming out a bit shaky.

"Then I applaud you. Most men cringe or shrink the first time they see one up close."

Kaletor had no response, and so said nothing.

Ockos smiled warmly. "Incredible, isn't she?"

He nodded. "Yes. How is it that she speaks our language? I thought yagars only spoke their own."

"She was born in Sparta," Ockos answered, moving slowly behind and around Sola, who remained silent and still as a statue. "Right here in the palace, in fact. She speaks our language because it's the only one she has ever heard."

He stopped on her left side and touched a hand to her arm. "I have been her caretaker since the day she was born. She is like my own child."

Kaletor struggled to contain the impulse to act. All his life he had been told that yagars were mindless savages who killed for sport. To see the emperor so close to one, unguarded and totally vulnerable, sent sparks of readiness through his body.

And yet Sola looked down at Ockos with what appeared to be fondness, and the emperor was completely at ease. They looked at each other in silence for a moment, and in that look, there was an intimacy and love that Kaletor recognized was beyond anything he himself had ever known.

Then, without a word or gesture, Sola turned and walked away, disappearing into dark shadows.

Kaletor hadn't realized just how taut his body had become. With the yagar gone, he let out a ragged exhale and felt his muscles relax.

"You did well to conceal it."

He forced his gaze away from the last spot he had seen Sola and looked to the emperor. "Conceal it, sir?"

"Your alarm," Ockos supplied, his hands clasped in front of his waist. "Everyone reacts the same. I suppose we can't help it. Yagars are so clearly more powerful than us, so we see them as dangerous, a threat to be guarded against. All because we are inferior."

"Forgive me, Emperor, but I thought yagars attack humans whenever they have the chance. Isn't that a good reason to be cautious around them?"

"Sola could have killed you in an instant. Did she?"

Kaletor shook his head.

Ockos released a sigh. "Everything isn't always black and white. Yes, yagars are dangerous, brutal, and violent people. But they're also beautiful, powerful, majestic, and proud. Perhaps they deserve our black hatred and violent opposition. But perhaps not."

Once more, Kaletor was stuck for words. He shifted his weight onto his right side but said nothing.

"I'm sorry," Ockos soon said, running a hand along the gold-flecked diadem atop his head. "These are problems I wrestle with, but they do not concern you." He stepped forward to close the gap between them. "You must be wondering why I brought you here."

Kaletor nodded. "Yes, sir."

"Sola is my biggest secret," Ockos said, his tone suddenly low and somber. "Very few people know of her existence, let alone the nature of our relationship. Most people still believe that every yagar should be killed or imprisoned, so naturally, I keep her hidden here, where it's safe. But you are different than most people, Kaletor. Most people aren't brave enough to sacrifice their life for their emperor. For this reason, I know I can trust you, even with my most precious secret. Am I wrong to do so?"

"Of course not, sir," Kaletor said, his head starting to spin. "You are my emperor. You can trust me with anything."

Ockos smiled. "I thought so. In the interest of building that trust, I would like to ask you a question."

The beginnings of a lump formed in Kaletor's throat. "Of course," he said around it, his voice thick.

A brief moment of silence ensued. Ockos's dark eyes held steady on Kaletor until he broke it.

"I care for Sola more deeply than anyone else in this world," he said, starting to pace slowly around Kaletor. "I will always do everything in my power to keep her safe. But what if I can't? What if I fail? This possibility is something I've dwelled on in the dark of night. One thing I know for sure is that I would hate anyone who caused her harm, more than I have ever hated anyone before. And I would inflict unspeakable pain on them if given the chance."

At this point, Ockos was back in front of him.

"I spoke with your father," he continued, their eyes locked. "He told me what happened with your friend. He told me you fought him so that she could escape. He also told me you've never disobeyed him before. This leads me to believe that you care for this girl as much as I care for Sola. Am I right to think so?"

The lump in Kaletor's throat was making it difficult to breath. Untrusting his voice, he answered only with a nod.

"Yes, I can see it in your face. You truly do love her. How long did you say she's been missing?"

The words came out in a harsh husk. "A week."

Ockos shook his head solemnly. "You poor boy. You may not believe me, but I can imagine what you're feeling. As emperor, I have become skilled at putting myself in the minds of others.

"And so I come to the question I wish to ask you. It could be argued that your father is the reason you are now separated from the one you care for most in this world. If I were you, I would hate him with every bone and muscle in me. So, tell me the truth now, son. Do you hate your father?"

The moment the question was asked, Kaletor realized it was a notion that had never crossed his mind. He felt his hands ball into fists and his jaw clench tight.

Forgetting to consider what the emperor might want to hear, he answered in a low, quiet tone. "I do not hate my father. He was only doing what he thought was right. My anger is with myself. I hate my failure and my weakness."

Ockos's expression shifted in response, turning into something hard and rigged.

Kaletor blinked and his breath caught. He had said the wrong thing.

All his hopes for fast promotion and important military postings, all that he wanted besides Vaseus, seemed to vanish like smoke.

How could I be so stupid—

"It is a rare thing," Ockos said, disrupting Kaletor's thoughts, "for an emperor to receive an honest, genuine answer. It is rarer still for a man to find another who shares the same struggles in life."

He stepped in closer, eyes boring into Kaletor's. "I too hate my weakness. I have spent my entire life trying to overcome it, both as a man and as an emperor. I seek to strike it down at every turn."

He paused, as if hesitant to say anymore.

But then, after a moment, he said, "I'm going to tell you something that I've never told anyone else."

He brought a hand up to settle on Kaletor's shoulder. "The Empire is dying. Weakness has spread to every corner, a weakness born of disobedience, free thinking, and disloyalty. I blame myself for allowing this. I have not been a strong enough emperor. But I love Sparta. I will not be the one responsible for her demise. I have come to realize that there is only one way to save our glorious Empire; by the sword and spear. We must deliver blood and death to all lands. We must instill terror in all those who would defy the strength and power of Sparta."

The emperor's words sent something dark and alive crawling down Kaletor's back. It felt as if his skin were prickling to life. It was a dark thrill, and he turned to it fully.

A response came to him then as if on its own. "Violence is the only thing people understand. When they feel like they can do whatever they want without deadly consequences, there is chaos."

"Ha!" Ockos laughed, slapping Kaletor's shoulder before turning aside. "I knew it. I knew you would understand. The Empire needs order and justice, stability and security. If that means hundreds or thousands must die, so be it. Sparta is worth any sacrifice. People will fear me, and many will hate me. My weakness has held me back and kept me from doing what needed to be done. But no longer. The Empire's survival is more important than how much I am loved. From now on, I will be much stronger.

"First, traitors will be hunted down and executed. Free thinkers will be silenced. Uprisings will be crushed without mercy. Then, we'll turn to conquering the west. Now that Rome has all but destroyed Carthage, their Republic is stronger than ever. Our alliance with them will end and we will conquer their lands for the Empire. All who stand against us will fall."

The emperor's voice had grown more and more powerful as he spoke. Now he looked back to Kaletor, eyes afire and arms spread wide. "I have seen your loyalty, your strength, and your bravery. I have also seen your rage. Pledge your life to me, and I promise to unleash it. Together, you and I will make Sparta greater and stronger than ever before. Together, you and I will conquer our weakness."

Kaletor was speechless. Visions of glorious battle filled his mind, of victory after victory. He also heard a small voice, a voice that might have been Vaseus, a voice pleading with him to remember his promise.

But as he looked into the fierce eyes of his emperor, he saw what his future could be.

Dropping to a knee, he said, "Glory is the only thing I want that I can still have. My life and my spear are yours, Emperor. I swear, that from this day forward, I will kill every enemy of Sparta."

As he bowed his head, Ockos released a low laugh, and the last whisper of Vaseus's voice faded away.

BOOK TWO

THE
WAR
WITHIN

179 B.C.E.

SIXTEEN YEARS LATER

TWELVE

In those early days, no one was ever banished, and there was no such thing as Clanless. But at some point, someone realized just how powerful the threat of banishment could be. So, in the name of motivating everyone to become better warriors, it was decided that those who fought poorly could be sent away forever.

The Spoken Tales

J arka moved slowly between the trees, eyes wide and ears rotated forward. He stayed low, his spear gliding just above the forest floor. The carpet of pine needles silenced his steps.

It had rained throughout the night, and chill drips still clung to the budding canopy of green. The smells of wet pine and old bark filled his nose as he breathed deep and steady. Squirrels scurried through the branches, claws clicking. Small red birds, recently returned from their winter nesting grounds, sang their songs.

The hunt had been long and uneventful, and his belly was grumbling its empty complaints. He was about to straighten out of his crouch and turn back—

But then, finally, a new scent on the wind. He paused to sniff.

Elk, and not far. He set off in a new direction, stepping carefully over gnarled, mossy roots.

It wasn't long before he spotted a mother and her calf, both drinking from a small stream. He moved from tree to tree, fast and silent, until he had an open throw.

He raised his spear—

And was blindsided. The impact sent him to the ground. He tried to roll away as he hit, but his attacker leapt on and pinned him down.

"I win."

Still unable to move, he could only grin into the pine needles. "Only because I let you."

Rox screwed an elbow into the back of his ribs. "You never let anyone win."

Jarka laughed. "Oh yes. I'd forgotten."

He thrust his arm up under her arm, grabbed hold of her shoulder, and pulled. This shifted her body weight enough to allow him a quick roll, and he spun her onto her back.

He finished the reversal positioned flat atop her front, their faces inches apart.

She smiled as they looked into each other's eyes. "You're lucky I love you so much."

"Oh yeah? Why's that?"

Her hand came up to cup his cheek, fingers brushing through his whiskers. "Because I could've killed you just now, if I'd wanted to."

He laughed again. "I don't think so. No one can kill me."

She craned her neck and planted her lips to his. He kissed back for a long moment, running his hands through the soft plume of white fur at her chest and stomach.

But then, just as his blood was starting to pump hot, she broke it off and sank back down.

He released a chuckling groan. "Come on, Rox. We rarely have this much privacy."

"Rarely?" she said, shifting her head slightly back, her eyes filled with amusement. "I don't think you know what that word means."

He brought his hand up to play with the purple gem necklace at her throat. "Sure I do. It means less than twice a day."

Her answering laugh was full and light, an intoxicating sound of sweetness. "Not here."

"Why not? I need to, Rox. I'm a young bull with more stamina and strength than any yagar you've ever known."

"A young bull who was just pinned by an even younger vixen."

"Oh, you cut deep," he growled, burying his face in her chest. "That wasn't fair. I was distracted."

She giggled and set her hands just below his ears. "No excuses, my love. A true warrior is always alert to her surroundings. Perhaps my skills have surpassed yours."

He collapsed down, the top of his head resting under her chin. "Rox, you wound me. You cut deep. How can you cut so deep?"

"Oh stop," she said, roughly rubbing his ears.

Growling, he slid himself up so that his face was back in front of hers. Without hesitation he kissed her again, long and deep, their tongues meeting and dancing together.

*   *   *

The sprawling village of the Clanless was visible through the thinning trees. Jarka walked leisurely beside Rox, his hand intertwined with hers.

Distant voices and the sound of cracking spears reached them when she said, "I hope you know how grateful I am."

He stepped around the trunk of a maple tree before glancing over. "Oh?"

"You accepted me so quickly. I feel so welcome here thanks to you. When I had to leave my Clan, I was terrified. All I heard about this place was how awful it was."

"I heard the same things, years ago," he replied. "I thought this place would be dark and lawless. I was nervous about coming here too."

Her eyes widened. "You, nervous? Impossible."

He chuckled. "Well, only a bit."

"That must have changed fast. Everyone seems to love you."

"I won't argue with that."

She laughed and squeezed his hand a little tighter. "I can't blame them."

They looked long at each other as they emerged from the trees and continued towards the village. Thousands of small, wooden huts sprawled across the wide, flat clearing, bordered on all sides by the forest wall of towering pines and oaks.

The village itself had grown gradually, so there was almost no order in its layout. Well-worn foot paths formed narrow, winding streets, snaking every which way through the shin-high grasses.

"Is there a Challenge today?" Jarka asked as they came around behind one of the huts and stepped onto one such path.

"I'm not sure."

Spotting someone walking up ahead, he called, "Oi!"

Whoever it was didn't react. They just continued on in the same manner, slightly hunched over and moving slowly.

He was about to call out again, but then realized who it was and held back. "I think that's Elder Imzen."

"Oh no," Rox said with a shudder. "She's so strange."

"But harmless. Let's sneak up on her, send a bit of life coursing through those old bones."

"Jarka, no—"

He raced ahead before she could protest further. He tread light, dancing on the balls of his feet, moving swiftly up on the plodding Elder.

The gap between them shrank. He made no sound as he rushed up behind her—

"Hello, young ones."

She hadn't turned around. She hadn't even stopped walking.

"Imzen!" he exclaimed, glancing back to Rox as he fell into step at the Elder's side. "How did you know I was coming?"

"I felt your footfalls through the ground," she answered, her voice weathered but gentle.

"Really? That's impressive. When did you learn to do that?"

Still walking at the same, slow pace, her attention straight ahead, Imzen said, "I did nothing."

"Right. Anyway, do you know if there's a Challenge today?"

"I do not."

"What a surprise. Well, we've got to get going. Thanks for your help, Imzen. Always a pleasure."

Her gaze still fixed straight on, the Elder said, "Goodbye, young ones."

He hurried by, shaking his head as he winked at Rox. "See. Harmless."

"True. But still strange."

He reached over to shove her shoulder. "Kind of like you."

She gasped and pushed back. "You're terrible!"

They continued their banter as they walked on, moving deeper into the village. As they progressed, they met many familiar faces. Jarka greeted one after another, laughing and smiling all the way.

When they came to the bustling square at the heart of the village, they halted. It was here, upon the wide, open space of stunted grass and hardpack dirt, that many yagars mingled. Most were sparring, either with or without spears. Others were standing together in small groups, talking and laughing amongst themselves. Youngsters dashed this way and that, chasing each other all through the square.

As he looked on the chaotic bustle, a deep chuckle rumbled in Jarka's throat. He glanced over to Rox just as she glanced over at him.

"I still can't believe how amazing this place is," she said.

"I wish the Clans could see it. We're not weak or immoral or anything like that. We all just lost one too many Challenges, or we had to leave our Clan for some reason.

"In any case," he added, nudging her in the side, "now that you're here, this place is even better."

She released a soft, musical laugh. "You certainly are a smooth talker. I wonder how many females before me have fallen prey to your charms."

Before he could reply, someone called his name. He would have ignored them, but Rox turned away. He released a long exhale as he turned with her.

From within the crowd emerged the one who had called out. As he neared, Jarka said, "Well if it isn't Relyk, the Unskilled One."

The younger, sleeker male bared his fangs in a mock snarl. "I think we will spar again soon so you can experience how much I've improved."

He let a pair of youngsters pass before joining them. "Rox," he said, inclining his head in greeting.

She returned the gesture. "Relyk."

"Why wait?"

Jarka quickstepped ahead and swung a high jab. Relyk weaved under it and wrapped his arms around Jarka's torso. They both eased up then, sharing a laugh.

Once they disentangled from each other, Jarka pointed to his friend's shoulder. "That's new. Antler or bone?"

"Bone." Relyk glanced down at the thick, single band of red-dyed bone coiled around his left shoulder. "From a deer's thigh. I just finished it last night."

"Yet another doomed attempt to attract the attention of a female, yes?"

Relyk's small, dark eyes flashed within his sparingly spotted face. "Maybe."

"Of course it is. I see right through you."

Rox jabbed an elbow into his side. "Don't be mean."

"He likes it. Don't you, old friend?"

"I wouldn't say that."

Jarka waved a hand dismissively. "Please. Anyway, how goes the hunt for a female?"

Relyk's glower lifted. "Better. Remember Lalath?"

"Oh, yes," Jarka replied, smiling wide until he caught Rox studying him.

"My age I believe," he hurried on. "Short but quick, kind of like you. So what happened? Did you ask her to spar?"

"No."

"Ask her on a hunt?"

"No."

"Tell her she was a beauty like no other?"

Relyk shook his head.

Jarka wheezed out a long, sarcastic breath. "Then what did you say?"

"Nothing."

He turned to Rox, his eyes wide. "He's hopeless."

The beginnings of a laugh slipped out before she stifled it. Looking to Relyk, she asked, "So what did happen?"

"We looked at each other."

Jarka doubled over laughing.

"Oh, my poor, poor friend," he said, straightening with tears in his eyes. "You truly are hopeless."

Relyk's glower had returned, but before he could retort, Jarka held up a hand and looked beyond him. "Hold that thought. Someone important approaches."

Jazith was picking her way through the crowded square, and she was moving fast.

"What a happy day," Jarka said, feeling his whiskers rise as he beamed. "All my favourite yagars in one place."

When Jazith was within earshot, he called out, "Greetings and well wishes, dear sister—"

"No time for that," she cut in like a cracking tree branch. "You must come with me. Now."

"How very impolite. When you meet someone you haven't seen in a while, it's best to start with a friendly—"

"Not now, Jarka. This can't wait. Are you coming or not?"

He tilted his head to one side and screwed up his eyes. "Do I know you?"

Jazith scowled before turning and storming off.

"Alright, alright," he called out, hurrying after her and motioning for Rox and Relyk to follow. "We're coming. What's put you in such a foul mood?"

She ignored him as she walked at a brisk pace across the square.

He glanced sidelong at Rox. Shaking his head, he said, "Sisters. They're not always so nice."

Rox shoved his shoulder. "Neither are brothers."

Remaining silent and maintaining her hurried pace, Jazith led them through the village and into the forest. As they went, Jarka pestered her for answers but received none.

They had been walking for quite some time when she finally stopped and faced them. "From now on, we all move in silence."

Jarka released a low growl. "Come on, Jaz. Just tell us what we're doing out here."

"There are humans nearby."

"This close to the village?" Relyk said.

"That's why I was in such a rush." She paused, but when no one responded, she said, "Follow me."

They continued on, moving slower and more cautiously through the tightly packed tangle of moss-soaked trees.

Jarka's heart quickened and his muscles tensed. If humans were close, they had to be ready to move fast.

They hadn't gone much farther when Jazith crouched low and hid behind a wide tree trunk. Jarka moved to crouch behind her. Out of the corner of his eye, he saw Rox and Relyk hide behind some neighbouring brush.

"Where are they?" he whispered, settling a hand on Jazith's shoulder as he scanned the tangled greenery that obscured nearly everything in the distance.

She inched her face slowly out to see, then pointed. "There. Through that gap."

Following her finger, he saw what she was pointing to. Within a small clearing of stunted brown grasses sat a dark tent. A thin trail of smoke twirled skyward beside it. Three humans were visible, all of them women. Two sat on the ground and were talking quietly. The third was focused on something near the tent.

"Is that all of them?" Jarka asked.

Jazith nodded.

"Where are the men?"

"There are no men."

"Oh. Well that's convenient."

He straightened and moved out from their cover—

Jazith grabbed his forearm and held him in place. "Are you crazy? Get back down here."

"They keep getting closer and closer. If we don't do something, they'll discover the village."

"You can't. You know the Warrior Code—"

"Yes," he cut in, yanking his arm from her grip. "I know the Warrior Code."

As he finished, he took off, feeling Jazith's grasping hand whisper through the fur of his back. He ran at the tiny camp, weaving around trees and hurtling logs without breaking stride.

As he sprinted towards them, the women stood and looked in his direction. When they spotted him, two screamed and bolted, but the third stayed where she was.

He hurtled on, breaking into the clearing at full speed. Even as he sped towards her, the third one held her ground. Her eyes were wide and she was unarmed. But she did not flee.

Jarka charged straight at her, opening his mouth to loose a roar—

"Peace! Peace!"

Her desperate plea hit him like a thrown spear. He stuttered his steps to slow down and stopped right in front of her.

He stood there, breathing hard as he glared down at this insane human. She met his eye directly, unflinching, standing a little taller, as if willing her fear away.

He stepped in to loom over her. "What did you say?"

The slender, puny woman clasped her hands together at her stomach. "I said peace."

"How do you know our words?"

"I am fluent in your language. I learned it from—"

"Why?"

Her green eyes flashed with what might have been anger. "Because I knew this day would come."

"What day?"

"The day that my people would need your help."

He narrowed his eyes. "Look, I don't know who you are or what you want, but there must be something wrong with you. Humans don't belong here. You're all afraid of us. You always run, like your friends just did. You run, yes? You don't talk. You run."

"No."

"No? What do you mean, no?"

The human brushed some of her golden hair away from her face and gave him a hard look. "I'm not leaving until I say what I came here to say."

Jarka shook his head, bringing a hand up to rub across the back of his neck. It was a moment before he thought of a response.

Drawing himself up tall, he stepped forward to tower directly over her. "I'm a savage you know. If you don't leave, I'll kill you."

The woman smiled up at him, exposing her little white teeth. "I don't think so. If you were going to kill me, you wouldn't have stopped."

Again, all he could do was shake his head.

He stepped back to study her more closely, crossing his arms over his chest. Her small body was clothed in form-fitting, pine-green cloth, plain and worn. Her face was unmarked and her pink lips were full.

"Did you get a good look?"

He snorted a laugh through his nose. "Do you have a name?"

"Of course I have a name. I am Vaseus, and I have come from a small village at the edge of the Forever Forest. What's your name?"

"I am Jarka, and I am Clanless. What is it that you want, Vaseus of the Small Village?"

Her eyes narrowed. "What happened to trying to scare me off?"

"You're not like the other humans. You know our words and you're not afraid of me. I want to know why."

"I've come to ask for your help. A rebellion has begun in my homeland. Thousands of oppressed people have risen up against their Spartan overlords to fight for their freedom. But the Spartans are strong, well-equipped, and well-trained. The war to come will be hard and costly. Many will die. But we must win. The Spartans are violent, corrupt, and cruel. If we ever hope to lead decent lives again, we must defeat them.

"That is why I am here," she carried on, her tone fierce. "We need warriors to lead us into battle. I've heard about your people's fighting skill. It's said that you live to fight, and that no human could ever be your equal. We need such warriors on our side in the war to come. Join us, and together we will destroy the Spartan Empire."

Jarka had listened closely. As she finished, he nodded thoughtfully, put a hand to his chin, and said, "Are you completely insane?"

Her eyes widened and her eyebrows rose. "Excuse me?"

The disgust writ so plain on her face nearly made him laugh aloud. He managed to keep it to a huge grin as he said, "You don't know this word? It means you've lost your mind. You're crazy—"

"Yes, I know what it means," she snapped. "Why do you think that?"

"Isn't it obvious?" he said, spreading his arms wide. "First, you stand your ground while your friends flee. Now you're asking me to gather my fellow yagars to join a rebellion against the entire Spartan Empire."

She crossed her bare arms just under her small breasts. "And?"

He couldn't stop a barking laugh. "Really? Humans and yagars working together? Fighting together? We can't even have a conversation, let alone fight at each other's side."

"We're having a conversation right now."

He shook his head. "This doesn't happen. This isn't normal. Don't you know that? I've never spoken to a human before."

"And I've never spoken to a yagar. But desperate times call for desperate measures."

"That may be, but it doesn't change the way things are. As always, humans and yagars either fear or hate each other. Aren't we just mindless savages to your people, no better than primitive beasts?"

"Just because something has been true for all time," Vaseus said firmly, "doesn't mean it can never change."

Jarka huffed a chuckle. *She certainly doesn't give up easily.*

"Okay, let's say that humans and yagars could somehow be friends. Why would we help you? We have no stake in whether your rebellion succeeds or fails. It's your fight, not ours, yes?"

He had expected this to finally trip her up, but her response was swift and sure. "The Empire has conquered all the lands to the south of the Forever Forest. With no one left to oppose them, it's only a matter of time before the Spartans attack you with thousands of warriors."

"That can't be right. Why would they do that? We have nothing they want."

"Yes, you do. The Spartans desire power, order, and above all, glory," she said, her hands moving to emphasize her words. "They also hate what they do not control. Yagars are something far beyond their control, and that frightens them. To conquer your lands would bring them everything they crave. Their thirst for more knows no bounds. If we do not destroy them first, they will destroy you."

Jarka crossed his arms, resting a thumb on the shortened, blackened antlers that encased his left shoulder. "Perhaps. But how do I know you're telling the truth? The Spartans are obviously your sworn enemy. You would say anything if it led to their defeat."

For once, she did not respond as sharp as a spear's edge. She blinked a few times and glanced away, some of her golden hair falling across her face.

Eventually, she said, "It wasn't always this way. I speak of the Spartans as if they aren't my people. But they were, once. I lived in Sparta throughout my childhood, where my wealthy, highborn parents raised me. But when I realized how immoral and violent the Empire is, I left Sparta and never returned."

He observed her closely, searching for any hint of a lie. But this, he decided, was no lie. There was only pain behind her words, true, deep pain.

He knew something about that. True, deep pain was something no one could fake.

"I see," he said, letting his arms down to dangle at his sides. "So you were raised to be one of them. That is your home, and yet you would see it destroyed."

She nodded. "Yes."

"I am impressed, Vaseus of Sparta. And I am convinced."

At first, her eyes widened, and she didn't reply.

But she soon recovered. "That's very good to hear, Jarka."

"Yes," he replied. "It is, isn't it? Unfortunately, there is one little, tiny problem."

Her expression darkened. "What problem?"

He brought a hand up to his chin. "I'm not exactly someone with a whole lot of power. You might even say that I'm at the bottom of the tree."

"Oh. In that case, perhaps you could arrange for me to meet with someone of higher standing."

"A fine idea, but not possible."

Her hands went to her hips. "Why not?"

"Because everyone I know is Clanless, and Clanless have no power."

"What do you mean?"

Jarka thought for a moment, searching for an explanation she might understand. "We are shunned, banned, exiled. Clan yagars think we're worthless, and they look down on us with disgust. This is why we live so far south and so close to you humans. It's part of our so-called punishment."

Her brow furrowed and her lips pursed, a look he was fairly certain meant that she was thinking.

After a moment, she clapped her hands together. "Okay, so I need to speak with someone who isn't Clanless. Can you take me to such a yagar?"

He shook his head. "No."

She crossed her arms with surprising speed. "Why not?"

"Because all Clanless are forbidden to re-enter what they call civilized society. We're not allowed to speak to any Clan yagars."

"Then I'll go myself. Just point me in the right direction."

"I admire your bravery, but that isn't a good idea either."

"Why not?" she demanded again.

"I'm not like the rest of my people. We are taught to avoid humans, and if that isn't possible, to kill them. So when they see you, they'll either disappear or throw a spear at you."

"You didn't do that."

"That's because I'm friendlier than most," he said with a smile. "And even I tried to scare you away. Trust me on this. If you go looking for other yagars, you'll end up dead."

"But I need yagar warriors," she growled, her hands firing back to her hips, "to fight with the rebellion. There has to be a way to make that happen."

"There isn't. It's impossible. Can't happen, won't happen, never will happen."

Despite his jovial spin, the look on her face only darkened.

He released a sigh through his nose. "Look," he said, taking a step towards her, "I love your determination. I really do. And I wish I could help. But some things just can't be done. Humans and yagars can't be friends. That's just the way it is. So, your best option is—"

She snarled, spun around, and started walking off.

He stared after her, blinking. "Hey! I'm not done my speech!"

His words fell on deaf ears. She continued on without so much as a backward glance.

"Where are you going?"

Again, she ignored him and walked on.

He shook his head even as a smile cracked his mouth. *Did that really just happen?*

He watched her until she disappeared among the trees.

When he finally turned away, Jazith, Rox, and Relyk were approaching.

"What have you done?" his sister asked as they all came together.

Still smiling, he looked at them all in turn. "I think I'm in love."

THIRTEEN

Feel no fear before the multitude of men, do
not run in panic, but let each man bear his shield
straight toward the fore-fighters, regarding his
own life as hateful and holding the dark spirits
of death as dear as the radiance of the sun.

Tyrtaeus of Sparta

Kaletor sprinted through the street, pulling away from his personal
guard. The clash of raging combat sounded all around him. Straight
ahead, a line of enemies was barring the way deeper into the city.

He loosed a roar and charged the line. As he arrived, several swords and
spears came at him. He swung his iron shield out to take them all. The metal
sang, and as it did, he thrust his spear out with all his strength. The leaf head
punched through a wicker shield and into a body.

Those beside the stricken man attacked again. Kaletor stepped left, avoiding
one sword while blocking another with his shield. A spear came at his face. He
dipped his head just enough so that the pike skittered off his gold helmet. As
it did, he swung his spear high on a horizontal arc. The iron head found its
mark, and another fell.

He roared in triumph, but then three Jews broke formation to rush in on his
sides. Kaletor lashed out wildly with his spear to keep the one on the right at
bay, then pivoted back, barely intercepting the incoming spear strikes with his
shield. Seeing that one of these two assailants was off balance, Kaletor thrust
his spear into the Jew's belly. The other swung for his extended arm. He let go
of his spear and twisted his body to slam his shield into the man's face.

Although it worked, the move had opened up his right side, an easy target for his third attacker. Kaletor craned his neck and leaned back to avoid the inevitable blow—

The Jew screamed as a spear took him in the side, and the sword he had raised to cut Kaletor down clattered to the cobbles. In that instant, a wave of red-cloaked Spartiates slammed into the enemy line.

Kaletor turned to attack with them, drawing his sword and closing with the nearest Jew. The man swung high. Kaletor deflected it wide with the edge of his sword, then followed quick with a slash at the chest. The counter was too fast for the Jew, and he cried out as he toppled.

A moment later, the phalanx line of his Spartiates finished cutting down the last of the enemy.

Kaletor moved ahead and turned to face his men. Holding out a hand, he barked, "Spear."

As the nearest Spartiate handed him a spear, Kaletor again noticed the chaotic clash of combat all around them, the screams of terrified women and children, and the stench of smoking buildings.

A grin came to his lips. *Things are going well.*

He turned and led his men deeper into the city.

*   *   *

The thick, grey clouds that had blanketed the sky were beginning to break up as dusk fell. By the failing light, Kaletor observed the sacked city from the balcony of a rich man's palace.

Fires blazed everywhere, the smoke billowing high in great, black columns. Several buildings that had evaded the flames were damaged or collapsed, the piles of rubble evidence of the many days of catapult bombardment. Thousands of hoplites swarmed every street, breaking into shops and homes as they went, taking what they wanted and killing anyone they found. Screams continued to sound on all sides.

It was a scene of carnage and death. Kaletor observed it all intently.

Footsteps at his back drew his attention. Without turning, he said, "What is it?"

"I'm sorry to disturb you, Commander, but General Hullis has returned."

"And?"

"He wishes to deliver his report."

Kaletor set his hands to the balcony's railing, sweeping his eyes across the city once more. "Very well. Send him up."

The Spartiate left swiftly, and soon there came another's approaching footsteps. With some effort, Kaletor pulled his gaze away from the burning city to face his childhood friend.

Grime and blood covered Hullis's pale face and arms. His short, chestnut-brown hair was slick with sweat and appeared slightly singed. His sculpted torso of iron was streaked in black char and blood, and his red cloak was torn down one side.

It was clear he had had an eventful day.

"Where's your helmet, General?"

Though the twitch of his head was subtle, Kaletor saw it and knew that Hullis was nervous. "I lost it in the fighting, Commander. There wasn't time to retrieve it."

"Pity. What do you have for me?"

"The last of the enemy soldiers are dead. Jerusalem is ours."

"Again," Kaletor added. "Jerusalem is ours again."

"Of course, sir. Shall we rein in the army to save what's left of the city?"

Kaletor shook his head. "No."

He turned back around to look on the death and fire once more. "These people rebelled against the Empire. They do not deserve mercy. Every subject of the emperor needs to understand that this is what comes to those who rebel."

"As you wish, Commander."

"Dismissed."

"Forgive me, sir, but there's one more thing."

Kaletor clenched his jaw tight as he glanced back over a shoulder. "What?"

Hullis averted his eyes as he said, "A kohort of hoplites was seen fleeing from the fight during the taking of the eastern gate—"

"Fleeing?" Kaletor snarled, spinning around and striding over. "Which kohort?"

"The 11th of the 8th Phalanx."

"Egyptians. Where are they now?"

"In the house neighbouring this one. I had them stripped of their weapons—"

Without waiting for Hullis to finish, Kaletor was past him, moving into the palace with powerful strides. He descended the stairs two at a time, walked out the front door, crossed the street, and came to the house next door.

To the four Spartiates standing guard, he barked, "Take me to the prisoners."

The men obeyed. Passing through dark halls, they led him to an open courtyard in the building's center.

Standing around a small, shallow pool were about sixty dark-skinned hoplites, each one adorned in a red cloak and a plain iron breastplate. Most had their helmets in hand or tucked under an arm. Not one had their shield or spear.

"Cowards!"

Kaletor's bellow cut off every conversation and drew every eye. He saw recognition come to many, followed closely by looks of dread or fear.

"Form ranks, you maggots! Your Commander addresses you!"

As the hoplites scurried into lines, Kaletor glanced over to watch Hullis arrive and stop a few paces behind him. He gave the general a quick nod before returning his gaze to the assembled men.

"Do you know why you are here?" he asked, moving forward to stand before the neatly ordered rows.

There was a long hesitation before someone finally called out the answer. "Because we retreated without orders, sir."

"You *ran*," Kaletor shouted. "You ran like cowards."

Many looked down, either in shame or fear.

"Spartans never run," he went on. "Never. Yes, I know you aren't truly Spartan, but your homeland is part of the Empire. Your behaviour and conduct, therefore, reflect back on the Empire. Do you understand me, you Egyptian bastards?"

Together, the kohort called out, "Yes, sir."

Kaletor crossed his muscled arms over his broad chest. "To run from a fight is the greatest shame and dishonour a hoplite can commit. When men in the Spartan army run, they bring dishonour not only to their fellow hoplites, but also to every Spartiate, every general, to me, and to the emperor himself. Your shame is our shame. Your weakness is our weakness. And if there's one thing I hate more than anything, it's *weakness*."

His shout echoed through the wide, still courtyard as he glared at these pathetic excuses for soldiers. They all kept their eyes downcast.

"Weakness is why we're at war," he snarled, uncrossing his arms to pace in front of them. "All these rebels think the Empire is weak. That's why so many have risen against us. They think they can overthrow Sparta by force, and they will if cowards like you are allowed to infect the army. But I will not let that happen. The Empire must not fall. The world needs order and stability. Your cowardice and weakness cannot be allowed to spread. I will not allow it!"

As he bellowed this last statement, he pulled his sword from its scabbard, stepped up to the Egyptian closest to him, and drove the point through the man's chest. When he collapsed to the floor, the Spartiates who had been watching from the courtyard's fringes interlocked their shields and closed in with spears poised to strike.

The Egyptians cried out in panic and begged for mercy. Some fell to their knees, hands raised in surrender.

Without hesitation, the Spartiates attacked on all sides, cutting down the defenseless men. Screams full of pain and terror erupted.

Eventually, there were none left to kill.

Kaletor's chest heaved as he stood there, looking down at the corpses all around him. The stench of blood filled his nose. He closed his eyes and breathed it in deep. It was a smell he knew well, and one he welcomed.

It was the smell of victory.

FOURTEEN

Even though Clanless are looked down upon,
there is great resilience among them. It may be
a different kind of strength than what we have
always valued, but it is strength nonetheless.

The Spoken Tales

"I still can't believe she didn't run."

Jarka chuckled as he bounded up onto the mossy trunk of a fallen tree. "And yet it happened, dear sister. You saw it yourself."

Jazith joined him atop the horizontal trunk, just as lithe and balanced as he. Her gold and black fur flowed from the cool, lazy breeze drifting through the forest. Sabres of sunlight stabbed down through the canopy, shimmering in her deep brown eyes.

"It's just so absurd. Why didn't she run?"

"I don't know. Maybe she's mad."

"And she really wanted yagars to fight alongside humans?"

He laughed louder this time. Ever since his encounter with the strange human two days earlier, Rox, Relyk, and Jazith had asked him many questions of this kind.

This time he decided to have a little fun. "Nope. I just made that up."

Her eyes widened. "Really?"

For a moment, he just stared at her, a wide grin exposing his fangs. Then, without a word, he leapt down from the tree and raced away.

"Hey!"

He loosed a whooping laugh and continued on, running through the forest.

He darted this way and that as if evading attacks. He ducked branches, hurtled shrubs, and dodged the incoming tree trunks of pine and oak trees.

For some distance he ran on in this way, only slowing when Jazith came up alongside him.

"What are you doing?" she demanded.

"Being a thorn in your side."

She shook her head. "As usual. But did you really make it up?"

"Come on, sis. You sound as gullible as Rox right now."

"How's that going by the way?"

"How's what going?"

"You and Rox."

"Couldn't be better. She's great in bed, almost as good as—"

"Not that!"

He barked out a laugh. "You asked me how it was going. What'd you expect?"

"You know what I meant," she said, giving him a shove.

"So that's really why you wanted to get me out here, yes?"

Her answering smile was coy. "Perhaps."

He pushed her back. "I say, you've become a devious one. Here I thought you just wanted to spend some time with your favourite brother. I must finally be rubbing off on you."

Her smile remained unchanged.

They walked on in silence, and Jarka noticed how quiet the forest was. Even the near-constant chirps and songs of birds had ceased.

He did a quick scan of the surrounding brush and trees. There were only the green pine needles, budding leaves, and wide tree trunks. He rotated his ears forward and sniffed the air. He still heard nothing, and he smelled nothing but the pines.

"So?"

Satisfied that they were alone, he looked over. "Hmm?"

Jazith huffed a laugh through her nose and smoothed down her whiskers. "You and Rox."

"Ah, of course. Your ulterior motive. You know how it is. Up, down, highs, lows."

"Yes, I do know how it is. But I never imagined you would."

"I don't, really," he admitted. "It's just something you say."

"And yet I don't recall ever hearing you say such things," she replied, her tone easy. "What's happened to you?"

"I thought you'd approve."

"I do. I'm just surprised. You've never tied yourself to one female for so long. Why her?"

"I don't know, Jaz," he said, extending a claw to scratch his chin. "Maybe I've grown tired of the game. It's almost become routine, drifting from one to the next to the next. It's all fun and games, passion and excitement, lust and pleasure."

He paused a moment, remembering many of his escapades over the years.

"On second thought, perhaps I'm not cut out for this whole serious relationship thing . . ."

Jazith gave a soft chuckle. "Focus, Jarka. There must be a reason you've stayed with Rox for so long."

He shook his head to try and banish the lurid stream of thoughts. "Yes. Right."

After a brief moment, she said, "Could it be because she's kind, intelligent, and warmhearted?"

He slowly nodded. "Yes."

"And maybe she's fun to be around? Maybe she makes you laugh?"

Memories of Rox came to him, and he nodded again. "She definitely makes me laugh."

"Is she generous of spirit?" Jazith went on. "Is she open and honest?"

"She *is*. I'm always happy when I'm with her. I mean, I'm usually happy anyways, but with her it's different. Usually, I'm always looking to the next one, the next opportunity, the next challenge. But she's smart and fun and playful. I feel so alive when she's around."

As he spoke, he had surged ahead. Noticing that she no longer walked at his side, he slowed and glanced back. At that moment she caught up, placed a hand to the back of his head, and stopped.

Her eyes locked with his, and with a smile, said, "That's wonderful, little brother. You finally know how it feels."

He made a puzzled face. "How what feels?"

"How it feels to fall in love."

"Is that what's happened to me?"

She nodded, her smile widening to reveal her fangs as she placed both hands on his shoulders. "Yes. You're in love."

He smiled too. "Really? This is love?"

This time her nodding was vigorous. "Yes," she said excitedly, pulling him into an embrace. "You're definitely in love."

He wrapped his arms around her as he laughed. "I didn't think I had it in me."

"Neither did I! Mother and Father would be—"

Jarring shouts snapped apart the air.

They stepped away from each other and looked in the direction of the noise. In that look, Jarka saw at least twenty men sprinting straight at them through the forest. They wore red cloaks and golden armour. They were armed with spears and shields.

They were human warriors—warriors called Spartans.

Jarka looked back to Jazith. "Go, get back to the village. I'll lead them away—"

"No," she cut in. "That's my job."

Before he could stop her, she took off, going straight at them. His insides lurched as he ran after her.

Knowing he wouldn't catch her, he focused on the humans. Three were ahead of the rest, charging at a full run. He ran hard, weaving between five trees without breaking stride. As he cleared the last tree, he made straight for one of the leaders.

The sprinting Spartan raised his spear high, ready to strike. Jarka roared and leapt, leading with his shoulder. He slammed hard into the metal shield.

Sharp pain stabbed down his arm. The Spartan went spinning away as Jarka hit the ground on all fours.

Gritting his teeth, he scrambled back up in time to meet the next one, rotating his upper body to one side. It was just enough to dodge the thrusting spear, which drove by within inches of his chest. In that same motion, he batted the shaft of the spear up and away with one hand and swung the other at the Spartan's head. The open-palmed strike passed over the rising shield and slammed into the helmet. The man collapsed to the ground.

Sensing a gap, Jarka looked around for Jazith. She had already downed three and was engaging two more.

He glanced beyond to the rest of them. Having entered a clearing, they had formed a solid line, their shields overlapped to form a wall of iron. Less than ten paces separated them from Jazith.

Desperate energy surged through Jarka's legs as he charged the line's left side.

"Run, Jaz," he shouted at her. "There's too many!"

He veered out sharply to get wide of the advancing line. Once he was level, he turned in and attacked the edge.

The Spartan peeled off from the line surprisingly quick and lanced his spear out beside his shield. Already committed, Jarka snarled as he planted a foot and dove forward, arms extended.

Fire split down his side even as his hands found the man's throat and helmet. He dragged the Spartan down to his back. When they hit the ground, he ripped the helmet off and pushed down on the throat with all his strength. The Spartan went still.

Heat was seeping from his side and pain burned in demanding waves, but he had no time to stop. Loosing a roar, he pushed himself back up to his feet.

The line had continued past, so he charged after it. Coming up directly behind the one on the edge, Jarka snagged the Spartan's red cloak and pulled him down with it. The act put the unsuspecting man flat on his back and sent a fresh wave of burning fire through Jarka's torso. He howled as he dropped a knee on the man's throat.

From that position, he glanced down at his midsection. His fur was soaked red, and a jagged gash revealed dark blood leaking down the left side of his belly. Hissing, he put a hand over it and grit his teeth as he stood.

He looked up and saw the shields of the wall knock Jazith down.

He loosed an exploding bellow and took off. The Spartans started kicking and smashing their shields into her. He charged, roaring as he launched himself at their backs—

Just as he left his feet, a shield rammed him from the side. He spun through the air, then crashed and rolled across the ground. He ended up on his back, unable to breath, his chest seized, the fire in his side obliterating his mind.

He tried to roll onto his front. He couldn't. His body would not move.

Clenching his jaw tight, he managed to raise his head to look for Jazith. He caught a glimpse of her curled up on the ground as the Spartans battered her on all sides.

Spittle spewed from his mouth as he pulled his elbows under him—

Gold flashed on his right, and something smashed into his skull.

FIFTEEN

Learn to love death's ink-black shadow as
much as you love the light of dawn.

Tyrtaeus of Sparta

The night air was close and thick. Sweat coated Kaletor's face and streamed beneath his breastplate as he moved cautiously through the darkness. Torches blazed here and there, but the flames were small and weak.

Unable to pierce the dancing shadows, he kept his eyes wide and his spear ready as he proceeded along the narrow, unfamiliar streets.

He was crossing an intersection when he heard a foot scuff the cobbles. He spun towards the sound, arms tensed, poised to fight.

Seeing nothing but darkness, he growled, "Show yourself."

Someone ran by and tore the spear from his hands.

Tracking the small figure through the gloom, he barked, "Stop!"

The answering laugh belonged to a small boy.

Kaletor ran after him. "Give that back, you little shit!"

The boy laughed again and kept running. Kaletor gave chase through the empty streets, nearly blind in the oppressive darkness. The kid was surprisingly quick, darting left or right at every intersection.

Kaletor ran harder, pumping his arms. Gradually the gap closed.

After a long run, he finally caught the boy and snagged his scrawny arm. Pulling him round, Kaletor raised a fist to strike—

And froze. Dripping blood covered the boy's face and throat. But this wasn't what rendered Kaletor immobile.

It was the boy's identity.

"You were supposed to use this for good. You were supposed to be a hero," the boy cried, yanking his arm free to take the spear in both hands. "But you're no hero. You're a monster!"

Kaletor couldn't move or speak. He could only watch as his ten-year-old self drove the spear straight into his belly—

He jerked upright with a shout, hands going to his gut. For a moment he sat there, blinking and breathing fast.

Understanding came that he had been sleeping. It had all been a dream.

"Did you have a nightmare, Commander?"

He looked over to the woman lying next to him. "I told you to leave."

She propped herself up on an elbow, her long black hair spilling down to sweep across her bare breasts. "Oh, don't be like that, honey," she cooed, reaching out to caress his hard, muscled torso. "I was thinking we could have some more fun this morning. Last night was incredible—"

"Enough," he snapped, grabbing her wrist to fling her arm away. "Get out."

She gave him a pouty smile. "Too bad. You're delicious."

"Just get out."

Giggling softly, she rolled out of bed and started dressing.

Kaletor looked out the window to a grey sheet of solid cloud. It was early, and Jerusalem was quiet beneath the bleak sky.

All of a sudden, he saw his ten-year-old self driving the spear at his gut. He shook his head and dragged a hand down his face.

As the image faded, he ground his teeth. *Stupid little bastard. I'm stronger and more powerful than you ever dreamed of becoming. I'm the hero of the entire Empire. I'm the greatest Spartan alive.*

Kaletor continued to stew as more thoughts of this nature streamed through his mind like a raging river. The whore was long gone by the time he drove every vestige of the unsettling dream away.

He released a snarl, got out of bed, walked across the purple rug, and pissed in the copper pot beneath the open window.

When he finished, he called out, "Talos!"

The old, bronze-skinned Athenian came limping in from the adjoining room. He bowed his bald head and said, "Yes, Master?"

"Help me get my armour on."

Kaletor stood tall at the center of the rug while his slave strapped his iron greaves, gauntlets, and sculpted breastplate into place.

Talos had finished tying his sandals and was bringing over his red cloak when there was a knock at the bedroom door.

Kaletor took the cloak and said, "See who it is."

The Athenian nodded and crossed the spacious, ornately decorated room.

As he neared the door, he called out, "Who is it?"

The answer came swiftly. "Captain Ackadus."

Talos looked back with a questioning look. Kaletor suppressed a groan and gave a forced nod before twirling his cloak around to fall upon his shoulders.

"Ah, you're dressed," the teenager said as he strode in through the opened door. "So much better than seeing you naked again."

Kaletor fastened the golden broach at his throat. "What do you want?"

Ackadus clicked his tongue and raised his small, pointed chin. "Now now, is that any way to address the emperor's son?"

"I outrank you, boy."

"Doesn't seem right, does it? You outranking the Prince of Sparta."

Kaletor glared at him but said nothing.

"You're never any fun, Kaletor. Why is that? I would have thought that sacking this city in an orgy of violence, followed by a night of sexual pleasure, would have lightened your mood."

Still, Kaletor just glared.

Ackadus ran a hand over his short bristles of blonde hair. "But apparently not! You're just never happy, are you?"

"What do you want?"

"Fine," Ackadus said, his dark eyes flashing. "Have it your way. News just arrived from Rhodes."

"And?"

"The people there have turned against us. They've massacred the garrison and declared for the rebellion."

Kaletor loosed a savage roar.

"*That's impossible,*" he snarled, jaw clenching tight and hands balling into fists. "They're Greeks. Greeks can't rebel!"

"Apparently they can."

He released another throat-burning roar. "Those treacherous bastards. I'll kill every last one of them!"

"That doesn't seem to be working."

"What?" he snapped, fixing his glare on the puny prince once more.

Unlike most everyone else, Ackadus looked back without a hint of fear. "All you ever do is attack and kill those who defy you. But just like the hydra, for every enemy we defeat, two more crop up—"

"And what would you have us do instead?" Kaletor spat, stepping close to tower over the emperor's brat. "Negotiate? We are Spartans, boy. We fight all those who stand against us. That is Spartan law."

"But rebels are everywhere—"

"Your father assigned you to me so that you might become a true Spartan," Kaletor cut in. "Don't make me teach you the hard way."

A twitch spasmed down Ackadus's cheeks and upper lip. "You wouldn't dare."

"Don't tempt me, boy. I'd love nothing more."

His expression darkening, the teenager seemed ready to fire something back. But after a long moment, he turned on his heels and stormed from the room.

Kaletor watched the spoiled brat leave, teeth grinding once more. Without turning, he barked, "Talos."

"Yes, Master?"

"Where's Hullis?"

"Downstairs, sir."

"He'd better have every rebel bastard in this city rounded up." Glancing over a shoulder, he added, "Get my spear and shield and meet me downstairs."

Without waiting for a reply, he set off, striding fast through the silent palace. His footsteps echoed off high ceilings of intricately carved plaster, much of it painted gold and purple.

Reaching the wide staircase, he looked down to see Hullis speaking quietly with someone else.

"General," he called as he took the stairs two at a time.

Hullis turned and straightened to attention. "Commander."

"Are all the rebels gathered?"

"They are, sir."

"And the people are assembling?"

"The men are escorting them as we speak."

"Good," he said as he stepped off the bottom stair. For the first time, he looked to and recognized the older man at Hullis's side. "Belisar."

The famous general, who's silver-streaked black beard was thicker than usual, flinched ever so slightly at the omitted rank before bowing his head. "Commander Kaletor. I was just speaking with General Hullis of our victory—"

"*Our* victory?" Kaletor interrupted. "If it weren't for my plan of attack, we'd still be outside the walls, baking under the desert sun."

Belisar's smile revealed the wide gap in his bottom row of teeth, but it was empty and grim. "Yes, of course. I come to offer my congratulations—"

"And weren't you positioned at the very rear of the army? I doubt you took part in any of the fighting. But perhaps that was for the best. You're not as quick as you once were."

The general's small, brown eyes flashed at the insult. Visibly swallowing his pride, the rich aristocrat ground out the appropriate response. "I suppose not, Commander."

Kaletor couldn't keep the satisfied grin from his lips. He loved making distinguished and self-important men squirm.

Revelling in his power, he walked on. "Time to go, Spartans," he said loudly. "I have a city to punish."

*   *   *

In the crisp light of morning, the recent violence and destruction were stark and obvious. Dying fires still burned in homes and shops. Buildings on most streets were charred and broken, their innards exposed, blackened beams jutting out of a blanket of ash. Corpses were everywhere, scattered like discarded trash. Dark pools of blood filled most every dip and low spot in the cobbles. The smells of burnt flesh and acrid smoke mixed to form a strong reek of death.

Kaletor, his two generals, and his personal guard of Spartiates had proceeded through these scenes of carnage to arrive at the city's main gate. Crammed at the feet of the high walls, and filling the open square behind the collapsed gate, was a crowd of thousands. Rank upon rank of hoplites and Spartiates choked all three streets leading to the huddled mass of humanity.

Passing through one of these Phalanxes, Kaletor asked Hullis, "Is this all of them?"

"Yes, Commander."

They soon came to the gatehouse in the wall just to the left of the collapsed gate. His Spartiates remained outside as he led his two generals up the tight, winding staircase to emerge atop the rampart.

Ignoring the gathered crowd below, he went to the parapet to gaze upon the desert sands. He imagined what it must have looked like from that spot two days earlier. He saw his massive army of perfectly ordered lines, the red cloaks of his hoplites and Spartiates stretching on and on. For the enemy, it must have been a terrifying sight.

The idea brought a grin to his lips.

He kept scanning the barren sands as Hullis announced to the crowd, "Commander Kaletor, leader of the Empire's Phalanxes, has conquered your city. In the name of Emperor Ockos, he will now decide your fate."

Kaletor turned away from the empty sands and moved to the ramparts' inner edge. Utter silence and upturned faces greeted him.

Drinking in the crowd's palatable fear, he raised his hands and boomed, "Good morning, traitors."

He waited, casting his gaze over them all. The silence remained absolute.

"The emperor is disappointed with you," he went on. "Very disappointed. He gave you order, peace, stability, and justice. He gave you the chance to lead decent, civilized lives. You were part of the greatness of Sparta. We kept you safe from harm, and as a result, your city flourished. All we asked in return was your loyalty and cooperation."

He paused again, inviting the crowd to lash out, to release their anger. But they didn't take the bait. His reputation, it seemed, was known even here.

Clasping his hands behind his back, he started to pace. "But instead of loyalty, you betrayed us. You killed your protectors. You joined a lawless rebellion, bringing about chaos and death. Instead of thanking and honouring your protectors, you sought to be rid of us. You spat in the face of Sparta, despite all that we've done for you. This, you must now realize, was a grave error.

"Your city *is destroyed*," he burst. "The blood of your people flows beneath the flames. This is what comes to those who betray Sparta. You turned against us. You tried to destroy us. Now, we will destroy you."

With the echo of his bellowed words still on the air, Hullis shouted, "Ready phalanx!"

The hoplites choking all three streets levelled their spears and locked their shields, the sea of red and gold stretching away in great columns. The silence was broken as a murmur of fear swept through the crowd.

Gathering his voice, Kaletor bellowed, "Kill them all!"

Screams of terror erupted in answer as the hoplites closed in on three sides. The mob of people recoiled in on itself as those at the fringes tried to get away from the advancing walls of shields and spears.

But they were hemmed in and surrounded. There was nowhere to go.

The moment the killing began, screams of panicked fear seized the entire crowd. Some men proved themselves cowards, knocking others over as they bulled their way into the safety of the center. Some rushed the shield wall to fight back, but it was a disorderly and wild counterattack of unarmed nobles and peasants. They were easily repelled and died at the hoplites' feet.

Absolute terror gripped every person in that vast multitude. The stricken screamed as they were cut down. Men shouted as they rushed forward or scrambled back. Women hugged their children close as they cried and wailed.

Standing high above, Kaletor watched it all unfold.

He did not look away.

SIXTEEN

She was a Warlord like no other. Yes, she was
the greatest warrior alive in her time. But she
was also good. The purest good. She was,
simply put, the greatest of us all. This world
will never know another like Okanix.

The Spoken Tales

The moment Jarka opened his eyes, it felt like a spike of stone was
slicing through his skull. He groaned and brought both hands to his
face, squeezing his eyes shut as he rubbed, his fingertips sliding over
a bump on the side of his head.

He stayed like this, eyes shut, hands rubbing his face and head, lying flat on
his back, for some time.

But then, as the grogginess of sleep dissipated, his mind flashed to the last
thing he remembered.

*Spartans attacked. A desperate fight. Jazith was down, curled into a ball as they kicked
her—*

He snarled as he surged upright. "Jazith!"

"Easy, my friend," someone urged from behind, coming close to set firm
hands against his shoulders. "Slow. Easy."

The jerky movement had sent stabbing shards of stone down his right side.
With his head swimming, he sank back down.

Blinking away the blotchy, shifting colours speckling in his eyes, he looked
to the yagar who held him.

"Relyk," he gasped between breaths, his voice hoarse. "Spartans. My sister.

Where is she?"

"I'm sorry, my friend. She was already gone when I found you—"

"Where?" Jarka growled, struggling to sit up again. "Jazith! Where are you? Get off me, Relyk. I must . . . help her . . ."

"Please, Jarka. You need to rest."

"I cannot rest. I need . . . to . . . know . . ."

But even as he struggled to rise, his head and body screamed. Heavy blackness came on fast and he collapsed.

*   *   *

Fitful, fractured dreams plagued him in sleep. Some hours later, he woke again. He was burning hot and his vision was blurred. He heard voices that sounded far away, but before long, he succumbed to the pull once more.

The next time he woke, there was only darkness. Instead of voices, there was silence. He blinked over and over, unsure if he had gone blind. The fog, sharp pain, and fever remained, but he tried to push through and sit up. The moment his head left the pillow, the black wave swarmed up and knocked him out.

This went on and on, the same snatches of horrid wakefulness interrupting short spurts of fevered, restless sleep.

He had no concept of passing time. He could do nothing but endure.

Eventually, he awoke without the all-consuming pain dominating his entire world. At first, he simply lay there, unwilling to move for fear of invoking yet another agonizing black spasm of his mind.

But as the moments stretched on and it did not come, he realized that the delirium of his fever was gone.

Moving careful and slow, he pushed himself into a sitting position. Once he was vertical, his head swam and dots flooded his vision. He shut his eyes and braced himself with his arms.

He remained stiff for some time, not daring to move as his laboured breath and pounding heart gradually slowed. When at last he felt he could, he opened his eyes.

At that moment, Rox walked through the open entrance of his hut. When she saw him, she dropped the basket in her arms and rushed over, tears already welling in her eyes.

"My love," she breathed as she wrapped her arms around him. "I can't believe it. I thought I'd lost you."

"Shh," Jarka rasped, gently bringing his arms up to hold her. "It's alright. I'm alright."

Rox cried into his shoulder, or laughed, or both. They held each other for a long time as she let it all out.

But the instant he knew contentment, memory of the attack returned.

Speaking softly, he said, "Where's Jazith? Is she alright?"

Rox brought a hand to the back of his head, her fingers pressing through his fur. "Now's not the time, my love. You need to rest. Eat. Recover your strength."

"I need to know," he said, shifting back in the bed so he could look her in the eye. "Tell me, Rox. Where is she?"

Her tears had matted the black and yellow fur of her cheeks and left drips in her whiskers. But where before her eyes held relief, now they held sorrow.

"Relyk did all he could. You weren't moving, maybe dead for all he knew. If he hadn't fought them off, you would be—"

"My sister, Rox."

Fresh tears welled in her light-gold eyes as she shook her head. "We're not sure. Relyk said some of them were disappearing into the distance when he arrived. By the time he killed or drove off the ones around you, they had vanished into the forest."

Jarka closed his eyes and let his head drop. The wave came on fast, and unable to do anything else, he cried.

Rox wrapped her arms around his head and pressed his face to her chest. "I'm sorry, my love," she whispered through his gasps and shaking. "I'm so sorry."

For a long time, there were only tears, and something like tearing inside.

At some point, as he wept, a single, clear thought sounded in his mind.

She's not dead. She's not.

Slowly, gradually, the thought swelled. His sobs eased. He extended each inhale and exhale to slow down his breathing.

Eventually, once it had slowed enough, he rasped, "How long?"

Rox was a moment in responding. "How long?"

He took another steadying breath and brought his head up. "How long since they took her?"

Her hesitation was longer this time. She slid her hands from the back of his head to his cheeks. "You still need to rest—"

"How long, Rox?" he interrupted, grabbing her wrists to take her hands away.

She sighed and relented. "Three days."

It felt as if a rolling boulder had slammed into his gut. "Three days?" he gasped. "Has anyone been out looking for her?"

"Of course we have. We looked everywhere, all through the forest in every direction. A few search parties have not yet returned, but so far we've found no sign of her."

Jarka's mind worked slower than usual, as if he were moving through a deep swamp. Still, a solid truth soon came.

"That means she's still alive. Otherwise, someone would have found her by now."

"We don't know that—"

"She's not dead, which means they have her. I must find them."

He moved to get off the bed—

"You can't get up," she said as she got in his way. "Your wounds need more time to heal—"

"I'm fine," he insisted, nudging her aside and shimmying to the edge of the bed. "I'll take it slow—"

"Don't," she fired back, blocking him again. "Please, Jarka. You must stay in bed—"

"I've been in bed for too long already," he snapped. "I can't just lay here while my sister is being held by those monsters. I will not lay here any longer."

"I understand, but just wait. Just wait, and I promise to go find her myself—"

Shifting quick, he bulled through her as he lurched from the bed. The moment his legs took his weight, they buckled. He staggered and fell to his hands and knees.

Rox gasped and crouched beside him. "Please, Jarka, you can't. You lost a lot of blood, and you haven't eaten. Your wounds are still healing. Your body needs rest."

Blood pulsed in turgid bursts through his head, his side burned, and his stomach was twisted into knots. With his mouth wide to gulp air and his head hanging, the need to lay down pulled at him, begged him to give in.

But just as he was about to let himself collapse, an image of Jazith being dragged away flashed in his mind.

He clenched his teeth and surged up, roaring as he pushed through the demands of his body.

Without really knowing how, he was outside. The sunlight was blinding, stabbing his pounding head like a thousand dagger tips. He staggered on with eyes squinted so tight he could barely see.

"Jarka," Rox called after him, "please stop. You can't help her if you're dead."

He ignored her pleas and rushed forward, arms extended for balance. Eventually, his eyes adjusted enough so that he could relax his squinting.

He saw that he was in the middle of a wide street lined with the mud-caked wood huts of the village. Six yagars was standing in front of one such hut, talking amongst themselves.

When they all started laughing, Jarka hollered, "Hey!"

As the group looked his way, he made straight for them. "What do you think you're doing?"

Blank or confused looks answered him.

His stomach burned and his head pounded harder than ever, but he kept going.

"Someone's been taken by humans," he growled between quick, harsh breaths. "How can you just stand there doing nothing?"

"What's that?" said one.

"Who's been taken?" another chimed in.

"My sister."

"What's her name?"

"Jazith."

"Don't know anyone by that name—"

"*I don't care*," he roared. "A fellow yagar is a captive of humans, violent Spartans that attacked us for no reason—"

Black dots blotched his vision and his left leg buckled. He fell to a knee, only just keeping himself from going all the way down. His chest seized up as he gulped air, shaking his head to try and push through.

Desperate to breathe, he forced out, "She needs . . . our help. We mu-must . . . f-find . . ."

The black swarm engulfed him, and he toppled.

*　　　*　　　*

"I'm sorry, my friend. I wish I had better news."

It was late afternoon the next day, and Jarka was back in bed. His head no longer throbbed, and the pain all over his body had eased. Still, his speedy recovery did nothing to comfort him in the wake of Relyk's words.

"Unbelievable," he muttered, shaking his head and crossing his arms over his chest. "How can they give up so easily? How can they just abandon one of their own?"

"It's been four days," Relyk said, stepping from the foot of the bed to stand at the side, "and there's still no trace of her. They've likely taken her into human lands—"

"I don't care," Jarka growled. "I will get her back, with or without anyone's help."

"It's too dangerous. You know what happens to us in human lands. You'd be killed or captured."

Though he hated to acknowledge it, he knew the truth of Relyk's words. Seeing the concern in his friend's expression, he released a ragged sigh and settled back, his shoulders pressed against the wall.

"Yes," he said, his tone less harsh. "I know. If it means sending more yagars into danger, it cannot be done. But I will find her myself."

"Alone?" Relyk said, his dark eyes instantly stern. "Are you mad? They'll kill you the moment they see you."

"Maybe," Jarka said, already feeling better as the beginnings of a plan formed in his mind. "Or maybe not."

"You're talking crazy," Relyk snapped, a scowl marring his sparingly-spotted face. "You can't do this. I won't let you—"

"It's not up to you, my friend. Jazith is my big sister. She's the reason I'm still alive. I will get her back."

"How? How will you find her? There are thousands of humans out there, and they'll all be afraid of you or want to kill you. And even if you did, how would you free her?"

He didn't have any answers. His mind raced, trying to think of possible solutions. He soon realized it was an impossible task, and doubts leaked in, eroding his resolve.

At a loss, he gave up thinking for a moment.

And then it hit him.

A smile slowly curled the corners of his mouth, raising his whiskers. "The woman."

Relyk squinted up his eyes. "What? What woman?"

Jarka's only answer was to smile wider.

*   *   *

The night was getting old when Jarka slipped out from under his blanket and got out of bed. Although the hut was in total darkness, he could see clearly, everything a different shade of black or grey.

He stood motionless for a moment, waiting for the pounding in his head to subside. Then he moved silently across the room, donning the blackened antlers that encased his left shoulder.

A small, stone knife sat on the table in the corner. He grabbed it and pushed it down into the sheath that was strapped to the antlers, wincing as a hot wave seared through his stitched side.

When it passed, he did a final check of the room, but saw nothing else he needed.

He turned to leave, but as he did, he noticed a small bracelet of deer bone on the bedside table. It was Rox's favourite.

He paused as the reality of what he was about to do settled like a weight in his stomach. *Can I really do this? Can I just leave without saying goodbye? Rox will not understand. She'll be hurt. Relyk too. They will feel betrayed.*

It would be easier to go back to sleep, wait another day, then ask Rox and Relyk to come with him. He knew they would, and it would be easier with their help.

But even as he considered this, in his mind's eye, he saw an image of Jazith imprisoned in some dungeon. In that instant, he knew he had to go, and that he had to go alone. Finding the woman called Vaseus meant going into human lands. It would be dangerous, and he was not about to put his friends in harm's way.

So, releasing a sigh filled with silent apologies, he turned and walked out into the cool night. He moved quickly through the dark, sleeping village, collecting a spear that was leaning against a fence as he went. There was no one else about, and before long, he came to the edge of the tree line.

He stopped and cast a final look back to the village. His lungs felt like they were constricted as he stood there, observing all that was his home.

Eventually, he released a grunt, turned, and set off into the forest.

His strides were long and powerful, and his progress was swift as he followed the southernly path he had taken hundreds of times before. He heard the occasional nocturnal creatures scurrying away in the undergrowth as he passed, but otherwise, all was calm and quiet.

An hour or so into his journey, the dull pain in his side worsened, as did the throbbing in his skull. He slowed his pace in the hope that his body would soon recover. When it didn't, he settled into the sedate pace.

Hours passed, his walk steadily devolving into an ever-worsening limp.

When at last the first hints of dawn pushed back the darkness, he was exhausted. Leaving the path, he staggered into a dense cluster of trees, sat with his back to a wide oak, and sank into sleep.

When he woke, the sun was at its peak. Hungry, sore, and chilled to the bone, he returned to the path and continued south. Clutching his side, he managed a slow, steady pace along the winding trail.

Though it took him nearly all of the remaining daylight, he finally arrived at the southernmost edge of the Forever Forest. Crouching low behind a spindly tangle of twiggy branches and tiny, orange leaves, he eyed the human village that was fifty paces beyond the tree line. Stone buildings poked up from behind a wall of sharpened sticks that circled the entire area. Through tiny gaps, he could see humans moving within, and he heard their voices on the breeze. Due to the walls, he could see nothing else.

Jarka's hunger and fatigue melted into the background as he watched and listened with eyes wide and ears rotated forward. He had never been so close to a human village before. The threat they posed was suddenly very real.

He felt the fur stand up on the back of his neck. He remained still, alert, waiting some time before starting to ponder his next move.

He had imagined watching from a safe distance until he spotted Vaseus, then somehow signalling her over. But seeing the village, he knew that strategy was unlikely to work. He tried to think of something else, something clever that kept him hidden.

It didn't take him long to realize that there was no such solution. If he stayed in the forest, he would probably never find the woman.

There was only one option.

When he decided to move, a powerful need to stop froze him in place. Humans killed yagars. It was an undeniable fact that he had known all his life. If he walked up to that place, he knew without putting it into words or thoughts that he would probably die.

His heart beat fast and his mouth was dry as sand. He was too weak to win a fight or run away. To walk up to the wall and announce his presence seemed like it could only end in a painful, violent death.

These rational arguments churned through his mind, over and over. As the purple gloom of evening deepened and the air cooled, he remained still and silent within the safety of the forest.

With every fiber of his being locked up by fear, he forced himself to remember why he had come to this wretched place. *Jazith. Jazith needs me. She's been there for me all my life, especially when I needed her most. Now I need to be there for her. I have to. I have to. For Jazith.*

He shook himself and said the two words under his breath. "For Jazith."

He lay his spear on the ground, straightened to his full height, and walked out into the open.

SEVENTEEN

After their victory over the Athenians, the Spartans turned from controlling Greece to conquering the world. The Peloponnesian War had set them on the path to empire.

Androdamos of Boeotia

K aletor set the silver goblet to his lips, tilted his head back, and downed the last of his wine. He then held the goblet out to one side and said, "More."

Talos stepped up from behind his seat and poured. Despite the ship rocking this way and that beneath them, the slave did not spill a drop.

"Oi," Ackadus said from his seat along one side of the rough-hewn, rectangular table. "Me too."

Kaletor had never liked sea voyages. Too unpredictable. Although they were enclosed within the confines of the captain's quarters, he could hear the water smacking into the hull, and he could feel the dips and tilts of the ship beneath them.

His gut rolled and squirmed in response. The table was laden with food, but he had no desire to eat any of it.

Those sitting with him, it seemed, suffered no such discomfort. Hullis and Belisar had eaten the bread, salted pork, and cheese with ravenous zest. Ackadus had sat tall on the table's bench, talking and drinking more and more as time passed. Most recently, the arrogant brat had babbled on about his family, highlighting the skills they had displayed to successfully remain atop Spartan society for generations.

"But enough about that," the teenager said once his cup was filled. "What are we going to do about Rhodes?"

Though the question had not been directed at anyone in particular, both Hullis and Belisar remained silent and looked to Kaletor.

When Ackadus took the hint and did the same, Kaletor met his eye and said, "The same thing we do to every traitorous city. Smash our way in and kill whoever's inside."

"But these are Greeks. Surely we can't treat them as harshly as the barbarians—"

"They turned against Sparta," Kaletor cut in, "which makes them traitors. There's only one way to deal with traitors. Isn't that so, Belisar?"

The aging fool gave a sharp nod. "Yes, Commander."

"My father needs to be consulted," Ackadus argued, leaning forward to rest his arms atop the table. "He's the emperor. It's his decision—"

"Unnecessary," Kaletor said. "I know he would agree. It's Spartan law."

"Word should still be sent. This has never happened before."

"It wouldn't hurt," Hullis pitched in. "And there will be time. Taking the city will not be easy."

Looking to his childhood companion, Kaletor allowed the ensuing silence to stretch. He clenched and unclenched his jaw repeatedly.

Eventually, he took a sip of wine, eyes never straying from Hullis's. As he swallowed, he slowly set the goblet on the table. "Ockos will not be bothered with this. Rhodes will be punished the same as any other rebellious city. That is my order."

Ackadus shook his head. "No, you can't just make that decision. The emperor—"

"Gave me sole command of the Empire's Phalanxes long ago," Kaletor cut in, his tone jagged. "In matters of war, he trusts my judgment. Seeing as this is a matter of war, my command is law. If you defy the law, you will suffer the consequences."

This time there was no retort, but Ackadus glared at him with daggers in his eyes, and Belisar and Hullis shared a look that, although subtle, was laden with disapproval.

Kaletor knew why. They thought he was overstepping his authority and wielding power he did not possess.

But whether he was or wasn't didn't matter. There was nothing any of them could do about it.

The realization brought a grin to his lips, and for a time, he enjoyed the oppressive silence weighing heavy in the room. Waves continued to crash into the ship, rocking her to and fro.

But there was more to discuss, so he said, "How will we take Rhodes?"

It was a moment before anyone spoke up.

Not surprisingly, it was Ackadus who did so first. "With an all-out frontal assault. Our fleet of warships is the greatest in the world. We should surround the island and attack the coast with every vessel we have."

"To what end?" Belisar challenged.

Ackadus answered quick as a snapping whip. "To strike fear into the heart of everyone on the island. When they see our vast armada encircling their homeland, delivering death and destruction, the entire population will be consumed by fear. They will see that there is no escape, and the prospect of death will make them beg for mercy."

"Preposterous," Belisar countered, his silver-streaked tangle of black beard quivering. "These are fellow Greeks we will be facing, not some barbarians that chop wood and herd goats all day. They will know what's coming, and they are braver than you think. Greeks are not spineless cowards—"

"They are," Kaletor interrupted. "The days of Themistocles and bold Athenians are long gone. We Spartans crushed such strength when we took their lands and conquered their cities. These Greeks no longer have such will."

When he finished, he shifted his gaze to Hullis. "What say you?"

Hullis tilted his head slightly before responding. "There is a wide beach on the southeast edge of the island. The fleet should sail straight for that point to disembark the army—"

"A beach?" Ackadus cut in, his tone scathing. "With this many ships and men? It would be chaos and confusion. We would be exposed to attack while we land. The Mandrakion Harbour would be much better suited."

Seeing Hullis struggle to find a counter, a rush of heat flooded Kaletor's face and neck.

"The Rhodians will be expecting that," he snarled, leaning over the table towards Ackadus. "They'll have archers ready to rain arrows down on our heads. They'll have hoplites ready to cut us down as soon as we step onto the docks. Such a direct, frontal assault would be difficult, and costly. What they won't be ready for is a beach landing, which gives us the advantage."

Ackadus seemed ready to retort, but Kaletor glared him down. It was enough to silence the welp.

In the brief glance Kaletor directed to Hullis, the pale man gave him a subtle smile.

The point settled, Belisar moved the discussion on to the ongoing war effort in Thrace, around the Hellespont, in Mesopotamia, Phoenicia, Egypt, and Cappadocia.

But while the others talked, Kaletor receded inward. He leaned back into his chair and sipped his wine, seeking to uncover the source of his sudden melancholy. He stewed for some time, unable to determine where the inner disturbance had come from.

It wasn't until Ackadus brought up the rumour that the Lycurgans had recently orchestrated another failed assassination attempt on the emperor's life. At that moment, the gentle voice of a young girl sounded in his mind.

"I knew there was still good in you."

Kaletor nearly choked on the wine flowing down his throat. He swallowed painfully and sat up straight, setting his goblet to the table as he was consumed by disbelief. It was a voice he rarely heard, and only ever in dreams.

It was her voice. Vaseus's voice.

But why? Why now? What could have triggered it? He hadn't seen her since the day she ran away and abandoned him. She was just a distant memory, one of many that had faded into oblivion. She was a memory that had no place in his life.

As he struggled to understand, his gaze drifted to Hullis. It was then that the reason for her words came.

I defended Hullis, and not because I agreed with his strategy. I defended him because I felt bad for him.

The realization made him grit his teeth. *Compassion is for the weak. I am not weak.*

"Compassion is good," the voice of Vaseus countered. *"You are good—"*

No, stop. You're wrong. Go away. I don't want to hear it.

"My dear Kaletor. Don't you know that I'm still part of you?"

"Enough!"

Seeing that Ackadus, Belisar, and Hullis were all looking at him, he realized he had bellowed the word aloud. His breathing raced as he glared them down.

"What are you looking at?" he snarled, snatching his goblet back up to drain the rest of his wine.

The ensuing silence was broken when raised voices sounded out on the ship's deck.

Baring his teeth, Kaletor spat, "What the hell is that about?"

He slammed his goblet back to the table, stood, rushed across the room, and barrelled through the heavy door.

In the instant of stepping outside into the bright sunlight, he saw dozens of sailors standing around on deck, every one of them watching two men fighting near the main mast.

"Stop!" he hollered over the cheers and goading calls, all of which quickly subsided.

The combatants ignored him and fought on.

Baring his teeth in a snarl, he took long strides beneath the red and gold sails billowing overhead. The sailors moved aside to let him through.

Over the steady wind, he shouted, "Stand down, you dogs!"

One of the men obeyed, letting go and slumping to the deck. The other used the opening to swing a fist into his opponent's unprotected gut.

Kaletor arrived and delivered a kick to the disobeyer's ribs. "You two picked the *wrong* day."

His boot had separated the pair, revealing one to be a young sailor, the other a hoplite. Both sprawled on the deck, they eyed each other like angry children.

"On your feet," Kaletor barked.

As they picked themselves up, Hullis, Belisar, and Ackadus arrived.

The young sailor was tall and lanky with black hair and a bloody mouth. The hoplite had three deeply creased lines running horizontally across his forehead and a pink swell under his left eye. Both breathed heavily as they glared at each other.

"Look at me, Spartan," Kaletor snarled. "Explain this, and be quick."

"Yes, Commander. This worthless filth mocked Spartan honour. When I moved to put him in his place, he attacked me—"

"Lies," the young sailor shouted. "It was you who attacked me, and just for looking at you the wrong way. I was defending mys—"

Kaletor's fist cracked into the sailor's throat. The boy choked and collapsed, gagging for air on all fours.

Looking to everyone all around him, Kaletor called out, "No one strikes a Spartan. Ever! We are the masters of the world. I don't care how wronged you feel or how unjust something seems. We can do whatever we like. For those who disrespect us, this will be your punishment."

As he finished, he pulled the dagger from the sheathe at his right hip. The sight of the blade made the boy's eyes open wide.

He tried to scramble away. Kaletor stepped close, tangled his fingers firmly in the boy's thick black hair, and yanked up. Still gasping for air, the sailor gurgled and flailed wildly. In one quick motion, Kaletor slashed the blade across the boy's cheek.

The answering howl was a choked sputter. Kaletor released him. He went down to his stomach, hands going to the bloody gash.

With the sailor moaning and writhing at his feet, Kaletor turned around, looked at Ackadus, and said, "Fetch a whip."

The emperor's son had gone a ghastly white. Now plain confusion narrowed his eyes and creased his forehead. "A whip? Wasn't that punishment enough?"

"It's not for him."

Ackadus's confusion deepened. "Then why do you want a whip?"

"To teach this disgraceful hoplite a lesson," Kaletor said, glancing over to the aging man. "A Spartan should never allow himself to be struck by a sailor boy."

Anger flashed across the hoplite's face, but he quickly banished it. "Where do you want me, Commander?"

"At the rail."

Kaletor looked back to Ackadus. "Do you understand now, Captain?"

Ackadus's expression of confusion was gradually replaced by one of somber gravity. "Yes."

"Then what are you waiting for? Fetch a whip!"

As Ackadus scurried to the hole in the deck and disappeared below, Kaletor noticed the utter silence that gripped his audience. The only sounds were the groans of the boy as he rolled on the deck and the wind snapping through the ship's two massive sails.

No one spoke as they looked on, their gazes shifting away as Kaletor looked to the many faces all around him. Seeing and feeling their discomfort or fear was a dark pleasure. He drank it in with a grin on his lips.

Ackadus re-emerged, a black whip coiled in his hand. Stepping around the moaning boy, he offered it to Kaletor.

Instead of taking it, he crossed his arms over his chest. "I didn't say it was for me. Give him fifteen."

"Me?" Ackadus said, eyes going wide. "But I've never done this before."

"Exactly. Time for you to learn."

"There's a reason I've never done it. I'm the emperor's son. It's beneath me—"

"Are you disobeying," Kaletor cut in, "the direct order of your superior?"

"This is not an order you're allowed to give me—"

"Say one more word and your back will be as bloody as his!"

The outrage in Ackadus was obvious as his jaw clenched and his eyes filled with hate. In that instant, it looked like he would fire something back.

But then he turned away, let the whip unfurl, and moved to stand directly behind the hoplite waiting at the rail.

Kaletor's grin, which had vanished, now returned.

That's right, boy. Fear me. I am all-powerful here.

"Remember," he said smoothly, "fifteen."

Ackadus shot him a sidelong glance full of fury, but didn't reply.

Releasing a low laugh, Kaletor looked once more at his silent audience. His eyes fell upon Belisar and Hullis standing side by side. The older, refined aristocrat had his thick arms crossed over his wide chest and a scowl on his face. Hullis hid his disapproval better, but it was there, behind the mask of neutrality.

Kaletor understood. His actions went beyond what was expected of him. No Spartan, not even the commander of the empire's Phalanxes, was supposed to wield power so nakedly. Only the emperor could do that.

He knew why his generals disapproved. Still looking at them, his grin widened.

You think that what's happening here is wrong or cruel or improper. Yet you cannot stop it. It is my will that rules here, not yours. This is my world.

Revelling in his power over powerful men, Kaletor turned to watch as Ackadus swung the cracking whip into the hoplite's back.

EIGHTEEN

It's not entirely clear when or why the Clans started fighting each other. It's assumed that the War Season evolved gradually over many years. At first, neighbouring Clans skirmished sporadically and randomly. As this happened more and more, it became formalized into something that resembled the Challenge.

The Spoken Tales

Beneath the chill gloom of early night, Jarka interlaced his fingers and rested his hands atop his head. In this position he waited, staring at the village's wooden wall of sharpened sticks and the gate directly before him, listening to the hurried movements and biting voices on the other side.

There was still time to run and leave the humans behind, a notion that was extremely tempting. Instead, he stayed where he was, pulling in deep breaths through his nose as he fought the urge to flee.

The gate swung open. Twenty or more men in two lines choked the opening, each holding a levelled spear.

One of them barked out three words, but in the human's language, so Jarka didn't understand.

"I surrender," he said quickly. "No fight. I'm looking for a woman named Vaseus—"

The same man cut him off by shouting the three words louder than before. At the same time, the two lines moved closer, brandishing their spears.

It was just as he feared; they didn't understand either.

He said the only word they might know. "Vaseus."

The stern-faced men didn't respond. They kept their spears down and advanced, many of them shouting the same three words.

"Vaseus," Jarka repeated, holding his ground despite the overwhelming need to run.

Still, they came on, gradually closing the gap.

"Vaseus," he said again, hearing the rising panic in his voice. "I'm looking for Vaseus. No fight. Is Vaseus here? Vaseus!"

No response. The outer edges of the lines rushed around to surround him, and like a tightening noose, they closed in, spears level, most still barking the same three words.

With nowhere to go and nothing else to do, Jarka lowered himself to his knees, hands still pressed firm to his head. Every muscle itched to move and fight, but he forced himself to stay still.

Once the points of their spears were a foot away, the men went silent and stopped.

Jarka's heart was racing as he eyed them. Many of their faces were gaunt and streaked with dirt, their heavy clothes were old and dishevelled, and they reeked of unwashed filth. It was clear that these people were not prospering.

As this somewhat bizarre observation went through his mind, someone stepped up behind him and grabbed his wrists. He clenched up, every muscle tightening and demanding that he resist. But, as before, he denied the urge to fight and allowed his hands to be bound together at the small of his back. He tried to exude calm as he met the gazes of the serious and nervous-looking men training their weapons on him.

As whoever was binding his hands finished, someone behind him said something. A moment later, a heavy cloth bag was pulled over his head, plunging him into darkness. Only the presence of so many spears inches from his body stopped him from growling or jerking away.

More words were barked out, and there was a flurry of movement around him. Hard fingers dug into his arms to pull him up. Jarka swallowed his burning pride and allowed himself to be steered into the village.

Walking blind proved to be an uncomfortable experience. He stumbled again and again as they progressed, only remaining upright thanks to the two men squeezing his arms. Making matters worse was the sour reek of the bag that filled his every breath, which was getting more and more laboured as they walked. Shouted words sounded all around him, creating a chorus of unknown phrases that hounded his imagination.

After what seemed like a long distance for such a small village, his escorts stopped, spun him around, and pushed his shoulders to make him step back. When he bumped into something thin and taller than himself, they pulled him to his knees. His hands were tugged back. When his wrists collided with what felt like a wooden pole, more ropes were secured around his forearms.

Before long, they finished. Jarka tested his bonds and felt that he was tied to the pole. The ropes were so snug he could barely move.

Minutes passed. He could smell that many were close by, despite their now muted voices.

His neck became sore. He let his head down to dangle in front of his chest and closed his eyes. He tried to focus on evening out his breath.

Suddenly, the voices silenced altogether, and a lone voice spoke words that he understood.

"Is that you, Jarka?"

"Vaseus?"

The bag was lifted from his head and there she was. Her blonde hair spilled out to frame her delicate, smooth face, and the torchlight surrounding them dazzled in her green eyes.

He released a gusting laugh. "Vaseus," he repeated, smiling as wide as his cheeks allowed. "I've been looking for you."

Either confusion or shock spread her eyes wide as she took a step back. "Have you lost your mind? What are you doing here?"

"It's great to see you again too. You look good, at least for a human—"

"Jarka," she cut in. "What is this? You've frightened my entire village. All the children have been sent indoors, and everyone wants to kill you."

For the first time, he looked beyond her to what surrounded them. They were in an open square filled with a tight circle of thirty or more humans, their collective attention fixed entirely on him. By the flickering light of torches that many held in hand, their fear was obvious.

He turned his head from side to side. He was completely surrounded.

Noticing all the swords, spears, and clubs held by the men, he let out a low whistle. "How many weapons do your people have?"

Someone in the sea of bodies shouted a few angry human words.

Jarka looked back to Vaseus. "What did he say?"

She seemed to be making eye contact with someone directly behind him. After a moment, she glanced down and said, "They want to know if you're alone."

"Well, not exactly. I'm sort of seeing someone—"

"This isn't a game," she snapped, hands going to her hips. "Didn't you hear me? Everyone is afraid of you. They want to kill you."

"And what about you? Is that what you want?"

Her gaze softened some, but only briefly. "Just answer the question. Did other yagars come with you?"

He shook his head. "No. It's just me."

She looked back to whoever was behind him and said something in human. The man's response was clipped and hard.

She returned her gaze to Jarka and said, "He wants to know why you're here."

"To find you."

"Why would you want to find me?"

"I need your help."

"My help with what?"

The question triggered memories of Jazith being taken, and all of a sudden, his head felt heavy. He let it hang, and with his eyes on the dry dirt beneath his knees, said, "Five days ago, I was walking in the forest with my sister when a group of Spartans attacked us. They took her, and she hasn't been seen since."

Vaseus didn't respond, and silence reigned. But not for long.

The man barked out more harsh words. Vaseus responded calmly. But when the man barked again, her tone turned angry, and the two went back and forth, practically shouting at each other.

Eventually, they stopped. Jarka brought his head back up and said, "Are they going to kill me now?"

Vaseus glared the man down for a long moment, arms stiff at her sides, chest heaving.

With her nostrils still flared, her venom-filled eyes dropped to look at him. "Not yet. I told them to wait."

"Very good. You really are—"

"But it won't last long," she said, stepping forward to crouch so that their faces were at the same height. "They'll still kill you if you don't prove useful."

Jarka grunted a sarcastic laugh. "And how am I supposed to do that?"

"By helping us defeat the Spartans."

"What? No, I can't. I'm not here to join your rebellion. I just want to get my sister back."

"And there's only one way you can do that."

"How?"

She inched a bit closer, those green eyes of hers wide and sharp. "Your sister is being taken to Sparta. The men who attacked you are yagar hunters. They travel to your lands for the sole purpose of capturing females."

"Why would they do that?"

Her expression turned grim. "The emperor has an obsession with the females of your kind. He rewards anyone who brings them to Sparta. Those he deems the most beautiful fetch the biggest payouts.

"Once a yagar enters Sparta, they never leave. He keeps them like pets, caged and on display. Sometimes he brings one or two with him to public events so he can show them off to the people. He's even had them fight to the death for his and the crowd's entertainment. When I saw this happen years ago, the yagars weren't even armed."

"No," Jarka growled. "That cannot be. It cannot."

The ring of onlooking people responded to his harsh tone by pressing in closer, weapons levelled and poised.

Vaseus cast about, hissing something in her language. The mass of humans halted, but they remained poised to strike, as ready as a crouching hunter.

"I can't hold them back much longer," Vaseus said, speaking more quickly than before. "You must agree to help us. It's the only way you live until tomorrow, and it's the only way you'll ever see your sister again. Without an army, you won't get within two hundred miles of Sparta. The moment you're seen in the Empire, you'll be reported and hunted down. You can't even hope that she'll escape. No yagar has ever escaped from Sparta."

Jarka's head spun as he tried to take everything in. He needed time to think, time to process and plan. But time was something he did not have. The spear tips were getting closer, looking ready to plunge into his body at any moment.

Refocusing intently on Vaseus, he said, "How do I know that what you're saying is true? How do I know she's being taken to Sparta?"

Her response was immediate. "You don't. All you have is my word. You must choose to trust me or not."

She was right. His mind raced in a desperate attempt to determine the correct course. He kept his gaze on her eyes, trying to catch any hint of dishonesty. All he saw was firm determination staring back at him, unflinching and open.

"I trust you, Vaseus. Tell me what I must do to bring my sister home."

A slight smile tugged at the corners of her lips. "Help us defeat the Spartans. Only then will your sister be free."

"And you know how to do that?"

Her smile broadened as she nodded. "The war is already underway. Rebellious towns and cities are battling the Spartans all across the Empire. Their army is spread thin. If your people join the fight, we can march straight for Greece, crushing the few Phalanxes we meet along the way. But we must move quickly, before the Spartans can suppress the rebellion."

He saw a fire ignite in her eyes as she spoke. It sounded like a great plan, but he immediately recognized its flaws.

One was that The Ten Clans were divided against one another. They would never band together into anything like an army. Another was that every yagar hated humans. They would never fight for any human cause.

He opened his mouth to point this out—

But stopped. Something sharp and cold had been pressed to his back, sliding through his fur to settle on the skin beneath it.

The man behind him spoke again, his volume indicating that it was his spear that Jarka felt.

This time Vaseus did not argue. After nodding to the man, she looked back at Jarka. "Last chance. Will you help us? Will the yagars join our rebellion?"

Never.

The answer went through his mind as clear as water flowing down a mountain stream.

But to say it aloud meant death. And even worse, Jazith would be a prisoner until she died, alone in a foreign and cruel place. He could not let that happen.

Into this moment, a clear thought sounded in his mind.

Challenge them all. Become Warlord of every Clan.

Jarka blinked as the idea struck. *What? That's unheard of. Is it even possible? Does the Warrior Code allow for such a thing? I'm Clanless. Has a Clanless ever challenged a Warlord? Has the Warlord of one Clan ever challenged the Warlord of another? Even if I could become Warlord of all the Clans, could I really bring them together to fight as a single army? And would they follow me into a human war?*

"Jarka," Vaseus snapped. "What's your answer?"

Her voice pulled him from the vortex of swirling thoughts. Become Warlord of every Clan. It was the craziest idea he'd ever had, far beyond anything he or anyone else had ever known.

It was impossible and sure to fail. But it was all he had.

And so, he swallowed, pulled in a deep breath, and gave his answer. "The yagars are with you. We will help you defeat the Spartans."

NINETEEN

It was then that Spartans first encountered the strange race of people known as yagars. They lurked in a seemingly endless, dark forest, an ever-present threat beyond the newly established frontier of the Empire.

Androdamos of Boeotia

"What should we do, Commander?"

Kaletor glared at the black sky directly ahead, pacing back and forth behind the wheel that the ship captain held steady. A bolt of lightning arced down, followed closely by a booming roll of thunder that rumbled across the choppy water.

"Damn you, Poseidon," he growled, slashing an arm out toward the storm. "Damn you!"

"We have to go around," Ackadus called over the ever-increasing wind. "It's the only way."

"Not necessarily," Hullis spoke up, his red cloak snapping around his body. "Look how far the clouds stretch to either side. Even if we turn ninety degrees, part of the fleet might still get caught in it."

"We have to try," Ackadus argued. "We could even turn around, angle our way towards its edge—"

"You want to flee from some wind and rain?" Kaletor scoffed. "Have you no courage at all?"

The teenager's expression darkened, his lips becoming even thinner than usual. "I have as much courage as I have sense. At best, sailing into that storm will scatter the fleet. At worst, every ship goes down and wipes out three entire Phalanxes."

Kaletor barked a mocking laugh. "Sounds like you've lost your nerve, boy. Perhaps you should join Belisar in my quarters."

"It's not fear that grips me. It's reason. Look at those clouds. Our ships won't survive."

Kaletor turned to eye the storm once more. The wind picked up as another boom of thunder reached them.

"Rhodes is there," he called, pointing straight out, "just beyond this little storm. I'll not run in the opposite direction."

"But the fleet—"

"We're at war, *boy*," Kaletor roared as he spun back round. "Risks must be taken. I'll not give the treacherous people of Rhodes any more time to prepare."

He looked to the ship captain. "Signal the fleet. Maintain our present course."

While the thick-limbed African relayed the order through hand signals to his first mate at the main mast, the prince appeared ready to explode. Yet despite his bulging eyes and downturned eyebrows, he kept his mouth shut.

Kaletor grinned at him. *That's right, boy. Know your place, and remember what happens to those who displease me.*

With that thought lingering in his mind, he moved to stand beside Hullis and watch the sailors on the lower deck. Some were filing below to join the slaves on the oars in the bowels of the ship. Others were tying off sails and tugging on lines. All appeared chaotic, yet everything ran smoothly.

Among this seething mass of activity, one sailor raised the black-and-red striped flag, the signal that told the other ships to continue straight ahead.

Kaletor folded his arms over his breastplate, and keeping his gaze steady on the black storm, said, "What do you think, General?"

"It's a bold choice," Hullis replied after a moment. "One worthy of a true Spartan. The historians might well compare you with Leonidas himself."

"Yes. Yet Leonidas marched to Thermopylae knowing he and his men would die. Have I condemned my men to the same fate?"

As he finished, he glanced over. Hullis struck a stoic figure, peering steadily at the storm, red cloak streaming out behind him.

He seemed deep in thought as he turned his head to make eye contact. "Ships will go down and men will die. But with your iron will pulling us onward, most will make it through. The gods have always been on your side."

The words filled Kaletor with ideas of glory, and he grinned so wide it felt as if every one of his teeth were exposed. "Nothing, not even Poseidon can stand in my way. Nothing can stop us."

Remaining straight-faced, Hullis nodded his agreement. "As you say, Commander."

Thanks to the added muscle on the oars, the ship had picked up the pace. The wind was intensifying, and the sky was darkening. Kaletor checked on the rest of the fleet. Those to the left maintained good spacing between each other and were keeping up. Those to the right were slightly bunched up, yet remained in the checkerboard formation. From what he could tell, they were in good shape.

A white flash of lightning illuminated the darkness, and a deafening clap of thunder exploded through the air. A pounding downpour of rain followed. The wind picked up even more, sending those still on deck scrambling for the rails.

Watching this, a solitary thought passed through his mind. *So it begins.*

Both Hullis and Ackadus struggled against the wind to get to the rail running horizontally between the two outer staircases. Kaletor refused to be so cowed. He spread his legs wide and bent at the knee. He grit his teeth in a snarl, squinted his eyes against the slanting rain, and looked up into the huge mass of black clouds.

"Come on then, you bastard. Come on!"

As if in answer, another incredible boom of thunder split the air. Many covered their heads as if to protect themselves from an incoming blow. A wave slammed into the left side of the ship's hull, tilting the deck high and to the right.

He was thrown off balance and landed hard on his side. Before he could recover, the ship crashed back down flat, and he was tossed through the air. He bounced and rolled across the deck, completely out of control. As he tumbled, he glimpsed the seething water below and expected to be thrown clear.

Instead, he slammed bodily into solid wood, ending up face down on the deck.

For a moment, he couldn't move or breathe. His lungs were seized up, and stabbing pain prickled down his left side. All he could hear was the incessant pounding of rain and wind.

But before long, as the shock of being tossed around like a rag doll subsided, he felt heat flush his neck and face. There had been fear in him, and it had been all-consuming.

He thought he had purged himself of such weakness. To know that it still resided within him was infuriating.

He clenched his jaw and rolled to his knees. Snarling against the shooting pain, he forced himself back to his feet.

The ship lurched hard, knocking him back down. He kept a knee under him and caught himself with both hands, every muscle screaming from the strain.

Once he was steady, he roared and surged back to his feet.

"I will *not be defeated,*" he bellowed, staggering once before standing firm. "Nothing can stop me! Do you understand? Nothing!"

Another sweeping gale of wind blasted him, but he held his ground. The pounding rain slanted into his eyes. He was soaked to the bone. The sky was black, almost as dark as night, and he could barely see anything. All he knew was the battering wind, the icy rain, and the never-ending thrashing of the ship beneath his feet as waves slammed into the hull.

Into this hell came a blinding flash of white and an earsplitting boom of thunder. Kaletor brought both hands up to cover his ears, but too late. With his head ringing, a bloom of orange light caught his eye.

He looked over to see that the neighbouring ship was on fire. The flames were already devouring the main mast and licking across the deck.

At first, he was confused. Were they under attack?

But after a moment, he realized that the ship had been struck by lightning. Still, it was unbelievable. How could the fire be so strong when everything was soaking wet?

He could see men running from the blaze, some on fire themselves. Over the howling wind and pounding rain came their screams.

As he watched the fiery chaos, Kaletor noticed something else. By the light of the flames, he saw a towering wall of water coming straight at them.

"Brace!" he hollered, rushing towards the rail. "Brace for impact!"

Keeping one eye on the black wave, he sprinted across the deck. But everything was slick, and he slipped. He stuttered his steps, stumbled, and barely managed to stay upright.

He scrambled forward, reaching out for the rail—

The wave hit with the force of a thousand catapults and he was thrown, lifted bodily into the air. His gut clenched as he careened clear of everything, weightless, flying. He spun out of control, expecting to slam into something.

He didn't. He felt himself falling, dropping like a stone.

He knew what was coming. He squeezed his eyes shut as he plummeted.

He hit the water hard and went under. Tiny knives of ice lanced every inch of him, and the slamming impact rendered him immobile. The dark water crushed in on him, heavy and impossibly cold. All was muted. There was only the roiling, raging sea, and distant thunder somewhere above.

He floated there, motionless, struck numb.

Before long, he realized he wasn't floating. He was sinking.

Shaking himself, he thrashed into action, arms sweeping out and legs kicking. Still he sank. He kicked harder and clawed at the water, pulling his arms through the cold with all his strength.

But it made no difference. The crushing water weighed down on him, too heavy and too strong.

Despite the burn in his lungs, a thought pushed into his mind.

My armour. Get it off!

Frantic, he brought his hands to his throat and ripped the broach that held his cloak. As the garment fell away, he yanked at the straps on both sides of his breastplate.

He released the first six, but when he went for the last two, his fingers fumbled. Black dots crowded the corners of his vision.

Clenching his teeth and needing air, he pulled again. They didn't release.

He tugged again—

TWENTY

If just one came, a thousand yagars could not
defeat it. They are nearly indestructible. Only
their wings can be pierced by a thrown spear.
If just one came, we would be doomed.

The Spoken Tales

You have to tell her. Even if you don't, she'll figure it out soon enough.

Jarka rolled his shoulders, hoping to shrug off the unpleasant
thought. It didn't work. He glanced down the line of seven humans
walking alongside him through the Forever Forest. Before long, his gaze settled
on Vaseus.

She'll be a lot more upset if she finds out on her own.

He shook his head and looked forward. That voice in his head had barely
shut up ever since he declared that all yagars would join her cause and fight
alongside humans.

What had he been thinking? He was Clanless, the lowest of the low, completely without power, influence, or status. Yet here he was, leading a group of
humans to his village under the expectation that he would muster a massive
yagar army from The Ten Clans to take on the Spartan Empire. The absurdity
of it had dominated his mind for the day and a half they had been travelling
together.

But what choice did he have? They would have killed him if he hadn't
promised to help. It was an act of desperation for the sake of saving both
himself and Jazith.

He didn't know how long he could keep the façade going. What would happen when they learned he couldn't deliver? It felt like he was hunting blind, barely able to make his way, and on the brink of failure.

But he had to keep going. Somehow, he had to find a way.

He was consumed by this dilemma, continuously trying to come up with solutions as they progressed between the trees, hardly noticing the passage of time or his surroundings.

It came as something of a shock when he heard someone calling his name.

Blinking as he shook himself, he glanced left. "What was that?"

Vaseus had shifted down the line and was now right beside him. "I said we need to stop. We haven't eaten in hours."

He huffed out a breath. "Right, yes. I'd forgotten how often you humans need to eat."

She gave him an unimpressed look before calling in her strange language to her companions. They all stopped, unshouldered their packs, and sat down.

Jarka moved off several paces, taking in their surroundings. The random jumble of pines, maples, and birches remained an unending maze of thick trunks and budding leaves. He sniffed deep, smelling the moss and decay of the undergrowth. All was calm save for the back-and-forth calls of two unseen birds.

He was unsure exactly where they were until he spotted a lone grey stone beneath the dangling fingers of an ancient willow. In that instant, everything became familiar. He remembered hunting here on a few occasions, stalking the elk and deer that called these woods home. The village was no more than a few miles away.

As all this became clear, something clicked in his mind, and he knew what to do.

Spinning on his heels, he returned to the group. Most were sitting on the trunk of a fallen tree, drinking from their waterskins as they chatted.

Moving closer, Jarka called out, "Vaseus!"

She had been listening to one of the men, the one named Dacio. Now she shot him an annoyed look. "What?"

"I need to talk to you."

"Talk then."

He glanced to Dacio, noticing his hard glare.

"Not here. In private."

"But they can't understand a word you're—"

He turned away to cut her short, moving off quickly and not stopping until he had pushed his way through a dense tangle of tree limbs and bush.

He turned around in time to watch her emerge from the foliage, her thin arms raised to shield her face.

"What are you doing?" she huffed between breaths. "We don't have time for lengthy delays."

"It would appear your friends still don't trust me."

Her brow creased in a frown. "Did you expect differently? They've feared or hated yagars their entire lives, just like their parents did, and their parents before them."

"I'm just not used to being disliked. Everyone likes me."

"Everyone?" she said, her light eyebrows rising.

He flashed her a grin. "Is that so hard to believe?"

"In my experience, no one can be liked by all."

"Perhaps I'm the exception."

He looked past her shoulder, back in the direction of her companions, and brought a hand up to tap two fingers to his chin. "I wonder why they don't see me for what I am. Is it the brilliant arrangement of my richly coloured gold fur and black spots? My towering, impressive physique? Maybe that's it. The simple fact that I'm so much bigger, stronger, and faster makes them feel intimidated. Or maybe they're in awe—"

"Jarka."

He blinked and returned his gaze to her. "Hmm? Yes?"

"You said you wanted to talk to me. Get to the point."

He crossed his arms and studied her for a brief moment. Her green eyes were as piercing as ever, utterly focused and clear.

She's not easily distracted, this one. I wonder if all humans are like her.

While he considered this, she too crossed her arms, and with a slight tilt of her head, said, "Well?"

Still looking at her closely, more thoughts came to him. *She's also quite impatient. And fiercely determined. Like a honeybee.*

The idea was amusing, but sensing her burgeoning ire, he stifled the chuckle that was about to bubble out.

"Before we arrive at my village," he said, "there's something you should know."

Her eyes narrowed, instantly suspicious. "I don't like the sound of that."

All at once, his amusement evaporated. He cleared his throat. "Remember when we first met and I told you that I was Clanless?"

"No, you didn't."

"Did I not?"

"Well, whether you did or didn't, why are you bringing it up now?"

Heat flooded his face. But why? She was just a little human that could never beat him in a fight. Why did he feel warm?

He swallowed and forced his dry tongue to form words. "I . . . I'm Clanless. Do you know what that means?"

"Yes, I understand. You're Clanless. You don't have a Clan. Can we go now?"

"Yes. I mean no."

He snorted a laugh at himself, but regretted it immediately. Shaking his head and releasing a long exhale, he did his best to rein in his spinning thoughts. "There's no easy way to say this, so I'll just say it. We're not on our way to convince my people to join your war. But—"

"What?" she sliced in. "You said you would help us. You gave your word!"

"I know, I know, and I will, I promise. It's just going to take a little bit longer than you probably hoped."

Her expression darkened. "How much longer?"

"Oh, not too long," he answered brightly, flashing his most charming smile. "So long as we move quickly and everything goes according to plan, it'll be no more than a few months."

"A few months?" she spat, arms jerking down stiff to her sides. "That's too long. My people are fighting and dying every day. The Spartans have already recaptured several settlements and slaughtered thousands of innocent people. We need your warriors now."

Jarka's smile faded away. "I understand your rush, but you need to be reasonable. Yagars hate humans. We want nothing to do with any of you. Every one of us would rather kill you than talk to you. Getting my people to fight for your rebellion is going to be more difficult than you could possibly imagine. It's going to take time to change that. This is something you need to accept, just as I have."

"Why do you care how long it takes? It's not your people who are fighting a war for their freedom."

"My sister has been taken against her will," he growled, stepping close to her and straightening to his full height. "She's afraid. She's surrounded by humans that hate her. Her world is pain or misery, or both. All I want to do is run south, find her, and bring her back home. Instead, I'm here with you, doing what you say is the only way to save her. I put my trust in you, Vaseus, against my every instinct to rescue Jazith myself. Is it too much to ask that you trust me in return?"

As he finished, he was towering over her, arms taut and poised as if ready to strike. She held her ground, though her eyes had softened.

"Forgive me. I'd forgotten about your sister. I'm just so wrapped up in this war, sometimes it's all I can think about. You're desperate, just as I am. Let's work together, and maybe we can both get what we want."

He stepped back, allowing his tensed muscles to relax. "Thank you."

She gave him a small smile. "Of course. But how do you plan on getting your people to fight for us? How will you get them from hating my people to cooperating with them?"

"I will travel to The Ten Clans and challenge every Warlord for the right to rule. Once I defeat them all, I will be the sole leader of every yagar alive. I will then lead our warriors south to join your armies and help you destroy the Spartans."

It was the first time he had told someone his audacious and insane plan. As he spoke, any hope he had that it would sound better aloud than it did in his mind died. If anything, it made it more real, and even more daunting.

But he must have been hiding his misgivings well.

Vaseus set her hands to her hips as she nodded, appearing satisfied. "Okay then. How difficult will it be to defeat a Warlord?"

Almost impossible. This answer snapped instantly across his mind.

He pushed it aside and spread his arms wide. "You're looking at the best of the best, honeybee. I have never been defeated."

She tilted her head to one side. "Really?"

No.

"Yes. I'm unstoppable with a spear in my hands."

"And it's really that simple? You can just walk into any village, challenge the Warlord, win the fight, and become their new leader? Just like that?"

Once again, he couldn't prevent the true answer from flashing across his mind. *It's never been done by anyone, let alone by a lowly Clanless.*

"Just like that."

Despite his confident responses, she didn't seem convinced. She started tapping her fingers to her belt. "Has anyone ever attempted this before?"

This time the truth slipped out. "Never."

"Why not?"

He had no good answer, so he just stared at her.

"Maybe," she picked up, "it's because there's nothing to stop someone from turning around and challenging *you* right after you've won."

He kept his gaze steady on hers. *I wonder if all humans are as clever as this one.*

"Details, bee," he said aloud, clapping his hands in front of his chest. "Details that we need not concern ourselves with right now. In any case, this is the only possible way to get my people to help us."

She seemed to consider this statement for a time, one hand coming up to smooth down her hair. "Unless," she said slowly, "I found one of these Warlords and enlisted *their* help. It sounds like any one of them has far more power than you."

He forced out an exaggerated gasp, clutching at his chest and leaning back. "Cut me straight to the bone, why don't you? You humans don't mince words."

"Some do. I don't."

He chuckled. "I see. In that case, I don't know whether to be offended or amused."

"Amused? What could be amusing?"

Jarka smiled, his fangs poking free. "The idea of you going straight to a

Warlord and asking for help. It's quite funny."

She crossed her arms. "What's funny about that?"

"Have you forgotten how yagars feel about humans? You'd be dead long before you got anywhere near a Warlord."

"If that's true, if all yagars hate humans so much, why haven't you killed me yet?"

"Because I'm not like other yagars, remember? You'll understand soon enough."

She answered with a low laugh. "Very well. Looks like I'm stuck with you and your . . . ambitious plan."

"And I'm stuck with a human. A fair trade, yes?"

She laughed again.

*　　*　　*

"Everyone else needs to stay out of sight for now. Just you and me from here."

"Is that really necessary?"

Jarka looked away to scan his village one more time. All was calm beneath the deepening gloom of a purple dusk. From the forest's edge, he could only see a handful of yagars moving through the streets. He rotated his ears forward but heard nothing.

"There's no time to argue," he said, looking back to Vaseus and her waiting companions, their faces shaded by the dangling canopy. "We need to announce your presence without causing a panic. Tell them to stay here and remain hidden. Once it's safe, we'll come back for them."

She hesitated for a long time, lips tight and eyes wide.

Eventually, she relented. "Fine."

Following a brief exchange, the humans began unshouldering their packs, giving him nasty looks and grumbling as they did.

He nodded and said, "Well done. Now follow me and keep quiet."

"Why do I have to be quiet?"

"Just trust me."

He struck out then, moving fast to quickly cover the open ground between the edge of the forest and the nearest huts. Keeping to the village's outer limits, he proceeded around the edge.

Without being spotted along the way, he arrived at the rear of the hut he was heading for. He paused to listen. Hearing nothing, he motioned for Vaseus to follow and crept around to the front.

Leaning his body tight to the flimsy door of cracked wood, he hissed, "Relyk. Relyk, you bag of meat. It's Jarka. Are you in there?"

A muffled response filtered through the thin walls. "Someone there?"

"It's Jarka. I'm coming in."

Not willing to wait any longer, he turned the door handle and moved into the hut. In the middle of the central room stood Relyk, the sweet smell of fresh meat and the hint of red on his lips suggesting he had just left the table at the hut's back wall.

He opened his mouth to speak—

But froze when he saw Vaseus.

"What's this?" he blurted, his small eyes bulging.

"It's okay, my friend," Jarka said, reaching his arms out with palms down. "She's with me. She's here to help—"

"What?" Relyk rasped, whiskers twitching as his face screwed up in confusion. "What's wrong with you? That's a human. What's she doing here? Have you lost your mind?"

Before Jarka could reply, Vaseus stepped to his side and said, "A pleasure to meet you as well. Relyk, was it?"

His mouth fell open as he gawked at her, and silence prevailed.

Eventually, he said, "What's going on?"

Jarka looked over at Vaseus. "What are you doing? Didn't you hear me when I said I'd do the talking?"

She crossed her arms. "You never said that."

"Really?" he said, tilting his head slightly. "Well, I meant to. Yagars have never heard of a human that can speak our language. It's unnerving. So no more out of you."

She responded only with a smug smile.

He returned his attention to Relyk, who was staring wide-eyed at Vaseus.

"It's alright, my friend," he said, moving slowly to stand closer. "I know how this looks—"

"What's going on?" Relyk repeated, his expression severe. "Why did you bring her here? And where have you been?"

"Yes, I understand. You have questions, and I will provide answers. But first, I need you to find Rox and bring her here. I need both of you—"

"No," Relyk snarled. "I will do nothing until you tell me what's going on."

"There isn't time," Jarka shot back. "I'm asking you as a friend. I need your help. You know me, Relyk. You know you can trust me. I came here because I know I can trust you."

A low sigh rumbled somewhere in Relyk's chest. Following a short silence, he released a harsh exhale and stepped around Jarka.

He said over a shoulder, "You'd better still be here when I get back." He strode to the door, opened it just enough to slip out, and was gone.

Jarka hadn't noticed how tense his body had become. With Relyk's departure, he relaxed and released a shaky breath.

"Well that went well."

His answering laugh was choppy. "Yes, I thought so too. Didn't I say this was going to be easy?"

She responded with a low chuckle before moving to sit in one of the chairs at the back table. "As long as it works, you do whatever it is you have to do."

"I like your thinking."

"So what's next? And who's this Rox your friend is going to fetch? Why do you want her here?"

"All in good time, honeybee. All in good time."

With fingers intertwined, she rested her forearms on the table. "Alright. Can we at least light a lantern or something? I can barely see anything."

"Really?" he said, looking around the hut. "I can see fine."

"That doesn't help me any."

"Do all humans have this problem? Or just you?"

"You mean can humans see in the dark? No, we can't."

He couldn't help but chuckle. "How unfortunate. Perhaps this means you can't hear or smell or taste as well as us either."

"Perhaps," she snapped. "Can we just get some light in here?"

"As you wish, Unseeing One."

She was silent as he went about lighting a fire in Relyk's small stone hearth.

The flames had just come to life when he heard someone approaching the front of the hut. He looked to Vaseus, put a finger to his lips, and crept silently to the door.

Whoever approached did so quietly. Jarka planted his feet far apart and tensed his legs, ready to move.

A single moment of still quiet.

Then the door was opening—

And in stepped Relyk, followed closely by Rox.

"There she is," he exclaimed, straightening out of his crouch and spreading his arms wide.

"Where's the human?" Rox snapped as she rushed past him.

When she saw Vaseus at the table, she shook her head. "Unbelievable." She turned and fixed Jarka with her light-gold eyes. "You're unbelievable, you know that?"

"Well, actually—"

"Shut it. First, you disappear without telling anyone. Without telling me. Now you return with one of them? What's wrong with you?"

"That's what I said," Relyk seconded, moving to stand between where Rox stood and where Vaseus sat.

"One of them? You can't talk about me like that—"

"Vaseus," Jarka growled. "Not a good time."

"Explain yourself," Rox growled. "And be quick, before I lose my patience and kill her."

"Alright," he said, raising his hands in surrender. "Just take it easy. I'll explain everything."

Talking fast, he told them why he left and what had happened since. As he spoke, the harsh looks he was getting from them only worsened. It was surprising that they held their tongues until he finished.

Shaking his head, Relyk spoke first. "You've lost it. Those Spartans must have hit you harder than I thought."

"I know how it sounds—"

"I don't think you do," Rox interrupted, the flickering firelight dancing in the purple gem of her necklace. "Becoming Warlord of *every* Clan? Yagars joining together to fight alongside humans and destroy an empire? It's impossible. It's beyond any delusion, hope, or reason. You can't be serious."

"I have no other choice," Jarka countered. "It's the only way I can save Jazith. She's the reason I'm still alive. She has protected me my whole life. She has never abandoned me or let me down. I will not abandon her now."

"But it's too much, Jarka," Rox said, her tone softer now. "It cannot be done."

"You don't know that. You can't know that until somebody tries." He paused to release a shaky breath. "She's the only family I have left. I have to try."

Silence followed his words. He looked to the fire, unable to meet the dismay in their eyes any longer.

Before long, the quiet became unbearable.

Dragging a hand down his face to clear away the tears, he said, "I came here because I need your help." He looked back up to meet their eyes. "Will you help me?"

Relyk gave a terse nod. "I will."

Jarka released a deep exhale and nodded back. "Thank you."

Rox was hugging herself, eyes filled with disappointment or remorse. It was a long moment before she said, "You won't be talked out of this, will you?"

He shook his head. "No."

"Even though you will fail?"

He shook his head again but said nothing.

"Please, Jarka," Rox said, her voice regaining some of its edge. "Don't do this. Don't throw your life away. I know you think you don't have a choice, but you do. Sometimes we lose those we love and there's nothing we can do about it. Sometimes, no matter how badly we want to, we can't bring them back. But even when we lose those we love, all is not lost. You still have many friends that love you. I still love you. You don't have to throw that all away—"

"Stop," he cut in, the word coming out husky and thick. "Please. No more. Are you going to help me or not?"

"You know I would do anything for you. But not this. I can't help you destroy your life. I love you too much—"

"Then you need to leave. If you won't help me, I need you to leave."

It was as if he had struck a crushing blow to her very core. She seemed to collapse inward. The light dimmed in her eyes. Her mouth hung slightly open as she stood there, somehow smaller than she was a moment before.

Seeing this, Jarka's gut clenched, and his throat constricted. But before he could even attempt to ease her pain, she walked out without a second glance.

For a long moment, he just stared after her, his chest seized up so tight he could barely breathe.

At some point, Relyk moved close and said, "So what do you need me to do?"

Jarka blinked but didn't look at him. Swallowing to loosen the walls of his throat, he said, "We need supplies. Water, tools, tents, weapons. Food, if there's any to spare."

"Understood. Is this the only human, or are there more?"

Now he did turn to glance at Vaseus. "How many?"

She leaned into the back of her chair, setting a hand to her chin as she pondered the question.

"I'm not sure," she said after a moment. "I'll need to know how the war is progressing, which means maintaining communication with my people, which means they'll need to know how to find me."

She paused, tapping two fingers to her chin.

Eventually, she said, "Two or three. But they'll be coming and going all the time—"

"Got it," Relyk cut in, moving to the door. "I'll see what I can find. Sit tight."

Jarka shook himself and turned to say, "Thank you, my friend. I don't know what I would have done without your help."

Relyk looked back to meet his gaze. He gave a quick nod, then was gone.

Silence reigned once more. Jarka's breath remained sharp and quick as he stood there, not knowing what to do with himself.

The minutes passed slowly. The crackling of the flames was the only sound that filled the gaping void.

"I'm sorry," Vaseus eventually said, mercifully ending the excruciating silence.

He glanced over. "For what?"

Her bright green eyes were soft with sadness. "I know pain when I see it. Loss is something I'm far too familiar with. She loves you, and you love her. I may not be yagar, but that doesn't matter. It's plain to see."

His throat squeezed tight, his jaw clenched, and his ears strained. Unable to speak, his gaze faltered, and he brought a hand up to cover his face. It was all he could do to cry without sobbing.

*   *   *

Some time later, Relyk finally returned. "Come on," he said quietly from the doorway. "Help me with this."

Desperate to do anything to get his mind off of Rox, Jarka lurched into action. Stacked against the hut's back wall were four packs, two spears, and a clutch of hunting knives.

He slung two of the packs over his shoulder, hearing the slosh of water within. He took up the spears and hurried back inside. Relyk followed with the rest and shut the door.

"Were you seen?" Jarka asked as he set the packs on the floor.

Relyk also lay down what he carried, his mouth hanging open as he tried to catch his breath. "No," he managed. "But nearly. At one point I thought I was done for, but it was just Elder Imzen. She couldn't have seen me with her failing eyesight. Other than that, I had to hide a few times, and I was sprinting everywhere."

"I owe you one, my friend, but there's no time to waste. We've already lingered here for too long." He looked to Vaseus. "Time to go. Carry what you can. I'll take the rest."

He expected resistance to such blunt demands, but she complied without complaint. She must have understood just how precarious their situation was.

"I'm going with you."

Jarka looked back to Relyk. "What? No you're not—"

"Yes I am," Relyk cut in, hefting two of the packs onto his back and taking up a spear. "And there's nothing you can do to stop me."

Jarka shook his head. "No. No way. One Clanless returning to the Clans will upset them enough, if they find out. Two would just be asking for it."

"I don't care," Relyk said. "You'll need someone else to hunt if you want to move fast. Without plenty of food, you'll weaken and lose, and if you lose, it's all over."

"What?" Vaseus said, stopping beside Jarka, her eyes wide with alarm. "What does he mean, if you lose it's all over?"

Jarka hesitated as he struggled to find an answer. "Uh . . . Well—"

"You didn't tell her?" Relyk interjected. Looking at Vaseus, he continued. "When someone challenges a Warlord and loses, they—"

"Alright," Jarka blurted out, "you win. You can come with us."

"Hold on," Vaseus persisted. "Explain what happens if you lose—"

148

"No time for that," he said, dumping a pack in Vaseus's arms as he headed for the door.

"Just wait—"

He ignored her and went outside, moving to the back of the hut and stopping there. He swept his gaze over the surrounding area. All was dark and quiet, and there was no one around.

A moment later, Relyk and Vaseus joined him. Glancing over at them both, he said in a hushed voice, "Stay silent and follow me."

The possibility of being detected was stark, almost palpable. It was probably the only reason Vaseus refrained from questioning him further, though the ferocity in her eyes expressed her displeasure. Relyk simply nodded his understanding.

After one last sweep of the area, Jarka pushed off from the back of the hut to make for the safety of the forest. The packs bounced and dragged on his body, but he kept stride.

It wasn't far, and after a short sprint, they crossed the tree line.

Running around a wide bush for cover, he took a knee. While the other two did the same, he peered back at the village. He hadn't heard any voice or movement, nor could he see anyone now. Everything indicated that they had gotten away clean.

A smile came, but it disappeared quickly. Still looking at the village, the last image he had of Rox flashed in his mind's eye. His chest tightened and he suddenly felt cold.

I'm sorry, my love. I never meant to hurt you.

"Jarka," Vaseus hissed through the darkness. "Let's go."

He closed his eyes and swallowed.

Goodbye.

With that silent farewell resounding in his mind, he forced effort into his legs, stood, and set off.

TWENTY-ONE

One of the many strengths of Sparta was its attitude toward women. Unlike the rest of their Greek counterparts, Spartan girls were trained to be physically fit. This was traditionally done so that women would bear strong sons. And since Sparta has always desired and lauded strong men, their women were valued and respected.

Eurydemos of Corinth

Kaletor clawed his fingers deep into the wet sand, dragging his numb body towards the shore. The white-crested waves helped to push him up onto the beach, as if the sea wanted no more to do with him. It took all his remaining strength to keep his face clear of the shallow water.

When at last his chest dragged along the sand, he rose to his hands and knees. His arms shook as he crawled up the gentle slope.

Finally clear of the sea, he collapsed.

Solid land. I never knew it could feel so good.

At last, somehow, his struggle to survive was over. It seemed impossible. He had thought it would never end.

Without attempting to, he knew he couldn't get up, nor did he want to. He just wanted to breathe and be still.

He remained on his front, sprawled flat, with one cheek resting on the sand.

I'm alive. I'm still alive.

As he lay there, totally motionless, exhaustion overwhelmed him, and time lost all meaning.

At some point, he must have drifted off. When he woke, the dim light of dawn was gone, replaced by the bright sunshine of early morning.

Though his limbs were still stiff, some feeling had returned to his hands and feet. His arms shook from the effort, but he managed to push himself up to a sitting position.

The beach he had ended up on was littered with grey stones and dark driftwood. Beyond the beach, the ground flattened out into a barren stretch of straw-like grass, with a few small clusters of trees here and there. There was no sign of civilization save for one very distant structure, which appeared to be a small farmhouse.

Despite the lack of landmarks, Kaletor knew he could only be in one place—the island of Rhodes.

This thought moved him away from the need to recover. First to the fore was the fleet and the army it carried. He twisted around to eye the sea, but there was nothing visible on the endless stretch of dark blue. Just as the storm that had raged for hours was gone, so too was everything else.

Were they all at the bottom of the sea? Had he led over fifteen thousand men to their deaths?

He brushed the sand from his face as he turned away. *Impossible. They can't all be dead. Scattered, yes, but not dead. And those that are dead have only themselves to blame. I made it out alive, just as any man of worth should. The Empire doesn't need anyone that can't survive a little storm.*

Dismissing the unknown fate of his army, he considered his own situation. He was in enemy territory. If he was found and identified, imprisonment and death would surely follow. The fleet's approach would likely have been picked up by now, meaning the rebels could already be scouring the shoreline for survivors. Alone, unarmed, and exhausted, he realized he had only one option.

Hide.

He scanned everything in his vicinity once more. The sporadic bunches of trees might work, but they would offer shelter and nothing more. His gaze soon found the distant farmhouse. Looking more closely, he saw that it was a squat, stone building less than a mile inland.

As if on cue, his stomach groaned its longing to be filled. Kaletor nodded to himself in agreement.

Yes. Food, water, and supplies. I need them all, and with any luck, I'll find them there.

Ignoring the potential risks of his decision, he rocked onto all fours and pushed himself up. His legs were like water, and he crumpled back down to the sand.

Snarling his frustration, he brought his feet back under him and surged upright. The muscles in his legs burned in protest. He growled through grit teeth and forced his body to hold. Though his knees almost buckled, he managed to stay standing.

For some time, it was all he could do to remain upright. Each ragged breath rattled through his chest and ribcage.

When the intense burn in his legs finally eased, he started to walk. He progressed slowly, holding out his arms to keep from stumbling. Every step loosened things up, and some vitality flowed through his body. Before too long, he was able to pick up the pace.

As he walked, the feel of his wet clothes clinging to his skin suddenly sent his mind back to the horror from which he had just emerged. He remembered how the waves crashed down on his head, forcing him under again and again. Water choked him, making him cough and gasp, barely able to draw breath. He remembered how the shocking cold stole into his bones and sapped his strength.

At first, he had considered swimming to the nearest ship. But the sky was dark. No one would see him. Besides, the waves were so powerful that all his efforts went to keeping his head above water. All he could manage was to keep from drowning as the storm raged overhead and the sea heaved all around him.

He lost all sense of time as a continuous cycle of breathless hell ensued. Pulled or pushed under, hold his breath, break the surface, gasp and sputter and choke, arms and legs always churning. Back under, lungs on fire as they demanded air—

"Enough," he hissed through clenched teeth. "No more. It's done."

The enormous power of the memories lost some of their hold on him, but not all. Like infuriating flies buzzing around the head, they remained, impossible to eliminate completely.

It wasn't until he approached the farmhouse that they faded into the background. He squinted his eyes to peer through the two square windows on either side of the front door. He saw nothing, no movement or passing shadow. Was it empty? Abandoned? Were the inhabitants away, or hidden somewhere within?

It didn't matter, as there was only one thing to do. Hearing nothing and seeing no one, he did not slow or hesitate. He went straight to the door, turned the black handle, opened it, and stepped inside.

He was in a narrow entranceway, the blue walls marching straight ahead to form a long, tight hallway. At the end rose a staircase that took a sharp left five stairs up. Along the way were three doorways. One was a few strides in and on the left. The other two were further along and on the right.

He took this all in as he eased the door shut behind him. He listened intently, staying still with his back to the door. There was nothing, no sound and no movement. He sniffed the air, picking up a faint smell of old smoke and cool ash.

His conclusion came quickly. *Someone lives here.*

Stepping lightly, he moved to the first doorway, which opened to a small kitchen. A stone counter lined the left-hand wall with cupboards above. The back wall had a larder half in the stone floor. A wooden table with four, rough-hewn chairs occupied the right side of the room. Three plates sat atop the table, each covered with crumbs and indiscernible smears.

The sight of the larder made Kaletor's gut clench and groan. He shifted his weight onto his heels to peek down the hall. Still nothing but silence.

Satisfied, he strode to the back wall. Once there, he reached down, pulled the doors of the larder open, and peered inside.

Food of all kinds lined three shelves: carrots, potatoes, bread, apples, olives, cheese, even salted meats. At least thirty pots were lined up in neat rows, as well as two jugs of water.

There was more, but Kaletor dismissed the rest. He snatched up one of the jugs, pulled out the stopper, and tipped it up to drink.

With his thirst quenched, he set the jug on the floor and began filling his arms with food.

Soon he was at the table, biting into a block of cheese, chewing quickly. He gulped down water. He bit into an apple. He drank again. He attacked it all with ravenous haste.

Before long, the empty void in his gut was filled, and he felt some strength starting to flow through his body. He leaned back, massaging the overworked muscles in his jaw. His eyes wandered to the counter, which was bare except for a wooden cutting board and the small knife laying atop it. The bread was tough, so he rose to retrieve it.

"What are you doing?"

He froze, his breath catching as he looked to the doorway. Standing there was a small boy, dressed only in a long, white nightgown, rubbing a fist into an eye. His question asked, he seemed content to wait for an answer.

Kaletor straightened and released an amused sigh. "I haven't been startled like that in a very long time. Not since I was a young boy like you."

As he finished, he went to the counter.

The boy watched him, appearing unconcerned. "Who are you?" he asked casually.

"Kaletor. What's your name?"

"Antoninus—"

"Who are you talking to?" someone called from the hallway.

Kaletor didn't hesitate. He snatched up the knife, rushed over to the distracted child, and punched a fist into the side of his head. The boy went limp and collapsed to the floor.

An alarmed shout filled the house. Kaletor stooped low, grabbed the back of the boy's neck, and dragged him up. In one fluid motion, he continued into the hall, dropped to one knee, and draped the boy over it.

Setting the knife to the exposed throat, he looked up and barked, "Stop or the boy dies!"

Halfway down the hall was a woman, her eyes wide and her mouth stuck open. She fell to her knees, tears flooding out as she spread her arms wide and lowered her head.

"Okay okay okay," she babbled, the words spilling out impossibly fast. "I'll do whatever you want. Just please, *please* don't hurt my son."

"Is there anyone else here?"

"My husband."

"Where is he?"

"Upstairs."

"Get him down here."

The woman nodded and shrieked, "Mammot! Come down here now!"

"Why?" came the man's response. "What's going on?"

"Just get down here, you stupid bastard!"

The thud of heavy footsteps sounded overhead as the husband moved across the floor.

Kaletor maintained his position, eyes fixed on the mother. Her upper body began to shake, causing her uncombed nest of brown hair to quiver like reeds in the wind. Tears continued streaming down her cheeks as she stared wide-eyed at her unconscious son.

Soon there were heavy footfalls on the stairs. He looked beyond the woman to watch a shirtless man emerge, his arms, legs, and chest heavily muscled and covered in dark hair.

The moment their eyes met, the man shouted, "What's this? Take your hands off my son—"

"I have a knife at his throat," Kaletor growled. "If I flick my wrist, he dies."

The burly man's dark eyebrows drove down as he said, "If you harm him, I'll make you wish you had never been born—"

"Silence," Kaletor snapped. "Do as I command, or he dies. Understood?"

The man continued to glower as he gave a single nod.

"Good. Now, we're all going to move into the kitchen. The boy and I will go in first. You two will follow, slowly and calmly. Got it?"

"Yes," the mother said quickly, rising to her feet. "Yes, okay. Let's do that."

Kaletor looked past her. "And you?"

The man's jaw was clenched tight, but he nodded once more.

Kaletor wrapped his arm around Antoninus's torso, braced his legs, and stood. He turned, moved quickly into the kitchen, and lay the boy on the table. He then sat on the chair facing the doorway, placing his free hand on

Antoninus's chest while guiding the knife to his throat.

A moment later, the couple came in, the husband holding his wife's shoulders. She was still shaking, and her gaze immediately went to her son.

"Now," Kaletor said, "here's how this is going to go. Woman, you will go fetch a rope to tie up your husband. Then—"

He cut himself short. A faint but unmistakable sound had reached through the stone walls, a sound that sent a chill slithering down his spine.

"Riders are coming," he snarled, rising from the chair. He was about to stride over to the lone window, but then caught himself. Already, in that split second of distraction, the burly man had moved to within three paces.

"Hey!" he barked, laying the knife back across the boy's throat and glaring at the husband. "Get back! Back!"

The man released a pent-up exhale as he held his hands up and backed away. "It's fine—"

"Don't be *stupid*, Mammot," the wife shrieked, coming forward to pull him back. "Just do what he wants."

"Try that again and I'll kill him," Kaletor snarled, sitting back down while glaring at the man, who allowed himself to be dragged back to the doorway.

The sound of thundering hooves was already much louder. Kaletor's mind raced to come up with a plan.

"Go to the window, woman," he said, barely keeping his voice steady, "and tell me who is coming."

Nodding profusely, she did as instructed.

Kaletor kept his eyes on Mammot as he snarled, "What do you see?"

"R-riders," she sputtered. "I see riders."

"How many?"

"I don't—I—I'm not sure. Ten. Maybe fifteen—"

"Are they coming towards the house?"

"I don't, uh, I don't know—"

"*Yes or no!*"

"Y-yes, yes. I think so."

Kaletor swore loudly. "Get out there and get rid of them," he barked at the husband. "If anyone comes into this house, your wife and son will both die. Go!"

Mammot bared his teeth in a silent snarl before turning away and exiting through the front door. Freed to do so, Kaletor looked past the woman's shoulder and out the window. But from his angle, he could only see the blue sky.

Feeling helpless and at the mercy of someone else was almost too much to bear. He snarled another curse as the thundering horse hooves grew ever louder.

Then, abruptly, they stopped.

Though he was desperate to see, he stayed seated. "What's happening?" he growled at the woman.

Her voice trembled as she spoke. "They're lined up in front of the house. One of them just dismounted and is saying something to Mammot—"

"How many are there?"

He watched her count, her lips moving as she did. "Eleven."

Too many to fight off.

He shook his head and grit his teeth to silence a roar. *If only I were armed and at full strength. I'd go out there and cut them all down. Instead, I have to hide in here like a pathetic weakling.*

The fire that coursed through him brought him to his feet as he resolved to charge out the front door and fight.

But before he took a step, reason returned to stop him. There was no sense in dying just for the sake of his pride. It would accomplish nothing. No, such a pointless, inglorious death would not do.

And so, despite the need to fight that was burning through him, he sat back down and waited.

While he struggled to restrain his will to act, he noticed the woman's face start to tremble.

"What's happening now?" he rasped.

Still staring out the window, she opened her mouth, but nothing came out.

"Answer me!"

"The—the man. He—I—I think he's coming in—"

"No," he growled, surging to his feet to rush towards her. "I'll not go down without a fight—"

"Wait," she hissed just as he reached out to grab her. "Wait. Mammot stopped him. He's turning around—"

"Silence," Kaletor spat, stepping close to wrap an arm around her shoulders and touch the knife to the side of her neck. She released a gasp and shrank in his grip, but otherwise didn't move.

While standing directly behind her, he could see over her head and observe what was going on outside. Mammot and a tall man in an old, mud-stained cloak were walking away from the house, mouths moving as they spoke. Facing them was a line of men sitting on horses, each one wearing different types of helmets and leather straps of armour. They appeared a young and impatient bunch, keen to leave this lonely place behind.

When Kaletor looked back to their leader, the man was shaking Mammot's hand. He then turned away, returned to his horse, mounted up, and rode off with his men.

Without realizing it, Kaletor had been holding his breath. Now he let it out and shoved the woman towards the doorway. She staggered and fell to her hands and knees.

"Be silent," he growled over her sobs as he returned to the table and set the cutting knife to the base of the boy's throat. "And go get that rope."

She was wiping at her face and struggling to stand when the front door opened and closed. A moment later, Mammot appeared.

"What did you do to her?" he demanded, rushing to help her up. "I did what you wanted. I got rid of them—"

"Leave her," Kaletor snapped, "and come sit down."

Mammot's eyes flashed. "Why?"

"My patience is running out," Kaletor replied, raising the knife to point the tip over Antoninus's heart. "So do as I say. Do it *now*."

His face blanching, Mammot moved quickly and sat in the chair at the other end of the table. While the woman scurried through the house, they glared at each other in charged silence.

Before long, she returned with a rope in hand.

"Tie his hands behind the back of the chair, then tie his feet together," Kaletor instructed. "And make your knots tight."

She set to work, tears again rolling from her eyes. Her fingers fumbled more than once as she bound her husband to the chair.

Through the sobbing and trembling, eventually, the task was done.

Kaletor glanced down at the boy to confirm that he was still out cold.

Satisfied, he said, "Step away."

Once the woman had retreated to the doorway, he stood and moved to inspect the knots. Each one was tight and secure.

"Why are you doing this?" Mammot said, his chin jutting and jaw clenched. "What do you want?"

Twirling the knife in his hand, Kaletor ignored him and looked at the woman. "Fetch me some clothes and something to carry supplies in."

She nodded and hurried down the hall to ascend the stairs.

"I asked you a questi—"

Kaletor punched a fist into Mammot's temple. His head bounced off his far shoulder and stayed there.

"Your questions are insignificant," Kaletor said, flexing his hand as he moved to stand directly in front of his hostage. "But mine are not. Now, where is your city?"

Like a listing ship, Mammot slowly brought his head upright. He blinked away the tears in his eyes and said, "If I help you, you must promise that you will not harm my family."

"Done."

"I want your word."

"I give you my word."

Mammot looked at him intently for a long moment.

Eventually, he slumped down and released a ragged sigh. "Eight miles northwest of here."

"I need to board a ship so I can get off this island. How would I do that?"

The burly man thought for a moment before answering. "Pose as a sailor, go to the Mandrakion Harbour, and declare that you're looking for work. It shouldn't take long to find a captain who needs more hands."

"What about security?" Kaletor asked, crossing his arms as he leaned against the table. "Isn't the city prepared to fight the Phalanxes? Won't it be full of hoplites?"

"Hoplites?" Mammot said, looking and sounding puzzled. "We don't have an army here. Rhodes may have declared for the rebels, but we have no military might."

"But then how did you overthrow the garrison?"

"The mob. Thousands of angry citizens with clubs and table legs. A few have declared themselves leaders, a few more think they're soldiers, but the city is unorganized. The mob isn't interested in becoming an army."

Hearing footsteps in the hall, Kaletor moved to sit with the boy again.

When the woman reappeared, he said, "Put the clothes on the table and fill the pack with food and water."

Still looking like a startled hare, she dumped the shirt and trousers on the table and hurried to the back of the room. Kaletor set the knife down beside the boy's head, and while keeping an eye on the woman, stripped off his damp undergarments and donned the dark brown, loose-fitting clothes. Then he sat back down and waited.

When the woman finished filling the pack, he said, "Leave it here," pointing to the floor at his feet, "and go stand in the doorway."

Again, she cooperated without a word. Kaletor knelt to peer into the worn canvas pack. Seeing it stuffed full of bread, carrots, apples, and water, he nodded to himself.

"You have what you need. Now take it and leave us alone."

Kaletor looked up to meet Mammot's glare. "You are in no position to be making demands."

"But we've done everything you wanted. You gave me your word."

Kaletor nodded, a slight smile coming to his lips. "You're right. I gave you my word."

As he finished, he stood, snatched the knife from the table, and focused on the woman.

"No!" Mammot bellowed as he strained at his bindings. "Run, Veera. Run!"

"Stay where you are or your son dies!"

The woman fell to her knees, arms reaching out, tears spilling from her eyes. "Please, sir. Have mercy. You don't need to hurt us. W-we're no threat to you."

"Oh, but you are," Kaletor said, stepping towards her. "You know where I'm going. You could tell someone what happened here. I can't have that."

Sobs racked through Veera's chest as she cried harder. "N-no. Not my boy. Kill me if you must. Just don't hurt my boy!"

Kaletor didn't reply. He continued closing in, twirling the knife in his hand.

"I'll make you pay for this, Spartan!" Mammot shouted. "In this life or the next. I'll make you suffer more than you could ever imagine!"

Again, Kaletor said nothing.

But with the harsh fury of Mammot's shouts and Veera's desperate wails filling the room, a voice whispered in his mind.

"*You don't want to do this.*"

It was unmistakably Vaseus's voice.

He released a harsh exhale through his nose. *Yes I do.*

Now he moved quickly, grabbed Veera by the hair, and dragged her to her feet. She screamed and flailed her arms. With merciless strength, he yanked again, this time to expose her throat.

Gripping the knife tight, he brought it high and drove it down—

"*Stop!*"

The tip of the blade was an inch from reaching its mark. He snarled through grit teeth, hating his hesitation.

As Veera wailed and Mammot bellowed, he clenched his teeth harder, throttling the handle of the knife in a death grip.

"*Don't, Kaletor. She's an innocent Greek. Please. Don't do this. You don't have to do this.*"

Kaletor closed his eyes and shook his head. *You're not here, Vaseus. You abandoned me a long time ago. You don't know me anymore. You don't know what I've become.*

He opened his eyes and raised the knife high once again. Releasing a ragged bellow, he drove the blade straight down.

TWENTY-TWO

The War Season is about keeping your spear
strong. The Warrior Code applies here as well.
That means there are no ambushes. There's
no unnecessary killing. Only armed warriors
can be attacked. Honour remains above all
else, even when facing a bitter rival.

The Spoken Tales

Head tilted back, Jarka peered up through the forest canopy to gaze at
the silver stars in the night sky. All was calm and quiet, save for the
crackling fire behind him. The air was still and cool.

Six days had come and gone since they left the Clanless village behind, and
they were drawing close to the Home Village of the Dark Stone Clan. Being so
close to their first encounter with Clan yagars had brought all his doubts and
misgivings around his insane plan back to the surface.

It seemed, now more than ever, overwhelmingly impossible. And if it didn't
work, if his Challenge was not accepted, Jazith was lost forever. This stark truth
hounded him, and it was almost more than he could bear.

He looked down at the ground and closed his eyes. *I miss you, sister. And Rox
too. I thought she would understand. But how could she? I didn't tell her what happened to
my parents, what happened to me and Jazith. Maybe I should have. Maybe if I had, she'd
be here.*

He shook his head and rubbed a hand through the fur of his neck. "Okay,"
he said aloud, "enough alone time."

He opened his eyes, spun on his heels, and returned to camp. Surprisingly,

Vaseus was sitting across the fire from Relyk in obvious conversation. Her two remaining companions were nowhere in sight, likely because they had gone to sleep in one of the tents.

"What did I miss?" he asked, stepping around a tangled bush to sit back down on the rotting log.

The pair glanced at him, and Vaseus said, "Nothing, really. We were just talking about you."

He flashed a grin. "How wonderful."

"Is it true that you don't practice very much?"

His grin faltered and he looked at Relyk. "And I thought we were friends."

Relyk shrugged, the yellow of his fur shimmering a deep gold in the firelight. "She was asking about your chances tomorrow if your Challenge is accepted. You know I have no talent for deception."

"So it's true," Vaseus said. "You hardly practice at all."

"That depends on how you look at it. When I was young, I hated practising, so I avoided it whenever I could. To this day I don't enjoy it, so it's not like I spar for hours on end. Still, combat is part of our way of life, so most days, I force myself to do something."

Vaseus crossed her arms over her green, form-fitting tunic. "I guess that's better than nothing. But this time you'll be facing a Warlord. Won't he or she be a difficult opponent?"

"I suppose," he said with a shrug.

"Have you ever fought a Warlord?"

"I know a few former Superiors back home. I've sparred with them many times."

"But have you ever faced an actual Warlord?"

"No."

Her arms and shoulders sagged in response. "Have you ever even seen a Warlord fight?"

Without warning, the question pulled forth a buried memory in his mind. In that instant, he remembered his father's death. He felt a remnant of that unbelievable anguish that had never fully healed.

Then it was gone, as quick as it came.

Noticing the sympathetic look from Relyk, he rolled his shoulders and stared into the dancing flames. "Yes, I've seen a Warlord fight," he answered. "Long ago."

Vaseus must have picked up on the change in mood, for she now spoke in a softer tone. "I still don't understand. Aren't you forbidden from entering yagar society?"

"I am. But I was not always Clanless."

"You weren't? What happened?"

The sight and sound of his mother screaming before being stabbed in the back flashed next.

He set his hands to his thighs and looked down at the ground. "Stop," he breathed. "I don't want to talk about it."

"Why not? What's wrong—"

"I said I don't want to *talk about it.*"

His growled words seemed to still the very air itself. His breathing was harsh as he glared at Vaseus. She met his eye and gave a subtle nod.

He let his gaze fall back to the fire as a long silence stretched. He didn't like his sudden loss of control. It wasn't like him.

I'm just stressed, he reasoned to himself. *Rox, Jazith, humans, this impossible task. It's too much. What have I gotten myself into?*

It took some time, but eventually, he managed to return his breathing to normal.

His thoughts turned to Jazith. *She saved me that day. If she hadn't stopped me, if she hadn't dragged me away, they would have killed me. Now it's my turn to save her. I'm her only hope. She needs me, and I cannot fail.*

Fresh determination warmed him, and he felt his mood lighten.

"No matter who I fight," he said, breaking the heavy silence, "I will win."

"As long as they let you fight," Relyk said, his arms dangling over his knees. "I still don't know how you plan to convince their Warlord to accept your challenge."

I don't know either.

Jarka allowed this answer to come and go in his mind. "You'll see soon enough."

"So you do have a plan?" Vaseus chimed in.

He looked to her. "Of course. Nothing to worry about."

A slight tug at the corner of her mouth gave away her amusement. "You better."

That's some wishful thinking, bee. Some very wishful thinking. He gave a low chuckle and kept the answering thought to himself.

"May I join you?"

Jarka's stomach flipped and he nearly jumped out of his fur. In that same reaction, his eyes went to the source of the voice.

There, standing to Relyk's left and just visible at the edge of the firelight, was a yagar he recognized.

"Imzen? Is that you?"

"Hello, young ones," the Elder said softly, moving slowly into the light. "May I join you?"

"What are you doing here—"

"Who is this?" Vaseus cut in. "What do you want?"

"Easy, honeybee," Jarka said. "She's a friend from our village."

"I've come to help," Imzen said, lowering herself to her knees and folding her hands in her lap.

"What makes you think we need your help?"

"There's no need for that, Vaseus," Relyk said.

"No need for what?"

"I apologize," Imzen said, "for startling you. Perhaps it would be best if I step away for a moment to give you a chance to calm down."

"That won't be necessary," Jarka answered before Vaseus could. "You'll have to excuse her. Apparently humans are quite suspicious."

Vaseus shot him a look that burned hot as coals. "Can you blame me? She came out of nowhere! How can you be so nonchalant about an unannounced intruder?"

"She's one of us," Relyk answered, his tone a little harsher than usual. "We've known her for years, and she's an Elder. We trust our Elders."

"But where did she come from? And how did she find us? And what's she doing here?"

"I saw the three of you leave the village that night," Imzen said, her bright orange eyes moving steadily to Jarka, Relyk, Vaseus, and back through again. "By dawn I was prepared, and I set out. I found and followed your trail. I thought I'd soon catch up, but you have been moving very fast. I'm not as young or spry as I once was."

"But why?" Jarka asked. "Why did you follow us?"

Her gaze shifted to settle on him. "I go where I am needed. Right now, I am needed here. I do not ask why. That is unimportant."

"What makes you think you're needed here?" Vaseus asked, her voice less erratic but still sharp. "You don't even know where we're going or what we're doing."

"Show some respect," Relyk growled. "Imzen is an Elder—"

"It's alright, Relyk," Imzen interrupted smoothly. "She is human and thus unfamiliar with our ways.

"A shift is coming to my people," she went on, looking to Vaseus. "A shift that must occur if we are to survive. I have known this for many years. When I saw two yagars slipping away from the village in the company of a human, I knew the time had come. I knew that you are the ones who can bring about this shift. For that reason, I have come to help."

As she finished, she looked back to Jarka and held his gaze. He couldn't tell for sure in the dancing firelight, but he thought he detected a subtle smile lifting her whiskers and creasing her wizened face.

After a moment, she broke eye contact and looked steadily into the fire.

To his surprise, the need to dissuade the strange Elder from joining them did not come. It felt natural and right that she accompany them. It didn't make sense, but he didn't resist.

And so, flashing Vaseus a smile despite her disapproving glare, he said, "Why not? We could use the help. Welcome to the team, Old One."

*   *   *

Dawn broke cool and gray, the solid blanket of clouds threatening rain. Upon waking, Jarka saw that Imzen was gone. He roused Relyk and they ate the cold remnants of the two rabbits they had caught the night prior, speaking little under the damp coat of the sleepy morning.

Vaseus and her pair of friends emerged from their tent. "Where's Imzen?" she asked, running her hands over her head to smooth down her golden hair.

"We don't know," Jarka answered, tossing away the bone he had just finished picking clean.

"Well seeing as she's apparently part of our little group, shouldn't she be here?"

"Imzen has always kept to herself," Relyk answered. "She often leaves our village for days at a time. But she always returns, sooner or later."

"In other words, she will come and go as she pleases," Jarka added. "You'll soon learn to accept this and trust her as we do. Now, we need to get moving."

Vaseus met his eye, steady and discerning. After a moment, she simply said, "Agreed."

Her casual compliance was unexpected. He smiled to himself as she turned and disappeared into the tent.

I can't get a read on you, honeybee. I wonder if all humans are so difficult to get a feel for. You're intriguing if nothing else.

While this curiosity mulled through his mind, Vaseus and her silent companions packed up their tent. When that was done, everyone shouldered their packs and they set off, continuing north through the damp forest.

It was about two hours later when Relyk said, "We're close."

Jarka, who was in the lead, stopped and looked back over a shoulder. "How do you know?"

Relyk pointed ahead. "I remember that fallen tree. It was felled by the Clan to serve as a marker for those returning to the village."

"Right. How many villages did you say you've visited?"

"I'm not sure exactly. Twenty or more Small Villages, and eight Home Villages."

Jarka nodded. "Good."

Looking beyond Relyk to Vaseus and her two male friends, he said, "Time to lose some humans."

Relyk snorted a laugh. "Have fun."

Following a lengthy explanation and much convincing, Jarka, Relyk, and Vaseus were once again moving toward the village. But she wasn't going quietly.

"What if they're spotted?" she demanded, referring to her companions who were now making camp somewhere behind them. "Won't your people kill them on the spot?"

Jarka ducked under a low-hanging branch and answered without slowing. "Probably."

"I won't allow it. We have to go back—"

"I warned you of this. Our lands are dangerous for humans. It's one of the risks you agreed to take."

"Yes, but I thought we'd be facing any threats together."

He shook his head as he swept aside some branches to continue in Relyk's wake. "Like I said, it's bad enough that we're showing up with one human. Three would make things far worse."

"But now if they're seen, they'll be mistaken for unwelcome intruders that weren't guided here by yagars."

"They'd be seen as unwelcome intruders regardless, whether in our company or not. Outsiders are met with almost as much hostility as humans."

"So then there was no reason to leave my friends behind!"

Jarka pulled up to glance back at her. "Are all humans as stubborn as you?"

She scowled and released an exasperated sound. "Oh, that's cute. Are all yagars as flippant as you?"

He scratched two fingers through the soft fur at his throat as he shook his head. "No. But neither are they so charming, confident, or savvy."

"I think you mean unbelievably frustrating," she growled before pushing past him.

He felt the tips of his fangs poke free as he smiled after her. "Yes, that too."

Feeling it to be a wise move, he allowed a small gap to stretch between them before he followed.

As the morning wore on and they continued north, the forest became more and more congested, forcing them to pick their way around tangled brush, thick clusters of tree trunks, and hanging branches. The canopy above was thick, and the air was damp. Tiny droplets of water clung heavy to everything. Budding leaves all around them hung low, pulled down by the droplets.

At some point, the ground began to climb. Not long after, Jarka saw Vaseus and Relyk standing in a small clearing at the foot of a steep-sided hill.

As he joined them in the clearing, he saw a dark, gaping hole at the base of the hill.

"I've always wanted to come here," he said as he arrived.

Vaseus turned to fix him with her green eyes, her brows driving down. "Huh? You've always wanted to come to a hole in the ground?"

"This is the home of the entire Dark Stone Clan," Relyk supplied.

She cast about as if looking for something. "Where? I don't see anyone."

"They live underground."

Jarka heard something and looked left in time to watch Imzen appear from within a nearby cluster of tangled brush.

"Where have you been?" Vaseus demanded.

"Waiting for you to arrive," Imzen said smoothly, hands clasped behind her back as she joined them. "This Clan has lived underground for a very long time. They feel removed from the rest of the world. They will likely be less welcoming than most others."

"Not a problem," Jarka said, moving towards the mouth of the cave. "I know exactly how to handle this."

"Wait," Vaseus called after him. "Shouldn't we all know how we're handling this before we go in?"

He glanced back over a shoulder and waved her concern away. "No need, it'll be simple. Just follow my lead."

Without waiting for her response, he walked into the darkness of the cave. Rock walls pressed in on all sides, and the ground sloped into a steep decline.

"Jarka!" Vaseus snapped at his back.

Again, he glanced over a shoulder. "What now?"

"I can't see in here."

"Oh yes, I forgot about your human shortcomings. Better take my hand then, Unseeing One."

"Can't we light a torch?"

"We don't have time. I'll guide you."

"But I don't want to be so dependent."

"Okay, you can walk blind. But we won't wait—"

"Fine! Where are you?"

She was directly behind him with arms outstretched and eyes staring at nothing.

He reached back to take her hand in his. "Here."

She gasped at his touch. "I had no idea you were that close. You better make sure I don't run into anything."

He leaned close. "Oh, I'll make sure, bee."

He continued on, leading her down the narrow corridor, Imzen and Relyk close behind.

It was the first time he had ever touched a human. His heart beat faster, and he became acutely aware of how pleasantly soft and smooth her hand was.

They descended for a long time, the path twisting and winding continuously, the air gradually cooling as they progressed.

Jarka sniffed deep. He smelled the subtle scents of rock, spider webs, and dust. The only sounds were Vaseus's sandals scuffing across the bare rock.

Finally, the ground levelled off, and shortly after, the air began to warm. They rounded a few more bends before a faint glow bloomed on the rock walls.

"I can see light ahead," Vaseus exclaimed.

"Quietly," Relyk whispered at their backs. "We don't want to . . ."

He didn't finish. At that moment, they emerged from the unending narrowness of the tunnels onto a platform at the edge of an enormous, open chamber. A long, shallow ramp led down to a village of rock that sprawled across the floor of the vast open space. Hundreds of squat, square structures were illuminated by the light of torches and fire pits that were burning in their holds on every street. The ceiling of the cave was so high above that the light did not reach there. It was as if the village sat squarely within the heart of a towering mountain.

"That's," Vaseus slowly said, "incredible."

Jarka felt her squeeze his hand a little tighter. He smiled to himself, and keeping his gaze on the sprawling village awash in firelight, said, "You've got that right, bee."

"We shouldn't linger," Imzen said, moving past them to start descending the ramp.

Relyk followed. "She's right. Let's keep moving."

But Jarka stayed put, marvelling at the sheer enormity of it. "I've never seen anything like this. It must be miles across."

When he finished, Vaseus slid her hand from his. "Come on. We better keep up."

The smile that had remained on his lips slackened as he brought his eyes down to meet hers. "Right. Let's go."

The four of them proceeded close together and in silence. As they descended and neared the edge of the village, he kept his eyes wide, watching for any sign of movement. But there was none.

"Where is everyone?" Vaseus asked in a hushed voice.

"At the Challenge Ring," Imzen answered.

"How do you know?" Relyk asked.

At first, the Elder didn't respond. Then, in the barest of whispers, she said, "Listen."

They stepped off the bottom of the ramp. Peering down the long, straight street that stretched ahead, Jarka rotated his ears forward. It was distant and faint, but he heard the crack of spear against spear echoing off the dark rock.

"She's right," he said quietly. "I hear combat. Perfect. This could work to our advantage."

"How so?" Vaseus asked.

He surged ahead. "You'll see."

Thankful that no one questioned him further, he led the way into the village.

Far away, a tall structure rose high above the rest, most likely the Warlord's Hall. The buildings closer at hand were all one story of black or grey, the blazing firelight dancing shadows across the smooth surfaces of rock and stone. Most were obviously homes. Some were without a roof. Each one was quiet and barren. It was as if the whole village had been deserted.

The street they came in on ran straight through the heart of the village, and they followed it all the way to the Challenge Ring. A massive formation of rock rose up behind an open forum, a dark mass towering above the street like a small mountain. Into this was carved a rising semicircle of benches, upon which sat several hundred black-furred yagars. At the bottom of the rising semicircle, a pair clashed in a dance of spears, appearing like shadows in the light of the torches aligning both sides of the forum.

Upon seeing such a familiar sight, Jarka felt his shoulders relax and his breath flow more easily. *They're just like us. Strength is what matters, more than tradition or ritual or anything else.*

As they approached, the fight ended in a spectacular flurry of blows. The one with red bands around his forearms had emerged as the victor, and the crowd erupted into raucous applause.

Jarka slowed his steps, considering how best to announce their presence.

But before he had an answer, Vaseus sneezed. The sound seemed to echo everywhere.

"Oh no," Relyk groaned under his breath.

The noise from the crowd died down, then morphed into a hushed wave of murmuring. With many of the black-furred yagars pointing down at them, twenty or more from the bottom row moved into the ring.

"Halt!" one of them bellowed. "What is this? An attack? It's not yet the War Season."

"Peace, my friend," Jarka answered, holding out his hands. "We are lone travellers. We bring no threat to your village. My name—"

"Is that a human?" someone in the crowd cried out.

"It is," another boomed. "Kill it!"

Many more spectators on the lower benches sprang into action, rushing forward—

"Hold," the one who had spoken first, the sleek male in the middle, bellowed in a commanding voice. In perfect synchronicity, the forward movement ceased, though the group glared across at them with ferocity in their eyes.

Jarka, who had stepped in front of Vaseus, said, "I thank you for—"

"What do you want, stranger?" the male cut in. "And who are you? Why have you led a human into our lands? Answer true and be quick!"

"Yes, alright," Jarka said, taking a few steps forward to shrink the gap between them. "It's a long story, but I'll give you the short version. My sister was taken by humans, and the only way to save her from imprisonment and death is to destroy the Spartan Empire into which she was taken." He pointed to Vaseus. "This human is leading a rebellion to overthrow the Spartans, a rebellion that will only succeed with the support of our warriors—"

The male burst into laughter, and many more joined him.

When it died down, he said, "Have you completely lost your mind? Or is this some elaborate new scheme to defeat us?"

"It is no scheme," Jarka replied, feeling heat flood his face.

"Then what? Have you come to ask us to join your absurd quest? Did you really think we would pledge our spears to such an insane cause? I wouldn't agree to it if one of my own proposed such a thing, let alone an outsider and his human."

Jarka shook his head. "No, my friend. I did not come to ask for your help. I came to claim it." Raising his voice, he called out to everyone, "Warlord, I challenge you."

The few remaining hushed conversations died out, and there was only silence.

The condescending smile on the male's lips was replaced by a scowl, and his pale blue eyes appeared to glow hot within his black face.

"You *have* lost your mind," he said as he crossed his arms over his chest. "As you must know, the Warrior Code dictates that only the Second Superior of this Clan may challenge me. Who are you to break one of the laws that govern our way of life?"

"So you are Warlord, yes?" Jarka replied, moving forward again so that only a few paces separated them. "You're the best warrior of the Dark Stone Clan. Do you accept my challenge or not?"

An oppressive silence seemed to hang heavy while the crowd waited for the answer.

After a long moment, the Warlord spoke. "I must at least know who you are and where you come from before I give my answer."

Just like that, Jarka's hope of fighting as an unidentified outsider was gone. And so, with a straight back, he said, "My name is Jarka, and I am Clanless."

"Clanless?" the Warlord echoed, his expression changing into outright shock. "Then you are forbidden to challenge anyone, let alone a Warlord. You are forbidden to even be here. You dishonour the Warrior Code. I will not cross spears with a disgraced Clanless."

He turned to the warriors standing at his back and said, "Arrest them."

The warriors closed in, their spears levelled. Inexplicably, something ran through Jarka's mind then, a feeling or a memory. He couldn't place it, but something felt familiar.

As the warriors arrived, he had it.

That day in the forest. The Warlord had black fur . . .

"Corthak was my father!" he cried out. "And you knew him, didn't you, Alarix?"

Obvious shock alighted in the Warlord's eyes. At first, he just stared.

"Wait," he finally said, the command halting his warriors. He narrowed his eyes. "What was your name before you were Clanless?"

"Jarka of the Western Woodlands Clan."

Alarix paused for some time. Then, looking to his waiting warriors, he said, "Watch the others. I will speak to this one alone."

With his instructions given, the Warlord walked into the street. Jarka felt some of the tension in his body melt away as he followed.

When they were about forty paces away from everyone else, Alarix stopped. "Your Clan has never been the same since that ill-fated day," he said, his tone low. "They've been less honourable in war, and more bloodthirsty. If your father had lived, things would have gone differently.

"Even after all these years, I've only ever heard rumours," he went on, taking a step closer. "But they didn't make sense. Warthux could never have defeated your father."

Jarka swallowed. "He didn't. My father won their Challenge easily. It was when he turned away that Warthux speared him in the back."

"I guessed as much. Perhaps it would please you to know that that dishonourable coward died several years ago."

Jarka nodded, but not trusting his voice, he said nothing.

"I understand your mother was killed in the melee. How did you survive?"

"My sister," he said, wiping at the tears in his eyes. "She stopped me from charging Warthux. If it wasn't for her, the Superiors would have cut me down."

Alarix turned back, his blue eyes filled with remorse or sympathy. "It should never have happened. I still wish it didn't. Your father and I also hoped to unite the Clans."

"He told me. I saw you two meet, and I confronted him afterwards. He said he was doing what he felt was right."

"Did he tell you why?"

Jarka nodded. "The humans. He said that one day, they would destroy us if we remained divided."

"I still believe he was right," Alarix said. "But after his death, I couldn't see a way forward. Warthux only ever cared about his own power. Now his sons rule together, and they're worse than Warthux ever was. Under their leadership, your Clan has become more powerful than any other. During the War Season, the twins attack without regard for the Warrior Code. They utilize ambush, and they kill far too frequently. Yet despite their dishonour, they cannot be stopped. They have the protection of warriors loyal only to them, and to challenge them is forbidden."

He paused, looking back towards the waiting crowd, and sighed. "I'm concerned about the survival of my Clan. Should the humans invade, we will not stand a chance. If it's not the humans, I fear it will be the twins. They are without honour. Since they do not follow the Warrior Code, there's nothing to stop them from attacking us here."

Jarka could hear the worry in the Warlord's voice.

"So let me help you," he said. "We want the same thing. Accept my challenge. I am my father's son. I will do what I feel is right."

"But how? It's impossible."

"I will challenge the other Warlords and unite the Clans under my rule. I'll have to save the twins for the end. Once I have that much power, they won't be able to resist the temptation of claiming it for themselves."

Alarix crossed his arms and seemed to hesitate, his eyes searching. Eventually, he said, "You know this idea is insane, right?"

Jarka grunted a laugh. "I still don't know how I even came up with it. But maybe, if we're lucky, it'll work."

"Well, if anyone were to pull something like this off, it would be Corthak's son. He was the greatest warrior I've ever met. In his honour, I will accept your challenge."

The Warlord's pronouncement sent a thrill through Jarka's core, and his breath flowed more easily.

"But this plan is a huge risk," Alarix continued. "If you manage to defeat all the other Warlords, the twins could take that power from you in a single Challenge. That cannot be allowed to happen, so I will not just let you win. I must be sure that you're good enough to defeat them."

Jarka gave a single nod. "I'd be disappointed with anything less."

"The extent of all this must stay between us," Alarix added, stepping closer. "If you do win, I will support you however I can. But for both our sakes, no one can know what we've spoken of."

"Agreed."

"Come," the Warlord said with a slight smirk. "Let's give them a show."

Together, they returned to the Challenge Ring. Nothing had changed in their absence. The warriors still watched Relyk, Imzen, and Vaseus, and the crowd still waited on the rising semicircle of benches.

"I have decided," Alarix called out, silencing the few conversations, "to accept this outsider's challenge. However, I have one condition."

"Which is?" Jarka asked.

"When I win, you will return to Clanless lands and never challenge anyone else again. The Warrior Code demands it."

"Done."

"Now, join me in the ring. Let us see if you are as skilled as your father."

Jarka slowed to check on his companions. Relyk and Imzen met his gaze, their expressions neutral. Vaseus, however, appeared impatient or irritated.

He thought to say something, but seeing that Alarix already stood waiting on the far side of the ring, he continued by in silence. As he approached, he noted that the Warlord was by no means an imposing sight. Six bands of string with small, white stones were spaced evenly down his entire left arm. He was shorter and sleeker than most opponents Jarka had faced.

And yet, he was Warlord.

Don't underestimate him. He'll be quick, and stronger than he looks.

Spears were brought forth by two young males. Jarka accepted his without taking his eyes off of Alarix.

As he felt the well-balanced wooden shaft in his hands, his mind quieted, and his body stilled. Sensing the familiar calm that came before a fight, he allowed his eyes to close and lowered himself into a crouch.

For Jazith.

From somewhere nearby, someone shouted, "Begin!"

Jarka opened his eyes and charged ahead. Alarix's sprint across the ring was incredibly fast. Jarka had only taken four steps before their spears met.

In those first moments, he knew why Alarix was Warlord. His spear was a blur as he attacked. Jarka barely kept up, blocking each lightning strike with both spear and forearm.

He had to backpedal beneath the onslaught, already nearing the edge of the ring. He tried to push Alarix left or right as he parried, but the Warlord was too well balanced. He was relentless, his every strike perfectly placed, denying Jarka any opening to counter or slide away.

Jarka could barely match the Warlord's speed. His arms were tiring fast as he tried to keep up, reacting without thought, barely blocking or deflecting every blow. He took another step back and felt the rope beneath his foot. Another step meant defeat. He was out of room.

Desperate panic fired through his entire body, fuelling him to swing harder and faster than he knew he could. He blocked and parried, trying to create an opening in Alarix's relentless attack.

But it was no use. The Warlord was too balanced and too quick. Nothing Jarka did interrupted the onslaught.

Before long, the energy flowing through his arms lessened. He clung on, frantically searching for a way out, refusing to give in.

And yet the truth was inescapable.
He couldn't hold on much longer.

TWENTY-THREE

Because, for the Spartans, loyalty was everything. "Show no mercy to those who have shown no loyalty," as their saying went.

Eurydemos of Corinth

Kaletor stepped clear of the trees and proceeded onto the road. Ignoring the puzzled looks from a passing group of tattered travellers, he turned north and walked on. The city of Rhodes lay ahead, less than a mile away.

Several hours had passed since he left the farmhouse behind. To his surprise, the voice of Vaseus had not yet attempted to torment him. Was it possible the act of killing innocents had proved that he no longer believed in her childish ideals? Was he finally free of her judgments and infuriating resistance?

Determined that it be so, he had resolved to stay focused on the task at hand. Keeping to empty fields and virgin forest had allowed him to move across the sparsely populated countryside undetected.

But he had to take more risks if he wanted to get off the island. He needed to board a ship, and the only way to do that was at the Mandrakion Harbour, which was on the far side of the city.

With any luck, the evidence of his visit to the farmhouse remained undiscovered. Yet there was every chance that the opposite was true, in which case there might be a hunt for outsiders.

Either way, he needed to move quickly.

As he drew near the towering walls of the city, traffic on the road grew more and more congested. Four-wheeled carts pulled by either oxen or horses bounced and creaked over the wide, black stones. Their drivers shouted at the beasts to move, snapping an angry whip or stick over their backs when words weren't enough. Between these bulky transports moved an endless stream of peasants, chatting noisily as they entered or exited the city.

He listened for any mention of the war, but heard none. The faint but unmistakable stench of shit was an ever-present distraction.

Moving amongst these disgusting people made his skin crawl. He rolled his shoulders and neck to shift the weight of his pack and quickened his pace.

He was nearly to the yawning gate when he caught sight of armoured men. Though they wore chain mail and held spears, it was obvious in an instant that they were raw recruits. They stood in a circle, backs exposed to the passing crowd as they chatted amongst themselves. Not one was keeping an eye on the peasants streaming by. If he were so inclined, he could knife two of them and disappear before the others even noticed.

Pathetic, traitorous Greeks. They shouldn't be allowed to bear arms. I could kill you all singlehandedly, even if I were stark naked and drunk. One day soon, I'll make you and your city pay for turning on the Empire.

Gnashing his teeth with hands balled into fists, he walked by the ignorant fools, passed under the arched gate, and entered the city.

Rhodes, he quickly realized, was like Sparta, only smaller. The streets were wide and ran in straight lines, each one lined with shops and homes of either brick or wood.

But there was one major difference that distinguished one from the other, and that was colour. Most everything in Sparta was gold, red, and black. Rhodes was far more diverse. Walls were painted different shades of blue, yellow, red, orange, purple, and green. The mix of colours was endless and vibrant, and not just the buildings. The men and women moving about were adorned in colourful tunics and dresses of every shade and hue.

It was clear that these traitors were radical freethinkers. As Kaletor looked on them, it felt like lava was sizzling through his veins.

During his progress through the noisy, lively city, he eyed every corner, every alley, every stretch of street. Though some places could be made into dangerous chokepoints if barricades were set up, he soon concluded that once his Phalanxes were inside the walls, Rhodes would fall quickly.

Glorious images of the colourful buildings being consumed by flames while the wretched people were cut down filled his mind as he walked. *Soon you will regret turning your backs on Sparta. I will bring death and fire to this place, and every single one of you will know terror and pain.*

His thoughts of blood-soaked victory were interrupted when he heard the emperor's name. Blinking, he refocused his attention on the two men walking leisurely a few paces in front of him.

". . . it'll be Athens," the taller of the pair was saying. "No other city has more to gain than she."

"Impossible," the squat, bald man at his side replied. "They're too close to Sparta. If they tried anything, the Spartans would crush them in a matter of days."

"Alright, then which Greek city do you think will follow our lead and join the rebellion?"

"I don't know. Perhaps none."

"Perhaps none? What's wrong with you? How can you be so pessimistic?"

"I'm not being pessimistic," the bald man retorted. "I'm being realistic. Look what happened to Chersonesus. Every man and boy killed. Every woman and girl raped and taken as slaves."

"An exaggeration, no doubt," the tall one said, though there was a hint of uncertainty in his voice.

"Even if it is, I can understand why people are reluctant to rise against the Empire."

"And yet we did it. Many towns and cities have done it. Thousands of people have risked everything to become free of Spartan oppression. Why not other Greeks? Do you imagine that we're special, or braver than others?"

The squat, bald man wagged his head from side to side. "Like I said, I don't know. All I'm saying is that I don't expect other Greeks to do as we have done. Fear can be overpowering. When you hear stories about cities burning buildings with their own people inside to avoid Spartan terror, you might think twice about rebelling."

"But fear is what got us here in the first place," the tall man argued. "We were afraid to speak out when they raised taxes, and we were afraid to say no to an armed garrison, and we were afraid to do anything about the excessive abuse, the slew of arrests, or the unjust executions. The Spartans have created an empire that's built on fear. As long as we're afraid of them, corruption, injustice, and death will go on and on without end. I don't want to live in such a world anymore. It's better to fight for what's right and good—even if it means we die—than to live and allow such horrors to prevail."

At this point, Kaletor's teeth were clenched so tight that his jaw felt ready to snap. Balling his hands into fists, he moved close to the pair, bringing his right arm up to strike—

And froze. Dazzling sunlight reflecting off water flashed in his eyes, a momentary distraction. But seeing the sea and the ships floating upon it reminded him just how tenuous his situation was.

He released a ragged breath, let his arm down, and forced his hands to open.

"Soon," he said quietly to himself, "I will return and kill you both myself."

The vow made, he veered away and walked swiftly towards the Mandrakion Harbour.

Thirty or more wharfs extended from the shore like stiff wooden fingers, fingers that were reaching out over the calm water. Most were occupied by ships of varying size, their high masts looking like a sparse forest of skinny tree trunks. Further out, the leg stumps of the fallen Colossus of Rhodes jutted up at the mouth of the Harbour's entrance, and the sea beyond was empty of any activity or movement.

Squinting as he looked towards the sun-splashed water, Kaletor guessed this was due to the ongoing war. The uncertainty of things bred fear and discontent, not to mention piracy. Traders were far more reluctant to carry their valuable goods across the Aegean without the presence of Spartan patrol ships. And now that Rhodes had rebelled, all official trade with the island would have ceased.

Taking this all in, a concerning question occurred to Kaletor—what if the ships were barred from leaving?

As he neared the Harbour's small, arched entrance, he cast his gaze from ship to ship, searching for signs that one was preparing to leave. All was quiet and lifeless, save for one. Down at the far end, he saw a few men scurrying on and off one of the smaller ships, carrying sacks or crates in their arms. From his distant vantage, it was impossible to tell if they were loading or unloading.

The streets by the waterfront were less crowded, so it was easy to approach the Harbour's entrance. A small, plain archway of stone served as a gate of sorts, beyond which stretched a flat bridge of narrow wooden planks.

Barring the way were six men, each wearing different combinations of leather or metal breastplates and helmets. Most were armed only with four-foot spears.

This sorry bunch, all of whom had been sitting on the ground or leaning against the archway, stiffened in response to Kaletor's direct approach.

"Harbour's closed," a fat man with greasy red hair and a mustache grumbled.

Kaletor almost rushed forward to ram a fist into the pudgy man's throat. But he caught himself in time, remembering that talking was his best chance of getting off the island.

"I'm with that ship," he answered, pointing to the far end of the wharves. "I need to get aboard before she leaves."

"Is that a fact?" the greasy man said, his mustache riding his upper lip like a wave. "Strange that they didn't mention you'd be coming. Any idea why?"

Kaletor struggled to keep his expression from darkening. "They must have thought I intended to stay. But I was just held up."

"Oh? What held you up?"

"Visiting family. Lost track of time."

The fat one nodded, crossing both arms over his protruding middle. "I see. Where in the city do they live?"

"It doesn't matter. I just need to get to my ship."

"Answer the question and we'll let you pass."

"Somewhere in the western district," Kaletor growled. "I'm not very familiar with this city."

"Of course you're not," the leader said, motioning to his men with one hand. "You Spartans hardly ever leave your precious capital. You and your emperor don't pay attention to Rhodes, or Persia, or anywhere else in your so-called empire. But now you do. Now you send a fleet filled with hoplites to destroy us. But the gods are on our side. That's why Poseidon killed you all in the sea. What was it like? What was it like to watch all your companions die?"

Kaletor launched himself forward with a snarl, left fist arcing high. The fat man's reaction was swift but foolish. The attack was a feint to create a gap, a gap that Kaletor exploited. He slammed his right fist into the soft flesh of the fat man's throat and felt the thin wall collapse beneath his knuckles.

With the fat man sputtering, he twisted away, avoiding a thrusting spear aimed at his midsection. He rushed the two that were moving to flank him. He shifted his torso beside a clumsy thrust, simultaneously slapping a hand into the spear's shaft. He bashed a rising elbow into the guard's chin. As he staggered, Kaletor yanked the spear from his hands.

The second would-be flanker closed and swung his spear horizontally at chest level. Kaletor ducked low, stepped in, and planted a kick to the man's gut. He sagged around the blow. Kaletor followed with a quick spear thrust that found flesh.

He barely heard the resulting scream as he spun around to meet the remaining three guards. Two were on him, their spears jutting out. Kaletor sidestepped one while deflecting the other high and away. At that moment, the third arrived, rushing close with a short sword. Kaletor spun aside, swinging his spear along with him. The metal tip whipped around to slash through one of the other's cheeks.

He glimpsed blood as he pivoted hard. A thrusting spear flashed right beside his face, a close miss. He stepped in and cracked the shaft of his spear into the swordsman's skull. The strike sent the man straight to the cobbles.

The last one standing, the one who had just barely missed, attacked with desperate power. Off balance, Kaletor managed to parry the blows, backpedalling to keep up.

He soon recovered, and after surviving a short flurry, sped up and countered with two quick jabs. The guard parried both. Kaletor released a ferocious roar as he came out of this with an overhead smash. The guard blocked, but not strong enough. The leaf head end pushed down to the top of his ear, and when Kaletor yanked back, the metal sliced through. The guard howled as he collapsed to the ground.

Panting, Kaletor looked around, ready to fight on. But they were all down.

A barking shout pulled his attention around to the nearby streets. Several armed men were coming.

He turned and ran towards the ship.

TWENTY-FOUR

Slowly, our numbers grew. Some struck out to forge their own paths in new lands. One Clan became two, then four, then five. Eventually, a few ventured beyond the Forever Forest. The North Lands were tough and cold, but still, some found a home there.

The Spoken Tales

J arka had managed to avoid, deflect, and block the Warlord's spear with his own, but only just. His arms were tiring, and he was on the brink of being forced from the ring.

Alarix jabbed high, then swung left, then went high again. Jarka blocked each, then dove forward. Alarix twisted left, but not far enough. Jarka wrapped his arms around the Warlord's middle and dragged him down. His bones jarred as they hit the ground in a tangled heap.

Alarix snarled as he rolled away and surged back to his feet. Seeing him go for his fallen spear, Jarka swept out a kick. His foot caught Alarix's calf and sent him sprawling. Jarka scrambled over, snatched up one of the spears, and jabbed the point to the Warlord's chest.

In that moment, they stared at each other, breathing harshly but otherwise still. Jarka saw shock or disbelief in Alarix's eyes.

He shouldn't have been able to do what he had just done. They both knew it.

Arms feeling like they were full of stones, he slowly took the spear away and let it fall to the ground. He glanced up to the crowd. Everyone was looking back in absolute silence. They were all witness to something unbelievable, something without precedent.

A Clanless had defeated their Warlord.

Jarka rose to his feet, eyes sweeping over the silent, midnight-black sentinels. Then he looked down to Alarix and offered his hand. "Well fought, Warlord."

Alarix just stared up, motionless, his eyes still wide.

After a moment, he said, "Warlord no longer."

He took hold of Jarka's hand and rose to his feet. "It's been years since my last defeat. For it to come in this way, not from a Superior, but from a Clanless . . ." He trailed off, slowly shaking his head. "Even though Corthak was your father, I still didn't think such a thing was possible."

Jarka shifted his grip to clasp Alarix's forearm. "Thank you for accepting my challenge. I know it went against the Warrior Code."

"Yes, it did," Alarix agreed. "But only the strong may lead. And you have proved yourself stronger than I." He stepped in close and quietly added, "When the time comes for you to fight the twins, make sure you beat them."

Jarka gave a subtle nod. "I will. Your honour does you credit. Now, I need to address your Clan."

Alarix winked before rotating at the hip and extending an arm toward the crowd. "You are Warlord now. May strength and honour serve you."

Jarka bowed his head before stepping towards the silent onlookers. Raising his voice, he said, "My name is Jarka, and I have defeated Alarix in an honourable Challenge. I am now your Warlord. I know this isn't how things are normally done, but we must adapt, and quickly if we are to preserve our way of life.

"The humans have grown far more numerous, and the Spartans have become very powerful. If we sit idly by, they will destroy every Clan, one by one, until every yagar is dead or captured. I do not want that. None of us want that. We must join together and fight this foe. It is the only way to protect our homeland.

"That is why I came here," he continued. "And that is why I will travel on to become Warlord of the other nine Clans. Once I have achieved this, I will call on all our warriors to march south, and together, we will defeat the Spartans before they ever set foot in our lands."

As he spoke, he expected defiance or outrage in response. Instead, with his incredibly lofty ambitions voiced, total silence remained. A mass of black-furred faces and hundreds of glowing eyes stared down at him, intent but unreadable.

He met their attention with what he hoped appeared to be unflappable confidence. *Do they think I'm mad? Are they reeling in shock? Or do they believe in this insane vision of mine? I don't know. Is this what it's like to be Warlord?*

These and other uncertain thoughts raced through his mind. They went round in circles, questions without answers.

*   *   *

"What was all that?"

Ignoring Relyk's question, Jarka looked around the simple hut they had just been led to, noting the large dining table dominating the back wall. A rug of dark brown fur lay spread before it. Antlers and bones adorned the black stone walls. He breathed in deep through his nose, smelling the smoke that rode the air, as well as the subtle scent of rock—

"Jarka."

He turned around to face his three companions. "Hmm? Yes?"

"What did the Warlord say to you?" Relyk repeated.

"Second," Jarka corrected. "I think he'll be Second Superior now. That should make the transition smoother."

"Yes, fine," Relyk said, "but what did he say to you?"

"And how did you know his name?" Vaseus added.

Jarka looked to Imzen. "Do you have a question as well?"

The Elder met his gaze with steady eyes, not speaking at first.

"I remember when you first arrived in the Clanless village," she eventually said, "all those years ago. You didn't talk about it, but I saw that you were suffering from profound pain, you and your sister. I believe this path you are on will cause some of that to resurface, and with a bit of luck, those deep scars will heal. However, there will be plenty of time for that. For now, let us simply enjoy your success on this day."

Jarka kept his gaze on her as silence followed her words. He wasn't sure what to make of what she had said, but he was glad for them. He inclined his head slightly to convey his gratitude, and she returned the gesture.

"You almost had me convinced," Vaseus said into the silence.

Jarka looked at her. "Convinced of what?"

"That you believed what you were saying about the Spartans. It seemed like you realized how much of a threat they are, and that if we do not stop them, the world will become a barren wasteland of iron, ash, and misery."

He nodded slowly before replying. "They took my sister, which is cause enough for me to hate them. Perhaps, then, I'm starting to see things the way you do."

She smiled as he finished, and though she quickly looked away, there was something familiar about that look, something unmistakable. Jarka had seen that look in many females, and so he recognized it immediately as warm affection.

The implications sent a tangled mess of thoughts and considerations rushing through him. Dominating all the rest was the clear impossibility. Humans were to be avoided or killed, not cared for.

Yet along with this resistance came a tempered thrill. She was no ordinary human. She had just stepped into the midst of several hundred yagars without a hint of hesitation or fear. It was unheard of.

We are breaking rules with every step we take, bee. I've already done what was thought to be impossible. I was Clanless, and now I am Warlord. It seems we can accomplish the unthinkable. Perhaps, together, we can even dissolve the hate and bridge the gap between humans and yagars.

Even as these thoughts passed through his mind, he knew them to be absurd. Yet as he looked at Vaseus, that fact didn't seem to matter. She was fierce and brave, qualities every yagar admired. And yet caring for a human was forbidden and unnatural.

What to do? Nurture this delicate, budding affection? Or keep her always at arm's length?

More questions without answers. He was Warlord for a mere handful of moments, and things were already more complicated.

TWENTY-FIVE

Not long after the death of Lysander, the Messenians, who had been the slaves of Sparta for over three hundred years, were gradually granted their freedom. At the same time, many people in the southern Peloponnese became full Spartan citizens. This allowed the size and strength of the army to swell immensely, and in turn, the state to grow in power.

Androdamos of Boeotia

Kaletor stepped off the ship, the merchants that had ferried him across the Aegean already dismissed. He was glad to be rid of them. Despite his best efforts to dissuade them, they had sailed to Karystos, a backwater of a port town. Thessaloniki, capital city of the province of Makedonia, was not far to the north. Sparta, however, was at least a week's travel away.

As he walked across the boards of the wharf, he surveyed the town. There wasn't much to see. Small houses of stone and brick sat along narrow, winding roads. Smoke twirled skyward from a blacksmith, and a wooden sign hung over the entrance to a tavern with the word *Aphrodite's* carved into it. Most of the yellow paint of the letters had flaked off.

"Gods, I already hate this place," he muttered to himself. Noting how near the sun was to the horizon , he shook his head.

Too late to get very far.

Resolving to continue his journey at first light, he strode over to the tavern, pulled the door open, and stepped inside.

Like the town itself, there wasn't much to it. Fifteen round tables with four chairs surrounding each one filled the room. A plain stone hearth was set into the left-hand wall, and a faded painting of a ship adorned the other. A bar fronted by several stools lined the back wall, behind which stood a toned young woman, her black hair flowing and her dark eyes looking straight at him.

"Ah, first of the night," she said, setting a hand to a hip. "What can I get you, stranger?"

"Do you have rooms?" he asked as he walked over.

"No, but the inn does."

"Where?"

"A couple of streets inland. It's the tallest building in town, you can't miss it."

"Fine. I need food and wine."

"What kind of food?"

"Just bring me something, woman."

She gave him a long, stern look.

"Alright," she eventually said, turning on her heels and disappearing into the back room.

Several hours later, the tavern was full. Torches bathed the room in orange light, and many voices jostled with each other, each trying to be louder than the rest.

Kaletor, now sitting at one of the tables in a corner, paid them no heed. Slowly swilling his glass of wine around and around, his thoughts swirled.

He needed to find a horse and get back to Sparta as fast as possible. The worst part of his absence was not knowing how the war was going.

Not well without me, I'm sure. If they think I'm dead, the rebels will have more people willing to join them. I could have fifty thousand more enemies to kill by the time I return. I suppose that wouldn't be such a bad thing.

Although he felt a thrill pass through him with the idea of even more glory, the truth was that the Empire didn't need any more enemies. They needed to win the war—that was all that mattered.

So, what must I do when I return? If Hullis is dead, I'll need a new second-in-command. And the emperor will be none too pleased. I'll have to talk to him—

"Greetings, stranger," an old man with a bushy white beard said before sitting across from him. "What brings you to our humble town?"

Kaletor looked him dead in the eye, noticing a few age spots on the old man's cheeks. "Just passing through."

"The name's Genrius. Travellers are pretty well the only ones we see showing up around here. I've lived here all my life, all seventy-two years, and I've seen all manner of folk. You remind me of myself when I was your age: strong, muscular, fierce, and handsome."

As he finished, he lifted the mouth of a jug to his lips and drank deep.

Kaletor could feel his jaw starting to bunch. "Yes. If that's all, I have—"

"Have you heard what happened to the fleet near Rhodes?" Genrius cut in. "Last we heard, a storm wiped them out."

Kaletor took a drink as he considered how to reply. Once he swallowed, he said, "I heard most of the men went down with the ships."

Genrius wagged his head from side to side. "That's a damn shame. A damn shame. All those good Spartan hoplites, gone, just like that. It's not right.

"I don't understand people these days," he continued after a brief pause. "So many seem unhappy with the Empire. But why? Sure, things can be tough, and the rules can be harsh. But what about all the good? Look at this place, for example. Before the Empire, there was chaos here. No one trusted anyone. Theft and murder were common, at least that's what my grandfather said. Now, people thrive. We have order, stability, and peace. We can walk down the street without fear of being robbed or stabbed. That counts for something. But people don't seem to realize how good they've got it."

Kaletor nodded. "The idiots that started this war don't know anything. They don't know how far they would fall without the Empire."

"Finally, a man of my own heart," Genrius said, his grin revealing some missing teeth. "We seem outnumbered these days. Even here in Greece—"

"Not going on about the Empire again, are you, old man?"

The large man who had spoken stepped up behind Genrius, accompanied by a short, skinny one. Both were young, probably no more than twenty.

"Don't mind him," the scrawny one said. "He's just an old fool."

"Run along, boys," Genrius said, half-turning in his chair. "This traveller and I are having a pleasant conversation."

"About what?" the same one said. "The greatness of Sparta? The majesty of the Empire? The benevolence of the emperor? All lies, old man. Lies to keep you compliant and silent, no matter what they do to us."

"The Spartans don't care about you," the large one chimed in. "They don't care about any of us. All they care about is keeping their boots on our throats. It needs to end. The Empire needs to die. Understand?"

Kaletor clenched and unclenched his hands, something he had done several times already. With jaw bunched, he waited for Genrius to reply. But the old man bowed his head and said nothing.

"The Empire needs to die," he repeated back, unable to refrain any longer. "Is that right?"

"Yeah," the short, skinny one said, tilting his head to look down his long nose. "That's right."

"And what if," Kaletor said, pushing his chair back as he stood, "the Empire needs *you* to die?"

Before either of them could reply, he surged into action. Coming around the table, he grabbed the wide-eyed scrawny one by the collar and threw him across the room. The large one watched, his expression turning nasty as he advanced. He swung high, but it was slow. Kaletor ducked and quickstepped close in the same motion. Another slow punch was coming as he straightened. He raised his left forearm to block, then lashed out with a right hook. His fist slammed into a soft cheek and the bone beneath it.

The large man staggered to the side, nearly going down. With arms spread wide for balance, he managed to straighten. As he did, Kaletor was there to hammer him in the face again.

Like a felled tree, the big man went down, crashing into a table.

Chest heaving, Kaletor looked up and found the skinny one. There was terror in his eyes as he stood and ran for the door.

"Where you going, coward?" he bellowed after him. "Aren't you going to defend your idiotic ideas?"

The worm didn't slow as he barrelled through the door.

Kaletor shook his head. "Pathetic."

He looked back to his fallen opponent. He was groaning as he rolled around and held his head.

"Who are you?"

The voice came from behind and belonged to Genrius.

Kaletor turned to look back at the old man. His mouth was hanging open and his eyes were wide.

"You wouldn't believe me if I told you."

With that, he left the old man behind, walked past the other dumbstruck customers, and left.

TWENTY-SIX

Many believe that Tarkoz was the greatest
hunter of all time. The story that best explains
why is the one about the five bears. One day,
as was his custom, he was out on a hunt alone.
Suddenly, through the trees, he spotted a bear.
Then another. Then another.

The Spoken Tales

"I told you this would work. Two Warlords down, eight more to go."

"And I told you that that arm needs attention. Look, it's still bleeding."

Jarka looked down. The wound from the Warlord's spear was a few hours old, and though it wasn't deep, it had soaked the fur of his forearm red. He could smell the iron tang as he breathed.

"It's fine," he said, looking up and noticing that Relyk was heading toward the forest. "Oi! Where are you going?"

"Hunting," Relyk said without slowing.

"I'm coming too—"

"No, you're not," Imzen cut in, stepping into his path. "The human is right. That needs to be bandaged."

"It's just a scratch—"

"Sit down over there," Vaseus commanded, pointing to a lone boulder within the sea of grass.

Seeing the unwavering determination on her face, he said, "Well, if you insist."

He went to the boulder while Imzen sat cross-legged on the ground beside him. Vaseus unshouldered her pack and knelt to rummage through it.

From their vantage, the Home Village of the Shaded Meadow Clan was mostly obscured. They were just on its western edge, so only the perimeter huts of mud and wood were visible. Beyond the village was a ring of flat, open grassland that soon gave way to the branches and roots of the Forever Forest.

"Hold out your arm," Vaseus said, straightening with a bundle of cloth in hand.

Meeting her gaze, Jarka did as instructed. He watched as she worked one end of the cloth free, tucked the bundle between her arm and body, and set the end to his arm. She pressed it just below the wound, flattening his fur as she started wrapping. Her fingers worked deftly, and there was care in her movements. Her eyes were clear and intent. Even when she tightened it, there was no pain.

"There," she said as she tied it off. She looked up then, and her eyes met his. After a moment, she looked away.

"Thanks."

"How'd he get you, anyway? Everything happened so fast, I didn't even see."

He held her in his gaze a moment longer before he too looked away. "It was right before I forced him from the ring. He fought back hard then, and he almost got inside to put his spear to my throat. Instead, he got my arm."

"Only because you became too eager," Imzen chimed in. "You must remain balanced, no matter how close you are to victory or defeat. We will have to work on that."

"Oh? Does that mean that your many words of wisdom will be complemented by bouts of combat?"

"Yes."

"How excellent."

Silence prevailed between them for a time.

Hearing the cry of a bird, Jarka looked up. It was a lone, dark-feathered hawk, its wings beating as it rose high above the trees. Even as it faded in the distance, its silhouette was clear against the solid sheet of grey clouds.

"This Clan seems far less hostile than the last," Vaseus said.

"Yes," he replied, "oddly enough."

"They have always been more open-minded than most," Imzen said. "They're less rigid and more accepting. It feels quite pleasant to be here."

He looked over. "Why?"

The Elder continued looking straight ahead as she said, "It doesn't matter why."

He turned to Vaseus. "I should have known she'd say that."

She gave him a brief smile. "You should have. So, when do we head to the next Clan?"

"Tomorrow."

"Then you better talk to the Warlord now."

"You mean Second, yes?" he said, widening his eyes a little. "You *are* talking to the Warlord."

Again, she gave him that brief smile. "I'll go get him."

"On your own?"

She stood and set off, calling back, "Why not?"

He chuckled and shook his head. "She's something else."

"Yes," Imzen said. "She's sharp as the stone's edge. We must be careful."

"Now those are some words of wisdom."

It wasn't long before Vaseus returned with Pythax at her side. The now ex-Warlord looked very similar to Jarka. The same shade of gold fur with black spots. The same medium height and build. Three dark-blue rings of bone were wrapped around his left forearm.

"Come," Imzen said, motioning to Vaseus as she stood. "We will let them speak privately."

Vaseus gave them a disapproving look before allowing Imzen to lead her away.

"Your human has courage," Pythax declared. "To walk alone among us is no small feat."

Jarka rose to stand with him. "I didn't know her kind could be so fearless."

"Indeed. You wanted to speak with me?"

"Yes," Jarka said, facing him directly. "I would see the life of the Clan continue on as normal. As Second Superior, you will lead in my absence. Daily combat and Challenges will continue. Lessons to the young will continue. The Warrior Code is to be followed as always. The only difference is that the Warlord cannot be challenged. I know this is not our way—"

"Done."

His quick agreement caught Jarka off guard, but the sincerity in his eyes was obvious.

"Thank you," he managed after a moment. "I thought it would be difficult to persuade you."

"I understand the necessity of what you're doing," Pythax replied, his light-green eyes softening a little. "I would have attempted it myself if I thought I was good enough. Your father's warning reached us years ago, and I had hoped he would be able to unite us. He was the greatest warrior of our age. Until, perhaps, you."

"You knew my father?"

"No. I wasn't yet a Superior then. But our Warlord at the time did, and she greatly respected your father. She was ready to ally our Clan with yours, if the call had come. Now, I'm honoured to aid the son of mighty Corthak."

Jarka could feel the walls of his throat tightening as memories threatened to consume him. He knew what could happen if they did.

"Thank you again, Pythax," he managed, meeting the ex-Warlord's eye while they gripped each other's forearm. Then he stepped aside and walked away.

Don't let him see, the thought came. *Focus on your breath, just like Imzen does. Breathe. Just breathe.*

TWENTY-SEVEN

The Spartans' need for more knows no end.
More power, more glory, more lands, more
hoplites, more weapons, more conquests. It is
an unquenchable thirst, an unyielding ambition
that will go on until they swallow the whole
world.

Eurydemos of Corinth

Sitting atop his horse, Kaletor looked down into a sprawling valley. The road he travelled ran straight through its middle, a barren wasteland of stunted grass, gnarled shrubs, and scattered rocks. A nearby mountain range towered high above, still blocking the rising sun.

He knew this land. He was in Attica, less than four days ride from Sparta.

After descending the hill, he was riding across the valley, keeping the beast beneath him at an easy canter. The sun peaked over the mountains. He glanced over, squinting up at the yellow light. It reminded him of the previous morning.

He had been walking along the road when he came upon a small farm. Within a fenced-off enclosure were some chickens, ducks, and a pair of horses. The peasant farmer was at the far end of his field. Seeing the opportunity, he had leapt the fence, mounted the larger of the two horses, and rode away. All the peasant could do was shout obscenities at his back.

Not for the first time, he considered his ongoing choice to remain anonymous. There had been several towns and a few cities along his route. It would have been a simple thing to go to one of the local garrisons, declare who he was, and command an armed escort to accompany him back to Sparta. Yet still he hadn't.

Why not?

"Because that would be too easy," he muttered to himself. "And the easy path is for the weak."

As he neared the southern end of the valley, he noticed a lone tent just to the side of the road. Before long, he spied a man and a woman moving around it.

They heard him coming and watched him approach. Kaletor patted the dagger sheathed at his hip, then dismounted.

"Greetings and good morning," the man said, his face creased and his hair messy. "My name is Isadoss, and this is my wife, Rhea. So nice to meet a fellow traveller all the way out here. Are you hungry? We have a bit of bread, though I must admit, it's quite tough."

"No," Kaletor said, stopping about five paces away. He glanced at the woman. She smiled at him, revealing teeth that were stained brown.

Returning his gaze to the man, he said, "But I will have your drachmae."

As he finished, he took hold of the dagger's handle and revealed its naked blade.

The mirth exuding from Isadoss instantly turned into fear. "Please, sir," he said, his face turning as ashen as his hair. "Please have mercy. We have so little."

"That's fine," Kaletor said, stepping towards him. "I don't need much."

He twirled the dagger in hand, looking back to the woman. Her smile was gone, and like her husband, her face betrayed her fear.

When neither of them moved or spoke, he stepped closer to the man.

"Go get it. And be quick!"

Isadoss shrank away, his eyes wide as he turned and hurried into the tent. His wife remained where she was, still as a statue.

Before long, he reappeared with a small leather pouch in hand.

Kaletor sheathed his dagger. "Throw it here."

The man hesitated, glancing over to his wife.

"Please," he said, turning back, "reconsider. We might starve without—"

"Now!"

Isadoss visibly shook beneath the force of Kaletor's bellow. Without another word, he tossed the pouch.

Kaletor caught it in one hand and turned away. He shook it, hearing the clink of several coins within. Satisfied, he tucked it into his belt, remounted his horse, and continued on his way.

He didn't bother to look back.

TWENTY-EIGHT

Those who left the Forever Forest disapproved of banishing yagars from their Clan. That's one of the reasons why they left; they wanted to live free of that dark shadow. Most yagars living in the Forever Forest today don't know this. They don't know that no yagar living in the North Lands has ever become Clanless.

The Spoken Tales

Jarka stepped over a fallen branch and continued on, doing another scan of their surroundings. The forest was calm and quiet. Almost everything was green: the leaves, the grass, the moss-soaked rocks and roots. Beams of sunlight filtered down through the canopy. He took a deep breath through his nose, smelling the moss and trees and nothing else.

Satisfied that nothing and no one was nearby, he slowed his pace. He was leading the group, Vaseus second, Imzen third, and Relyk bringing up the rear. He looked back over a shoulder to watch Vaseus catch up.

"What is it?" she asked as she drew level.

He noticed that her breathing was somewhat laboured, and that a few strands of her hair hung down to brush her neck.

Matching her pace, he said, "I was just thinking that we haven't seen any of your friends in quite some time."

"Oh," she said with a wave, "that's okay. They know how to find us. I'm sure someone will bring us an update before too much longer."

"I'm glad you're so confident, but humans don't know our lands. The Forever Forest is vast. Aren't you worried they'll get lost in here?"

"They'll be fine," she insisted. "Most of them are excellent trackers. They know how to follow a trail."

Jarka allowed silence to stretch in answer. He listened once more, rotating his ears forward, then back, then forward.

Hearing nothing, he said, "I have a question for you."

Her green eyes narrowed a little. "Okay."

"You seem to care about others, including those you've never met. Is this common for your kind?"

She shook her head. "Not really."

"So why do you care so much? Why go to all this trouble?"

She looked him in the eye for a moment. Then she looked forward, and after ducking under a low-hanging branch, said, "That's not easy to answer. There isn't one single reason. My whole life holds the answer, and that's not something I can just put into a few words."

"Tell me how, then. What led you here? How did you end up walking into our lands seeking our help?"

"Why do you ask?"

"I guess I'm curious. Can you blame me? Everything about this is unheard of, and, really, should never have happened."

She gave a slight smile. "True."

He stepped around a cluster of rocks. "So. How did it happen?"

When she didn't reply, he glanced over. She was looking straight ahead as they walked on, seemingly intent on something. He wasn't sure if she was considering her response, or just listening to the bird song that had started somewhere in the treetops.

He looked forward, not wanting to distract her. Between the rise and fall of the bird song, he listened for the scuff of a footfall behind them. He didn't hear anything, and he hoped their companions would remain out of earshot.

"After I left Sparta, I didn't know what to do or where to go," she said, her voice silencing the birds. "For years I wandered across the Empire, drifting from one place to the next. Sometimes I found kindhearted people who offered me food and shelter. Not often though. Mostly I was ignored. A few times I was attacked. As time went on, I knew what kind of person I wanted to be. I had always known, but those years made me more determined than ever. I wasn't going to be someone that stood by and did nothing.

"Eventually, I made my way further and further north," she went on, "helping and befriending the poor and downtrodden along the way. I learned how to fight. I learned how to lead. Once I had enough support, I organized an underground resistance, and it grew quickly. We undermined tax collection.

We sabotaged underhanded deals. We even assassinated a few corrupt government officials. All the while, we spread the word to neighbouring cities, towns, and villages, asking others to join us. The more we did, the more support we gained. Before we knew it, the flame of rebellion ignited, and the war began."

While she spoke, Jarka had mostly kept his gaze on her as they walked. As she finished, she met his eye, and he saw within them a blazing passion.

Glancing away, he said, "So that's why you weren't afraid when I charged you."

"What do you mean?"

"You've risked your life before. You know what that feels like. You've faced danger and death, and you know how to survive."

"Kind of like you," she replied, looking sidelong at him with a smirk.

He nodded. "Is this the life you imagined for yourself when you were young?"

The corners of her mouth flattened out and the light in her eyes dimmed. "Yes. And no."

When she didn't elaborate, he opened his mouth to say more—

But stopped himself. He pushed his ears back to confirm. Sure enough, Imzen had caught up.

"You should be scouting ahead," she said. "Go, get back out front."

Jarka looked at Vaseus. "Well, the Wise One has spoken. Should I do as commanded, even though I'm a Warlord?"

She nodded, her expression unreadable. "Sure."

He hesitated, held her gaze for a brief moment, then surged ahead. As he did, his unasked question sounded in his mind.

Who did you lose, Vaseus? Who did you lose?

TWENTY-NINE

Spartans do not ask how many, only where the
enemy are.

Agis II, King of Sparta

Kaletor scratched dirty fingernails through the matted mess of facial
hair on his cheeks and neck as he passed under the north gate of
Sparta. The company of eight hoplites posted on either side paid him
little attention. To them, he was just another dirty peasant with filth on his
clothes, reeking of unwashed body odour.

And so, the Empire's greatest ever Commander returns home, the bitter thought
came. *Alone and anonymous. How glorious.*

A solid sheet of grey clouds covered the sky, but the late spring heat was still
stifling. Though his gut rumbled and his mouth and throat were beyond
parched, he walked quickly through the crowded streets without seeking food
or drink. He had been gone for too long, and there were questions he needed
answered. And although his haggard appearance was both infuriating and
disgraceful, he planned to use it to his advantage. For all anyone knew, he was
either captured or dead. It was a rare chance to discover what some people
truly thought of him.

He made his way towards Hullis's house, and when at last he arrived, he
could hardly believe his luck. Both Hullis and Ackadus were in the street,
garbed in their red cloak and gold armour, intent on their conversation.

So you survived, young brat, he thought as he slowed his steps to blend in with
the ever-moving crowd. *How disappointing.*

Before long, he was within earshot.

". . . to me about squabbling Lycurgan filth?" the prince was saying.

"Because they still pose a very real threat," Hullis replied. "My intelligence suggests that they are preparing another attempt on the emperor's life—"

"Your intelligence? You mean Kaletor's informants? His terrified band of middle-class weaklings not man enough to do what real Spartans do?"

"They have their uses—"

"Please," Ackadus cut in, disgust curling his thin lips. "Let them fade away like the memory of their master."

At this point, Kaletor was passing right beside them. He made a smart turn within the cover of the moving crowd and continued back the way he had come. Moving even slower and with his focus remaining on the pair, he continued to listen.

"We have bigger problems to deal with right now."

Hullis raised his eyebrows. "Bigger than the safety and security of your father?"

"More towns and cities rise against us every day. My father won't have an empire left to rule if we don't win this war."

"Everything that can be done is being done—"

"Wrong," Ackadus snapped, his arm jerking out to one side. "Our Phalanxes are scattered. They're fighting too many enemies at once. We cannot win decisive victories when we're spread so thin."

"What other choice do we have? Every threat must be countered."

"Yes, but the major ones should be dealt with first."

"What are you getting at?" Hullis asked, his arms now crossed.

"We should be focusing on those who started all this. If we destroyed Sarmizegetusa, it would rip the heart out of this rebellion's chest. With their lead city back in our hands, every rebel would be filled with dismay and fear."

Kaletor squeezed his hands into tight fists. *Idiot! We would lose thousands, even if we did somehow manage to win.*

"Such a course would be unwise," Hullis replied. "Have you already forgotten Kaletor's strategy?"

"He was wrong," the teenager snarled. "I know it's a risk, but this is war. We must risk all to win."

"Kaletor was many things, but when it came to war, he was exceptional. He could see things clearly long before anyone else could. I think we should heed his words—"

"Did he foresee his own death?" Ackadus barked, looking like a madman with eyes wide and head tilted. "Did he see that storm wiping out our entire fleet? No, he didn't. Not everything he did or said was right. He was an arrogant fool who believed himself all-powerful and almighty, but in reality, he was nothing more than a violent, angry brute—"

Kaletor's right cross cracked into the back of the prince's head. He crumpled to the ground.

"Stand down, General," he snarled at Hullis, who had drawn his sword and was poised to swing. "That's an order."

Hullis froze. With his mouth hanging open, he looked Kaletor up and down.

Eventually, he said, "Kaletor? Is that really you?"

"Don't be a fool. Who else could have done that?"

"But I thought you were dead! The storm. You went over—"

"You thought a storm killed me? Ridiculous. Now take me inside. I need to clean myself up before I see the emperor."

Apparently unable to speak, Hullis turned and led the way to his front door. They were nearly there when he half-turned and said, "What about Ackadus?"

"Leave him," Kaletor growled. "He deserves to wake up alone and in pain."

Hullis gave a sharp nod. "Yes, sir."

*   *   *

Two hours later, he was bathed, cleanshaven, and fully girded for battle as he strode into the emperor's throne room. Ockos was speaking with three men standing at the base of his raised platform.

"The Empire's Commander," Kaletor called across the sprawling space, his voice echoing off the high ceiling, "needs to speak with his Emperor."

All four fell silent and their attention shifted to the unexpected interruption. Ockos's eyes narrowed, and for a moment there was only the sound of Kaletor's footfalls.

Then he leaned back into his iron seat and said, "Leave us."

The three men, after giving Kaletor dark looks, exited through one of the side doors.

"What took you so long?" Ockos said, his tone laconic.

"I was busy clawing my way out of hostile territory," Kaletor answered as he arrived to stand before the throne.

Though he was dressed in the same gold-trimmed, blood-red robe, and the same gold-flecked diadem of ivory rested on his brow, the emperor looked different. The corners of his eyes were more crinkled, and his hair had thinned and turned white. It seemed the war, or maybe the constant Lycurgan threat, was taking its toll.

"I sent you to punish Rhodes," Ockos said. "Instead, you led my ships and men into a storm that wiped them out. Why?"

"Aggression," Kaletor answered without hesitation. "And rage. I wanted to kill those traitors before they were properly prepared. If I had turned and fled like a coward, the attack would have been delayed a week or more. That I could not tolerate."

"A *week?*" Ockos exploded, rising to loom large atop the spire of marble. "You could not tolerate a week's delay? How long has the delay been now? Almost a month? Rhodes remains in the hands of rebels, and all because you were too stupid to avoid some wind and rain!"

Kaletor grit his teeth to stifle a scathing retort, glaring up at the old man who dared to insult him.

"Did you know that Athens has also joined this cursed rebellion?" Ockos went on, his voice ringing loud off the high walls. "Athens! A city on the mainland! If many more Greek cities rise up against us, Sparta will fall!"

"I will never allow that," Kaletor snarled, unable to contain himself any longer. "Sparta cannot fall. I will lead an assault on Athens, smash through their walls, and kill every living thing inside. Once every Greek man, woman, and child knows what happens to those who turn on the Empire, none will dare make the same mistake."

"And what if you fail? What if you fail me again?"

"I have *never lost a battle in my life.* Give me an army and I will destroy every settlement in my path. All will remember that Spartans cannot be conquered. Give me an army and I will *win this war.*"

In the face of Kaletor's outburst, Ockos's demeanour shifted. His dark eyes brightened, and a smile tugged at his lips as he straightened to his full height.

"Unrelenting will," he said, his tone now even and firm, "is what this empire was built on. It's what makes Spartans greater and stronger than everyone else. It's what we need now more than ever. I'm glad to see that your fire still burns.

"I lost hope when I heard what happened to you and the fleet," he went on, hunching at the shoulders as he sat back down on the throne. "'How can we possibly win without my greatest Spartan?' I thought. Who will lead us to glory and victory? I believed the Empire was doomed, and my days have been dark ever since. Now you've returned, but is it enough? We are assailed on all fronts, and there's no end in sight . . ."

He trailed off with a slow shake of his head.

Kaletor had never seen the emperor burdened by such despair. It was more obvious than ever that Ockos was not all-powerful. He was a pale shadow of what he had once been.

With this realization came an undeniable truth; the fate of the Empire rested solely in Kaletor's hands.

In that instant, he saw a vision of his future. He would lead Sparta out of the depths of darkness by spilling oceans of blood and bringing fire to all. He saw victory after victory, every one led and orchestrated by himself. All would come to know and fear him. He would make the Empire stronger and more powerful than ever. He would become the greatest Spartan of all time.

Never before had he known such a feeling of destiny, a feeling of such incredible potential, of such limitless power. It was beautiful.

Turning his fierce gaze to Ockos, his voice full and alive, he asked, "What forces do we have in the Peloponnese?"

The emperor's eyes were watery, and he blinked a few times before answering. "The 16th is garrisoned in Corinth. The 9th is split between Mycenae and Argos."

"And in Sparta?"

Ockos blinked some more, clearly hesitant.

Eventually, he slowly said, "My Elites. As always."

"I will gather them all and march on Athens," Kaletor declared, ignoring the alarmed look the statement earned from the emperor. "Once I've taken the city, I will continue north, attacking every rebel army and stronghold along the way. You will send supplies and reinforcements as I request them."

Ockos's face had darkened considerably. "You presume to tell your emperor what to do?"

"Do you want to keep that thing on your head or not?" Kaletor snarled, unwilling to back down this time.

Ockos sat taller on his throne of Spartan shields, shoulders bunching and eyes wide. But instead of saying whatever he was about to say, he released a hissing breath and eased back down a bit.

"Summon the Elites, the 9th and 16th, and lead them to Athens," he said, the words strained and tight. "Once you have taken the city, continue north and conduct the war as you see fit. Supplies and reinforcements will be sent to you when possible."

Kaletor managed to keep the scowl from his face as he bowed his head. "As you wish, Emperor. I will deliver victory after victory until the war is won."

Without waiting to be dismissed, he turned and walked away.

And when I return, we will discuss my reward for everything that I've done.

With this thought bringing a grin to his lips, he left the emperor on his throne, each stride long and powerful.

THIRTY

At first sight, the North Lands appear to be a lifeless, barren, and inhospitable place. But yagars found a way to thrive there. What was their secret? They became experts at hunting in the water.

The Spoken Tales

Jarka spun left, lashing his spear out horizontally. Vaseus ducked under it and jabbed her spear at his face. It missed by inches, so he was free to swing his spear diagonal to her throat, stopping it just before the stone leaf head reached her skin.

"Good," he said between breaths, "you're getting faster. But your footwork's still holding you back."

She gave him a deadpan look. "So kind of you to say. But it doesn't matter. I'm not the one fighting Warlords."

"No? In that case, perhaps we don't need to keep doing this. I have won all four of my Challenges quite easily, yes?"

She barked a short laugh as she stepped away. "Easily? Is that what you call it?"

"You disagree?"

"Honey, without your streak of luck, you would have lost the first one."

"Luck?" he cried, stepping forward to give her a shove. "Come on. You're just sour cause you still can't beat me."

She twirled away from his outstretched hand with another cutting laugh, her blonde hair tossing. "With all this practice, it's only a matter of time."

"No more practice then. I can't have you getting any better," he said, moving away from the clearing to pass through the trees.

"I don't think Imzen would approve," she called after him. "And don't tell me that the Warlord of four Clans is afraid of being beaten by a mere human."

He released a laugh in response and continued on.

Pine trees towered all around them, casting much of the forest floor in shifting shadows. He moved smoothly across the bed of brown needles underfoot, the sweet scent of oozing sap filling his nostrils. The blackened antlers around his left shoulder snagged on a low-hanging branch. As he readjusted to get loose, he heard footsteps behind him.

Smiling to himself, he took off, weaving past tree trunks and dodging branches as if they were flying projectiles. When he glanced back, he saw Vaseus running after him. He laughed and ran on.

Soon they emerged from the edge of the forest just to the left of their camp. Jarka slowed to a walk as he stepped onto the open plain of stunted, dry grass. The cool breeze felt good as it pushed through his fur.

Seeing movement amidst the dark tents, he called out, "That was a short hunt."

"Of course it was," Relyk answered. "I'm the best hunter there is."

Jarka chuckled. "And so humble."

As he moved into camp, the iron tang of blood stuck to his tongue. He breathed it in deep, savouring the smell. A large, black boar was laid out on its side. Imzen was sitting cross-legged on the ground to one side, her back straight and eyes closed.

Jarka looked to Relyk, noting the absence of his spear. "Did she charge you?"

Relyk nodded as he wiped the back of his hand across his forehead. "My spear snapped in half. Nearly tore my shoulders out of their sockets."

"That's odd. Why didn't she run?"

"That's how these mountain boars defend themselves," Imzen chimed in. "The white lions that hunt them are too fast to outrun. Their only chance is to drive them off."

Jarka glanced north to eye the distant peaks of towering rock capped in snow. "This already seems like a strange place."

"Is that a dead animal I smell?" Vaseus called from behind one of the tents.

He shared a smile with Relyk. "Is that a problem?" he called back.

"You know it is. Move it out of sight."

"But why? It can't hurt you now."

"Jarka!"

Laughing together, he and Relyk moved to hoist the carcass up and carry it behind one of the tents.

"Do you think all humans have such weak stomachs?"

They let the boar drop to the ground and Relyk shrugged. "Maybe. Maybe it's just the smaller ones."

"Why would that be?"

Relyk shrugged again. "Just a guess."

"How did sparring go?" Imzen asked as they returned, her eyes now open.

"Just excellent, my old friend. She never even touched me."

"I was close," Vaseus piped up.

"You and I will spar in the morning."

"Again? But Imzen, you might get hurt this time. I could never forgive myself—"

"It's time you learn what I'm here to teach you," she said, her tone even.

He narrowed his eyes. "Oh? As opposed to what you've been doing for the past month?"

Instead of replying, she closed her eyes and sat in silence.

"Alright then," he said. "Good talk."

Over an hour later, they sat around a small fire, a slab of boar cooking on a spit, the occasional hiss announcing a glob of fat hitting the flames.

Jarka's stomach grumbled its longing to be filled. They had taken to cooking their food for Vaseus. His belly was still struggling to adjust.

He glanced over to her. She was bundled within two or more blankets. "Warm enough, honeybee?"

"No," she growled, her eyes as hot as the flames. "I'm freezing. I didn't know it could ever be this cold."

Relyk said, "And it's going to get colder. Much colder."

Vaseus shook her head. "Great."

"Worse than the cold is your mind's resistance to it," Imzen said, her gaze holding on the fading sun. "Your body is cold, that's all. But the mind says it doesn't want to be cold. This gap between what is and what you want only worsens your suffering. It serves no other purpose."

"So I should just accept that I'm cold?"

"Yes. Or take action to change the situation. Anything else is futile."

Many times prior, such statements had earned Imzen a cutting remark from Vaseus. But this time, the human did not argue.

She must be too cold, Jarka thought, smiling to himself. *Perhaps going further into the North Lands will be a bit more peaceful.*

Silence reigned then. With the purple of dusk deepening all around them, it started to snow.

Some time later, Vaseus said, "How many more Clans must we visit?"

"Six," Relyk answered.

"And how long will it take?"

"Hard to say. Depends how much ground we cover each day. Assuming a decent pace, about seven weeks."

Upon hearing the answer, she seemed to shrink even smaller into her blankets. "Must we go to them all? The war drags on, and every day more of my people face terror, pain, and death."

"I'm sorry, bee," Jarka chimed in, "but I must unite all yagars for this to work. Facing the cold and the Clans that live here is something we must do."

She met his gaze. "I know. I just want to save as many as I can."

He nodded but didn't know what to say, and so silence reigned again, the snow falling gently around them.

And here all I wanted was to save my sister, the thought came to him as he glanced from the fire to Vaseus. *Perhaps humans aren't so bad after all.*

*   *   *

The next morning broke cool and clear, though a blanket of snow covered everything. Jarka convinced Imzen to postpone their sparring session since the snow promised slower going and they needed to get moving.

They ate a few cold bites of the leftover boar, broke camp, and set out.

The plain stretched flat in all directions. Everything was concealed beneath the snow, except for a few dark boulders that poked free here and there. In the distance, the mountain dominated the horizon.

It was a long, cold walk, but eventually, they drew close to their destination. The plain continued all the way to the foot of the mountain. Home Village of the Northern Mountain Clan spilled onto it, and even though the village was large, its outermost edge lay within the shadow of the mountain. The Warlord's Hall rose high above all the other structures, but it was dwarfed by the wall of rock and snow towering high above it.

Relyk, who was leading the way, pulled up about two hundred paces short of the village. Into the still, crisp air, he said, "We are expected."

Jarka looked past Imzen and Vaseus and saw that a party of eight yagars had emerged from amongst the snow-covered huts.

"Finally," he said as he came alongside his companions. "A Clan with some manners."

"Are you sure that's what this is?"

"Ever the skeptic, bee," he answered, shrugging his shoulder to adjust the straps of his pack. "We yagars can be civil. Right, Imzen?"

The Elder kept her gaze fixed straight ahead and did not reply.

Relyk gave him a sidelong glance. "I'm not so sure about that."

"We all know what to do," Jarka said, choosing to ignore the comment. "Just follow my lead."

Vaseus gave a snort. "Because that's worked so well before."

Jarka chuckled and moved out ahead, narrowing his eyes to study the approaching party. Surprisingly, many of them wore animal furs wrapped about their necks and torsos. Beneath these coverings, the yellow of their fur was light, and their black spots were smaller and fewer than Jarka's own. They also appeared thicker at the chest and neck.

Noting all this as they came together, he raised his hands and said, "Greetings, my friends. My name is—"

"Jarka," one of the females finished for him as she and her group halted. "Yes, we know who you are."

"Oh," he said. "Does that mean you know why we've come?"

"Yes. You're here to challenge our Warlord for the right to rule another Clan."

"Actually—"

"Even though you're a dishonourable Clanless, and a soft forest-dweller that doesn't belong here."

Jarka brought his chin down to look at her more directly. "You're not the first to disapprove of me. Is this because you are Warlord?"

The female crossed her arms over the white fur that encased her chest and shoulders, both her forearms entirely covered in wolf and bear fangs. "No."

Jarka waited for her to continue, but instead, she fell silent.

He looked to the rest of the party. "What about one of you? I wish to issue my challenge, but I need to know who is Warlord."

"She's not here," the female snarled, arms uncrossing with a jerk. "She sent us to . . . welcome you."

"How kind of her. So who might you be?"

"I am Jynx, and I am Fourth. These are the other Superiors."

"A great pleasure to meet you, Jynx. This is Relyk, one of my dearest friends. This is Imzen, our wise and fearless leader. And this is—"

"The human," Jynx spat, sounding as if the word tasted bad.

"Vaseus," Jarka said. "Her name is Vaseus."

"Is it true that you do as she commands? Are you here doing her bidding? Are you really her slave?"

"We are allies," Vaseus chimed in, her voice as hard as stone. "We are both free to do whatever we please."

Jynx cast her near-black eyes to Vaseus, her face twisting into a vicious snarl. "Be silent, human. You may not speak unless spoken to. Your every step in our lands is a trespass. You have no place here."

"She travels in the company of a Warlord," Jarka said. "You will treat her as an honoured guest."

"I will *not*," the Superior growled, dropping into a fighting stance, both hands on her levelled spear. "None of you belong here, especially this one. Humans are our sworn enemies. We should kill her now!"

"Stand down," Jarka barked, stepping over to put himself between Vaseus and the Superior. "She is under my protection. To threaten her is to threaten me."

Jynx's mouth opened, her fangs exposed as she released a hiss. "So be it. Attack—"

"Enough!"

The shouted word came from somewhere behind the Superiors. Jarka kept his focus on Jynx, who still glared at Vaseus and remained poised to strike.

Before long, a tall, lithe female wearing a white bear fur stepped through the line. "I said enough, Jynx."

Releasing a low growl, Jynx relaxed out of her fighting stance.

"So you are the famous Jarka," the newcomer said, "who comes to claim another Warlord's title."

Jarka straightened and met her silver-blue eyes. "Are you the Warlord of this Clan?"

"Yes. I am Tavyka."

"Then yes. Warlord, I challenge you."

"I accept your challenge," she snapped. "Tomorrow morning we will fight. For now, rest from your travels. The Superiors will escort you into the village. Do not leave their company. There are many here who share Jynx's resentment."

She turned away then and walked smoothly back towards the village.

Jarka looked back to Vaseus, Relyk and Imzen. "Another warm welcome."

*   *   *

The hut they were led to was small, cold, and empty. It was obvious no one had occupied it for some time. A pile of furs lay heaped in the middle of the common room, the only objects within the four walls of wood and dried mud.

While their escorts left without a word, Jarka moved to stand by the barren, blackened stone hearth. He breathed in deep, smelling the cold, grey ash. "What glorious hosts we have."

"Really?" Vaseus grumbled, arms crossed as she stood there shivering. "Still with the sarcasm?"

"Why not? We're not dead yet, which is good."

"Look at this place," she snapped. "They obviously don't want us here. They're hoping we'll freeze to death."

"Not to mention the looks we were getting," Relyk chimed in as he peered through a crack in the reedy front door. "I've never felt so much hate directed towards me through so many eyes."

Jarka looked to Imzen, who had already planted herself cross-legged on the floor. "How about you? What do you think about all this, Wise One?"

Her eyes remained closed as she said, "There is nothing wrong with this moment."

"So helpful." He shrugged off his pack and laid it down. "There's nothing to worry about. Their Warlord accepted my challenge. No one would dare violate the Warrior Code."

Relyk was shaking his head as he turned to face them. "I don't know, Jarka. There was so much hostility in everyone we saw. I don't like it."

"Me neither," Vaseus seconded. "Can't we just skip this Clan and move on to the next one?"

"No, we need everyone. We knew it wasn't going to be easy up here. But it's going to work. Trust me."

Neither of them appeared convinced.

After a moment, Relyk said, "I hope you're right."

*　　*　　*

"Please. Help me!"

Jarka spun around, looking in every direction, frantic to find who was calling out. "Where are you?"

"Please, Jarka!" she cried. "It hurts so much. Help me!"

He cast all around, but a thick cloud of smoke obscured his vision.

"Where are you?" he bellowed, unable to keep the fear from his voice.

This time the only answer was her scream.

He didn't know where she was, and he could do nothing as that scream sliced straight through him.

He woke with a start, his body jerking. Orange light flickered across a low ceiling directly above. He tilted his head to the right. There lay Relyk and Imzen, both asleep beneath white bear furs. Seeing them, he realized what had happened.

"You were dreaming."

Sucking in a sharp inhale, he jolted upright and looked left. But it was only Vaseus. She was sitting cross-legged, ensconced in two or three dark furs. She was gazing at him with an unreadable intensity.

He released a rattling breath. "Perceptive as always, honeybee."

He peered about the silent hut, noting that the fading sunlight was no longer spilling in through the reedy door. "How long was I out?"

"What did you dream of?"

"That's rather nosy."

"That bad, huh?"

He shot her an annoyed look before turning to the blazing fire. He stared at the flickering flames for a time, feeling the warmth billowing out from the little inferno. The wood split and crumbled, and sparks burst forth like speeding fireflies.

Eventually, he roused himself to say, "Someone was in pain. They were suffering. They begged for my help, but I couldn't see them. I couldn't help them."

He glanced back to her, and when their eyes met, she asked, "Who was it?"

"I'm not sure. I think it was Jazith."

He paused, releasing a heavy exhale. "I hope she's alright."

Vaseus clasped her hands in her lap. "How do you do it?"

He frowned and tilted his head. "Do what?"

"All of it," she answered, extending an arm out to one side. "This village is full of yagars that hate us, you most of all. Yet here you are, facing that down without flinching. You're going against traditions and principles that your people hold dear, defying the natural state of things, and risking your life with every Warlord you face. Yet I never hear you complain. You never despair or lose hope. I've never known anyone like you."

Jarka brought a hand up to rub the back of his head. "I have to. I'm the only one who can save Jazith. But I'm not special. That's how most of us are. Once we decide to do something, we see it through. Aren't humans like that?"

"Only a few. Most of us start down a path, but then something happens to disrupt our original intention."

"Something?"

"It could be anything. They'll doubt themselves, or suffer a setback and give up, or they'll decide it's too hard. Don't you feel these things? Don't you ever doubt yourself or worry that you'll fail?"

Yes.

The simple answer stuck in his mind like a thorn in the side.

He forced it aside and shook his head. "I can't. I have to believe that I will succeed. That's how I win these Challenges."

A slight smile played on her lips as she tucked a strand of golden hair behind an ear. "Turns out I picked the only yagar who could help me save the world."

He smiled back. "And I picked the only human who could help me save my sister."

After a moment, he rose to his feet, strode over to the pile of logs, and tossed three more into the fire. As the flames consumed the dry wood, he returned to sit on his fur.

"I meant to thank you," she said after a moment.

He looked over. "For what?"

"For defending me today. I knew it wasn't going to be easy, given our people's history. But it's even worse than I expected. So, thank you."

"We're in this together, bee," he said. "I'll always protect you."

She held his gaze for a moment before turning to the fire. A comfortable silence prevailed before she spoke again.

"Tell me a story."

"A story?" he echoed. "What kind of story?"

"Any story from your past."

He studied her for a moment, an amused smile crinkling his whiskers. "I don't think you've ever made such a request before."

She shrugged, her lower lip pursing. "Maybe I want to get to know you a bit better."

"Did I really just hear that?" he gasped. "Does a human want to get to know a yagar on a deep and personal level?"

"Is that not allowed?"

He chuckled and bared his teeth to feign nervousness. "Well, it's certainly unheard of. We are told to despise your kind. A far cry from swapping stories."

"What would our parents think?"

Seeing her broad smile and the lightness in her bright green eyes, a deep warmth spread through his chest.

"Nothing good, I'm sure," he said. "No one wants their son or daughter breaking the rules."

"I never have been very good at doing what I was told."

"Really? I never would have guessed."

She rocked to one side as she loosed an easy chuckle, her golden hair brushing against her knee. "I have a feeling you weren't the perfect son."

"You've missed the mark on that one."

"Really?"

"No. Not at all, in fact. I tested every boundary and pushed against every restriction. I was always trying to do things my own way. This one time I told my mother—"

He faltered there, the words becoming ash in his mouth. He turned away and looked at the flickering flames. Heat rushed into his face as a heavy silence dominated everything.

"What happened to her?" Vaseus asked after a moment, her voice a tender whisper.

Jarka pulled in a deep breath and let it out, hoping to release the tension in him.

The image of his lifeless parents flashed in his mind. His hands involuntarily squeezed into tight fists. His breathing intensified.

Keeping his gaze fixed on the flames, he eventually managed to speak. "It was years ago. It still hasn't gotten much easier."

He heard a slight rustling, and a moment later, she settled down next to him. "Have you ever talked about it?"

He shook his head. "No point. Talking wouldn't change what happened."

"Not even with your sister?"

"She was there, right beside me. She knows that there's nothing to say."

There was silence then, and it felt like time stood still. When she reached out to place her hand on his, he did not shrink away.

"You can talk to me, if you'd like," she said, her voice gentle. "It might help. We're in this together, right?"

He turned to meet her gaze. Her eyes seemed to bore straight through him, yet it was a soft, tender gaze. A fresh surge of heat coursed through him as the sweet smell of her filled his nose.

Releasing a heavy exhale, he gave her a small nod. "Good to know, bee. I'll keep that in mind."

She seemed to hesitate for a moment before smiling and withdrawing her hand. She stood and returned to wrap herself in her furs.

Jarka looked back to the fire, his heart pounding in his chest.

This is a dangerous game we play, bee. A very dangerous game.

THIRTY-ONE

Do you want your name to live through the ages? The names of heroes survive. Be like them, and yours will too.

Thrasilaus of Thebes

Beneath a dawn of grey gloom, the 16th and 9th Phalanxes had formed ranks in front of the camp. The Emperor's Elites followed, their gold cloaks distinguishing them amongst the sea of red.

Kaletor shifted in the saddle, teeth clenched and fingers itching. From his position atop the pinnacle of a steep-sided hill, he looked beyond his army to the city of Athens.

It remained just as it had the day before—silent and shut. The towering stone walls protecting those within appeared unmanned.

He glanced left and growled, "Where are their defenders, General?"

Hullis, also mounted and fully girded for battle, kept his eyes on the city as he replied. "Hard to say, sir. Maybe hiding inside the towers to deceive us."

"Or still asleep in their beds," Ackadus chimed in from the line behind them. "They always were a bunch of weak fools—"

"Silence, Captain," Kaletor snarled over a shoulder. "If I wanted your childish opinion, I would have asked for it."

The demoted prince still sported scrapes on his nose and forehead, the result of falling on his face back in Sparta. Though his eyes burned with hate, he kept his tongue still.

Dismissing the insignificant brat, Kaletor looked right. "Any thoughts, Belisar?"

The grizzled veteran, his black beard streaked with more silver every day, gave a grim look. "This reminds me of when I stormed the city of Tylis. Like the Thracians we fought there, the Athenians will be ready to fight. But it won't matter. Only the strong prevail, and no one is stronger than we Spartans."

Kaletor nodded. "Agreed."

He looked back to the army in time to watch the last of the Elites exit the camp. He released a hot, gusting breath and bellowed, "Sound the advance!"

The trumpets blared a solitary note, and he heeled his mount into a walk. At his back, his handpicked personal guard of five hundred Spartiates followed.

Thousands of crimson-cloaked hoplites marched steadily across the open plain, keeping in tight rows that stretched over two hundred across and twenty deep. The 16th and 9th led the way, side by side, each Phalanx forming six blocks that were separated by narrow gaps. The Elites, far fewer in number, followed in a long, single line, a sheet of gold carrying a forest of black pikes.

Kaletor looked from his army to the towering walls. The front ranks had moved within bowshot range, yet still the ramparts remained empty.

"You see," Ackadus called over the lazy clop of horse hooves. "Cowards. They think stone walls will stop . . ."

The fool went silent as hundreds of figures suddenly appeared all across the top of the wall. A cloud of arrows rose with them, silently arcing high, then diving towards the Phalanxes.

"Charge!" Kaletor yelled.

Howls of pain erupted all across the line as the deadly missiles struck. Dozens staggered and fell. Another volley was in the air when the horns blasted two short notes. More hoplites went down as the rest broke into a sprint.

The urge to charge with them burned through Kaletor like a hot wave. He balled his hands into fists and squeezed it away. He had to coordinate things from afar if they were going to breach the walls.

"We need to retreat," Ackadus shouted from behind. "Our men are sitting ducks—"

"Spartans never retreat, boy," Kaletor snapped, his helmet jostling from the force of his words. "Now be silent or I'll cut out your tongue."

They had come to a stop just beyond bowshot range, and from atop his horse, he watched things unfold. Arrows continued to rain down in volleys, but fewer hoplites were falling prey to the deadly missiles. Most had angled their iron shields over their heads as they ran.

Though it seemed an eternity, the front ranks finally reached the foot of the wall. Rocks and spears were hurled down on their heads from the defenders above.

"The ladders," Kaletor spat through clenched teeth. "What are you waiting for?"

As if hearing him, the ladders carried by both Phalanxes started going up. All across the wall, they were anchored and heaved upward to lean against the ramparts. A few were pushed right back down, but the rest soon had men on them, scurrying up like red-backed beetles.

Kaletor looked on with fists clenched and jaw bunched, barely able to sit still.

"Come on, climb, climb. Faster. Hurry up and *take that wall.*"

But even as he willed his men up, the Athenian archers started targeting the climbers. Though they held their shields overheard as they climbed, the sheer number of arrows was overwhelming, and all it took was one to get through. Men started falling all across the line, plummeting to the ground.

Four more ladders were pushed down, the men on them jumping off or clinging to the rungs all the way down. One hoplite of the 16th did reach the top, but as he stepped onto the rampart, an arrow struck him in the chest. He fell end over end and disappeared amongst his Phalanx.

Kaletor loosed a wordless roar as he watched the assault falter. He swept his gaze across the battle scene, desperately looking for a solution while the arrows continued to decimate his Phalanxes.

"Should we pull back, sir?" Hullis asked at his side. "The ladders are not enough—"

"The Elites," Kaletor interrupted. "Send them to attack the gate."

"Attack the gate? But they have no way of breaking through—"

"The Athenians don't know that. An attack on the gate will draw their fire away from the ladders. Do it now!"

Hullis nodded and barked the order down the line. The horns blared once more.

Before long, the emperor's prized gold-cloaks had coalesced into a block on the road running between the 16th and 9th. Then, with their shields raised in an unbroken, horizontal wall of iron, the Elites advanced on the gate.

Kaletor turned to Belisar and said, "When they reach the gate, follow them in at the gallop. Call the Phalanxes to you as you go."

The silver-encased aristocrat swallowed and hesitated, doubt plain in his watery eyes, clearly no longer the general he had once been.

After a moment, he gave a terse nod. "As you wish, Commander."

Kaletor turned to Hullis. "Follow me."

He dug in his heels and his horse bolted forward. He urged the beast into a fast gallop, pumping his arms in rhythm with its bobbing head. It wasn't long to cross the empty plain and come up to the rear ranks of the 9th.

As he reined in, he took one last look at the assault. Most ladders were down, and those still standing had few climbers. Arrows and spears continued to rain down all across the wall, though not as constant or thick as before. Off to his right, the Emperor's Elites were approaching the gate, and as he predicted, were drawing fire from the archers.

With a growl, he leapt from the saddle and looked back to Hullis. "We're taking the wall," he shouted over the screams and clamour coming from nearby. "Clear us a path to a ladder."

Hullis swung his leg over and dismounted, his cloak snapping out and around his body. "Yes, sir.

"Open ranks," he bellowed as he rushed up on the backs of the forward-facing hoplites. "Commander Kaletor needs to get through! Make way, you dogs! Your commander comes to bring us victory!"

Confused looks from within golden helmets turned to meet them. No one moved.

Hullis ran and smashed bodily into two of the hoplites, knocking them flat. "Clear a path, I say, or I'll start using my spear!"

This time, Hullis's enraged demand resulted in action. Nearby hoplites squeezed against their neighbours, many hollering at those around them to move for their commander.

A narrow gap opened. Hullis bulled his way into it, and Kaletor followed on his heels.

They soon came upon a fallen Spartan. Hullis stooped to retrieve the man's shield and passed it back, saying, "Watch their arrows, sir."

Kaletor fed his left arm through the loop and took the grip at the edge firmly in hand. He brought the solid disc of wood and iron to just below his chin, then hollered, "Keep us moving."

With Hullis shouting and issuing threats, they pushed their way through the tightly-packed ranks of the Phalanx. Arrows were flying into their vicinity, so Kaletor kept his focus locked on the wall, muscles poised to react if one came their way.

Those near the front were slower to part ranks, but eventually, they reached the second row.

Spotting an upright ladder as he peaked over the rim of his shield, Kaletor shouted over the noise, "On me, Spartans! Your commander has arrived!"

An uproar of cheers erupted in answer as he ran to the ladder, jumping over arrow-studded hoplites as he went. He spied an arrow coming and ducked low. It skittered off the ground behind him.

He reached the base of the ladder, wedged his spear between his left forearm and the inside of his shield, and began to climb. Holding his shield overhead, he bolted up the rungs, spurred on by the threat of an arrow punching into his body. Knowing speed was his best chance, he kept his focus on the climb.

The muscles in his arms and legs were burning when he heard a yowl above him. He looked up and saw a stricken hoplite near the top clutching an arrow as he fell. Kaletor pressed himself against the ladder as the man plummeted, his tumbling body coming within inches of Kaletor's back.

He grit his teeth and resumed climbing, moving even faster than before. An arrow sang just beside his ear. He looked up to the rampart. A lone archer was leaning out, less than ten feet away and directly above, aiming his arrow straight down.

Kaletor braced and raised his shield high overhead. His right foot slipped from the rung as the arrow punched into his shield. His arms burned and he growled from the strain, swinging his wayward foot back onto the rung.

Keeping his shield where it was, he climbed quickly and gained the top.

In one fluid motion, he stepped onto the rampart and brought his shield to chest level. The archer was there, standing at the wall's inner edge, another arrow nocked.

He drew back his bowstring and fired—

THIRTY-TWO

Some were taller than trees, even when standing horizontally. Their wings stretched out wide, flying higher than any bird ever could. They passed through soaring clouds. They breathed unquenchable fire. They were an unstoppable force, according to the legends of old.

The Spoken Tales

Jarka awoke with one side of his whiskers pressed against the floor. Vaseus slept a few feet away, buried beneath her heap of furs. Her face was a picture of tranquil beauty as she slept.

Looking at her brought the memory of their intimate conversation flooding into his mind. He rubbed his eyes and resolved to put it aside.

Though he was loath to leave the warmth of the furs, he stretched and rolled up to his feet. The early morning air was frigid. His breath plumed heavy from his mouth as he rubbed his hands through the fur of his arms.

The stone hearth was a dark pit of cold ash. He moved to reignite it.

"I wouldn't bother."

He stopped and looked over. Relyk was sitting cross-legged on the floor by the door, a white bear fur drawn about his shoulders.

"Why wouldn't I light the fire?" Jarka said, his voice quiet so as not to wake Vaseus or Imzen. "It's cold in here."

"They'll be here soon."

"Now how could you know that?"

"I've remembered something. Something that was gnawing at me all night."

Jarka frowned and crossed his arms over his chest. "What are you talking about?"

"Their Warlord's name is Tavyka."

"Yes. And?"

"She has another title besides Warlord; The Undefeated One."

A chill snaked its way through Jarka's torso. He managed to force out a scoffing sound, though it was limp as a wet branch. "Please. Where did you hear that?"

"I was here when I was young. Even then, Tavyka was known throughout the North Lands for her exceptional skill. Some say that she's the greatest warrior of our time."

The chill seemed to sink deeper, penetrating down into his bones.

"Why would you tell me that?" he snapped.

Relyk's gaze hardened. "Sorry for trying to help. I thought you should know what you're up against."

Jarka opened his mouth to argue, but then stopped himself. He heard Vaseus stirring behind him, and in that instant, a thought sliced through his mind.

I might lose. If I do, she'll be in danger.

He glanced back over his shoulder. She had sat up and was looking directly at him. Imzen too was awake and watching them.

"If I lose," he said, stepping close to Relyk and dropping his voice, "I want you to get Vaseus out of here."

Relyk's small dark eyes narrowed. "Why?"

"It won't be safe. You saw what these yagars think of her."

"No, I know that she won't be safe. What I don't know is why you care so much about her well-being."

He realized his mistake too late. Still, this was no time to worry about Relyk's opinions. "Just get her out of here if I lose."

An exploding bang at the door shattered the still quiet in their little hut.

Still looking directly into Relyk's eyes, Jarka said, "I want your word."

Though obviously reluctant, his friend finally gave a subtle nod. "Fine. Just make sure you win."

More banging on the door, louder than before.

Jarka patted Relyk's shoulder as he moved by, grabbed the handle, and pulled the door open. A rush of icy air and swirling snow swept in, followed closely by Jynx. She, like the eight Superiors just behind her, was cloaked once more in a snowy animal fur.

"Time to go, Clanless," she growled, getting in his face.

Jarka held his ground. "And good morning to you, my friend. Please. Lead the way."

The Superior glared at him before spinning away and stepping back outside.

He glanced back to Relyk, then to Imzen and Vaseus, giving them all what he hoped was a reassuring smile. Then he turned to join their escort.

The biting wind blasted through his fur to sink icy fangs in his bones as they were led through the village. Thick snowflakes pelted them, obscuring all but the nearest shapes and structures. Everything was covered in a deep, unbroken blanket of white. He sniffed the air, but it was devoid of any smell. There was only the harsh cold.

Within minutes of leaving the hut, his pluming breath had become laboured. Every step was an effort as they trudged through knee-deep drifts.

His fingers and toes were numb when the Challenge Ring finally appeared through the whiteout. His step hitched at the sight.

It was unlike any Challenge Ring he'd ever seen. The seating was built into the sloping shoulder of the mountain, rising high in a semicircle around the ring below. Fronting this rose two walls of wood at least twenty feet high, marching diagonally away from the foot of the mountain in a v shape. They came together so close that only one yagar at a time could pass between them.

One by one, they all proceeded through this narrow gap. As soon as they entered, the wind slackened off considerably, revealing the purpose of the huge walls. The snow came down more gently, and Jarka could relax his narrowed eyes.

As soon as he did, he saw the number of yagars sitting on the mountain side. Hundreds, maybe even thousands of them. Most were wearing snowy white animal furs, the yellow and black of their own fur closer to white and grey.

Even through the snowfall, Jarka knew that every one of them was watching their approach. There were a few conversations here and there, but he couldn't hear what was being said.

"There's so many," Vaseus breathed.

He glanced over, noting the concern colouring her rosy face. "Yes."

"What does it mean?"

Keeping his expression neutral, despite her admirable vulnerability, he looked back to the waiting crowd. "It means that our army will be even larger than we thought."

The Superiors fanned out to take their seats on the two benches that bordered the Challenge Ring. Relyk, Imzen, and Vaseus followed and stood beside one of the benches.

Jarka moved into the ring, which had been recently cleared so that only a light dusting of snow covered the frozen dirt. The nearby crowd rising above him went silent and still, though it was a quietness infused with black hate and barely contained tension.

He looked up at them briefly, then turned so that they were on his left. He felt their pent-up rage, allowed it to flow through him, then let it back out.

Breathing deep, he brought his attention into his body. He rolled his shoulders, shook out his arms, and shifted his weight from one leg to the other.

Gradually, he felt his muscles loosen and relax.

This I know. This I can handle.

Tavyka emerged from amongst the Superiors and moved into the ring. The white bear fur she had worn at their first meeting was gone. Her own fur was a pale yellow, almost white. Her few, small spots were grey. A string of small black gems was fastened close around her throat, and below that hung a necklace of seven talons. Her face was set, silver-blue eyes hard as stone.

Seeing this brought a slight smile to Jarka's lips.

"Is it true," he called out loud enough for others to hear, "that you're known as The Undefeated One? Have you really never been defeated?"

The Warlord remained as silent as the onlooking crowd, taking the spear that an approaching youth was offering.

Without seeing who brought his or if they were there, Jarka extended his arm out to the side. The shaft of a spear was placed in his hand. He tossed the weapon into his other hand, spun it around his wrist, and caught it again.

"I wonder," he said, his gaze still locked on Tavyka, "if that scares you."

The Warlord remained mute, standing tall, the butt end of her spear resting on the ground. The snow continued to fall around her. The gentle wind pushed through her fur.

He brought his spear up and settled into a crouch. While one of the Superiors said the ceremonial words, Tavyka did the same.

In a frozen moment, they waited, poised and taut.

Then the word came.

"Begin."

Jarka exploded forward to meet her in the middle. As they met, he lanced his spear straight for her chest. The Warlord slid by, redirecting his thrust up and away with apparent ease. She then stuck a foot in the ground and whipped her spear around at his trailing shoulder. He ducked under and swept out a low kick. She stepped over, but he adjusted higher and clipped her feet.

Jarka quickly straightened and plunged his spear down at her throat. But somehow, impossibly, Tavyka rolled away in the instant that her back hit the ground. Using a knee levered on the ground, she sprang back up like a coiled branch being released.

Utter disbelief at the incredible speed of the Warlord killed Jarka's momentum.

Tavyka rushed in close with a rising thrust. He backpedalled as he swung his spear over to intercept. He sought to counter, but the next attack followed too quickly. He parried again, then again and again as Tavyka unleashed a furious flurry of blows. Their spears cracked together three times a second, a whirling dance of power and speed.

Forced onto the defensive, he gave ground and kept his arms in close. He blocked and deflected, alert for a chance to counter. Tavyka's attacks were strong and quick, a relentless barrage that was well balanced. Her style was complex and varied, always flowing from power to speed, high to low, sweeps to jabs.

Finally finding an opening, he jabbed high. She avoided it by bobbing her head to one side. Her counter was a quick jab at his thigh. He knocked this aside with the bottom half of his spear. He transitioned straight into a rising strike. Just before it struck her shoulder, she spun away, coming around with a sweeping attack. He blocked it dead. She stepped in and lashed out a punch. He ducked under and swung the butt end of his spear at her belly. She bounded clear.

A gap opened up, but barely. She closed it quick and swung horizontal at his chest. He blocked, then jabbed at her throat. She deflected it high and wide. Her counter came for his shoulder. He dipped low and went for her hip. She tucked her spear in vertical to block, then swung down at his head. He deflected this wide, but the power of it slowed him. She flowed into a rising sweep. He leaned back to avoid, but not far enough. The tip of the stone leaf head sliced across his chin.

He snarled from the burning sting and backpedalled. She kept coming, forcing him towards the edge of the ring. When she came close enough, he drove his spear straight out for her chest. She batted this away and attacked hard, forcing him to defend, forcing him back. He could feel his arms tiring as he held on, his bones jarring with every direct block.

He felt the ring's edge underfoot and stopped giving ground. Her spear came diagonal for his left shoulder. He batted it wide. She transitioned smoothly into a quick jab at waist height. He brought his spear down to knock the attack wide of his hip.

Again she swung, again and again. He met each strike in turn, his torso twisting and arms moving in a continuous flow. Each reaction was instinctive, guided by his body and nothing else.

The Warlord bared her teeth in a snarl as another flurry failed to get through. Instead of continuing her barrage, she reared back and kicked out a foot. Jarka twisted to one side, narrowly dodging the kick. In that same movement, he swung an arm high and pivoted towards the ring's center, his forearm striking Tavyka square in the face. Feet planted firm, he whipped his spear around wide and fast. She rolled beneath.

Now on the inside, he attacked with all he had. High jab at the throat, sweep down at the right hip, reverse sweep at the left shoulder. She parried each. He transitioned quickly to a two-handed overhead strike. She blocked with her spear horizontal in both hands. He stiffened his lower arm and sent it forward and up. The rising butt end of his spear uppercut into her chin. The connection forced her head to snap back. He leapt in, bent his knees, and kicked both feet hard into her chest.

They both went to the ground in an explosion of snow. Slowly, the cloud of white drifted off. As it cleared, he saw that Tavyka was outside the ring.

He allowed his head to settle back onto the snow. He noticed then how hard his heart was hammering into his chest. He felt a searing fire that was burning through his arms, shoulders, torso, and legs. He felt the sting of the gash on his chin.

He relaxed completely, watching his deep exhales pluming thick toward the grey sky. All was quiet and still as the softly descending snow.

Before too long, he heard the subtle crunch of footfalls. He remained motionless as Tavyka stepped to his side.

When their eyes met, the Warlord said between heavy breaths, "What you just did was impossible. I had you. I *knew* I had you. There was no way you could get out of that. There was nowhere you could go."

He gave her an easy smile. "Yes."

She shook her head. "I can't believe it. I've never lost. Tell me how you did that."

A brief silence hung between them, a frozen drop of perfect connection.

Eventually, slowly, Jarka tilted his head to one side, looked her dead in the eye, and said, "I have no idea, my friend. That's what made it so beautiful."

THIRTY-THREE

It was there, at the Battle of Damascus, that
the rebels made their last stand. After weeks
of stubborn resistance, the frustrated Spartans
showed no mercy, cutting them all down beneath a blood-red dawn.

Androdamos of Boeotia

The assault on Athens continued, yet all of Kaletor's attention was
focused on the archer and the arrow speeding toward him. He ducked
behind his shield, felt the arrow plunge into it, and rushed ahead. It
took four steps to close the gap.

The archer turned to run, but too late. On the final step, Kaletor reared back
and kicked him in the side. The force of it sent the man off the edge, and he
fell screaming to the street below.

Kaletor glanced left then right. A single row of archers lined the top of the
wall in both directions, every one of them firing arrows at the hoplites below.

Knowing the gate was to his right, he turned that way—

"Commander, behind you!"

Kaletor pivoted hard around to face the other way. An arrow slammed into
his shield where the middle of his back had just been. The next moment, he
watched Hullis step off the ladder and take the archer down with his spear.

"Cover me," Kaletor barked. "I'll carve a path to the gate."

Seeing Hullis nod and turn to face the other way, Kaletor wheeled back
around to advance.

The oblivious man nearest to him fired an arrow over the wall. As he reached for another, Kaletor lanced his spear out. The Athenian crumpled to the stone walkway.

His neighbour looked over at the sound, wide-eyed. He turned to flee.

Kaletor rushed after him and thrust his spear out again. The leaf head hit home, and the man dropped.

The next one down the line was waiting, and he fired an arrow the moment his fellow archer fell. Kaletor stepped forward and to one side, narrowly avoiding the missile while moving into striking range. He drove his spear straight into the Athenian's chest.

Kaletor released a rising bellow, the rush of battle firing sparks through his body. He advanced, striking again and again. One Athenian fell after another, their death cries filling the air. Arrows flew but did not find their mark. With spear and shield, he blocked and struck, an unstoppable force, cutting down every man in his path.

In the corner of his eye, he spied a Spartan clamber from a ladder and gain the top of the wall. He continued past the man, intent on his next target.

At this point, the call had gone down the line that the rampart was being overrun, and so the defenders had redeployed. Pairs of archers had peeled back from the outer edge to block his progress.

Kaletor sprinted forward, taking two more arrows on his shield. As he closed the gap, the pair of archers backpedalled, frantically nocking another arrow.

But Kaletor was already on them. He plunged his spear into the gut of one and bashed his shield into the face of the other. The blow was so powerful it knocked the Athenian from the wall, and he fell to the street below.

Pulling his spear free, he continued without slowing. Two hoplites had gone past him, forcing more of the archers back. He rushed into the midst of the melee, weaving through the combatants. Ahead was the gatehouse, its pair of towers rising high.

Seeing it sent a surge of energy into his legs. He ran on hard, eager to descend to its bottom and open the gates.

But as he cleared the melee, a gap opened up. Twenty feet away, bunched in front of the tower's side entrance, were fifteen or more archers, all with arrows nocked and bowstrings drawn.

Someone shouted, "Loose!"

Kaletor dropped to a knee and squeezed behind his shield, but there were too many. He braced for the fiery bloom of pain—

Two hoplites suddenly arrived at his sides and overlapped their shields with his. The volley of arrows pattered off the iron like rain on rock. Three more hoplites rushed up from behind and set their shields over the top lip of Kaletor's and his neighbours' shields. Another volley of arrows slammed harmlessly into the iron wall.

"We're with you, Commander," one of the hoplites boomed.

Kaletor released a heavy exhale. "We advance together. Break formation and attack on my signal."

"Yes, sir," the men answered in unison.

Staying within their shield wall, they moved forward at a measured walk. Another volley of arrows hit, clattering off their iron discs. Then another, and another.

Following the last one, Kaletor peaked through a tiny gap between the rims of his and two other shields. The archers were in the midst of nocking arrows to their bows.

"*Now.*"

With his bellow, the shield wall broke apart and they all charged. Seeing this caused the archers to turn and run, but in their panic, they choked the small entranceway. Kaletor and his fellow Spartans cut them down from behind. Only four managed to flee into the tower.

Kaletor was in the lead, and at his back, the hoplites started chanting, "Kal-etor! Kal-etor! Kal-etor!"

Glancing back over a shoulder and raising his spear overhead, he hollered, "On me! To the gate!"

While the men cheered, he led the way through the side entranceway and into the tower that comprised one half of the gatehouse. Only bundles of arrows lay within. The surviving Athenians fled into a small room on the far side of the tower.

Dismissing them, he went to the stairs that descended along the wall and rushed down. Clattering armour rang off the stone walls as his men followed.

The chant from the ramparts came in with them. "Kal-etor! Kal-etor! Kal-etor!"

He bared his teeth in a ferocious grin, chest filled with gusting breath and mind permeated by certain invulnerability.

Taking the stairs three at a time, he reached ground level and exploded through the door like a catapulted rock. There was a group of Athenians to his right, all of them facing the gate. Kaletor roared as he attacked. His spear was a blur as he drove it into the back of an unsuspecting traitor. The rest wheeled around, shouting out their alarm as they rushed forward to engage.

He roared again as he met them. He angled his torso so a jabbing spear skittered off his shield, then swung his spear sidelong. The shaft dented the man's helm. Another attack followed, high and quick. He ducked low and bulled into the Athenian's midsection, driving his spear into the man's chest. He pulled it back quick and rammed it into the next one's gut.

A sprinting Athenian arrived at that instant, swinging his sword at Kaletor's extended arm. In one fluid motion, he let go of his spear, spun aside, drew his sword, and swung the blade around. The iron edge cut across the man's shoulder.

It all happened in a flash. As the Athenian clutched at the wound and fell to the ground, Kaletor saw that his men had arrived and were finishing off the remainder.

Pointing with his sword to the massive gate of heavy wood, he called out, "Take those beams down."

While his men hurried to do as he commanded, he retrieved his spear and went to the wheel that worked the system of ropes and pulleys. At least twenty hoplites lifted and carried all three thick beams of wood away. Kaletor then turned the wheel. The ropes snapped into action, spinning round the pulleys, slowly dragging the huge doors open.

Before long, a great cheer came in from the other side. Kaletor grinned wide as the gold-cloaked Elites poured in through the gap.

Another cheer followed, this one from the men who had come over the walls. Within the raucous chorus returned the chant, and as it rose, more and more added their voices.

"*Kal-etor. Kal-etor. Kal-etor. Kal-etor. Kal-etor. Kal-etor.*"

Now that the gate was flung wide open, Kaletor stepped away from the wheel and raised his sword high. "The city is ours!"

Another roar answered as the men raised their spears in salute.

"Go now, sons of Sparta," he continued, "and make the Athenians pay. Burn their homes. Rape their women. Kill them all!"

A savage bellow erupted in answer as the gold-cloaks ran past.

Kaletor felt energy surge through him as he turned, added his voice to the earsplitting roar, and charged into the city.

THIRTY-FOUR

The Warrior Code is a wise, near-perfect system that encourages order and peaceful harmony within each Clan. But nothing can be absolutely perfect in this world. Now and then, yagars slip through the cracks and fall into darkness. Chalrog was one such yagar.

The Spoken Tales

"We're dangerously low on supplies."

Not wanting to turn away yet, Jarka kept his ears rotated forward as he stared at the mouth of the cave. Night had fallen, and a storm raged on outside their humble shelter. The driving snow obscured everything. The wind whipped and whistled, and though he thought he had heard something, it was impossible to know for sure.

"Jarka."

He strained his ears a moment longer, but it was no use. He sniffed deep, but could only smell the frostbitten air, the rock of the cave, and the smoke of the fire. Finally, he relented and turned back to his companions.

"I guess we didn't get enough from the Northern Mountain Clan," he said, moving to rejoin them at the rear of the cave.

All three were huddled around the small fire, their faces illuminated by the flickering, orange light. Each sat on the bare rock, as the cave was empty of anything but a few bones.

Relyk, who had spoken before, said, "It's because we didn't count on spending an entire day in here."

"This cursed storm," Vaseus said, linking her hands to hug her legs. "Why won't it end?"

Imzen, who was sitting cross-legged with her eyes closed, softly said, "Resisting the storm is futile. It is as it is, and there is nothing you can do to change it. If you don't want to suffer, you must accept—"

"Gods, not now," Vaseus growled. "It doesn't help anyone."

"I think what she's trying to say," Jarka replied before Relyk could, "is that we can't stay here much longer."

"If we go out in that, one of us could get lost," Relyk said, his frown furrowing the fur of his brow. "Or one of us could die."

As he finished, he looked straight at Vaseus.

Her eyebrows drove down, and her eyes darkened. "You think some wind and snow can kill me? I've survived more than you can imagine."

"You're just a human. Look at all the furs you need to stay warm. You wouldn't last an hour out there."

"You don't know what you're talking about. You're an arrogant yagar who can't see beyond his own shortsighted opinions—"

"Okay," Jarka cut in, raising his hands towards them both, "this isn't getting us anywhere. Let's focus on what matters. The Home Village of the Frost Ocean Clan is less than a day away. That means—"

The sound of crunching snow cut him short. He looked to the mouth of the cave as the last of five wolves emerged from the storm.

They all looked at him. In an instant, their white fur bristled, their lips peeled back, their ears flattened, and growls rumbled in their throats.

"Spear!" Jarka shouted.

At the sound of his voice, the wolves sprang forward, chomping and barking as they charged.

Jarka caught the spear Relyk threw him on the run. The lead wolf lunged, coming at him like a speeding arrow. It was there so fast, he had to thrust out the spear the moment he caught it. The stone leaf head struck home, and the wolf went down.

Before he could do anything else, the next wolf was lunging for his throat. He brought his free arm up to block. The wolf's teeth dug into his forearm. He bellowed as the ripping pain tore into him.

He let go of his spear, balled his hand into a fist, and punched the wolf's nose. It yelped and released him, backpedalling away and shaking its head.

The other three had run past, and Jarka turned to see. Relyk met one with spear in hand, lancing it in the chest. Imzen met the final two unarmed, positioned right in front of Vaseus. The pair of wolves lunged at the same time. Imzen lashed out with a fist, knocking one away. But the other sank its teeth into her side. She cried out, her eyes squeezed shut and face contorted in agony.

Jarka had started to run over, and arrived as she sank to her knees. He thrust his spear into the wolf's side. It released her and fell dead.

He pulled his spear back and turned, but the two surviving wolves retreated to the mouth of the cave and disappeared into the snow.

With the threat gone, he smelled the iron tang of blood. He looked down to Imzen, who had collapsed onto her side. The fur where the bite was, right along her ribcage, was already soaked red.

"Imzen," he breathed, going down to his knees to press both hands to the wound. He immediately felt warm blood flowing out.

He looked over to her face. Her eyes were steady on his, and the strain in them revealed how much pain she was in.

"It's alright," he said, holding her gaze. "You're alright. Just hold on, Imzen."

She gave a slight nod and closed her eyes.

Relyk arrived then, kneeling at her head to ease it onto his lap. Vaseus was there next, kneeling across from Jarka.

"Here," she said, reaching out with a torn piece of cloth. "Press this to the wound."

He took it from her and did as she said, putting pressure on where it seemed worst. Moving fast, Vaseus picked up one of her furs and tore off a thin strip. She tore off two more, then set to tying all three together.

"Lift her up a bit," she said as she finished. "I'm going to pass this under to you."

Again, he did as she said, though his chest was tight and his fingers didn't work at first. Once he had her up, Vaseus slid the strip of fur under.

"Here," she said, handing him the opposite end as he let the Elder back down. "Tie them together when I say. I need to make sure it's in the right place to slow the bleeding."

He nodded and brought the two ends close together at Imzen's chest. He watched Vaseus lean in to remove the bloodied cloth, and with eyes wide, carefully replace it with a fresh piece.

"Tie it now, and tight."

Jarka swallowed and again did as she said, taking care not to snap the makeshift rope apart.

He let out a harsh breath and looked to Relyk. "How's she doing?"

"Not good," he said, his eyes filled with worry or fear. "She already feels cold."

"She's lost a lot of blood," Vaseus said. "And what we have with us isn't enough to treat the wound. We can't stay here any longer. She won't make it."

Jarka growled as stabbing pain suddenly lanced through his left forearm. He brought it up to look. Blood had soaked his fur, and he remembered the wolf's bite.

"What is it?" Vaseus asked, concern coming into her eyes.

"It's not as bad as Imzen," he said, doing his best to conceal a grimace. "Are you sure we can't do anymore for her?"

"I'm sure. She needs stitches and a warm bed, at the very least."

"Then we must go."

"How?" Relyk said. "There's no way she can walk. And the storm still hasn't passed."

"We'll carry her," Jarka said, rising to his feet. "Leave everything behind that we don't absolutely need."

"And the storm?" Vaseus said. "Won't we get separated?"

"We go through it. We have no other choice. I won't sit here and let her die. Will either of you?"

They both shook their heads.

"Let's get her up."

With the help of Relyk, Jarka managed to drape Imzen over his shoulders. Fortunately she was on the smaller side, though the strain of lifting her still sent prickles of fire lancing through the gash in his arm. He couldn't keep a growl from escaping past his lips.

"You lead, Relyk," he said, walking towards the mouth of the cave. "Vaseus second. I'll follow."

Relyk moved in front with a spear in hand. "We won't be able to see anything. Once we get out there, I might not know which way it is to Home Village."

"It shouldn't be dark for too much longer. When day breaks, we'll see light and know which way is which."

He gave a nod. "Good enough for me."

Jarka looked to Vaseus. "You ready?"

She looked back as she wrapped one of the furs around her shoulders. "Let's go."

They reached the mouth of the cave. Without another word, Relyk went first, followed closely by Vaseus. Jarka went out after her.

The biting wind sliced through his fur and stole the warmth from his body the moment he stepped outside. Sharp daggers of ice stabbed into his bloody arm. He snarled, narrowed his eyes against the slanting snow, and followed Vaseus into the storm.

Soon the cold had completely consumed him. It sliced deep into his bones, jagged and sharp. Breathing was painful. It felt like his lungs were on fire or freezing up, he couldn't tell which. Making it worse was Imzen's dead weight. Her body felt heavier than it should have. She dragged on him, making it tougher to get through the snow.

He trudged on, willing his freezing body to keep moving, staying close behind Vaseus. She was all he could see, the snow was so blinding. The darkness of the night around them felt oppressive. It felt like they would never see the sun again.

Time ceased to exist. There was only the next step, the blasting wind, the snow and the cold.

At some point, his body started to crumble. Though his wound had become numb and painless, the weight of Imzen dragging on his shoulders was too much. His back ached and his legs burned. He let his head down to relieve the ache in his neck.

A couple of steps beside him, he spotted something protruding from the snow. He slowed and peered down through the snow slanting into his eyes. It appeared to be a skull, a huge skull with wide, flat pieces at the back.

He looked up and knew his mistake. His stomach clenched at the sight of no one in front of him.

"Vaseus!" he yelled into the wind, knowing immediately that she wouldn't hear him. "Relyk! Oi! Here!"

He rotated his ears forward, but there was only the howling wind. He looked down to find their footprints, but the blowing snow obscured everything.

"No," he breathed, the crushing weight of Imzen dragging at him.

He took a step forward, then another. Her weight was unbearable, forcing him down. He growled and took another step. The deep snow clawed at his legs. He snarled as he bent low, taking another gruelling step. His back screamed and his legs shook.

For Jazith.

With the thought sounding in his mind, he managed to hold on for a moment longer.

But his body couldn't take it anymore, and he collapsed to his knees. He tightened his arms and shoulders to hold Imzen close as he fell forward.

It was a gentle impact into the snow. His breath gusted harsh, and he could feel his pulse throbbing in his ears. He knew he had to get up soon, but it felt good to rest for a moment. The wind was weaker down on the ground, and the cold wasn't quite so sharp. His body ached, and being free of Imzen's weight was an incredible relief.

He nestled his cheek into the snow and relaxed, releasing one breath after another, feeling his heart slow and the ache slip away. His eyes grew heavy, and before long, he let them close.

Sleep descended on him, and though he knew he shouldn't, he allowed it to come.

Just at that moment, a voice sounded from somewhere. He couldn't tell what was said. Then it sounded again, closer this time. Then again, closer.

At last, he knew who it was.

"Jarka!" Vaseus was shouting. "Wake up!"

The wind and the cold returned as he opened his eyes. Vaseus was huddled over him, her face close to his. She brought a gloved hand up to tap his face.

"Okay," he growled. "I'm okay."

"You have to get up," she said into his ear. "We can't stop."

He shook his head, shut his eyes tight, then opened them wide. Splaying out his hands, he pushed himself up to his knees. After a few breaths, he looked up.

Relyk was standing with Imzen draped over his shoulders. Vaseus was crouched beside him. Both were covered in ice and snow.

"You alright?" Relyk shouted over the wind.

Jarka nodded. "Yeah. Let's go."

He pushed out a gusting breath and managed to get back to his feet.

"Do you want to lead?" Vaseus asked once she stood.

"No, I'm okay," he replied, then looked to Relyk. "Whoever is carrying Imzen should lead. I'll go last until we switch."

He nodded, and though Vaseus seemed about to argue, she did the same.

The wind and snow continued to batter them as they trudged on. Every step sapped away a bit more strength, and the inescapable cold pierced deeper than ever.

Before long, Jarka took Imzen back. He managed about thirty steps before he was near to collapse, so he stopped and allowed Relyk to take over again. More than once, they each staggered and fell, needing help to get up. Though they shared the burden that Imzen had become, it seemed like they weren't making any progress.

Jarka didn't know how long they had been out in the storm. He had never been so cold in all his life. His every muscle ached, and he was completely exhausted.

Will this never end? he thought as the weight of Imzen forced him to walk bent over. *We might not even be going the right way. We could die out here, and Jazith would never see home again.*

Staring down at the snow, he willed his legs to keep working, one step after another. The ache and pain consuming his body begged him to stop, demanding relief and warmth. He doubted he could go on much longer.

"Look!" Vaseus cried from close behind him. "Up ahead!"

He stopped and managed to bring his head up enough to see. He hadn't noticed, but the snowfall had eased, revealing a flat, open tundra of white stretching before them. In the distance, on the horizon, he could see tiny points of orange light.

He let himself collapse to his knees. As he looked to the distant torches, he released one laboured breath after another.

"We're almost there, Imzen," he eventually said, gently patting the back of her head. "We're almost there."

THIRTY-FIVE

The Third Persian War was the greatest of
them all. After twenty-seven years, the Persian
Empire was destroyed, and Sparta ruled over
its lands. It was then that the Spartan Empire
was born.

Androdamos of Boeotia

*T*his isn't you. You've lost your way. You promised you would do good. You wanted
to protect people. Who do you protect now?

Kaletor snarled inwardly at the voice of Vaseus to push her from
his mind. She had become faint and hollow during the previous days, and thus
easier to ignore, if not banish altogether. This time he managed to cast her out
quickly.

He set his hands to the balcony's stone railing and looked upon the city of
Athens. All was quiet beneath the early morning sun, yet the previous night's
assault clung to the streets like a weeping wound. Here and there, black
columns of smoke spiraled skyward. Bodies were strewn about haphazardly
along every street. Red pools of blood stained the grey stone and white marble.
The stench of burnt flesh clotted the air.

As Kaletor took in the scene of death, he grinned. "This is what comes to
those who defy me," he said, addressing the voice of Vaseus in his mind. "And
this *is* good. This is what they deserved."

Somewhere behind him, footsteps slapped off the villa's marble floors. He
let the grin fade as he turned around to watch Hullis, Belisar, and Talos
approach.

Noting the blood splattered on Hullis's breastplate, arms, and face, and the absence of such a mess on Belisar, he said, "Report."

"All resistance has been neutralized, Commander," Hullis declared. "The city is ours."

"Shall we call off the attack?" Belisar asked.

"No need. The men will decide when enough is enough. How many have surrendered?"

Hullis replied, "Some, but they are not yet counted."

"No matter," Kaletor said. "Kill them all except for a few women and children. I want this city an empty husk of its former glory."

Inclining his head slightly, Hullis said, "As you wish, sir."

Looking to his slave, Kaletor asked, "Did you find any yet?"

"Not much, Master," Talos said. "Just a few sacks of wine."

"That'll have to do. Bring it up."

As the leathery Athenian bowed and left, Kaletor ran his fingers through his hair. "Any idea how many casualties?"

"Nothing solid yet," Hullis answered, "but it's substantial. I'd say we lost almost a quarter from both the 16th and 9th."

"As I thought. We'll need reinforcements." He looked to Belisar. "Find Ackadus and deliver my orders. He is to return to Sparta and tell the emperor to send us the 7th Phalanx from Corinth and the 4th from Kydonia."

The famous general's wizened face scrunched up in confusion. "Reinforcements? But why? Athens is taken. We have accomplished what we were sent here to do—"

"And yet the war is not yet won," Kaletor snapped. "There are more rebels to kill, many more, and I intend on killing them all. I can't do that without more men."

The concern remained in Belisar's brown eyes. "Forgive me, Commander, but isn't how we proceed up to the emperor?"

"There isn't time for consultation. Ockos understands this. He has given me free rein to conduct the war as I see fit."

"Oh? He didn't tell me."

"He didn't tell you," Kaletor snarled, "because he expected you to follow the orders of your superior, just like every other Spartan. Is this not the case?"

Belisar stiffened, and for the briefest of moments, it appeared like he was finally going to voice his defiance.

But with the muscles beneath his silver-streaked beard bunched, the proud old veteran visibly swallowed his words. "Of course not, sir. I will do as you command."

"Good. Now go."

Staring straight ahead, Belisar saluted, turned, and walked across the balcony.

Kaletor watched him leave. "Can he be trusted?"

"Belisar has been loyal all his life," Hullis replied. "For a brief moment, he was the most famous Spartan alive. The Empire is his reason for breathing."

Kaletor crossed his arms as his most senior general disappeared into the villa. "It's not his commitment to Sparta that I doubt. It's his loyalty to me."

There was a pause before Hullis spoke again. "Does this mean you no longer answer to the emperor?"

It was a dangerous question. Kaletor looked back to his childhood friend, trying to gauge what he was thinking. "Would that be a problem?"

Hullis's expression remained neutral. "If you had asked me that two days ago, I would have said yes. But your deeds at the wall have spread through the ranks like wildfire. I've heard the men speak your name with awe and pride in their voices. They are comparing you with Leonidas himself. Some are calling you the Taker of Athens. Others have named you the Lion of Sparta. There's nothing Spartans love more than a victorious leader who brings them glory, honour, and wealth. Give them more of that, and they will follow you anywhere."

A grin split Kaletor's mouth as he nodded. "Yes. Soon our enemies will fear me more than ever before. Now, with all the Empire's resources at my disposal, nothing will stand in my way."

A flicker of something crossed Hullis's pale face.

When he remained silent, Kaletor said, "Speak."

The general shifted his weight from one foot to the other. "Are you sure about this? It's just . . . it seems like you're challenging the emperor's authority. What happens if he sees you as a threat to his throne?"

"He won't. I spoke with him before we left Sparta and we reached an understanding. As long as I bring the Empire victory in this war, Ockos will provide whatever I ask for."

Kaletor knew the true version of that conversation could expose his deepest ambitions and thus be more difficult to accept. Making it seem like everything had been mutual would allow Hullis, and hopefully others, to go along with him.

Sure enough, it worked. The tightness melted from Hullis's face. "That's good to hear, sir. How, then, shall we proceed?"

Kaletor turned to face the fallen city to hide the triumph that was surging through him. "Instruct the men to scour the city for supplies. Food, weapons, wine, water, horses, gold, pack animals, slaves. Have them take anything and everything of use. If we cannot take it, destroy it. I want Athens stripped to the bone. I want the few we leave behind to suffer, to starve, to struggle to survive. I want every Greek to know the fate of those who stand against Sparta."

"Very well, Commander. Anything else?"

He slowly swept his gaze across the burning scene as he replied. "Yes. Tell them to feast and celebrate our glorious victory tonight, for tomorrow we march."

"Where are we going?"

"North. Send riders ahead of us into Makedonia, Thrace, and Dacia. I want to know if any more Greeks have turned against us."

"Yes, sir."

"Dismissed."

With the sound of Hullis's footsteps fading away, Kaletor turned back around to watch him go.

He grinned to himself. *Now I will become who I was meant to be.*

THIRTY-SIX

No one knows for sure why he did. His mother was a Superior for many years. His father too was a respected warrior, though he was a Superior only briefly. Chalrog had no siblings, so he received plenty of attention from his parents. From the outside, they appeared a typical family. They worked hard, fought hard, and followed the Warrior Code. They enjoyed life within the Clan, and all seemed well.

The Spoken Tales

The gales of the afternoon had slackened with the fall of dusk. Above the barren, frozen tundra was a clear sky coloured in shades of deep purple and soft orange.

Standing within the limits of the coastal Home Village of the Frost Ocean Clan, Jarka gazed upon this beauty. He breathed the frigid air in through his nose, then released a heavy plume, allowing his mind to ease. Four days removed from their trek through the snow storm, he hoped to relax and enjoy what the coming night promised.

Nothing to accomplish tonight. Remember Imzen's teachings. Worrying about the future is futile. Let go of all the troubles that reside only in your mind. Just be here now.

The crunch of crusty snow underfoot drew his attention to the left. Vaseus was approaching, wrapped head to toe in white and grey animal furs.

Well, he thought with a wry smile, *perhaps not all my troubles.*

"What's that for?" she said, pointing a gloved finger at his face.

He held her gaze for a moment before replying. "Oh, nothing. How is she now?"

"Better. These yagars have great knowledge of healing. She's been sitting up most of the day, and the wound is coming along well. She's going to be fine."

"That's good to hear. What would we do without her?"

"What would we do without you?"

He was about to give a witty answer, but stopped himself. The slant of her expression was sincere, and he sensed this wasn't a moment to cheapen.

"We all help each other," he eventually said. "We're in this together, after all."

She smiled. "And together we can help others. Your sister. My people. We can help them all."

"I sure hope so."

"How's your arm, by the way?" she asked, setting her hands to her hips.

He held up his left forearm, which was swathed in animal skin bandages. "It's still sore, but it's getting better. As you saw, it didn't slow me down too much yesterday."

"Speaking of that, we'd better get going. I don't want to make the new Warlord late."

He chuckled. "How thoughtful of you."

Side by each, they set off. It wasn't long before they stepped onto one of the few main streets and fell in with the moving crowd of locals. Like the other two Clans of the North Lands, most were taller and thicker than Jarka, and the yellow and black of their fur was white and grey.

Despite their physical differences, he recognized himself in them. Many were laughing and chatting, with most clustered in groups of thirty or more. Youngsters darted all through the crowds, playing their games with youthful exuberance. And, to his surprise, many of those nearby congratulated him on his success.

"I've never felt this welcome in any of the other Clans," Vaseus said quietly after yet another yagar, this time a stout older male, had passed on his kind words. "Why are they so friendly here?"

Jarka glanced over. "I'm not sure. You'd expect them to be the most bitter, being stuck out here on this frozen wasteland. But maybe it's that very thing, their isolation from the other Clans and the lack of strife and warfare in their lives, that has made them so open and joyful.

"Or," he went on, allowing his voice to be a little louder, "everyone's in good spirits because tonight's going to be so much fun."

"What exactly is happening tonight?" she asked, a strand of her golden hair falling across her face. "Will you tell me now?"

"It goes by many names, and different Clans celebrate at different times. Back home, it's called the Celebration of Life, and it's celebrated twice a year."

"Why though? What's the purpose?"

He laughed, a sound that melded with the chorus of nearby merriment. "Don't worry, honeybee. You'll see soon enough."

That gentle smile of hers played across her lips, a smile that made her beauty shine even brighter. "If you say so."

He glanced away, doing his best to ignore the flutter in his stomach.

The site where the festivities were to take place came into view. On the open plain stretching flat from the edge of the village blazed at least forty fires, the fierce glow of their flames painting the snow in orange and yellow hues. Low benches had been placed around many, and while these seats were occupied, hundreds more were on their feet, scattered all across the flat, open area. Smoking carcasses of wolf, bear, fish, bison, and caribou cooked on spits above some of the fires, their juices dripping to hiss in the heat. At the very heart of it all roared three huge fires, arranged in a tight triangle, each one piled high with black and white logs.

"So," Jarka said, pausing at the edge of the village, "what do you think?"

Vaseus looked on the scene, the deep purple of dusk flushing her face. When she turned her gaze to him, a radiant smile revealed nearly every tooth.

"I love it."

He smiled back. "Now, come with me."

They moved to join the throng, the commotion and bustle of laughter and voices buffeting them all the time. He led her towards the center, cries of congratulations following them as they proceeded through the crowd.

"Look," Vaseus said, pointing to one of the many clusters. "Is that Relyk?"

Jarka followed her finger. Sure enough, there he was, talking and laughing with these jovial northerners.

"It is. Shall we go talk—"

"What's that?"

He looked from Relyk to Vaseus, who was craning her neck and looking toward the center. "What's what?"

"That sound. Do you hear it?"

He rounded his ears forward to listen. "It's a song."

"A song? Yagars can sing?"

Seeing the bafflement on her face pulled a laugh up from his belly. "Of course we can sing. It's part of tonight."

Her eyes narrowed. "What do you mean?"

He took her hand in his. "Let me show you."

He led her on, heading towards the triangle of large fires. Before long, the song had spread its tendrils out to everyone.

He joined in.

To fight a Challenge
Is oh so good
It brings honour
And glory

We fight and fight
To win and win
And the strong
Then lead us on

To arms, my friends
With spear and bone
We keep our home
Safe and full

An eruption of whoops, cheers, laughs, and applause went up as the lively little tune finished.

Jarka continued leading Vaseus through the crowds, curving and weaving his way between each group. Another song soon began, this one jaunty and long.

With the multitudes all around adding their enthusiastic voices to the loud, joyous chorus, they stepped clear of the chaotic sprawl. There, in neatly ordered rows running behind, beside, and in front of the triangle of raging fires, at least thirty yagars moved and jived in a synchronized dance.

"Even way up here they know it," he laughed, a surge of energy flooding his body. Looking back to Vaseus, he said, "Come. We dance."

"Whoa, hold on," she said, digging her heels in to hold him back. "I don't know how."

"That doesn't matter, bee. It's not about doing it right. It's about the joy of dancing and moving and laughing together. You'll see."

Her eyes flitted to the dancers, then back to him. Slowly, a hesitant smile spread across her lips, and her resistance ebbed.

He pulled her after him, and together they rushed to the end of the nearest row. He released her hand, positioned himself between the young neighbouring female and Vaseus, and fell into step.

Shoulders rolled, arms up, step left once, twice, slide back, bring a leg up and out, foot back down, arms straight, and three small hop steps.

In this repeating sequence he danced, hundreds of voices singing all around them. At some point, he glanced over to Vaseus. Though she moved differently, she kept with the rhythm, her arms, legs, and body weaving a fluid flow that melded with the group. She met his eyes as they danced, and together they laughed.

The song went on and on, as did the dance. Eventually, the end came with a final flourish.

"Wow," she breathed as the cheers and applause faded. "That, uh . . . that was . . ."

He laughed through laboured breaths. "I know. There's nothing else like it."

She smiled broadly, releasing a heavy exhale as she smoothed back some loose strands of hair with both hands. "You move pretty well for having such a large frame."

"Oh, how kind of you to say. And so much for not knowing what to do. I had no idea you could move like that."

A sly grin curved the corners of her mouth, and she stepped in so that her face was close to his. "You ain't seen nothing yet."

A thrill seared across his chest as he laughed.

Another song started up, followed by another and another. They danced to them all, with more and more of the crowd joining in all the time. Everyone moved together, keeping to the rows as if they all shared one mind.

Through it all, Jarka and Vaseus weaved with each other, close, then distant, then close again. For him, time ceased to exist. He knew nothing but the energy flowing between them, a tranquil blend of song, movement, and the sizzling heat of dancing flames.

*   *   *

The festivities went on into the night. Good-natured sparring contests spontaneously sprang up everywhere, and everyone either found a partner or formed small circles around the combatants to watch.

When exhaustion and laughter ended these contests, the cooked meat came off the fires and the feast commenced, everyone sharing and passing the hot food around.

With bellies full, the crowd gradually coalesced into a massive circle around the fires to watch the night's Challenge. It was between two Superiors, Fourth and Sixth. They were evenly matched, and they fought well. It went on for some time with neither one able to gain an advantage.

When at last Fourth defeated Sixth with an incredible finishing combination, everyone broke into wild cheers and applause.

"Is there only one?" Vaseus asked, the latest of the many questions she had asked throughout the evening.

Jarka nodded, still watching as the two Superiors bowed to each other in mutual respect. "Always. And it's always between two Superiors to ensure an impressive display of fighting skill."

"What about the Warlord? Can you be challenged for this event?"

While the Superiors moved away from the raging fires at the center of the ring, Jarka looked over to her. "No. I must deliver the final words to conclude the celebration."

She nodded her understanding, eyes lingering on his before shifting away. "And what happens next?"

"The Grand Tale."

"The Grand Tale?"

"Someone is chosen to tell an epic tale, which can be a legend, a hero's quest, or a recounting of a story from one's own past."

"Really? How is the storyteller chosen?"

"Simple. Anyone can call out a name, and if others want that yagar to speak, they add their voice to the chant. Whoever's name is chanted loudest and longest becomes the storyteller."

"Is that so?" she said, tapping a finger to her chin. "Can anyone call out a name?"

"Anyone."

Upon hearing his answer, she grinned, straightened to her full height, and shouted, "Jar-ka! Jar-ka! Jar-ka!"

"Hey now," he growled, reaching over to clamp a hand over her mouth. "None of that . . ."

He trailed off as the chant of his name rose like a rushing torrent.

"What have you done?" he said, gently shaking her head in his hands before letting go.

She was laughing as she swayed and clapped her hands in front of her chest.

"It's not funny," he called over the booming chant, smiling despite his words.

She laughed on as the call for him reached a fever pitch.

Wiping at the tears in her eyes, she said, "I think they want you."

Still he lingered, resisting the call even though everyone's attention was on him. "You're going to pay for this."

She laughed some more and shoved him away. "Go already!"

Grinning so wide his fangs were completely exposed, he finally relented. The moment he moved out of the throng and into the open space, the chant morphed into raucous cheering and laughter. He raised his arms high and laughed along with them, walking steadily around the central fires.

"Thank you, my friends," he called out when the noise finally died down. "You're very kind. But I'm not sure I was such a wise choice. After all, my life has been quiet and conventional."

Hearty laughter from all around rolled in response.

Settling into a slow walk around the blazing flames, he went on. "I suppose I can tell you the tale of how I ended up here. It all started when my sister and I were attacked by humans, the ones known as Spartans . . ."

From there, he told them all about what had happened since that day. He told them of his desperate trip to the human village and his meeting with Vaseus. He told them how difficult it was for him to leave his home and undertake what had seemed a quest sure to fail. He described the many Warlords he had defeated, and how he had known that each Challenge could be his last. He told of the prejudice and hate they had encountered as Clanless, both subtle and obvious, throughout the Clans. He told them of the wolves' attack and their struggle through the storm. And, finally, he thanked them all for being so welcoming, and for saving Imzen's life.

As he spoke, he recognized just how harsh their journey had been. He recognized the incredible odds they had overcome. More than once he had to swallow to keep his emotions at bay.

To his surprise, as he finished and his voice stilled, total silence was all that remained. He stopped and swept his gaze across the motionless crowd.

Then, as if on a given signal, they all dropped to one knee and bowed their heads.

Jarka stood there, unable to hold it in any longer. Tears welled in his eyes and spilled down his cheeks.

*   *   *

The crowd quietly dispersed into the village, apparently content to forego the customary concluding words.

From amongst the flow of moving bodies, Vaseus emerged. Though it happened less often than it used to, Jarka found he could not read her expression.

As she arrived, she said, "That was the first time I considered everything we've been through together."

"Same. Not bad for a few outcasts and their human friend."

Her answering smile was soft, and for a moment, she watched the yagars returning silently to the village. "Their reaction was not what I expected. Was that normal?"

He huffed a low chuckle as he dragged a hand across his brow. "No. I've never seen that before."

"I thought you might say that."

The unreadable expression remained on her face as silence stretched between them. It wasn't long before heat spread through his chest.

He cleared his throat and said, "Well, that's it, bee. Time to head back to the hut."

"Not just yet," she said, her tone gentle. "I want to go to the shore first."

"The shore? Why?"

She tucked her chin towards her chest and turned her head slightly to one side. "So I can see what the ocean looks like beneath the stars."

"I don't know, bee," he said slowly. "I doubt the Elders would approve."

Her smile was playful. "No, I don't think they would."

He made a show of checking the area for disapproving eyes.

"Quick, before any of them see. Go, go!"

They shared a laugh and took off, leaving the dying fires behind as they rushed across the open tundra. By the silver light of the moon shimmering across the snow, they reached the point where the land met the sea. Sprawling islands of ice bobbed all across the surface, appearing like lumbering giants moving with great care.

For a while they stood there in silence, looking out on the vast emptiness of shimmering white and dark water. It felt like everything was enveloped in a kind of peaceful stillness.

"What's that?" she suddenly asked, pointing towards the floating ice sheets.

"Where?" he replied, uncrossing his arms and rotating his ears forward.

It wasn't long before he saw a distant flash of motion on the horizon. "You mean that great white beast?"

"Yes. What is it?"

He squinted as he studied the distant animal. "It's a bear, though I've never seen a white one before. I'm not sure what name these Clans of the North Lands have given it."

To that, she did not reply, and silence reigned once more.

He rubbed his hands together and blew on them, his stream of breath pluming thick before him. "I bet you've never seen anything quite like this before. I know I haven't. Do you find it beautiful? Or do you see a hostile, frozen wasteland—"

"Did you mean what I think you did?"

She had blurted it out, almost as if it were beyond her control.

He glanced over to see that she had turned to face him directly. "Did I mean what?"

"During your story," she said, her eyes intent, "you talked about being in unknown territory in many different ways. One was becoming familiar with a human. You said that you felt conflicted, and you looked right at me. Did you mean what I think you did?"

Did I say that?

The thought shot across his mind like a bolt of lightning.

I guess I must have.

"Oh," he said, thinking to sweep it aside as nothing to get excited about.

But something stopped him. It was something in her eyes, something that he'd never seen before. There, in those perfectly clear green eyes of hers, he saw a reflection of his own desires.

"Yes," he said, an unexplainable ease coming with the affirmation. "I haven't known what to do. All my life I've been told to hate and fear humans, so that's what I've always felt. That's all I had ever known. I didn't know what to do when I felt something else."

The smile that spread across her lips was serene. She stepped in close and placed her hands on his arms.

"So you do feel what I feel," she breathed. "Even though we shouldn't."

A relief unlike any he'd ever known spread warmth through his very core.

Gazing deep into her eyes, he brought a hand up to her cheek. "I've fought this for so long, tried to convince myself it was impossible, that we could never be. But this feels right. I don't know why, but somehow, this feels right."

"I know," she said softly, now pressing her body to his. "I've been telling myself the same things. Everyone would condemn us, humans and yagars, which would destroy everything we've come so far to achieve."

He felt the heat of her body flowing into him, and he ran his fingers up into her hair. "Yes. But we can keep it a secret. No one has to know—"

The crunch of snow reached his ears. He looked towards the village as he stepped away from her.

A lone figure was approaching at the run. Whoever it was was small, wearing heavy furs, and unarmed.

He glanced back to her, and they shared a look of fierce disappointment.

"Dacio," she cried out as the runner arrived. "By the gods, what are you doing here?"

The man they had last seen several weeks ago stopped before them. His chest was heaving, and tiny icicles clung to his thick beard.

"Vaseus," he rasped through laboured breath, "I bring word from the war. The rebellion is failing. We are being pushed back. We are losing towns and cities that we had reclaimed. When I left Greece, most of our forces were retreating north."

"No," she said, despair or anger dripping off the word. "That cannot be. The Spartans were reeling. We were getting stronger every day."

"Not anymore."

"Why not?" Jarka jumped in. "What happened?"

Dacio shot him a dark look before directing his answer to Vaseus. "It started when Athens joined us. The Spartans attacked, and most of the city, over one hundred thousand people, were put to the sword. Only a few were left alive.

Word spread that this same fate would come to all rebels, since the Spartan commander is no longer being directed by the emperor. It's said that he's a man without a shred of love or mercy in his soul.

"Soon after Athens, many Greek towns fell to the ruthless bastard, and every one suffered the same horror. Fear and panic swept through the entire rebellion, and almost overnight, thousands defected back to the Empire. The Spartans have been pushing us back ever since. I don't know how much longer we can last."

A heavy silence hung thick on the chill air when he finished.

Jarka looked to Vaseus. Her arms were crossed, and her face was strained. The desperate urge to hold her screamed at him to act. But with Dacio standing there, he could only grit his teeth and watch her suffer.

After a time, she turned to him. "We need to go back." Her voice was harsh and raw, as if sand had been poured down her throat. "My people need our help."

Although he wanted nothing more than to ease her pain, he hesitated. Asking yagars to go to war with humans as their allies was a huge risk. Their traditions had already been shaken. Their Warlords had been replaced by a Clanless outsider. That alone was unprecedented. Would they be willing to do the unthinkable and fight alongside those they had always been told to despise?

I have to try, the answer came swiftly. *For Vaseus and Jazith. If the rebellion fails, I will never see her again. And Vaseus might never recover.*

"Of course, bee," he said firmly, hoping to give her strength with his answer. "We will head south in the morning. Imzen can stay here if she can't travel yet."

"And the Clans?" she asked. "Will they fight?"

"Yes," he answered, ignoring his doubts. "I will instruct the warriors here to follow us south and spread the word to all Clans that their Warlord requests their presence in Clanless lands."

Vaseus gave him a terse nod. "Thank you."

"There are three Clans left, but only two are on the way back to human lands."

"Which two?"

"One is the Ocean Lake Clan. The other is where I grew up. It's time for me to return home."

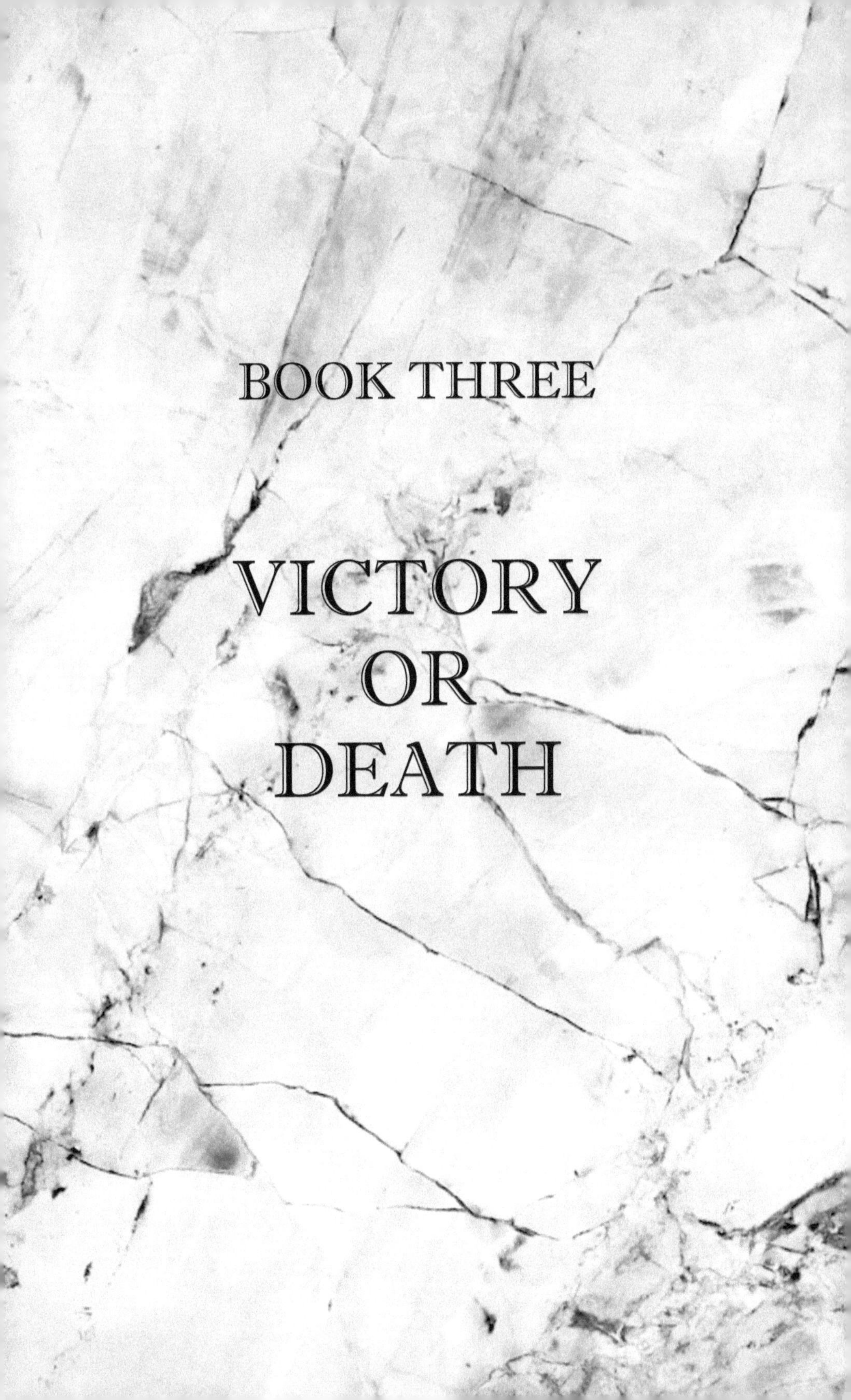

BOOK THREE

VICTORY
OR
DEATH

THIRTY-SEVEN

In the years following the Peloponnesian War, the Spartans and their allies moved north, conquering all Greeks who dared oppose them in one campaign after another. By the time they reached Makedonia, nearly all of Greece was under their control.

Androdamos of Boeotia

Elbow resting on the chair's armrest, Kaletor closed his eyes and rubbed them with thumb and forefinger. Faint sounds crept in under the canvas of his tent, a muted mix of voices, plodding horse and oxen, stone grinding across iron, and the constant thump of men's footfalls. The smell of churned mud mingled with sweat and smoke.

The living beast that was his encamped army moved and breathed outside, but Kaletor paid it little attention. Left alone with only his thoughts for company, he brooded on the war.

To any outside observer, it was going well. Many settlements across the Empire were back in Spartan hands, rebels were surrendering every day, and the army's confidence was restored.

But it wasn't enough. Tylis, Sarmizegetusa, and Bylazora remained in enemy hands, and most inhabitants along the northern frontier continued to resist. Total victory remained far from certain.

As he often did, he sought the best way to bring the war to a swift end. There were many possible strategies, but one was not obviously better than the rest. He went over each one in his mind, searching for a clear solution. But it was no use.

He snarled and barked, "Talos!"

His aging, bronze-skinned slave emerged from the front section of the three-room tent, limping in to stand at the long table's opposite end. "Yes, Master?"

"Summon my generals."

Talos bowed, his bald pate shiny in the flickering torchlight. "As you wish, Commander."

"And be quick!"

As the old Athenian limped away, Kaletor stood and started to pace. Back and forth he went, sometimes running a hand along the dark canvas wall, sometimes balling both hands into fists, sometimes grinding his teeth together. Before long, his mind was a tumultuous battlefield of chaos, completely devoid of clarity.

After what seemed like an hour, there was movement at the front entrance. A moment later, Hullis and Ackadus appeared, clad in their red and gold. Belisar followed, still wearing the silver and crimson from his days of glory.

They lined up at the head of the table, stood tall, and saluted.

"Are you all as slow as the oxen?" Kaletor snarled before they could greet him formally.

Without allowing an answer, he pointed to the huge cloth map of the Empire laid out across the table. "Tell me what you would do to end this war as fast as possible."

The three men positioned themselves around the table to study the map and the pieces arrayed upon it.

The teenager was first to speak, pointing a slender finger at the map as he did. "We have the strongest force, which means we can annihilate any army the rebels send against us. We should march on Tylis, take it, then onto Bylazora, and then Sarmizegetusa."

"We don't have the necessary artillery to take Tylis," Hullis countered. "How would we take it without imposing a long, drawn-out siege on the city?"

Ackadus shot Hullis a look of daggers. "By drawing them out."

"How? What would make them leave their high walls?"

"We could burn all the barns, crops, and homes around the city—"

"Burn crops?" Belisar cut in. "That would deprive our men of food."

"Who cares about food? We can always transport supplies from the south—"

"*Enough*," Kaletor bellowed, slamming a fist to the table. "Your plan is folly. Besides, you don't think I've already considered that? It would take too long and could fail too easily. I need something better."

A brief moment of silence followed.

Belisar pointed to a small force to the west of their position. "This is the 10th, right?"

"It is," Hullis supplied.

"Who leads them?"

Kaletor snapped, "Captain Heliodorus. Why?"

Belisar put a hand to his neatly trimmed silver-and-black beard, his small brown eyes darting around the northern reaches of the Empire. "I know these lands well from the Thracian rebellion. What if I took the 4th and joined the 10th in Thessaloniki. From there, we would march west, then up the coast to attack the town of Salona. Once we destroy the rebels there, we would head back southeast and converge on the western side of Bylazora. When the rebels see just two Phalanxes, I'll be able to lure them out into open battle. Once that happens, you attack the undefended city from the east."

Kaletor eyed these maneuvers, moving the pieces on the map in his mind. A two-pronged attack had its advantages, and it could work. But they would need perfect timing to pull it off.

"What about Tylis?" Hullis said, pointing to the huge city that was about fifty miles north of their camp. "The rebels have garrisoned a large force there. What happens if they realize we've gone west and come up behind us while we're attacking Bylazora? We'd be squeezed on two fronts."

"I think you forget who we're dealing with," Belisar said with a wry look. "Farm boys and dimwitted scum from the gutters. Their so-called leaders know nothing about tactics or strategy, and they're terrified of facing our undefeated Commander. That alone will keep them holed up in their city. And even if they somehow mustered up the courage to come after us, they'll take so long to make that decision that we'll have sacked Bylazora by the time they arrive. We could then crush them from that position of strength."

"That's a lot of assumptions," Hullis countered. "Many things could go differently than you just described."

"Any course we take will involve some risks—"

"You're right," Kaletor interjected, leaning forward with his hands on the table. "But some plans are riskier than others. Your best days are clearly behind you."

While Belisar's expression darkened, the prince jumped in. "That's why we should take each city one after the other—"

"*Idiot*," Kaletor snarled before the brat could say anymore. "Another word and I'll demote you again.

"Hullis," he went on, looking to his most intelligent subordinate. "What say you?"

The pale, ropy-muscled general studied the map, eyes flitting here and there. His mind worked fast, for he was soon pointing to one of the roads snaking northward. "We march on Tylis with the 4th and 7th, but here, at this wide stretch of open fields south of the city, we send the 8th, 9th, and 16th west to continue on to Bylazora. Each army then encircles and besieges both cities, constructing rams and siege towers to take the walls. Once both cities are in our hands, we march on Sarmizegetusa."

"Impossible," Ackadus declared as he wagged his head. "There's not nearly enough wood around either city for such towers to be built."

"This map doesn't show several small clusters of trees." Hullis leaned over to point at different points on the map. "There are trees along this stretch of road, at the base of the mountains here, and a small forest hides a village just here, a few miles from Bylazora. There's enough for at least four rams and six towers."

"How do you know that?" Ackadus challenged.

"Some of us have seen much more of the Empire than you."

"How long will it take?" Kaletor demanded.

Hullis straightened, considered the question briefly, and said, "Once our men start cutting down trees, we should be ready to attack in two weeks."

Kaletor rammed his fist back to the table. "Two weeks? For thousands of men to build some towers?"

Somehow, Hullis managed to maintain his neutral expression. "Only so many men can build at a time—"

"And what about Aquincum?" Kaletor snarled, referring to the large town northwest of Sarmizegetusa. "Or Segestica? How long until we deal with them?"

"They will surrender to us once we've taken the cities—"

"I don't want them to surrender! I want to break down their walls, ravage their women, and slaughter every living thing!"

Kaletor seethed hot breaths through clenched teeth, glaring at his useless generals, daring them to voice another foolish plan.

They didn't. His outburst had silenced them and dragged their gazes down to the map. Even Ackadus averted his eyes and remained mute.

The croaking voice of Talos came from the front of the tent like a splintering crackle of dry leaves. "Forgive the intrusion, Master, but a certain Captain Zagris has a message for you."

"What message?" Kaletor snapped, keeping his glare on the men standing around his table.

"He didn't say. All he said was that it is urgent."

Releasing a growling exhale, Kaletor relinquished his glare and stepped away. "Send him in."

Zagris was a thick man who appeared to have seen at least thirty years. His copper beard was short and trimmed, and his curly hair was pressed flat from the helmet now tucked under his arm.

He gave a smart salute, eyes high and staring at the back canvas wall. "It's an honour, Commander. I am—"

"Captain Zagris," Kaletor cut in, crossing his arms over his chest. "This better not be a waste of my time."

The captain maintained his professional air of composure and spoke in a clear voice. "A unit of thirty-five hoplites just returned from foraging in the woods to the north. They were ambushed by rebels firing arrows and hurling spears. Many were killed."

"How many?" Kaletor demanded.

"Twenty-one, sir."

"How many rebels were there?"

"The survivors say they couldn't tell. They say the arrows and spears came from all sides."

Kaletor grit his teeth and balled his hands into fists. "*Cowards.* They fight without honour. I want those bastards found. Have the survivors lead a cavalry detachment to the ambush site . . ."

He trailed off when he heard a commotion outside the tent.

"Talos! What's going on out there?"

The old slave limped in from the front entrance. "You'd better come see, Master."

Striding past Zagris, then Talos, Kaletor stepped clear of the tent's front flaps. Standing arrayed before his guards were ten or more ranking officers, all of them exchanging heated words.

He grit his teeth in a snarl. "*Spartans!*"

His bellow cut the noise off at once.

"Are you all here," he said, "because your men were ambushed?"

They all nodded or said, "Yes, sir."

He dug his fingers into the base of his hands. Unable to kill something, he roared.

THIRTY-EIGHT

But as he grew into a strong, talented warrior, Chalrog began to show the darkness within. At first, it was small things. Insults meant to wound. Attacking a bit too long. Shouting when he lost his temper. He was behaving dishonourably, but his skill as a warrior was undeniable. So most in the Clan looked the other way, dismissing his behaviour as just immature, youthful exuberance.

The Spoken Tales

"You're not good enough," Traz said, standing shoulder to shoulder with his twin brother. "You never were."

"You're just a weak coward," Vawk added. "You couldn't save your sister. You couldn't save your parents. You let everyone you care about die—"

Jarka roared and charged. They laughed as he approached. He lashed out at them, but they stepped aside and disappeared.

Blinding white light forced him to throw his arms up. He shielded his eyes as he walked forward. When the white light finally subsided, he let his arms back down. Straight ahead, within the shade of trees, he saw Spartans dragging Jazith away.

"No!" he bellowed, running after them. "Let her go! Jazith!"

He closed in on them. Soon, he saw that her eyes were closed, and her body was limp.

He ran faster, ready to attack—

But then tripped and careened down a hill. He bounced off a tree at the bottom and ended up flat on his stomach. He couldn't breathe. He couldn't even move.

Finally, his lungs opened, and air flowed in again. He looked up to find Jazith. Instead, he saw his father down in the mud, his body lifeless and still. Nearby was his mother, on her knees with a knife in her back. Traz was approaching, a spear in hand. Vaseus was there too, running towards him, pursued closely by Vawk.

When her eyes found his, Jarka saw that they were filled with fear.

"Jarka, help me!"

He struggled to stand, his arms shaking from the effort. He heard Vawk laugh. When he looked up, the twin drove his spear into her back—

He jerked awake, his mouth wide as he gasped for air. All was dark and calm around him. He looked for Vaseus. There she was, sleeping on the ground beside Imzen and Relyk.

He closed his eyes and released a shuddering breath.

Another nightmare. They seem to be getting worse. I just want them to stop.

*   *   *

A clear stream lapped over smooth, dark stones, winding its narrow path down between the towering pine and oak trees. The early morning sun splashed dazzling sparkles across its flowing surface.

Jarka crouched low, reached in with hands cupped, and splashed the water to his face. Cold little daggers pierced through his fur to poke the flesh beneath.

He looked up to the clear blue sky and released a measured exhale. As he did, questions came into his mind. *Do these nightmares mean anything? Are they just caused by my memories? Are they my fears? I don't know, and I don't understand.*

The soft snap of a twig betrayed someone's approach.

"Good morning, my friend. How did you sleep? Hopefully better than me."

As he finished, he straightened and turned around. The harsh pace of the past two weeks had taken its toll on Relyk. He was noticeably slimmer.

"I've put this off long enough," he said, halting beneath some low-hanging branches of pine needles.

"What are you talking about?" Jarka said, looking back towards their camp. "Where's Vaseus?"

"That's what I want to talk to you about."

With a thrill rushing through his chest, Jarka forced a broad smile. "What has she done this time? Did she handle your spear? I told her—"

"I know what's going on."

His stomach clenched. "What?" he managed, feeling his smile crumble.

"Don't bother denying it," Relyk said as he crossed his arms. "I know you better than you know yourself. And you've never been any good at disguising your feelings when it comes to females."

Jarka swallowed, searching for words of escape. But none came.

"I've spoken to Imzen, and she agrees," Relyk went on. "Vaseus has to go. You know that our people can only take so much change. They have accepted a single Warlord because the Challenge is our chief law. The Warrior Code demands that we follow strength and honour. And yet I'm sure some are looking for a way to bring you down. Should they find out about this, they'll use it against you. No one will follow a Warlord who has feelings for a human—"

"Vaseus is our ally," Jarka cut in, finally finding his voice. "Nothing more."

"Don't be a fool, Jarka. We're about to walk into a nest of vipers. The twins dominate their Clan through the brute strength of their warriors. They deceive and betray and lie at every turn—"

"Do not tell me what Vawk and Traz are like. I was the one they bullied. I was the one who watched Traz murder my mother. I was the one Vawk tried to kill."

"Then you know they'll do anything to hold on to their power. Vaseus must not be with us when we face them."

"This is my home," Jarka snarled, straightening to his full height and stepping in to tower over Relyk. "I know what I must do."

Relyk remained rooted where he stood, his face set and hard. "If you bring her, you risk losing everything. All the Challenges, all the toil and hardship, all of it will have been for nothing—"

"What do you care? You never thought this was a good idea anyway. Why do you want me to succeed now?"

Jarka saw the muscles of Relyk's jaw clench, the tell that he was about to attack. Jarka braced, ready to fight.

Instead, Relyk glared him down, then spun away and stormed off.

Jarka released a low growl. *You don't know what you're talking about. But you'll see. Soon enough, you'll see.*

*   *   *

A few hours later, the four of them were on the move, passing trees, streams, and meadows Jarka recognized from his youth. The late morning was warm, bright, and still, a sharp contrast to his inner reality. Relyk's words had left behind deep, dark troughs, and in those gouges he remained.

Similar to his nightmares, dark memories of his final days in these lands churned through his mind. Memories of the twins attacking him. Murky details of the day that had changed his life forever. All the moments of that day, moments coloured with the raw anguish of watching his parents die, an anguish long buried in the deepest recesses of his mind, struggled to mount the walls he had built to survive the pain.

His thoughts turned to Jazith. He imagined her imprisoned somewhere in a strange place, surrounded by humans that despised her, devoid of any hope of rescue.

It was all he could do to keep from howling.

"Are we nearly there?"

He blinked, taking a moment to notice that Vaseus was looking back and awaiting an answer.

"Yes," he replied, his voice low and thick.

She must have sensed something, for she slowed and allowed him to catch up. "What's wrong?"

Although Relyk walked ahead of them, Jarka could almost feel the judgment emanating from his friend.

"Nothing," he muttered out of the corner of his mouth, feeling his chest tighten.

At first, it seemed she wouldn't reply, and he had hope that that was it.

It was a short-lived hope.

"I know this can't be easy for you," she said, her tone gentle. "I can't imagine what it must feel like, being back here. But try to remember why we're doing this. We need as many warriors as possible on our side if we are to win the war. Once you defeat the twins, our army will be strong enough to take on the Spartans—"

"That's all you care about, isn't it?" he sliced in. "Killing Spartans. We yagars are just a means to an end. I doubt you care how many of us die, so long as you see the Empire fall."

"Where's this coming from? You don't really believe that."

"And what if I do?"

She snagged his arm and pulled up, bringing them both to a halt. "Then you are far crueler than you pretend to be."

"Humans believe yagars are mindless, bloodthirsty savages, right? Wouldn't it be best if we and the Spartans wiped each other out? Wouldn't that be ideal for your people?"

In an instant, her eyes were ablaze. "I've done nothing but help you get closer to what you wanted. You needed an army to get your sister back. Now, thanks to me, you nearly have one—"

"Thanks to you?" he fired back. "What have you done? Did you defeat all those Warlords?"

"Do you really think you could have made it this far without my help?"

"I don't need anyone's help to win Challenges."

She nodded, hands going to her hips. "Fine. Fine. You don't need my help? Then I won't help you. But know this, Warlord; without me, you'll never see your sister again."

She turned away and sped past Relyk and Imzen.

Jarka glared after her, shaking his head. He soon noticed that Imzen and Relyk were looking back at him.

"Not a word, Relyk," he growled when their eyes met. "Not one word."

*　　*　　*

She was standing at the edge of the forest, looking on the village beyond. Jarka kept his distance and stopped to do the same.

A rush of familiarity flooded him as he took in their surroundings. The layout of huts was just as he remembered, but this recognition was a fleeting thing, for the village was packed full of yagars.

From where they stood, he could see hundreds, some milling about on the streets and in between huts, others sitting in small groups. Youngsters ran and played through it all. A multitude of voices rode the air, a melding wave of constant noise.

He heard Imzen and Relyk stop beside him. "How can this be?" the latter said.

Jarka didn't reply at first. He watched the buzzing scene, unsure what to make of it.

After a long moment, he stepped out from the safety of the tree line, saying over a shoulder, "Only one way to find out."

Staying ahead of the others, he walked briskly through the open grasses to enter the village he once called home. A group of six soon noticed him, pointing and speaking to each other in hushed tones.

When he came within a few steps, one of the group, an adolescent female of slight build, stepped into his path. "Is it really you?" she said, her eyes wide. "Are you who I think you are?"

Jarka stopped before her, noting that her group was looking from him to Vaseus. "Are we expected?"

She nodded. "Word came that you intend to challenge the twins. Is it true?"

"Yes. Is that why there's so many yagars here?"

"It is. Everyone's come to watch you fight the twins. More and more are arriving all the time. Even Bex, the Warlord of the Western Waterfalls Clan, is here. It's rumoured that she will pledge her Clan to your leadership if you win."

The darkness that had brewed and clouded his mind started to lift. "Did you hear that, Relyk?" he said, glancing back. "They're all here because of us."

260

Noticing a shift in the noise level, he cast his gaze around to those nearby. Many more were pointing and talking amongst themselves, "Warlord" and "it's him" sounding loud enough to hear above the general din.

He looked back to the young female. "What's your name?"

"Pix."

"Do you know where Traz and Vawk are?"

"They're at the Warlord's Hall."

"Very good. How would you like to escort us there?"

The youth's jaw visibly dropped. "Me? Escort the most famous yagar that's ever lived?"

"That's right."

"Are you sure? I'm nobody important. I even lost my last Challenge, though I've been training harder and getting better ever since."

"That's all any of us can do. You may not be a Superior or a Warlord, but you're still yagar, and that's good enough for me. So lead the way, Pix. It's time for me to meet my old friends again."

The young female was smiling as she turned and set off. Jarka followed, hearing Relyk, Imzen, and Vaseus moving close behind him.

They passed through the crowded streets, keeping a steady pace as they proceeded deeper into the village. Every corner was familiar, and Jarka found himself remembering things he thought he had long forgotten. He recalled running and playing with his friends, being reprimanded by the Elders, and laughing so hard outside the weaponsmith that he was rolling on the ground. He remembered walking these streets with his mother, father, and sister. His chest and arms became warm, and his legs felt heavy.

He was so drawn into his memories that he didn't notice the way had become clear. Blinking, he saw that the crowd had coalesced into two lines, one on either side of the street, creating an open lane between them. This procession extended towards the towering structure that was the Warlord's Hall, which was even larger than the last time he saw it.

Down the procession they went, a tight corridor of bustle and lively voices. As he walked, a smile came to his lips. He looked at as many faces as he could, swivelling his head from one side to the other. There were young and old, stout warriors and caring Elders. It seemed like a thousand voices buffeted them on all sides. Jarka saw and felt their eyes on him, and his smile widened as he took in the excited anticipation of so many.

They came to the wide-open forum before the Warlord's Hall, followed closely by the crowd. Many more were there waiting, but Jarka barely even saw them. Dead ahead, at the foot of the Warlord's Hall with thirty or more warriors at their backs, stood Vawk and Traz.

In the moment of recognizing them, Jarka remembered the bullying, the cruel words meant to wound, the hard punches and kicks they had doled out. But this was just the tip. His mind returned him to that day that had changed his life, and he felt that helpless agony rushing back with the force of a hammer blow.

He saw the lifeless body of his father in the mud. He saw Traz stabbing his mother in the back. He saw Vawk moving to kill him and Jazith.

His vision and hearing narrowed as he stepped around Pix, muttered a thank you, and continued on alone.

Details beyond the twins became blurred and muted. They stood with arms hanging loose at their sides, dark sneers on their faces. They were much bigger than they used to be. The yellow of their fur stretched wide between their black spots due to the bulging muscles of their shoulders, chest, and arms. Traz had multiple bands of bone wrapping all the way up his arms. Vawk's torso was encased in nine boar tusks tied together. They both wore short black cloaks and a single band of yellowed bone on their heads.

Though much of their appearance had changed, one thing remained the same. Within those dark orbs that were their eyes, Jarka saw the same malice, cruelty, and violence.

When he was fifteen feet away, Vawk raised his arms for quiet. It was all Jarka could do to keep from charging them. Knowing it was not the time for that, he sucked in a harsh breath and stopped short as the noise of the surrounding crowd died down.

"Well, well, well," Traz said, crossing his arms dramatically over his puffed-out chest. "If it isn't our famous friend."

"It's been a long time," Vawk chimed in, his grin exposing fangs that were unnaturally sharp. "Last time we saw each other, you were running away like a coward. Do you remember that, little one?"

"Course he does," Traz sneered. "That's the day we killed his parents."

They both started laughing.

Jarka clenched his fists to fight the demanding need to attack. His voice shaking, he managed to say, "Warlord, I challenge—"

"Whoa, whoa, whoa," Vawk interrupted, holding his hands up with palms out. "Don't you think we should catch up before we get to that?" Glancing at his brother, he went on. "Do you remember his screams? You know, when you killed his mother."

Traz nodded profusely and loosed a wicked cackle. "He sounded so whiny and pathetic. I bet your friends don't know about that, do they, Jarka? What about all the Clans you've been to? If they all knew the truth about you—"

Jarka roared and sprang forward, but by his third step, someone wrapped their arms around him and held him in place.

"No," Relyk hissed in his ear. "Not like this. They'll kill you if you attack.

There's too many."

Jarka snarled and swung an elbow back into Relyk's face. His tight bear hug slackened, and Jarka broke free—

"Don't!" Vaseus yelled as she rushed into his path. "Please don't."

He growled at her but stopped short. Her desperate plea pierced through his rage like a knife. He stared into her eyes, chest heaving, struggling to restrain himself.

"I knew it," Vawk called out. "The human is his master. He does what she tells him to do. He is her slave."

"He's always been like that," Traz added. "It used to be Jazith that bossed him around."

"Where is that dumb sister of yours anyway?" Vawk asked. "Oh wait, I remember. The humans took her."

"You were there, weren't you? Traz asked. "You were just too weak to stop them."

Jarka roared and moved to speed past Vaseus. But Relyk grabbed him again, arms clamped heavy around his torso.

"Enough of this," Vaseus shouted as she spun to face the twins.

Jarka again tried to break loose, but this time Relyk held on even tighter.

"Jarka has come to challenge you both for the right to rule this Clan," Vaseus went on, her voice hard. "Will you honourably accept or refuse in disgrace?"

The twins fixed their attention on her, eyes dark with contempt.

It was Vawk who replied. "Be silent, human. You have no place here. If you speak again, we will kill you."

The threat sent another surge of fire burning through Jarka, and he resumed his efforts to break the bear hug.

"Challenge them."

This was Imzen. She sounded close, likely standing right next to Relyk.

"It's the only way," she said into his ear. "Challenge them now."

Jarka twisted left, loading all his strength onto that side. He snarled as he rotated hard to the right. The power behind the move threw Relyk off.

Free once more, he stepped around Vaseus and bellowed, "Vawk and Traz, I challenge you. Do you accept?"

"You would fight us both?" Traz said, a surprised grin alighting on his lips. "At the same time?"

"Yes," Jarka growled. He was less than ten feet away, and it felt like his entire body was begging him to attack.

The twins shared a knowing look. Then they looked back to him, and it was Vawk that said, "Very well. We accept your challenge."

"But when you lose," Traz quickly said, "all the Clans you now lead will belong to us. And you, having lost your position as Warlord, will return to Clanless lands to live out the rest of your life in shame and disgrace. That is, if we don't accidentally kill you. Agreed?"

Teeth grit together hard, Jarka nodded once, not trusting what might come out if he opened his mouth.

The twins laughed wickedly in response. Vawk waved a hand in the direction they had come. "Now get that human out of my sight."

Jarka stayed where he was, glaring them down, hands itching to grab hold of his spear.

"Come on," Vaseus said from just behind him. "Let's go."

"Tomorrow, you will both pay for everything you've done," he said, his voice low and hard.

"I'm sure," Traz scoffed before he too waved a hand dismissively. "Go on. Get."

Jarka gave them one final blazing glare before allowing Vaseus to pull him away.

Once he turned, he remembered the huge crowd surrounding them. They were all watching in silence, as if collectively holding their breath.

THIRTY-NINE

Courage, fortitude, strength, and martial prowess. These were the traits the Spartans valued above all else. Once innovative thinking bloomed and their population expanded, there was no stopping their march to empire.

Eurydemos of Corinth

The stench of death hung thick on the air, emanating from the corpses. At the edge of the killing zone, Kaletor stood with arms crossed, his red cloak snapping in the hot wind.

The harsh cawing of crows and vultures grated in his ears as thousands of the black-winged creatures continued to gorge themselves on the flesh of dead men. Most were rebels, indistinguishable in the massive sprawl. But amongst the filth, here and there, Kaletor spied a torn red cloak, a Spartan helmet, a golden shield.

Many in his army had wanted to honour their fellow Spartans by burning their bodies on a pyre. But he had forbidden this. They had allowed themselves to be killed by lowly peasants. They didn't deserve to be honoured.

He brought a hand up into his hair, sliding his fingers through to gingerly prod the bandaged wound on the side of his scalp. The rebels had been desperate to win, and so the battle had been hard. They had fought without the fear of death, hurling themselves with reckless abandon at the phalanx wall. The killing was fast and furious, challenging even his abilities. He had relished it, loved it, fighting alongside his personal guard of Spartiates, as unrelenting as they were unstoppable.

It had taken several hours, but eventually, they had cut their enemies down, for not one rebel surrendered. Not one rebel survived.

Thinking on that day filled him with glorious triumph. Finally, after so many battles, so much killing, every city was back in Spartan hands. The end of the war was near.

The pounding of horse hooves coming from Sarmizegetusa disrupted his reverie. He made one final scan of the carnage before turning to face the approaching riders. They were thirty Elites, led by Belisar and Hullis.

The company reined in, and his two generals dismounted. Both appeared weary. Their eyes were bloodshot, and their movements were sluggish.

"What do you have for me?" Kaletor asked without waiting for them to salute.

"A small band fled north from the city," Hullis supplied. "Mostly women and children. I've sent four hundred cavalry after them."

"Who leads that unit? And what orders did you give him?"

"Captain Heliodorus. I told him to kill them all."

Kaletor gave a sharp nod. "Good. Continue."

"Some scouts have just returned. They report that small pockets of fanatics are still holed up in the towns of Aquincum and Segestica, as well as a few villages scattered throughout the north."

"How many fighting men do they have left?"

Hullis said, "Hard to say for sure. Can't be any more than two thousand though." He gestured with a hand towards the corpse-covered battlefield. "This was their last real army."

It was exactly what Kaletor wanted to hear. And yet, for some reason, it did not deliver the anticipated satisfaction. Instead, he felt an odd mix of doubt and confusion.

Unsure what to make of this, he distractedly said, "Anything to add, Belisar?"

The older man's chin was tucked in, and his shoulders were slumped. Upon hearing his name, he straightened, scratching at his thick, silver-streaked beard.

"No, Commander. General Hullis covered everything. I would only say congratulations. Celebrations are in order to mark your great triumph. Thanks to your brilliance, the Empire is restored."

Belisar's words brought sudden clarity, and Kaletor knew why his reaction had been one of unease. For months he had focused solely on the war. It had consumed his every thought, all his energy, leaving room for nothing else.

But now that it was done, a new task was at hand. It concerned an enemy far less obvious than the rebels, and achieving victory would require even more skill. The Empire was indeed restored, but its strength was compromised.

The time had come to change that.

"You're wrong, General," he said, his mind afire, burning bright with the exhilaration of clear purpose. "Victory is not yet ours. The Empire is weak, vulnerable to attack from within and without. But I know how to fix it.

"You and Ackadus will remain in the north with the 10th, 7th, and 4th," he went on, looking at Belisar as he stepped closer to his weary generals. "I leave you in charge to finish off the last of the rebels. I don't want any of those filth to survive this war."

Belisar's bushy, black eyebrows on the protruding shelf of his forehead drove down. "I don't understand, sir. Where—"

"Hullis and I will lead the 8th, 9th, and 16th back to Sparta."

"Back to Sparta? To what end?"

Kaletor shifted his fierce gaze to Hullis and held his eye.

Eventually, he gave his answer in a low voice. "To receive a hero's welcome. And to be rewarded for all of our victories."

Hullis held the look for a long time. When he finally glanced away, there was understanding in his eyes.

That's right, Kaletor thought without releasing Hullis from his gaze. *My time has come. Even you have nothing to say.*

FORTY

It proved to be a mistake. As the years passed, Chalrog became more and more powerful, and his dishonourable behaviour worsened. By the time the Clan realized the danger he posed, it was too late.

The Spoken Tales

"Help me, Jarka! Please!"

The desperate cry was distant, the direction from where it came impossible to discern. Jarka spun around, trying to see where the female was. But there was only a tangled mess of dark vines all around him, stretching up from the ground of bare dirt and rock.

"Where are you?" he shouted, brandishing his spear as he looked in every direction, trying to peer through the tangled wall of vines.

"Please help me!" she cried, her voice seeming to echo on all sides. This time he knew for sure that it was Jazith.

The vines were close, choking the very air he breathed. Darkness cloaked everything beyond, and a red mist infused the gloom.

His inaction was unbearable. Still unsure where her calls came from, he picked a direction at random and sprinted down the narrow path.

He had only taken a few strides when a white jungle cat appeared and charged straight for him. It roared as it launched itself at his face, two long fangs poised to tear into his flesh. Jarka swung his spear in a rising uppercut as their momentum brought them to a bone-jarring collision. The impact sent him sprawling, and the spear was twisted from his hands. The cat's screech split the air.

Sharp pain stabbed down his left arm as he rolled to his hands and knees and looked up to locate the beast. It was lying motionless on its side, its white hide speckled red.

"Somebody, please! Help me!"

He surged to his feet, rushed over to retrieve his spear, and ran on. The path zigzagged, left, then right, then left again, forcing him to constantly cut side to side. He expected the oppressive tangle of vines to recede, but they seemed to go on forever.

"Where are you?" he shouted again, hearing the panic in his voice.

No answer came. He ran harder, eyes wide, trying to see what lay ahead—

A screaming Spartan appeared around the next turn, charging headlong with spear and shield. Jarka stuttered his steps, shifting just enough to slide past the thrust destined for his chest. Now beside the human, he swung the butt of his spear into the Spartan's helmet. The blow knocked the man down, and Jarka drove his spear into his enemy's gut. In that instant, he saw that the red mist speckled the man's arms, golden breastplate, and face.

A raging howl snapped his attention around. Another Spartan was on the path, charging just like the first. Jarka stepped left, causing his assailant to shift his shield. A quick thrust of his spear slid just beside the large disc. The Spartan grimaced as he collapsed.

Another came running from around the vines. Jarka yanked his spear out to fight on, striking the man down after deflecting a wild jab.

More followed, one after the other, the red mist clinging to them all. They attacked without fear of injury or death. He met each in turn, dispatching one after the other, arms gradually becoming more and more tired.

It seemed to go on forever, an unending tide of defend and strike, of gold and red, of iron and blood.

Finally, after felling more than he could keep track of, no more appeared. He stopped and hunched over. While he gasped for air, he heard the same plea for help, more distant than ever.

Gathering in a ragged breath, he cried out, "Where are you?"

A voice of cold stone sounded directly behind him. "Here."

Jarka twirled around to see a yagar driving a spear into him—

Suddenly, he was roaring in a dark room. The red vines were gone. He was in a bed, and as he blinked, he saw that at the foot of it, Vaseus had leapt onto a yagar's shoulders and was batting her fists at his face. The big male reached around, wrapped an arm around her body, and threw her into the wall. She bounced off and crashed to the floor.

"Vaseus!" Jarka bellowed as he surged from the bed. He dove at the intruder, lead shoulder ramming into his chest. Together they went to the floor, Jarka landing atop the male's front. He raised an arm and swung down, fist connecting with nose. He drew back again to strike another blow—

Something sharp pierced his thigh. He roared, looking down to see the handle of a knife jutting from his leg, the slicing pain demanding all his attention.

The intruder seized his chance by punching a fist into Jarka's throat. Choking for breath, he couldn't stop his assailant from throwing him off. Before he could recover, he was pinned to the floor.

Now on top, the intruder twisted at the hip, took hold of the knife handle, and yanked it out. Jarka howled as the blade slashed through his flesh.

Through the mind-consuming pain, he knew what was coming. He brought both hands up just as the male drove the blade down towards his chest. He snagged the intruder's wrists, freezing the driving plunge a few inches short of its mark.

In that moment, nothing moved. The knife was in limbo, hanging there, a thin pillar of sharpened stone.

Jarka's teeth ground together as he pushed up with all his strength, straining every muscle in his arms, shoulders and chest. He locked eyes with the intruder, seeing in them only intense determination. It was a face he did not know.

Soon, the unyielding pressure began to crush his resistance. Slowly, bit by bit, the tip of the blade sank down. His arms started shaking. He pushed up harder, demanding more strength, teeth clenched so tight they could crack.

But it wasn't enough. The intruder's entire weight was behind the knife. Despite all his power, all his will, Jarka could not stop it.

He held on, determined to keep death at bay as long as he could. A low growl rose into his throat, rumbling up from deep within him. He looked down as the blade touched the fur of his chest.

An image of Jazith suddenly flashed in his mind, and a wave of strength flowed in response. Impossibly, he stopped the blade's downward trend.

But the intruder pushed down harder still. It was an unrelenting weight that kept getting heavier.

Jarka growled as his strength ebbed once more. He looked back into his killer's eyes, loosing a final roar of defiance—

The crack of an impact, something smashing apart, dark shards falling in a scatter to the floor. The incredible pressure slackened. Jarka summoned the strength to push up and twist bodily to one side. The male collapsed face down to the floor beside him.

As he gasped in total release, he saw Vaseus on her knees at his feet. He understood that she had used something to strike the intruder in the head.

Releasing a ragged snarl, he rolled onto his side and scrambled bodily onto the male's back. He looked around and spotted the knife on the floor. He snatched it up, raised his arm, and drove it through the back of the male's neck.

The deed done, his body released, and he was still. He stayed where he was, breaths coming in ragged and harsh.

At some point he rolled onto his back and was staring at the dark ceiling. He felt a sharp, searing sensation in his thigh. He snarled and reached towards it, fingers touching just short of the wound.

"Jarka. Are you alright?"

Her voice was faint, as if she were far away. He allowed his head to tilt to one side so that the ends of his whiskers brushed the floor.

There she was, crawling towards him. He watched as she came to his side. Her gaze went to his leg, and there was obvious fear in her eyes when she looked back up.

"It's alright, bee," he croaked. "I'll be . . . fine. Thanks to you."

Tears filled her eyes as she took his hand in hers. "Why?" she breathed, the word dripping with darkness. "Who is that? Why did he try to kill you?"

An uncontrollable shudder swept through his body, and he squeezed her hand tight.

When it passed, he said, "I don't know. Maybe he didn't like me."

Hurried footsteps sounded down the hall and the bedroom door was flung open.

"What happened?" whoever it was demanded.

A moment later, Jarka saw that it was Relyk.

Gathering his voice, he said, "I was nearly killed . . . in my sleep . . . by this assassin. Vaseus . . . saved me. Perhaps now . . . you will count her . . . as your friend."

*   *   *

"It's not too late to go back. No one will blame you or think you weak—"

"This is happening," Jarka interrupted Vaseus, hobbling towards the ring he became so familiar with in his youth. "I issued a Challenge. I must honour that."

Her growl was pure frustration. "But you can't possibly fight. Look at you! Without Relyk, you would have toppled long ago."

She was right. His arm had been draped around Relyk's shoulders since they left their hut, for he was barely able to put any weight on his stitched and bandaged leg. Without that support, he couldn't have made it.

But she didn't have to know that.

Biting down a grimace from the persistent, hot pain, he said, "I could walk if I needed to. This way I save my strength for the fight."

"Your pride knows no end!" she growled as she threw her hands up. "It's infuriating!"

Once, he had seen an outburst like this as an explosion of uncontrolled anger. Now he knew it was caused by the worry assailing her mind.

Knowing he could do nothing to alleviate her concerns, he remained silent.

The Challenge Ring at the foot of the hill, as well as the hill itself, was covered with yagars. In all his past years of living in the village, he had never seen it so crowded. Every inch of the rising slope was occupied, and everyone was standing shoulder to shoulder. On the flat ground, the crowd wrapped all the way around the ring, row upon row stretching across the open grassland.

Many voices filled the bright, warm morning air as they approached. But when they were noticed, a wave of silence fell and the crowd parted, opening up a corridor through which Jarka, Relyk, Imzen, and Vaseus proceeded. Surrounded by attention on all sides, the throbbing pain in his leg eased.

Within the ring stood Traz and Vawk, their warriors standing around them in a semicircle. While the expressions of their brutes were severe, the twins appeared positively ecstatic.

"When we heard someone tried to kill you," Vawk called out, "we didn't think you'd show."

Jarka moved away from Relyk and straightened to his full height. "So sorry to disappoint, old friend. I had to come, for I am one yagar who honours the law of the Challenge."

Even with their dim wits, the twins noticed the barb within those words.

Their smirks twisted into snarls, and Traz beckoned him in. "Come on then. Let us show everyone what a fake you really are."

"Really? You still want to fight him?"

Jarka turned to Vaseus. "No," he hissed. "It's not your place—"

"Last night, an assassin tried to murder Jarka in his sleep," she called out so that many could hear her. She shrugged past his outstretched hand and moved into the ring to face down the twins. "Was he sent by you two?"

"What did we say about talking?" Traz snarled as he stepped towards her. "This is a yagar matter. These are yagar lands. A human has no voice here—"

"She prevented the unjust killing of a Warlord," Relyk cut in, moving to stand with Vaseus. "This human saved a Warlord from being murdered in his bed. She has earned a place among us."

"Was it you?" Vaseus demanded, the words coming out hot and fierce. "Was the assassin following your orders?"

The twins bristled, their hulking forms flexing and clenching in a ripple of muscled rage.

"You understand nothing, filthy human," Vawk growled. "I could kill you in a second—"

"*Enough*," Jarka bellowed, unwilling to allow it to go on any longer. "These words are pointless. Let us decide who is right the way we always have."

Vaseus shot a fiery look back at him.

"Yes," she quickly called out, projecting her voice for the whole crowd. "Combat is the only way to settle this. But the Challenge should not be today. Warlord Jarka is too honourable to say it, but the fight should be delayed until he is healed."

Her gaze returned to the twins. "Where is the honour in defeating a wounded opponent? Would it not be better to win a fair fight?"

Though the two brutes stared her down with rage in their eyes and muscles flexed, they did not respond.

As the silence stretched, a murmur rippled through the crowd. At first it was low and tentative. But soon it rose, higher, louder.

Before long, many voices joined the call, and what the call was rang out clear.

"Delay! Delay! Delay! Delay—"

"*No*," Jarka bellowed, pushing past Vaseus and into the heart of everything. The noise fell away in answer.

Looking to the crowd all around him, he called out, "There will be no delay. None of you have the power to decide that. A Challenge was issued and accepted. Honour demands we fight, here and now. The Warrior Code demands it."

A heavy silence followed his words. Jarka cast his gaze around to them all a final time before looking directly at Vawk and Traz. "Shall we?"

Sly grins revealed the tips of their fangs.

"Clear the ring," Vawk barked.

"And bring him a spear," Traz added.

Jarka suppressed a grimace as he pivoted and moved to the edge of the ring. Vaseus exited slowly, her face racked with anxious worry. He could only muster a whisper of a smile as she joined the massive crowd surrounding the ring.

A piercing throb surged all through his leg as he settled in. He sucked in a sharp inhale and couldn't help but wince.

As he let it out, he breathed, "For Mother and Father. And for Jazith."

A tall warrior arrived and gave him a spear. In that moment, as he eyed the two bulky brothers standing at the opposite side of the ring, Jarka knew something he rarely knew with a spear in hand.

He knew that he could lose.

"Begin."

The twins loosed exuberant roars as they charged. Jarka grit his teeth as he ran to meet them, an explosion of fire sweeping through him. Traz came hard on the left, swinging his spear overhead and down with both hands. Jarka deflected the heavy blow wide, continuing by and twisting right. Vawk swung for the knees. His spear still too high to intercept, Jarka leapt over the sweeping attack. His wounded leg gave when he landed, forcing him into a barrel roll.

As he came out of it, Traz was right there, bellowing a roar as he attacked. Jarka parried the diagonal strike, thinking to counter with an attack of his own. But the power of the blow was incredible. The bones of his arms shook, and it was all he could do to absorb it then bat away a rising jab.

In the corner of his eye, he spied Vawk about to flank him. He pivoted around, shifted his hands to grip the middle of his spear, and lashed the butt end out at Vawk's face. The twin pulled up to block. Traz sought to take advantage with a quick thrust at Jarka's chest. He quickstepped back and knocked the strike wide. Vawk came on with a high jab and a sideways sweep for the hip. Jarka parried both, giving ground to dodge Traz's incoming high swipe.

He snarled, furious that he could not go on the attack. Despite his all-consuming need to defeat the twins, he was forced back, barely keeping them at bay. His breath was laboured and his muscles were tiring. Their every strike was powerful, and absorbing them sapped his strength.

He fought on, fuelled by the demanding need to win. He roared as he stymied another of Vawk's side swipes, the wood of their spears cracking off each other. He pushed off his good leg to dodge Traz's high thrust, then lashed the leaf head of his spear around at Vawk's ribcage. This surprised the twin, for he was forced to jump back to avoid being hit. Jarka moved to press home his advantage, but Traz cut in with a sweeping kick. He leapt back, burning agony flashing in his gashed thigh. He snarled again, enraged with his inability to take advantage of the opportunity.

The next moment, Vawk was upon him, grinning as he resumed the attack. Jarka parried the short combo and was about to counter, but again was interrupted when Traz arrived with a two-handed overhead strike. Caught in the movement of an attack, Jarka could only twist to block. He absorbed the blow straight on, arms crumbling beneath Traz's raw power.

Vawk followed with a jab. Jarka had to let a hand come free of his spear to bat the driving jab aside with his forearm. Traz stepped in close and swung a right cross for Jarka's head. He barely ducked under the punch, and in the same motion, stumbled back.

He sensed he was at the ring's edge and tried to rush towards the center. But Vawk cut him off with a quick spear thrust. Traz came in too, boxing him in with a diagonal swing at his shoulder.

Trapped, Jarka could only defend, using the ends of his spear twirling back and forth to stave them off.

But it couldn't last. They all knew it. Without space to move, it was only a matter of time.

Jarka held out, somehow deflecting and blocking every swing and thrust of their spears, his reactions flowing without decision.

He grit his teeth, willing his wasting muscles to work. But the twins did not relent. They attacked with triumph in their eyes. They knew they had him.

His arms tired and his movements slowed. After blocking another strike from Vawk, he could not get back in time to meet Traz's spear. He had to drop to a knee, the weapon passing just over his head. Vawk thrust again. Jarka intercepted with his spear, but slowly. The opening was there for Traz to end it—

"Roll forward now!"

The voice sounding in his head coincided with a surge of energy in his legs, and he leapt into a diving roll. He passed in between the twins, Traz's spear whispering through the fur of his belly. In one fluid motion, he hit the ground shoulder first, barrel rolled, and sprang back to his feet.

"That's my son."

Though it couldn't be, it was. It was the voice of his father.

"We're with you, Jarka. And we love you."

This, his mother.

Tears welled in his eyes. In that frozen moment, he felt strength flow through him. The fatigue in his muscles lessened, and his anger dissolved like dust on the wind.

He turned around. Vawk and Traz were just standing there, looks of disbelief on their faces. Though he did not look, Jarka sensed that shock had rendered the entire crowd mute. All was still, and in that still instant, he felt the familiar ease of knowing one simple thing.

This I can do.

Traz broke the moment apart with a violent bark as he charged, followed closely by his brother. Jarka stood ready to meet them.

Traz lanced his spear straight out, all power and speed. Jarka dipped a shoulder and slid aside, slapping his spear down to the shaft of his opponent's. The move was so fast that Traz's left side was exposed. Jarka feinted a strike towards the opening. Vawk arrived there, lunging his spear to intercept. Anticipating this, Jarka shifted and rammed the butt end of his spear into Vawk's chest. There was a dull thud as the wood hit. Vawk groaned and went sprawling to the ground outside the ring.

Bellowing, Traz lashed out with a wild horizontal sweep. Jarka deflected this high, then blocked an overhead strike. Arms weaving, he countered with a series of high and low thrusts. Traz parried one after the other.

But then, after faking a quick jab aimed at the chest, Jarka brought his spear up to Traz's throat. The twin stopped, breathing harsh and glaring Jarka down. Slowly, he raised a clenched fist to yield.

It was done. Jarka straightened out of his fighting stance and regarded the twins, inhaling and exhaling deep, measured breaths. He had dreamed of this moment for years, the moment when he made these two pay for everything they had taken from him. Countless times, he had conjured up triumphant statements he would say to make their defeat that much worse.

But with the opportunity at hand to cut them down to size, he felt no desire to do so. There was no hate anymore. There was simply relief, and a quiet satisfaction that he had done what needed to be done.

And so, once Vawk regained his feet, Jarka inclined his head. "Well fought, my friends." He straightened and met their eyes, eyes that were full of rage or fear or both. "It was an honourable Challenge."

"How?" Traz spat. "How did you do that? You were trapped. There was nowhere for you to go. We had you. We *had you!*"

Jarka's only answer was a slight smile.

"Answer him," Vawk snarled. "I want to know. You must have cheated somehow. You must have. Tell us how you did that!"

A low chuckle rumbled deep in Jarka's throat. He looked at Vawk, then at Traz. Without a word, he let his spear fall to the ground, turned, and walked away.

Upon seeing all the eyes of those in the crowd peering at him, his smile broadened. He looked for Vaseus and soon found her amongst the vast multitude of black and yellow.

We did it, bee, he thought as their eyes locked. *Now—*

"*No!*"

Her scream split everything apart. Seeing the rush of horror contort her face, Jarka's stomach dropped. He twirled around, consumed with the dread of horrid pain.

It all happened in a blink. The twins were rushing in, snarls of black hate on their faces. As they arrived to cut him down, spears flew in from all sides. Many found their mark. The thrown weapons plunged into Vawk and Traz, and they collapsed to the ground.

His breath stuck in his throat, Jarka stared down at the twins, both already dead at his feet.

He didn't understand. What had just happened? How was he not dead? Who would save him here? And why?

Eventually, he forced his gaze away from the brothers and looked to everyone nearby. Most of the warriors around the ring had empty hands, warriors that were loyal to Vawk and Traz.

"What they were about to do was without honour," one of them called out, as if knowing Jarka's mind. "You are my Warlord now. That is why I threw."

Another called out, "That is why I threw."

"And I."

"And I."

Jarka looked on as each in turn added their voice of confirmation. A feeling unlike anything he had ever known consumed him, and once more, tears brimmed in his eyes.

FORTY-ONE

That city is well fortified which has a wall of
men instead of brick.

Lycurgus of Sparta

The sun was high overhead, the heat suggesting high noon, when
Kaletor lay eyes on home, on Sparta, the greatest city in all the world.
The scouts had already brought back word that no opposing force was
anywhere to be seen. It seemed like there would be no battle.

Riding alone at the head of the column, Kaletor glanced back over a
shoulder. Strung out along the road were his Phalanxes, the red and gold of
their armaments stretching on and on.

It seemed a shame that so many veterans, hardened survivors of many
battles, all at the peak of their fighting prowess, would not get to claim their
prize by force. It was not the glorious finale they deserved.

He had assumed Ockos would try to stop him. Surely, he must have
recognized the threat. Even after the scout's report, he had held out; it couldn't
truly be so easy.

Yet, as they neared the city and he saw it with his own eyes, the situation was
undeniably clear. The gates were open and the walls were unmanned. Sparta
was his for the taking.

It didn't feel right.

He scratched at the stubble on his cheeks as he scanned the city. Civilians
flowed in and out of the gates as if nothing out of the ordinary was happening.
It felt like their arrival was a minor and insignificant detail.

His jaw clenched to grit his teeth, Kaletor gestured with his left hand.

Directly behind him rode Hullis, and within a few moments, the general had urged his mount alongside.

"What is it, sir?"

Keeping his gaze fixed on the city, Kaletor said, "What game is he playing?"

"I'm not sure. Perhaps he knew he couldn't win."

"Unlikely. Ockos doesn't base his decisions in reality or reason. He only does what's best for him and his power. That's why this doesn't make sense. He wouldn't just give up."

"Maybe he thinks we aren't a threat."

Kaletor shook his head. "No. It's something else."

Nothing changed as the column gradually neared the city. Kaletor maintained a rigid focus on the gates and walls, ready to respond to anything. They moved within bowshot, but still nothing happened.

Peasants on the road either scurried into the city or moved off the road, dragging their oxen, mules, or runts with them. From there, they watched Kaletor and his personal guard pass in what seemed an intrigued, but unconcerned, silence.

As he observed their calm, the urge came to jump from his horse and kill some of the dirt-stained people. Although the impulse had an appealing pull, he refrained. He had come for Ockos, not the spawn of poverty.

When they were within about one hundred steps of the gate, Hullis said, "Perhaps we should send a unit of hoplites in first, sir. There could be an ambush—"

"No," Kaletor snarled, still keeping his eyes dead ahead. "I will not enter my city cowering behind other men. I never have before, and today will be no different."

"As you wish, Commander."

They continued on, and at the head of over twelve thousand men, they passed under the gate and entered the city. The square just inside was empty, save for two rows of twenty of the Emperor's Elites. They were at ease, spears pointing skyward, golden shields slung over their golden cloaks.

Standing just in front was the emperor himself, dressed in his gold-trimmed, blood-red tunic, which, oddly, was too large for him. His diadem of creamy ivory flecked with gold ringed his head of short white hair.

Kaletor slid from the saddle and approached. As he came closer, he saw that Ockos had changed. He was hunched over, more wrinkles creased his cheeks and throat, and deep purple bags had sunk craters under his eyes. It was as if he had aged twenty years in a few months.

"Welcome home, Commander," Ockos croaked, his voice thin as a dry wind. "You have done well. The war is won, and the Empire is restored. All of Sparta owes you a great debt."

Kaletor barely heard the emperor's words. He stopped and stared at this shrivelled shell of a man he had known nearly all his life. As he looked, he saw something in those dark, watery eyes he had seen in many others—a broken, desperate fear.

He had come to seize control by force. He had never considered this.

Struggling to cope, he shook himself and finally found his voice. "What madness is this? What's going on? What's happened to you, Ockos?"

The emperor's brow creased, the corners of his eyes crinkling into tiny slits. "I don't understand your meaning, Commander."

"I marched three Phalanxes all the way down from the northern frontier to take Sparta away from you. Why have you not prepared to defend yourself?"

"You did?" Ockos said, blinking as he looked towards the gate. "Where? Which Phalanxes did you bring?"

"Do not take me for a fool, Ockos," Kaletor growled, a blazing furnace rising in his chest. "There's no way an army of this size could pass through the Empire without you knowing about it."

"No, you wouldn't think so. But I've been rather busy these days."

"Busy? Busy with what?"

The emperor's sunken eyes widened, darting to meet Kaletor's gaze, before falling away and settling on the ground. "Nothing, nothing. So why did you bring so many men with you? Didn't you win the war?"

Though he wanted to know why Ockos was so listless, Kaletor forced himself back to the task at hand. "Yes," he answered. "I have crushed the traitorous bastards and ended their little rebellion. I have restored law and order to the Empire."

Ockos nodded to himself, still looking at the ground. "That's good, my boy," he muttered, nodding far more than was normal. "Hopefully now there will be more female yagars being brought in."

Biting back a snarl, Kaletor stepped closer and said, "Are you insane? Female yagars mean nothing. Forget about your obsession. I have brought the Empire back from the brink of destruction. I have brought glory and victory to Sparta, and I've returned for my reward."

These forceful words brought the emperor's eyes back up. "Yes. Of course. How can I reward the greatest commander Sparta has ever known?"

It was the question Kaletor had been waiting to hear. He could finally dispose of Ockos, take the diadem, claim the throne, and become the most powerful man in the world.

But instead of satisfied triumph, there was hesitation and bitter uncertainty. His clear vision of defeating an old, corrupt, and weak emperor was gone, stained and murky as a foul bog. There was no resistance to overcome, no glorious battle to win. All he had to do was kill Ockos and the Empire was his.

It was all wrong. The ease of it left a rotten taste in his mouth.

As he struggled to overcome the doubt in his mind, he noticed something had shifted in Ockos's eyes. Where before there had been fear, or madness, or both, now there appeared to be hope.

No, not hope. Deep within those dark, sunken eyes, there was a strangled plea for help.

His anger slackened then, and questions arose. Why? What had the Emperor of Sparta so desperate that he was hoping for someone else to take his place? Had someone gotten to him? Was his life under threat? Was he being controlled or manipulated? And if so, by whom?

These and other questions flooded his mind. He had to look away, pressing his fingers against his forehead.

"Is something wrong, Commander?"

Kaletor ignored the emperor's shaky question as his thoughts raced. He had to change tactics. Before long, a rough plan took shape. It wasn't perfect, but it would have to do.

"What I have accomplished deserves the highest possible rewards," he said, locking eyes with Ockos once more. "First, a triumphant parade and citywide feast will be organized in order to celebrate the victorious end to the war. I will lead my army in a great procession through Sparta so that the people can shower us with praise. After that, we will drink, feast, and watch all manner of spectacles.

"But the parade will end with my second and final reward," Kaletor continued, watching Ockos's expression closely. "In front of the people, you will name me the Emperor's Champion and your sole heir."

The declaration caused the old man's clenched face to crease even deeper. "I don't understand. What does that mean?"

"It means you and I will rule together, with equal power and authority. You will remain emperor, and I will be your heir and champion. There is nothing to fear. I will be your advisor, your confidante, and your protector."

The emperor's strained mouth and worried eyes softened. "Oh," he said, the word stretching out long and dripping with a relaxed release. "Oh, I see. Very well. This is how it should be. Sparta's greatest son should get what he wants."

Kaletor gave a single nod. "Together, we will make the Empire strong enough to last a thousand years. Sparta will rule all the world."

Though his voice was firm and absolute, he felt little triumph. He had come home expecting to snatch a diadem from a bloody corpse. But the emperor was already broken, defeated by somebody else.

His glorious return was spoiled, and someone was to blame.

He looked into the city and ground his teeth.

Someone's to blame.

FORTY-TWO

He became a Superior, and since he kept winning one Challenge after another, there was nothing anyone could do. Before long, Chalrog was Warlord, the greatest warrior and most powerful yagar of the Clan. No one could defeat him. Many tried. They all failed.

The Spoken Tales

From the summit of a steep, sharp-sided hill, Jarka looked upon the valley stretching away from the forest's edge. Across the swaths of thick grassland stretched a chaotic sprawl of humans and yagars, Clans and Clanless, enemies turned allies. The number of humans swelled every day as more and more fled from the approaching Spartan army.

Even now, in the midst of ongoing preparations, he still felt as if he were in a dream. None of it was supposed to be possible. But with Vaseus leading the humans, and himself leading the yagars, it had somehow happened.

Seated on a wide boulder, he breathed in deep, and as he let it out, closed his tired eyes. *We've come so far, far beyond anything I ever imagined. And yet there's still so far to go. Can we really do this? Can we really defeat the Empire?*

It was a question he had brooded on ever since defeating the twins. Challenging the Warlords of all the Clans had once seemed the tallest of tasks. Success had seemed distant and impossible.

Now, it felt minor. Challenging Warlords was straightforward and simple, despite the difficulty. What lay ahead was something else entirely. He had stepped into completely unknown territory. Every day brought problems. Sometimes it felt like he was drowning.

His thoughts reminded him of the last time he had seen Imzen, who had stayed behind in the Clanless village.

"Control what you can control," she had said. "That is all you need to do. But you already know this. You are different than you were when we left home. You have learned what I had to teach, and I am proud of you, Jarka. I knew I would be."

His brooding was interrupted by approaching footsteps. He shook himself and stood to watch a group of humans and yagars, Relyk and Vaseus among them, summit the hill.

Forcing a smile, he moved to meet them. "Greetings, my friends. How are we on this fine day?"

"I can't take it anymore," snarled Masos, the dark-skinned, broad-shouldered man who had been declared the human's war leader, partly because he was one of the few that understood yagar. "I refuse to go on like this."

"What's the problem now?"

"Them," the human spat, pointing at Relyk and the pair beside him. "All of your people. They constantly mock and insult us. We're weak and puny, they say. We'd be better served to run from a fight rather than face it, they say. One of them is equal to twenty of us, they say."

Tavyka, now Second of the Northern Mountain Clan, said, "We say these things because they are true."

"Twenty's too low," the female Elder Loriz pitched in, a sly grin spreading within the grey whiskers around her mouth. "It's more like thirty."

"You see? I won't allow my people to be so abused—"

"What Masos is trying to say," Vaseus cut in, her voice firm, "is that this division between humans and yagars needs to be mended. If we're to stand any chance against the Spartans, we have to trust each other. Everyone must see that we're on the same side—"

"We have bigger problems," Tavyka cut in, stepping forward to address Jarka directly. "More Superiors have been issuing Challenges to the Seconds, and fighting for a higher rank continues within most Clans."

"You see," Masos snarled, moving to stand right beside Tavyka. "This is exactly what I mean. You blithely disregard our problems to focus on one of yours. It's arrogance like this that keeps us divided."

Jarka glanced to Vaseus, giving her a look of exhausted helplessness.

Seeing a humorous glint in her dazzling green eyes, he passed over the two directly in front of him to address Loriz. "It seems my instructions to the Superiors did not get through. I would ask that you deliver the message to all Clans that Challenges must cease until the war is over. We can't have Seconds changing, not if we're to fight as a single, unified army. Perhaps if they hear this from one as respected as you, they will finally listen."

The Elder gave a single nod. "I will make sure that they do, Warlord. But our problems do not end there. Old rivalries between certain Clans run deep. Long-standing wounds remain. The bickering is constant, and more fights broke out last night. Worst of all are the Clanless. They are hated the most. If it weren't for their numbers, the Clans would turn violent."

"They still could," Tavyka added. "I don't think it wise to bring them any further. We would be better off without them."

"They make up a fifth of the entire army," Jarka contested. "We need those spears. Not only that, they are as much my family as any Clan. I will not forsake them."

A flicker of rage marred Tavyka's face, and at that moment, she and Masos wore similar expressions. "Then what is to be done? We cannot win battles if we're at each other's throats."

She was right. Things could not continue on this path much longer. Jarka knew of only one solution.

Again looking past the displeased pair, he asked Relyk, "Have our scouts reported back yet? Do we know how far away the Spartan army is?"

"They're two days away, pursuing some rebel humans from the southeast. If they don't know we're here yet, they will soon."

Nodding, Jarka brought his gaze down to Masos. "Tell me again how many warriors they have."

"You can't," Vaseus cut in, rushing forward to join them. "It won't work—"

"How many?" Jarka repeated, ignoring her despite the impulse not to.

The fire dimmed in Masos's eyes. He visibly swallowed and said, "Fifteen thousand. Maybe more."

"Barely more than our numbers. Spread the word to all in camp that tomorrow we move to destroy the Spartans."

Relyk, Tavyka, and Loriz each nodded and turned to leave—

"You can't do this," Vaseus said. "You don't know this enemy like I do. They're professional soldiers, trained to the same tactics, drilled to fight as one, and immersed in a world of violence. They know everything there is to know about battles out in the open. We cannot win by facing them head-on."

Seeing the desperation in her eyes and hearing the same in her voice caused him to pause.

But this was bigger than them. This was the only way.

So, pushing his feelings aside, he said, "You forget who we yagars are, bee. We train as soon as we can hold a spear. We live by the Warrior Code. Combat is at the heart of our way of life."

"But this isn't a Challenge. Individual bravery and prowess aren't all it takes to win a battle. It takes more."

"Even still, yagars never back down from a fight. We will not run, hide, or cheat. A direct solution is the yagar way. The Spartans need to be defeated, and so we go to defeat them.

"Not to mention," he went on, bringing a hand up to stop her with her mouth half open, "that attacking a common enemy will force our army to come together and fight side by side. This is how we stop all the infighting."

"It won't work," she said, her tone even more desperate than before. "Brute strength is *their* game. You're playing right into their hands. Even a well-trained, well-prepared army would lose in a head-on fight. An army divided against itself has no chance against their phalanx formation. We must learn to trust each other first, then how to work and fight together. That is our only chance of winning this war. Please, Jarka. Please don't do this."

Again, he couldn't help but pause. He sorely wished to tell her what she wanted to hear. He wanted to take her in his arms and tell her it was going to be alright.

But no matter how much he wanted to do these things, he knew he couldn't. He had to do what was right.

"I'm sorry, Vaseus. It's the right thing to do. We attack tomorrow."

Though he had intended to say it gently, there was a hard edge in his voice as he spoke.

Her pleading expression instantly morphed into something uglier. "You stubborn, reckless fool. You send us all to our deaths. The Spartans will crush us, and everything we've struggled so hard for will have been in vain. I can't believe I trusted a savage to help my people."

There were tears in her eyes as she spun on her heels and stormed off. He stared after her, knots tying in his stomach.

Sensing the attention of the others, he said, "That'll be all. Make sure everyone knows that we head southeast in the morning."

They all turned to leave, Relyk casting him a stern look from the rear.

Once they were gone, Jarka brought a hand up and rubbed two fingers into his temples. *What have I done? I'm sorry, bee. I don't know what else to do. Is she right? Am I leading us to our doom?*

He released a heavy sigh. *I wish you were here, Jazith. You would know what to do.*

FORTY-THREE

If they stand behind you, protect them. If they
stand beside you, respect them. If they stand
against you, kill them.

Thrasilaus of Thebes

"The hoplites are ready, Commander. Shall I give the order?"

Kaletor let his gaze pass by Hullis as he turned in the saddle. The twelve thousand men he had brought to take the throne lined the Southern Laconia road all the way back to a series of hills, an unending column of red cloaks and gold armour flashing under the late morning sun.

Once more, he thought of the glorious battle they could have won.

Releasing a gruff exhale, he said, "Very well. Let's get this over with."

From his own mount, Hullis signaled to the trumpeter, and a long, low horn blast echoed across the silent valley.

Kaletor faced forward and nudged his horse into an easy walk. Just ahead waited Sparta, a city poised to celebrate their victorious Commander and his Phalanxes. Yet as he peered through the yawning gates and saw the street beyond lined with onlookers, he found himself dreading what was to come.

The cheering erupted the moment he and Hullis rode through the gate. Men, women, and children looked on, rows upon rows of them filling every space. Long banners of red and gold hung from atop columns and from the windows of buildings, many reaching all the way down to the ground. Bright music played somewhere ahead, the lively notes adding a merry background to the commotion.

Everything was bright and polished, and the banners dressed up the plain stone and brick of the city. The people were adorned in the Empire's colours, all of them smiling, laughing, or waving to show their adoration and excitement.

Though surrounded by this wash of cheerfulness, Kaletor could not bring himself to smile. *Simple pawns. You celebrate something you cannot possibly understand. All you see are strong men upon whose shoulders you stand, men who have won a war that you hardly noticed. None of you have the faintest idea of the things we've done. You don't know how much blood we spilled to keep your little lives safe and comfortable. I bring you victory and glory, but you are all unworthy of it.*

His mind continued to swim such dark streams as his horse carried him deeper into the city. It was a long, slow ride through the never-ending crowds, and his disgust was a constant thorn.

After what felt like an eternity, they reached the emptied Central Forum. People were packed all around its edge, forming an unbroken perimeter.

There was a thunderous roar when Kaletor arrived. He managed to incline his head slightly in recognition.

As he crossed the cordoned-off space around which the crowd was bunched, he looked across to the far end. There awaited Ockos, seated upon a marble throne. Arrayed before the raised platform were several rows of Elites, shining gold and fully armed.

But Kaletor's attention was drawn to the only other figure atop the platform. It was a yagar, seated on Ockos's left, unbound and unguarded. Over her yellow and black fur, she wore a gold cloak and a breastplate of iron with carved images of Spartiates. Her cold, unwavering regard was fixed on Kaletor.

He remembered her. Sola.

Upon laying eyes on the savage, he sucked in a sharp hissing breath. He kept his eyes on her for a long time before finally looking to the emperor.

What madness is this? What game are you playing now?

With muscles taut, he dismounted, walked around the statue-like Elites, and climbed the stairs. The moment he cleared the top step, his eyes locked with the yagar's. Her steady gaze was unchanged. He felt his heart quicken as he stared into the dark, vertical slits that were her pupils.

It wasn't until he was halfway across the platform that Ockos noticed his approach. "Commander," he said, his voice barely carrying over the persistent noise coming from the crowd. "What an excellent idea this was. Come, sit and enjoy the spectacle with us."

Kaletor didn't bother with any formalities. He remained silent and kept his eyes on the yagar, ready to act if she made any move.

But she was motionless as he passed by, her intense eyes tracking him. Pivoting to avoid exposing his back, Kaletor took his place on the marble seat to Ockos's right.

"Your men certainly look the part," the emperor said, apparently oblivious to the tension around him.

Sitting taut on the edge of his seat, Kaletor snarled, "What is this?"

Ockos was frowning as he slowly rotated in his seat. "I'm sorry?"

"Why is your yagar here, out in the open?"

The hunched, old man blinked, looking like a sleepy owl. "I don't understand. Why wouldn't she be out in the open?"

"She's loose," Kaletor growled, digging his fingers into the arm rests. "As far as anyone else knows, she could kill you before anyone could stop her. Why isn't she in chains?"

Unbelievably, the emperor gave a crooked smile. "There's no need for that, Commander. Don't you remember? I've raised Sola since birth. She is my daughter, and our bond is strong. There's nothing to fear. She is one of us."

"That's not the point. She's still yagar, and as far as anyone else knows, she's as bloodthirsty as the rest of them."

Ockos shook his head. "My Sola isn't like the rest of them, Commander. She's just as civilized as we are."

It was like talking to a child. Gritting his teeth and wishing he could snap the fool's neck, Kaletor looked away.

It's one thing to say that the yagar was like *his daughter. But now he's saying she* is *his daughter. I should have known he was insane. How will Sparta forge the greatest empire of all time with this emperor on the throne? I should kill him here and now.*

Seething in silence, he was consumed by the need to act as he watched his army filling the Forum.

But slowly, as the minutes passed, his reason for keeping the fool alive filtered in. Ockos was no longer in control. Someone else was, and he needed to find out who.

His death grip on the arm rests slowly eased, though his mind continued to churn. It had been four days since he had arrived home, and during that time, he had watched and listened whenever anyone spoke to or about Ockos. But this had earned him nothing, no leads whatsoever. His hope of forcing the traitors out with his blatant bid for power had not yet borne fruit, and his patience was wearing thin.

A long time later, the Forum was packed full of hoplites as the last Phalanx finally completed the procession through the city. The crowd's enthusiasm had waned, and there was now a halfhearted cheer for the conclusion of the march.

Ockos, whose listing head suggested he had nodded off, suddenly sat up. Looking around and appearing thoroughly confused, he said, "Is that it?"

Biting down hard on a snarl, Kaletor said, "Yes."

"Ah. I suppose it's time for me to speak then."

Using the support of the arm rests, the old fool managed to push himself to his feet. "People of Sparta," he called out, his thin voice barely loud enough to reach anyone, "behold the brave men who have won us the war."

The crowd's applause, whoops, and whistles rang out in answer, and the hoplites raised their spears in acknowledgment.

"Our invincible Phalanxes," Ockos went on as the commotion died down, "were led by a man who's name you all know. He is the reason the rebellion has been crushed. He is the Taker of Athens, the Lion of Sparta. People of the Empire, I give you the greatest Spartan of our time, Commander Kaletor!"

This time, the Phalanxes added their voices, and the answering eruption shook the very ground.

For a moment, Kaletor remained seated, taking in the waving arms, the smiling faces, the swell of adoration.

It did nothing for him. He was far too intent on what might happen next.

Still eyeing the nearest rows of the crowd, he slowly got to his feet, his expression grim and hard as iron.

Gradually, the noise ebbed, and Ockos went on. "His heroic achievements and unshakeable service to the Empire deserve to be rewarded. This is why I, your Emperor, officially declare Kaletor to be my sole heir to the throne. I also name him the Emperor's Champion, making his power and authority equal to mine."

Ockos turned and bowed his head. Taking the cue, Kaletor moved ahead to stand alone.

Playing his part, Ockos cried out, "I present to you your new Champion!"

As wild applause and cheers answered the call, Kaletor made ready every fibre in every muscle.

Now. Now was the moment. He kept his eyes wide, darting across the multitudes, watching for the flying arrow, thrown dagger, or charging assassin. Each moment passed with slow, sparking uncertainty.

He waited and waited, the noise of the crowd a distant crash of waves on rocks.

But nothing came. Nothing happened.

Gradually, the applause died. Kaletor hesitated at first, unwilling to present his back to the crowd. But there was nothing to suggest any danger whatsoever.

Releasing a long, harsh exhale through his nose, he turned and strode back to his seat. *Impossible! How can this be? I was unarmed, unguarded, completely vulnerable. That was their chance. Do they think I won't come after them? Do they think I'll be taking orders from Ockos? Or do they think they'll be able to control me as well?*

Though his mind raced, he did not glean any answers. He had been sure that whoever was controlling Ockos would try something at his moment of triumph. It was clearly a moment when he would appear an easy target.

But they had done nothing.

Denied any leads, he could only clench his hands into tight fists and grit his teeth.

Ockos had strode forward and was addressing the crowd once again. ". . . to honour the Emperor's Champion, the new heir to the throne, I present this spectacle, a spectacle unlike anything anyone's ever seen before."

On that cue, the Emperor's Elites started to move. The entire formation came apart, the straight rows morphing into a hollow square.

Kaletor absently peered into the empty space of the new formation. At the center, sitting back-to-back and bound together by chains, were two yagars.

A murmur rippled through the crowd, many pointing at the pair.

When the Elites finished moving into the formation, they levelled their spears toward the prisoners. With the boundary set, four slaves moved in to remove the chains.

"Yagars fight in single combat to determine who has power over whom," Ockos called out, stilling the rising chatter of the masses. "Today, we witness one of these legendary Challenges!"

Ecstatic cheers and crashing applause rose in answer.

Despite his simmering displeasure, Kaletor couldn't help but be intrigued. Not only by the impending fight, but by the emperor's decision.

He had always been obsessed with female yagars, but he had mostly kept them to himself. Why the sudden change? Was this manipulation? Was someone forcing him to display what he had often kept hidden?

This stream of thinking caused him to look over to the yagar still seated on the other side of the emperor's throne. She was looking on the scene without expression, her face neutral and slitted eyes level. If it weren't for the breeze moving through her fur, she could have been a statue.

Clenching his jaw, Kaletor looked back to the pair of yagars. Like Sola, these two were covered in yellow fur with black spots. The smaller of the pair had a copper band fastened around its neck, and bone bracelets on its wrists. The other had a bit of red cloth tied around its left bicep.

Once the chains were removed and the yagars were left alone in the square's center, Ockos raised his hands for attention.

"These two females come from very different places in yagar society. Wearing the red is Dynith. She was once the Third Superior of the Eastern River Clan, a respected and powerful warrior. The other is Jazith. She is the daughter of a Warlord who was cast out as a disgraced Clanless. Who will win this fight to the death? Let us watch and see!"

A raucous commotion spread across the entire Forum as people clambered to get closer. The yagars had risen and now stood with a few paces separating them. Both were looking to the surrounding Elites with their levelled spears and the mob surging beyond them.

Two spears were thrown into the de facto arena. Though jeers and cheers encouraged them to take up the weapons, neither did.

"They won't fight," Kaletor said to Ockos as the old man walked back.

The emperor settled onto his throne, a malicious grin on his lips. "Oh, I think they will."

"Why? They'd much sooner fight us."

The old man kept his gaze steady on the yagars as he replied. "I had them told that if they don't fight, we'll kill them both, but it won't be quick. They will know pain for days before they die."

Even as he finished speaking, the yagars' wandering gaze settled on the emperor. In that frozen moment, despite how inhuman they were, Kaletor recognized what was in their eyes.

Fearful hate.

In a blink, Dynith sprang towards a spear. A great roar of excitement burst as Jazith snatched up the other. Dynith came on hard, lancing her spear out far ahead of her. Jazith was forced to roll away in the act of grabbing her spear. She ended up on a knee, blocking Dynith's downward strike. She swept her trailing leg around. Dynith hopped over it, slashing a diagonal strike for her shoulder. She spun through her kick, getting her just beyond the attack, and surged to her feet.

This all happened in just a few seconds. Their movements were unbelievably quick, and Kaletor could barely follow.

Now Jazith jabbed high. Dynith ducked under it, sidestepped, and swung horizontal for the ribs. Jazith parried and countered.

Their spears cracked into each other in rapid succession, a dance of grace and power. Jazith gained the upper hand, stringing a complex combo together, forcing Dynith back. But a slight overextension, a quick counter, and Jazith was backpedalling, fending off a ferocious barrage.

"Incredible."

Kaletor barely noticed Ockos's awe. Like the crowd, he was fixated on the fight.

Jazith kept giving ground, her defense almost too slow. Dynith pressed hard, swinging her spear with expert precision. A feint fooled Jazith, and Dynith scored a thrust that sliced into the outer edge of her opponent's right side.

Jazith roared and pivoted away, rotating around with a wild swing. Dynith stepped beyond it and closed with a high jab. Jazith batted this aside, but Dynith kept on, forcing Jazith back. Blood stained the wounded yagar's side.

They fought on, somehow sustaining their lightning pace. Jazith was forced into a tight corner of spear tips, fending off blow after blow.

Kaletor knew what was coming.

Dynith struck high, smashing Jazith's spear shaft down and away. Her follow-up thrust drove deep into Jazith's thigh.

Despite the blow, the stricken yagar moved in close, bringing Dynith within arms reach. Loosing a ferocious roar, she swung her head straight out. Her forehead slammed into Dynith's face. The force of it caused Dynith to release her spear.

She staggered back, trying to get clear. Jazith thrust her spear straight out. It drove clean through Dynith's middle. A hideous death howl cut the air as she collapsed.

Victorious, Jazith dropped her weapon and fell to her knees, staring at her fellow yagar. After a moment, she tilted her head back and screamed. It was a wretched sound of pure anguish.

When it died, she slumped and sank to her side. There she lay, her entire torso heaving as she clutched at the spear in her leg.

The silence that hung on the air was like a black void.

Into it, Ockos rasped, "Tend to the victor! Such a fearless warrior deserves to live."

As a group of Elites moved to take up the fallen yagar, slow applause began. By the time they had her on their shoulders and were carrying her away, the combination of claps and cheers was deafening.

Kaletor did not join in the jubilation. The momentary distraction gone, his thoughts returned to what still plagued him.

So they think they can leave me alive and control Ockos the same as before. So be it. If they won't come after me, I will go after them.

FORTY-FOUR

As Warlord, Chalrog's dishonourable behaviour continued. His first War Season was worse than anyone could have imagined. He led his Clan into battle, unnecessarily slaughtering all those he crossed spears with. When some from his Clan protested, he cut one of them down. The Third Superior stepped in to stop it, issuing her Challenge to prevent further bloodshed. Chalrog won, and even after the Superior yielded, he killed her anyway.

The Spoken Tales

Many were about to die. That much was certain.

An army of yagars and humans stretched across an empty plain of stunted grass. Jarka was in the center of the front line, studying the enemy. Less than a mile away stood thousands of Spartans, a mass of iron shields and red cloaks. They were positioned atop a wide, rising hill, a crest of pine trees at their back. There they waited, apparently willing to let the fight come to them.

"What now?"

Jarka looked left to Masos, who was himself adorned in the heavy iron breastplate and helmet of their enemy. "Isn't it obvious? They're right there."

The human leader tilted his head, looking to others nearby as if hesitant. "I guess, uh," he said slowly, "it isn't. What's your plan?"

Despite the tightness that had been in his chest all morning, Jarka gave a low chuckle. "It's quite simple, my friend. We attack."

Many yagars within earshot laughed.

But Masos was undeterred. "We can't just go at them head-on. They have the high ground and they're dug in. It's impossible to break a Spartan phalanx with a frontal assault."

"Impossible," said Relyk, who was on Jarka's right, "for humans."

Even as further laughter sounded in response, Masos said, "Impossible for yagars, too. I promise you, Warlord, that if we attack them there, we will be slaughtered."

It was a phrase he had heard a few hours prior. He looked back to the perfectly arrayed ranks of the enemy, very different than their own disordered sprawl of yagars and humans.

Forcing aside a swelling doubt, he gave his reply. "Yagars do not shrink from a fight."

With that, he set off. He rotated his ears back and heard those behind him follow.

Staying out front, he walked on, spear in hand, eyeing the army of Spartans waiting atop the shallow rise. Their golden shields were overlapped, forming a solid wall of iron.

It was now, committed as they were, that the heaviness he carried dragged him back to the previous night.

"Don't do this," Vaseus had said to him. "It's not too late to pull back north."

Looking on her beauty, made all the more fair by the silver starlight, Jarka remembered wanting so badly to say yes. But it wasn't that easy.

"I can't, bee. If I call it off now, without a fight, every yagar will think I'm weak and cowardly. To run away is dishonourable. The Warrior Code forbids it. I would lose all respect, and they would either challenge my authority or return home. If that happens, I lose Jazith forever, and you lose your rebellion."

Her hands went to her hips as she shook her head. "You still don't get it, do you? That Spartan army you're planning to attack is better in almost every way. They've been drilled and drilled and drilled to fight together, to move together, to follow an order without hesitation. Their officers have studied the arts of war their entire lives. They know tactics that have been perfected over hundreds of years. Even the common hoplites wear armour that is nearly impenetrable. Their wall of shields is unbreakable. It's as strong as the hardest stone. Nothing gets through.

"Fighting battles like this is how they gained an empire. Do you understand? This is what they're best at. This is what they want!"

Her boiling shout rang loud through the still night air.

Peering through the trees, he glanced to the nearby camp. "I know you're upset, but try to keep it down, bee. You know what would happen if anyone found out about us—"

"What does it matter?" she snapped. "They're as divided as ever. Humans against yagars. Clans against Clanless. I'm sick of it. Maybe they should see us. Maybe we should show them that it's possible not to hate each other."

"You're probably right. We should announce our love to the whole world. What could possibly go wrong?"

For the first time in days, he saw a hint of a smile on her lips. But it was short-lived.

"Don't do this," she sighed, shoulders collapsing down. "Please. For me, Jarka. Please. Don't."

Hearing the exhaustion and desperation in her voice strained his chest. A powerful urge to take her in his arms demanded that he act.

"You know I would do anything for you," he said, stepping in close and bringing a hand up to her face. "Anything. But this is bigger than the two of us. And we yagars only know one way. This is the only way."

The disappointment that darkened her eyes was deep. But even worse was the hurt he saw within that darkness. It was as if he had driven a blade into her heart.

It was the last image he had of her. She just turned and left, disappearing into the darkness of the night. He hadn't known what to do, and so he stood there, frozen. By the time he moved to go after her, she was concealed by a thousand tents and firepits.

Now, about to face death, he had no idea where she was. Was she in the front line, somewhere in the ranks, or gone altogether? He didn't know. It was all he could do to put one foot in front of the other.

"Wait!"

The panicked yell seemed distant. The last image of her lingered in his mind's eye for a moment longer before he blinked and glanced back over his shoulder. "What is it, Masos?"

The broad-shouldered, dark-skinned man rushed to catch him up. "If we're going to do this, at least give us a speech."

"A what?"

"A speech. It's when you address your army. You know, give them some words of encouragement, stoke a fire in their bellies. Inspire them to great deeds and extraordinary courage. Help them to face death without fear."

Jarka waved the man away. "Yagars need no such words."

"Perhaps they don't, but men do!"

Instead of responding, Jarka started to run. He focused on the enemy line at the top of the hill. The Spartans remained motionless, their long wall of iron shields locked together, their spears jutting out.

Now within thirty paces, he broke into a headlong sprint.

At that moment, Masos hollered, *"Charge!"*

An answering roar rose up like a storm.

Raw power rushed through Jarka's body, and with thousands thundering at his back, he closed to attack. Gliding between two spears, he leapt high and drove his spear past the top of a shield. Neighbouring Spartans jabbed their spears out. He sidestepped two thrusts—

And was slammed into from behind, the collision foiling his move to attack. It was a crush of bodies with everyone rushing the shield wall, and he was knocked flat. Feet stomped on his back and limbs.

Roaring, he pushed into the ground with all his strength. His arms shook until he regained his feet.

A jutting spear forced him to jump away. As he did, his heel caught on something and he fell hard, landing flat on his back. He careened down the hill into someone's legs. Hands grasped hold under his arms, and he was hoisted back up.

Dull pain laced his legs and back as he stood just behind the line of fighting. Panting, he looked on a scene of chaos. Yagars were attacking ferociously, using their speed and size to drive their spears over the wall of shields. Yet the Spartans held firm, pushing back, jabbing their spears out with ruthless efficiency. All was angry shouts, bellows, and cries of agony. The stench of piss and blood already choked the air as death came to both sides.

Jarka watched two yagars go down right in front of him. A boiling roar erupted from deep in his gut as he charged into the fray. Without aiming, he drove his spear into a shield, all power. The man holding it was staggered but stayed in line with his neighbours. Jarka caught sight of a spear coming at him on his left. He twisted aside, drove off one foot, and swung his spear around. The stone leaf head cracked off one of the helmets. He followed with a quick thrust to the stricken man's chest.

As he fell, Jarka moved to exploit the gap in the shield wall. But before he could, another Spartan rushed up to fill it.

Jarka attacked with a snarl. His spear deflected off a shield in the unyielding wall. Two of the nearest Spartans thrust their spears at his torso. Jarka twisted away, cracking his spear's shaft into theirs. Following a short exchange of blocks and counters, Jarka worked in close enough to land a fatal blow. But just as before, another from behind stepped forward to shore up the gap before he could exploit it.

Ignoring his tiring arms, he battled on. The wall of iron and pikes remained stout and unbroken, and he was constantly dodging, parrying, deflecting, and ducking. He weaved the unending dance of combat, teeth grit and body in ceaseless motion. There was only the next attack, the next spear thrust to deflect or avoid, the next sidestep, the next death blow.

He had struck down ten or more, but not one had been easy. Still the wall held, a stubborn mass of iron and flesh and bone. The Spartans were defying the onslaught and showing no signs of breaking.

"Warlord! Warlord!"

Jarka ignored the call. He blocked a high thrust, avoided another by stepping right, then countered with a downward diagonal strike. His spear came down between the shoulders of two shields and connected with the side of a neck. The man howled and spun away.

As usual, a neighbouring Spartan attacked. He slid aside, smacking the spear shaft by with his free hand—

"*Jarka!*"

The urgency of the shout reached in harsh fingers and drew his attention. He bared his teeth as he backed away, blocking incoming attacks until he could disengage.

With more yagars rushing in front of him, he glanced over a shoulder and called back, "What?"

"Our entire left wing has been repelled," the voice, which Jarka now realized belonged to Masos, hollered over the crash of battle. "Our line is nearly split in two. We must pull back before it's too late!"

Jarka looked left, straining to his full height. He saw only a huge, chaotic mass of bodies, human and yagar alike. There was nothing to suggest that anything was wrong.

"The battle remains undecided," he called back. "We must keep fighting."

"But we cannot win. The Spartans are too dug in. They will never yield. Once the left breaks, the phalanx will sweep around and take us in the flank—"

"Yagars do not run from a fight," Jarka snapped, pivoting around to face the human leader. "We aren't starting now."

Before Masos opened his mouth, Relyk suddenly appeared. "There you are. Our left is nearly spent. They cannot hold much longer."

Jarka shook his head as he throttled the shaft of his spear. "Then we must break through their line here before they outflank us."

"We can't," Masos protested. "It will take too long. Sometimes you need to retreat and fight another day."

"It's not the yagar way!"

"The yagar way will no longer exist if we don't disengage!"

Snarling, Jarka spun back to the fighting line. The shield wall remained intact, still resisting the assault. He watched as yagars all along the line were being cut down with alarming frequency.

The truth staring him in the face was too obvious not to see it.

They could not win.

He loosed a roar that scalded his throat.

"Retreat!" he bellowed. "Fall back! Yagars retreat! Your Warlord orders you to retreat!"

Nothing happened.

Relyk and Masos added their voices.

"Retreat! Retreat! Fall back!"

With many looking around, the warriors nearest to them slowly began backtracking.

Jarka beckoned them back with his spear. "Retreat! Yagars, on your Warlord! Retreat!"

Many were cut down as they tried to disengage.

Gritting his teeth in a snarl, he turned away and joined the run back down the hill.

FORTY-FIVE

The Spartans are the equal of any men when
they fight as individuals; fighting together as a
collective, they surpass all other men.

Demaratus, King of Sparta

The sand in the open courtyard of his house felt coarse beneath
Kaletor's bare feet as he paced from one side to the other. The sky
above was a grey wasteland, promising rain it had not yet delivered.

"This can't be," he snarled, shoulders tight, hands continuously unclenching
and clenching into fists. "It can't be."

Hullis, who was leaning against one of the evenly spaced columns marking
the boundaries of the courtyard, now moved onto the sand. "It does seem
unlikely. And yet desperation can make people do the unthinkable."

Kaletor shook his head, the breastplate encasing his torso shifting slightly.
"But they're yagars. They hate humans. They squabble amongst each other.
They're divided and leaderless. How could the rebels have assembled so many
so quickly? And how did they get those savages to fight *with* them? It's
impossible!"

As ever, Hullis maintained his stoic exterior. "I'm not sure, Commander. But
even if the rebels have allied themselves with some yagars, you heard the
messenger. They are no more than a disorderly mob with no stomach for a real
fight. Our victory was total—"

"Unlikely," Kaletor spat, pacing faster than before. "We may have won, but not
as easily as Belisar would have us believe. He wants the glory of ending the war
for himself. He'd say anything to convince me not to come with reinforcements."

"Are we marching back north then? Shall I summon the Phalanxes?"

The notion was painfully tempting. Day after day of inactivity, of waiting for his network of informants to find something hadn't been easy. He craved the simplicity of war. He craved the drive to attain greater glory and an even greater reputation. Sitting around doing nothing had proved harder than he ever remembered it being. Every day was a struggle to get through, and every night was a restless hell.

"No," he snarled, stopping with feet planted wide directly before Hullis. "The situation here is too unstable. I cannot leave until my authority is absolute, no matter how badly I want to spill enemy blood."

The general gave a quick nod. "A wise decision, Commander. I'm sure Belisar can handle a mob of farmers and mindless savages."

"I wouldn't count on it. But enough of that. Fetch our weapons."

At last, as they had been intending to do when the message interrupted them, they sparred. With sword, spear, and shield they trained, trading blows in rapid succession, only easing up to avoid inflicting grievous injury.

After a while, Kaletor forgot about his problems. He focused only on his opponent, defending and attacking, intent on the fight at hand. His muscles strained with the effort and sweat sheathed his body.

An hour or more passed, Kaletor prevailing over and over again. They were battling with sword and shield when he noticed his lead slave standing in the shadow of the columned ring. All his troubles rushed back in like a pack of wolves, and he drove all his power straight into a shield bash that sent Hullis sprawling.

"What is it now?" he bellowed.

"Forgive the intrusion, Master," Talos said quickly, "but there's a certain Charis here to see you. He claims it is urgent."

Kaletor released a ragged breath. "It better be."

Dropping his armaments, he strode across the sand. "On your feet, General. Time to hear what the insects have to say."

Moments later, they arrived at the atrium, the large, square room of red-and-black walls that served as the formal entrance. Just inside the front door stood a lean, dark-skinned man in his middle years.

As they approached, he bowed his head. "Greetings—"

"Tell me what you came here to say," Kaletor cut in, moving to tower over one of his most senior informants. "And be quick. I'm in no mood for an exchange of wasteful words."

Charis tilted his head back, revealing calm, hazel eyes. "As you wish, Commander. We have captured a man we believe knows the answers to your questions."

"Who is he?"

"His name is Illyrius, a wealthy merchant who originally hailed from Corinth."

"A merchant? How could he possibly know who is controlling the emperor?"

"You will see, Champion. If you follow me, I will take you to him."

Glancing to Hullis over a shoulder, Kaletor said, "Fetch our swords."

"Weapons will not be necessary," Charis said smoothly. "He is bound—"

"Are you telling me what to do?" Kaletor said, craning his neck as he brought his attention back to the middle-class worm.

Somehow, the man did not wilt. "No, my prince. You can do whatever you want."

"I already have."

Once their swords were sheathed at their hips, Kaletor and Hullis followed Charis into the streets. The sky was even darker, the sheen of clouds the darkest shade of grey. Although it was still near midday, the city was lifeless, as if the peasants were anticipating impending doom and so were cowering inside their little houses like frightened mice.

Sure enough, it came. A shock of wind blasted its way through the street, dispelling the last vestiges of the day's heat. Then came the sheet of rain. Everything was soaked in a moment. White flashes lit up the oppressive dark, and thunderous booms shook the city.

Pushing through the driving gale and chill, slanting rain, Charis led them into the southern district. Coming to a narrow alley, he turned, the skinny path of rough cobbles a sloshing stream. Midway along, he stopped and came about.

"He's down there," the informant hollered, pointing down to a circular grate.

"What?" Kaletor snarled, feeling the chill sink even deeper into his bones. "In the sewers? What idiot decided to drag him down there?"

"It was the only place we could go without risking detection."

"Ridiculous. Haul the grate off then. And be quick!"

The iron rungs of the ladder were slick in hand, and the rushing water poured continuously on their heads as they descended.

Dripping wet, Kaletor reached the bottom and stepped onto the narrow walkway of stone, a walkway that ran just beside the river of shit. The foul stench clawed its way down his throat.

"How far?" he growled.

"Not far, my prince," Charis answered as Hullis joined them. "Follow me."

The narrow chamber was dark and winding, the dim light from above barely illuminating their way. Kaletor kept a hand trailing across the cool, rough-hewn stone of the tunnel in order to know where to place his next step. Muted rumbles of thunder reverberated down, and flashes of white lightning stabbed continuously.

Through the dank, wet labyrinth of stinking filth, they eventually came to a cistern. Here, the narrow tunnels gave way to an expansive hall, though the ceiling height remained unchanged. The air was cooler but less foul.

Most of the floor was submerged in a large pool of stagnant water, a pool which was being fed by seventeen sewers. Four raised walkways led to a central platform at the pool's heart. There stood seven figures, most with torches in hand. They were standing around a man on his knees with his hands tied behind his back.

Without pause, Charis continued onto one of the narrow walkways. "Look alive, boys," he called out, voice echoing hollow through the damp chamber. "The Emperor's Champion is here."

Kaletor arrived on the platform and moved to stand over the kneeling man. "So, this is the merchant with the answers."

"Not exactly, my prince."

The words were spoken by Charis. Kaletor looked up to release a fiery tirade—

But what he saw froze the words in his throat. The informants had all drawn short swords or daggers and now held them at the ready.

Kaletor drove his eyebrows down. "What is this?"

The kneeling man spun on his knees and surged to stand with the others. He too drew a sword, eyes fixed on Kaletor.

In that moment, he understood.

"Treacherous bastards," he spat, drawing his sword and casting his gaze at them all. "Do you not know who I am? Have you not heard the stories? No one can defeat me."

"Lay down your sword," Charis said evenly, "and we won't kill you."

Kaletor bared his teeth and barked a laugh. "You expect me to surrender? You have no idea what you're doing. I'm going to kill you all, and it won't be quick. You will—"

Something hard slammed into the back of his head, and he crumpled. His knees hit the ground, then his hands hit and slipped. Someone stepped on his sword arm and kicked the weapon from his grasp. Hard fingers grabbed his arms and forced them behind his back.

It all happened in three heartbeats, so fast that he didn't know who or how. There was a ringing in his ears and a hot throbbing along the back of his skull.

Harsh fingers grabbed his hair and pulled his face up from the wet stone. At first, he only saw figures looming around him, dark shapes against the dim, orange torchlight.

But gradually, the blurriness cleared. There, standing with Charis and the other informants, was Hullis.

"You," he snarled, the word coming out ragged and vicious. "I'm going to kill you."

Hullis held up Kaletor's sword and studied it. "I've been waiting to do that for a long time," he said, his monotonous tone infused with a new, malicious satisfaction. "A *very* long time."

With a flick of the wrist, he tossed the blade. The splash of it hitting the water echoed through the chamber.

Kaletor roared and twisted to get free. The pommel of a sword cracked into the base of his spine. He grit his teeth against the fire exploding through his lower back.

"You must be very confused, *Commander*," Hullis sneered, starting to pace just in front of him. "Allow me to explain. We are Lycurgans, and we are the ones controlling that old fool on his golden throne. For years, we fought a losing war. We tried to turn the city against itself through force, but the Elites were too numerous. Our numbers dwindled, and defeat seemed inevitable. We were reduced to near total despair and complete annihilation.

"But then, something unimaginable happened. The emperor's favourite dog, the mighty Kaletor, turned against his master. You took his Elites far away, which gave us the opening we so desperately needed. Imagine our surprise when it was you, Kaletor, the very person who prevented our assassination of Ockos sixteen years ago, who rescued our cause from the depths of defeat—"

"I'm going to kill you," Kaletor growled. "I swear by all the gods, I will mount your head on a pike and tear your body limb from limb!"

Hullis stopped pacing as Kaletor's shout echoed hollow through the cold, damp chamber. He moved to stand a few feet away and crossed his arms. "You've always been fearless, Kaletor. It's the one thing I admire about you. But you're just a mindless brute who uses violence to solve everything. You cannot be allowed to rule. The Empire is broken, and the war has left Sparta weak and vulnerable. Now more than ever, we need to return to the glorious ways of our past. The Agoge. The Ephors. The Council of Elders. Sacrifice. Honour. Valour. These institutions and values are what won us an empire. Only by returning to these Lycurgan ways can it now be saved."

"You've lost your mind," Kaletor spat, glaring Hullis down. "All of you have. The old ways are dead. The Phalanxes are the Empire now, and I am their commander. One word from me, and every Lycurgan will burn—"

"But how will you give the word?" Hullis cut in, arms crossing over his chest. "Do you think my plan was to tell you all this and then let you go? No, Kaletor. You will never give another order again.

"But you do not need to die," he continued, the surrounding flames dancing in his eyes. "We could use your ferocity should anyone step out of line. Join us, pledge yourself to the Lycurgan cause, and help restore Sparta to her former glory."

Kaletor kept his glare fixed on one of the few men he had trusted, wishing he had a weapon to cut the bastard down.

"This isn't going to go the way you want it to," he said, forcefully pushing out each word. "The city is full of my men. Once he realizes I'm missing, Ockos will use them to hunt you all down."

"Oh, I don't think so," Hullis replied, another sneer spreading across his face. "We have several men close to the emperor at all times. He knows that if he does anything we disapprove of, they will kill him."

Kaletor felt something snap inside him. Strength surged through his body, and roaring berserk, he twisted hard at the hip. He pulled his right arm free, balled his hand into a fist, and swung a punch over his left shoulder. It connected square to the nose of the one clamped onto his left arm.

He brought his feet under him—

A crushing punch pounded into the side of his head. He pushed through it, fist coming around to counter—

But Hullis hit him first, a hard blow to the throat. Kaletor choked, snarling as he tucked his elbows into his sides. Before he could counter, someone kicked him in the back of the knees. His legs caved and he went back down.

The moment he hit the ground, kicks pelted him from every side. He tried to roll, but there were too many. Fiery pain scorched through his body. He roared in defiance, a sound that rose to join with a booming clap of thunder above.

His roar ended when a kick connected with his head.

FORTY-SIX

Many sought for a way to bring him down after that day. The problem was that the Warrior Code, which everyone else still lived by, demanded honour, and there was only one way to remove a Warlord honourably—the Challenge.

Year after year, one Superior after another tried to defeat him. But Chalrog was the greatest warrior of his time. Every one of them fell to his spear.

The Spoken Tales

The number had come back—about two thousand dead, most of them yagars. Jarka had put on a brave face. Now, sitting by himself fifty yards removed from the camp, the mask was gone.

He felt numb, suspended in some sort of limbo. He felt like he was no longer the yagar he had been. His eyes saw the tall maples and pines of the forest to the east, the scattered tents on the grassland plain, the trails of smoke swirling skyward, and the humans and yagars that were still alive. But even though he saw all of this, none of it seemed real.

He had no notion of time as he sat there, his empty gaze passing over the scene before him. All was quiet. Even the birds were silent. Even they must have sensed that this was no time for song, no time for anything but for grief.

Masos had assured him that without the retreat, they would have lost far more. Jarka was unconvinced.

He kept replaying the battle in his mind over and over again. *Surely, we could have won. If only I had done something differently. If only I had fought harder and killed more.*

Once again, he revisited every moment of the battle. He knew it wouldn't help, but he couldn't stop. He didn't deserve to stop.

The daylight was failing when he spotted Vaseus crossing the long, leaning grass of the plain. The impulse came to get up and run away. A burning heat bloomed in his face.

Cowardice. It's like a sickness, and I'm infected with it.

She was adorned in her simple green tunic, the tough fabric fitting tight to her slender frame. Her golden hair was unbound, and loose strands danced in the breeze.

It was the first time he had seen her since their argument the night before. Despite himself, he was struck by the perfection of her beauty.

"How you holding up?" she called out as she came close.

Seeing her and hearing her voice lightened him enough to bring a gentle smile to his lips. "You know me, bee. I'm good."

She came to a stop just a bit more than an arm's length away, her hands going to her hips. "Come on, Jarka. It's just us."

The words reminded him of his sister. It was something she used to say to him. *Jazith.*

All at once, he felt the full weight of his every failure, felt all the loss he had known in his life. He tried to fight it, tried to pretend it wasn't there. But it was no use.

The tears came then, and he brought his hands up to cover his face. He felt Vaseus kneel at his feet, then wrap her arms around him. He sobbed even harder, unable to stop it. All he knew was the drowning pain as Vaseus ran her fingers back and forth across the fur of his neck.

It went on until all his tears were spent. His breath was ragged, but gradually, slowly, it evened out.

Vaseus squeezed him close before coming away a bit, enough so that her nose was a few inches from his. "I know. I know it hurts. But we cannot lose hope. This is not the end."

His eyes locked with hers, and for a long moment he stared into them, those perfect orbs of soft green.

Eventually, he released a rattling sigh and shook his head. "I should have listened to you. This never would have happened if I had just listened to you."

A tender smile creased her lips. "Yes, you should have. Don't yagars know that females know best?"

He breathed a low chuckle. "We do. But sometimes males are just too stubborn to accept it."

She looked into his eyes for another long moment. It felt as if she were peering straight through him.

In a gentle voice, she said, "Tell me something about your sister."

He breathed in a deep breath through his nose, then slowly let it back out. "My sister. Why?"

"Humour me."

He nodded, then turned his mind to Jazith. Before long, the words came.

"She's always had my back. I remember one time, when we were quite young, we were playing with a few of our friends. I got a little bit too enthusiastic and accidentally hurt one of the females. A nearby Elder heard and came over to investigate. Jazith said that she did it.

"She was always doing stuff like that. She looked out for me every day, and I knew I could count on her. She was the only one who knew the real me. I didn't pretend or hide things from her. I could tell her anything. She didn't judge me or make me feel bad about something I had done or said. She was just there for me, helping me when I needed help, listening when I needed someone to listen. Even when I was young, I knew . . . I knew she loved me. I've always known."

Tears welled in his eyes as he finished.

Vaseus brought a hand up to caress his face. "That is why we must fight on. Your sister is worth fighting for. Many in this world are worth fighting for. For them, we must fight on. This war isn't over. We can still win."

"I don't know, bee. Our spirit is broken. All we have is darkness and despair. More yagars died today than on any other day in our history. And it's my fault."

"Oh, my love," she said, taking his face in both hands. "I know your hurt must be terrible. I know because I feel it too. But we can't give in. We can't let despair win. We can't allow the Spartans to make the world suffer any more."

"But how? How can we possibly win? You were right about everything. We are divided against ourselves, individual pebbles pushed into a pile. The Spartans are one, like the rock wall of a mountain. Pebbles cannot bring down a mountain."

"No. But maybe we don't have to."

He furrowed his brow. "What do you mean?"

"We don't have to attack them head on. We need to fight in a way that plays to our strengths and exploits their weaknesses. The phalanx is the source of their strength. It's the reason they beat us. But the phalanx only does well in wide open spaces, spaces where they can deploy in a solid, unbroken line. If we can lure them into the forest, the phalanx will break down. Once that happens, you and your people will be free to fight one-on-one, which gives us the advantage."

It made sense. The densely packed trees would split the Spartans up.

And yet, prickly thorns of doubt remained.

"There are too many of them. Their numbers are too much."

"Not if we split up," she said, dropping her hands to rest on his forearms. "If we split into groups of ten or fifteen, we can strike quick and melt away, over and over again. They will be stretched thin and moving in unfamiliar territory. We can lead them deeper into the forest, and as they follow, their supplies will start to run out. One by one, they will fall, and before long, we'll wear them down to nothing. This is how we win."

Again, her reasoning was sound and resonated true. Maybe it could work. Maybe they really could win.

But even as he felt hope swelling in his chest, the thorns remained.

"It all sounds great, bee. But there's a flaw in your plan."

"Oh?"

"I doubt this army of ours has the will to fight on. Not only that, but drawing the enemy deep into the forest will not appeal to my people. We would be leading them straight towards our homes and families. How could I possibly convince them to do such a thing?"

The brightness in her eyes seemed to dim. "I'm not sure. But we have to try, right?"

Jarka hesitated at first, but then nodded. "Right."

They embraced, kissed, then rose and headed back to camp.

"Thank you, bee," he said as they walked beside each other.

He glanced over to meet her eye. She didn't reply.

She didn't have to.

Yagars and humans alike were scattered haphazardly across the grassy plain. Some were hanging their heads. Others stared at the deepening sky of dusk with blank eyes. No one spoke or made any kind of sound.

As Jarka and Vaseus moved among them, he could feel the desolate anguish pulsing from them like a firestorm of pain. It was a heavy weight that pulled on him, and the thought came that their plan was weak and insignificant. Only the presence of Vaseus at his side kept him going.

Eventually, they came to what seemed like the center of camp. Slowly casting his gaze in all directions, he broke the oppressive silence.

"I am Jarka, Warlord of The Ten Clans, and an ally of our human friends. I would like to say something to all of you now."

As Vaseus translated this, he saw that hardly anyone looked up. He did not blame them.

"We have all suffered this day, and suffered harshly. Nothing I say will change that. Many of those we love are gone, and we are left with two choices. One is to give in to our grief and return home with our broken hearts. The other is to fight on and honour the sacrifice of our fallen brothers and sisters."

More silence answered him. He shared a resigned look with Vaseus as she finished her translation.

"I will not force anyone to any course of action. But we must decide. The Spartans will be here by morning, so let us choose now."

Before Vaseus could translate, an unknown female called out, "Why would we keep fighting? We cannot win."

Though he didn't know who had spoken, Jarka looked towards the area from where the bitter words had come. "No. We cannot. At least not fighting them the way they want us to. But there is another way."

When no one raised any objections, he relayed to them the plan Vaseus had just voiced. As he spoke, pausing every so often to allow Vaseus time to translate, more and more eyes turned to look.

By the time he finished, the steady, silent regard of hundreds was fixed on him.

"To fight like that would go against the Warrior Code," a coarse male voice stated into the charged silence. "It's dishonourable. And what if it fails? Our villages would be attacked. Our youngsters would be slaughtered."

Jarka nodded in agreement. "Yes, there is a risk. And yes, it breaks with our traditional ways of fighting. But there's an even greater risk if we do nothing. There's the risk that the Spartans will invade our lands anyway. When they do, no single Clan can hope to defeat them. We would all be crushed, one by one. Is that what our fallen warriors would want? Do you want their deaths to be in vain?"

When he finished, there was only silence, no movement or reaction of any kind.

But then, a young female stood, eyes locking with Jarka's. Slowly, she raised her fist and said, "I will fight."

A male, who was sitting nearby, rose to stand at her side. "I will fight."

A few more stood as well, rising like sentinels on the watch. Then more. And more.

"I will fight," another boomed.

"I will fight," came another, louder than the last.

"I will fight," another bellowed, even louder still.

"I will fight."

"I will fight!"

And then, a great roar split the air. "*Honour the dead.*"

The cry was taken up. "*Honour the dead. Honour the dead. Honour the dead.*"

The chant grew until it was deafening, filling the meadow, rolling into the nearby forest. Jarka could feel it in his chest, reverberating through his heart as he watched and listened.

The entire army had risen, every human and every yagar. Together they stood, weapons and arms raised high, roaring out the thunderous chant.

"*Honour the dead! Honour the dead! Honour the dead! Honour the dead!*"

Chills raked through every inch of him, as sharp as shards of stone. He looked over to Vaseus, and she looked at him. Her eyes were ablaze, as he knew his were.

An impulse came, and he couldn't have stopped acting on it even if he'd wanted to. He reached out and took her hand in his. With one final, fierce look, he lifted their arms up, faced forward, and joined the all-consuming chant.

"Honour the dead! Honour the dead! Honour the dead!"

Together they stood, their voices added to the chant, united, surrounded, and embraced in the deafening roar of their people.

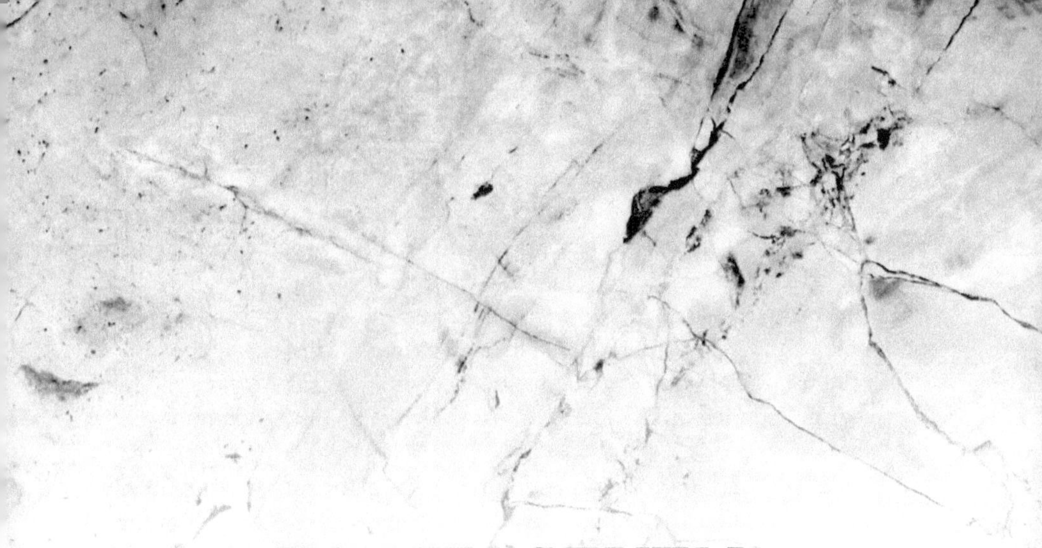

FORTY-SEVEN

Lycurgus had introduced many barbaric practices. One was leaving newborn babies to die if they didn't appear healthy enough to bear strong sons or become able soldiers. Another was the agoge, a school that saw boys taken from their mothers at the age of seven to receive brutal, violent military training. Perhaps these extremes were necessary for the times, but Spartans evolved. We no longer need to go to such lengths to ensure strength-at-arms. Rigorous training is required, yes, and harsh in the name of discipline. But the new system is enough. Idolizing and glorifying past heroes is enough. This is what the Lycurgans do not understand.

Podalinus of Sparta

You promised that you would do what's right. You promised me. But you broke your promise.

You said you would protect others. But who do you protect now?

Kaletor released a low growl and shook his dangling head. "Leave me be, Vaseus," he muttered into his lap. "A foolish boy said those words. He's long dead—"

"Quiet," Charis hissed. "Unless you want me to stuff the rag back down your throat."

The sound of his jailor's voice was a mercy. It pulled his attention away from the battleground that was his mind. He felt the ropes choking his wrists and the ache in his back and shoulders. He had no idea how long he had been down there, imprisoned in the sewers, tied to a chair that was hard as bone.

He licked his lips as he raised his head and tasted a tinge of iron, a reminder of the blood that had dribbled down from a gash in his forehead.

He felt a few flecks of the dried runnels come loose as he gave the man a savage grin. "Sounds quiet up there today. Maybe this time someone will hear my shouts—"

"Don't," Charis snarled, striding across the platform, footfalls echoing throughout the watery chamber. "Or I'll beat you even worse than last time."

"Unless you get too tired first," Kaletor mocked. "I think I'll take my chances."

The lean, dark-skinned man raised the club that he and the other Lycurgans had used to beat him. "Go on then. Maybe your skull will crack open this time."

Kaletor glared the traitorous informant down, hands balled into fists as he strained at the ropes. He was about to loose a bellow when the glint of torchlight flashed in the blood that stained the club.

Memory of agonizing pain stretching on for hours flooded in. A ragged breath rattled out between his grit teeth, but nothing more.

Charis snorted a laugh. "That's what I thought."

As he returned to the chair on the other side of the central platform, Kaletor glared daggers at the coward's back. He kept his rageful hate burning, sapping though it was, because he knew what would come if it subsided.

The internal war against Vaseus, a war he thought he had already won, was tearing him apart. As he sat there, unable to move or do anything, she assailed him day and night. Whenever he dozed or slept, she attacked. More than once, he had invited a beating just to escape her torture.

At first, he had fended her off, maintaining that everything he had ever done was for the greater good. But she was wearing him down, bit by bit. With every internal skirmish, he felt himself slipping towards madness. He had to escape, and soon.

Just as he felt his rage start to ebb, the distant echo of footfalls came from one of the connecting tunnels. He looked to the sound and watched Hullis emerge from the shadows, dressed in his military red cloak and golden armour.

"We have a problem," he declared while striding across one of the narrow walkways.

Charis stood to face his fellow traitor. "What is it now?"

"The Phalanxes are getting restless. We've nearly finished searching the city, and once we do, I don't know if I can stop the violent reaction that will likely ensue."

"So what? What will they do if he's not found?"

Hullis shook his head. "I don't know. They could start going from house to house, kicking in doors, threatening and abusing the people. It would only be a matter of time before they started killing—"

"Killing?" Charis cut in. "Surely they won't kill innocent Spartans."

The two were so involved in their conversation that Kaletor found himself unobserved. He started pushing and pulling with his arms, working to loosen the rope tied around his wrists.

"Just shut up for a second," Hullis barked. "Let me think."

"I thought you were second-in-command?" Charis said after a momentary pause. "Can't you just order them to stand down?"

"Yes, but that doesn't mean they'll listen."

"But you're the highest-ranking officer. Why wouldn't they lis—"

"Because," Hullis snarled, his chin jutting out, "he's the Taker of Athens, the Lion of Sparta. To them, he's like Leonidas and Achilles combined. They practically worship him. There's no telling what they might do to find him."

Kaletor froze in the brief silence. He had worked his left hand up an inch or so, but he couldn't risk drawing their attention. He stayed still and watched as Charis laced his fingers together and set both hands atop his head.

"Okay, okay, what about this. What if we let them find him?"

Kaletor resumed wriggling as confusion marred Hullis's face.

"What?"

"If they found him, the search would end. We should kill him and let them find the body."

"Kill him? Have you lost your mind? If the Phalanxes find him dead, they'll go on a rampage. They'll start killing everyone in the city they can find."

"What else can we do? You just said that you can't control them."

"If you'd just shut up for a second—"

Hullis broke off and looked straight down the tunnel he had just come from. "Did you hear that?"

Kaletor kept pulling as the patter of faint footfalls echoed into the wide chamber. It sounded like whoever was coming was moving fast.

"Who is it?" Charis hissed.

Hullis shook his head, turning fully to face the tunnel. "I don't know."

As the pair drew their swords, Kaletor grit his teeth and pulled, his right shoulder feeling like it was about to pop.

A sprinting yagar charged headlong into the chamber, hurling a spear as it appeared. The weapon sped through the air and punched through Charis's middle.

As the Lycurgan fell, Hullis rushed onto the walkway, raising his sword to attack. But before he could bring his weapon down, the yagar slammed bodily into him. The general landed flat on his back, head bouncing on the stone platform. He didn't move from there, and it was over as fast as it began.

With a snarl, Kaletor jerked his arm loose, but the savage was already advancing. He thought to stand and whip the chair out in front of him—

But stopped. By the flickering torchlight, he recognized that it was Sola.

She glided over to stand close, the vertical slits within her golden eyes fixated on him. "Hello, Commander."

He met her gaze. "What is this? What are you doing here?"

She paused a moment, seemingly to consider her answer.

Then, "I was hoping I'd find you down here. I need your help."

"My help?" he said, eyes narrowing. "With what? And how did you find me?"

"I followed General Hullis."

"Why would you do that?"

Her persistent eye contact remained unchanging as she replied. "I became suspicious of his motives and concluded that he might be a Lycurgan. Since your disappearance remained unexplained, I hoped he would lead me to you."

"For what purpose? Why me?"

"Because only you can free my father."

Kaletor's confusion cleared then. "So you know the Lycurgans have Ockos under their thumb."

"Yes. He has been living in fear every day for many weeks now. It took me a long time to figure out who was controlling him. But now that I do, I would see him free of their terror. I have observed that you are the strongest of your kind. Can you help me?"

He hesitated. Could he really trust a yagar? Could he ally himself with a mindless savage?

His gaze shifted and ended up settling on Hullis, who was still lying motionless on the floor. As he looked upon the man who had betrayed him, the answer came.

"Your enemy is my enemy. Get me safely to my Phalanxes, and I will send them through the city until every Lycurgan is dead."

"I want your word."

He looked back to her, this most unlikely of allies. "Name your terms."

Sola stepped closer to loom large over him, her scent of musty dirt reaching down his throat. "My father must be free from control and safe from harm. I want your word that this will be so when it's over."

Keeping his gaze steady on hers, he said, "I swear by Zeus and all the gods, Ockos will be safe."

Her eyes bore into his as if searching for dishonesty.

After a long moment, she moved behind him and snapped the ropes. As he stood, rubbing his wrists, he noticed Hullis was beginning to stir.

"Good," he growled, moving to press a knee to the traitor's chest. "You're not dead. I want names, you lying piece of shit. You're going to give me every single Lycurgan . . ."

He trailed off as Hullis's eyes rolled up in his head and his body went limp.

He straightened, stars dancing in front of his eyes. He massaged his temples and looked over to Sola. "Bring this filth with us. I want him to suffer before he dies."

The yagar dragged Hullis up and threw him over a shoulder as if carrying a sack of potatoes. Kaletor retrieved a sword and led the way toward one of the tunnels.

I'm going to do the right thing now, Vaseus. Watch and see.

FORTY-EIGHT

Eventually, after so long under his dishonourable leadership, some in his Clan had had enough. Three Superiors, along with seven others, conspired against him. They travelled to a neighbouring Clan to strike a deal. Even though it was against the Warrior Code, they felt it was the right thing to do. Their Clan needed a dishonourable solution for a dishonourable Warlord.

The Spoken Tales

Shifting his weight onto his left knee, Jarka peered out from behind the cover of an ancient, moss-covered tree. Through the hanging greenery of the forest, he watched the front of the Spartan column emerge. They were snaking along the skinny trail, no more than two abreast.

He sniffed deep, smelling their iron and sweat. Then he inched back behind cover and looked left. Crouched across the top ridge of the rising ground were seventeen yagars and nine humans, their weapons drawn and ready to charge down into the unsuspecting enemy.

The ambush was set. It was time to make it count.

He peered back down to the trail. The Spartans were moving slow and silent, their eyes roaming in every direction. Gradually, they progressed to the stretch of trail that curved around the hill.

Keeping his focus on the Spartans thirty feet away, Jarka reached the butt end of his spear out to nudge his neighbour. It was the signal for everyone to fix their attention on him, a signal passed down the line with the ends of spears.

Jarka waited, watching the Spartans getting closer and closer.

And he waited.

Now.

Without a sound, he stood and glanced to his unit. Seeing that everyone had followed his lead and stood with him, he faced forward and took off down the hill.

Their red cloaks and gold shields made them easy targets. Charging through low-hanging branches, he flew down the hill, spear poised in one hand. The Spartans didn't see him coming.

He burst silently from the trees and launched himself at the column. He dipped his lead shoulder and smashed it into the side of a man's head. At the same time, he drove his spear into another's neck.

He heard his unit arrive all down the line with an eruption of bellows and shouts.

The one he had shoulder slammed was sprawled on his back. Jarka took a quick step and finished the human off.

He glanced down the line and saw the yagar beside him kill a Spartan. But her spear stuck, and a nearby hoplite moved to cut her down.

Jarka brought his spear up and threw. It hit the mark and the Spartan fell.

He took off, running after his weapon while watching the enemy out of the corner of his eye. Seeing no immediate threat, he checked down the trail.

The ambush had worked. His unit had carved into the unprepared enemy, halting their movement and throwing them into disarray. Many had already been cut down.

His expanded focus was brought in close by a piercing howl. He watched one of his human warriors fall with a spear in his shoulder.

On the run, Jarka snatched his spear from the fallen Spartan, and in one fluid motion, jabbed it straight out. The stone leaf head punched into the Spartan's side, and he collapsed before he could finish the job.

Sensing that the female he had saved with the thrown spear was with him, Jarka pointed at the stricken human and yelled, "Get him out of here!"

He moved deeper into the fray, rushing into the midst of a small cluster of combatants. Two of his unit, a male and a human, were fending off three hoplites. Still on the run, he saw that the male was on the verge of being overwhelmed. He arrived there and swung his spear down, smacking a thrusting spear aside before it struck the male. Maintaining his speed, he tucked his arm in and rammed a shoulder into the Spartan's shield. The impact sent the man flying.

Pushing through the wash of pain, he ducked under a horizontal swipe from one of the other Spartans and lashed out a low counter. The Spartan took it on his shield, but it left him open. The male took advantage with a quick thrust, and the Spartan crumpled.

"Warlord!"

The warning shout came from behind, and Jarka twisted around. In that same movement, he reacted and dove aside. The slashing sword sang through the air. But the attacking Spartan came on, right there when Jarka rolled up to his knees, sword swinging at his face—

But it sailed high. The lanky human that had called out in warning had tackled the Spartan, and the two went to the ground. The lanky one took the worst of it, crushed on impact under the hoplite's full weight.

The Spartan rolled free, then came back, snarling as he raised his sword to deliver the killing blow. From his knees, Jarka cocked his arm back and hurled his spear. It struck the Spartan in the side, killing him before his sword fell.

Jarka rushed over to the human who had just saved him, stealing a look around as he did. The marching Spartans that were unaffected by the ambush had locked shields and were closing in.

"Fall back!" he bellowed. "Back up the hill!"

The lanky human had just got to his hands and knees when Jarka stooped down and dragged him up by the collar of his shirt.

"Run," he urged, using the human word. "Run!"

As the man staggered up the ridge, Jarka looked back up the trail. His unit had heard him and was disappearing into the forest. The Spartan column was hurrying down the trail, trying to cut them off.

Jarka watched as a wounded male was trampled underfoot. He loosed a ragged roar as he turned and ran up the hill before the advancing Spartans could reach him.

*   *   *

"Syvarx, Drofick, double back. See if they're following us."

The two males gave sharp nods and took off back the way they had come.

Jarka turned to the rest of his unit huddled beneath the dangling, wispy tendrils of a massive willow. Most were on a knee or sprawled on their backs, sucking air after the long dash through the forest. A quick count revealed that they had lost two yagars and three humans in the fight.

"It worked! I told you it would work."

Vaseus, who had been at the opposite end of their line to Jarka, was looking up at him from a knee. His stomach flipped upon seeing blood splattered across her face. But with the others watching and waiting, he had to swallow down what he wanted to say.

"I don't know. It was over so quickly. I don't think we did much damage."

"It's not so much about that," Vaseus said, "at least for now. It's more about getting inside their heads. They want a big, open battle where they can form their phalanx wall and send it straight ahead. By refusing to give them the fight they want, we neutralize their greatest strength. And with every ambush from all of our units, they'll always be on edge. They'll never know when the next attack is coming, and that's hard to live with."

"Yes, but we took losses too," Jarka pointed out. "Three or four more skirmishes like that and we'll be finished."

"Next time we'll do better. We won't lose very many, you'll see. And besides, they lost far more than we did. As long as the other units fare at least as well, bit by bit, we'll grind their army down to nothing."

Although he still had his reservations, Jarka couldn't help but feel heartened by her certainty.

He gave her a soft smile. *Maybe she's right. Maybe this will work.*

The thought made him think back to the skirmish they had just fought. He looked around until he spotted the human who had saved him. He was lying on his back, chest heaving up and down.

Jarka moved to stand next to him. "What's this one's name?" he asked, looking back to Vaseus.

She released a huff, pushed herself up to her feet, and moved to join him. "Orzon."

Hearing his name, the human opened his eyes. In a rush, he scurried to his feet, a look of doubt colouring his narrow, bony face.

"Orzon," Jarka repeated, "you fought well. Thank you for saving my life back there."

The lanky man looked to Vaseus as she translated.

When she finished, he met Jarka's eye with a warm smile and replied in an even tone.

"He says we're all on the same side now," Vaseus relayed. "And he imagines you'll soon have the chance to return the favour."

Jarka released a low chuckle through a wide grin. "Yes, I'm sure I will."

The man nodded, and Jarka was about to leave it at that. But then, he sensed that many of the others were watching.

Acting on a sudden impulse, he stepped in close and extended an arm out to Orzon. When he hesitated, Jarka held his eye and gave a small nod. The human seemed to recognize the intended respect. He reached out to meet the offer, and they gripped each other's forearm.

Warm power swelled in Jarka's chest, like a burgeoning fire.

"So," he said to Vaseus as the embrace ended, "what's our next move?"

She was beaming, seemingly as swept up in the moment as he was. Slowly, as if soaking it in, she turned her delight towards him.

"Now we really strike fear into their hearts," she said, her voice afire. "They're not going to know what hit them."

FORTY-NINE

Greece is poor, but brave and free. Spartans will
fight to the death even if vastly outnumbered.

Demaratus, King of Sparta

The warm night was black, devoid of moon or star. Beneath this inky shroud, the city of Sparta quietly slept.

But not for much longer.

Alongside Sola and her burden, Kaletor approached the lone gate of the wall that surrounded the second-largest barracks complex in the city.

As soon as they stepped into the dull, orange light of the gate's torches, someone barked, "Who goes there?"

Kaletor stopped and looked up to the shadowy rampart ten feet above. "I am Commander Kaletor. Open the gate, and quickly."

The hoplite, who was shrouded from view, didn't respond.

But just as Kaletor was about to issue a threat, the man called down, "You can't be him. The commander is missing—"

"I was held prisoner in the sewers by Lycurgan filth," Kaletor cut in, "and I just escaped. I'm sure you can smell it on me from there. Now let me in or I'll have your head."

Again, there was a long pause before an answer came back. "If you really are the commander, what are you doing with a yagar? And who is that draped over its shoulder?"

"I am Sola, daughter of Emperor Ockos," Sola called out, "and I carry—"

"General Hullis," Kaletor interrupted, the muscles of his jaw bunching. "He betrayed me. He's Lycurgan. Now open the gate before I kill you *myself.*"

This time, the guard responded right away. "Yes, Commander."

As they strode towards the large fort that sat atop the manmade hill, accompanied by the eight hoplites and three Spartiates that had been posted at the gate, Kaletor spoke quickly. "Rouse the Phalanxes, but quietly. I don't want any Lycurgans to know we're coming. Spread the word that every man is to assemble here in full battle kit. Let me know when it's done."

"To what end?" one of them asked.

Kaletor stopped short and looked at them all. "We're going to seal the city gates so that no one can escape," he said, feeling his heart quicken at the thought of what was to come. "Then we're going to purge Sparta of every Lycurgan with iron and fire."

The men dispersed, and Kaletor led Sola into the fort.

The long, rectangular entrance hall was deserted, empty save for two long tables and the low benches that ran alongside them.

"Put him on a table," Kaletor said, standing aside as the yagar did as instructed. He went to the nearest high, thick stone wall to remove one of the flickering torches from its sconce.

"Now," he said as he returned, "go to the palace and barricade Ockos inside your room. When the killing starts, the Lycurgans will come for him. Don't open the door for anyone but me."

Sola had been studying him as he spoke. Even now that he had finished, she continued to do the same.

"What?" he snapped.

She tilted her head slightly to one side. "What exactly are you going to do?"

"What I said I would do."

"Defeat the Lycurgans and set my father free?"

"Yes."

"How?"

He turned a glaring eye to Hullis as he answered. "My Phalanxes will treat Sparta like any other conquered city. It's the only way to get them all."

"Does that mean innocent people will also die?"

"Yes. Many."

As he spoke, he returned his gaze to her once more. Despite her hulking form and emotionless features, there was unmistakable sadness in the vertical slits of her eyes.

"Just save my father."

With that, she turned away and took off, disappearing into the night.

Knowing the fort would soon be abuzz with activity, Kaletor didn't wait. He stepped close to the table and brought the torch low.

Hullis was still out cold. Something slick shimmered on the table under his head. Kaletor leaned in to confirm that it was blood.

He grunted and guided the flame to within inches of Hullis's face. The muscles beneath the skin began to twitch.

"Wake up, you bastard!"

Hullis woke with a piercing cry, twisting away from the flame.

Kaletor grabbed him by the chin and forced his head back. "How long? How long have you been one of them?"

Instead of answering, Hullis squeezed his eyes shut and brought his hands up to his head. A low groan seeped through a manic smile of clenched teeth.

"How long?" Kaletor roared, pounding a fist into the traitor's chest. "How long? *How long?*"

But Hullis paid him no heed. The pain from the wound in his head was apparently too great to ignore. All Kaletor could do was glare down at him.

Eventually, the excruciating agony must have passed. Hullis released his hair and his face relaxed. His bloodshot eyes slowly opened, blank as still water.

Then he blinked, and looking around, muttered, "Am I dead?"

Kaletor seized him by the throat and squeezed. "Not yet."

Their eyes locked then, and when they did, Hullis's focus hardened into something Kaletor had never seen from his most trusted general—pure, dark hate.

Eventually, he let go and straightened. Hullis coughed and sputtered as he gasped for air.

Once the fit passed, Kaletor loomed over him and snarled the same question. "How long?"

Breathing harsh and ragged, Hullis looked up with teeth bared. "How long?" he rasped. "The whole time. Every campaign, every battle, every day and every night—"

"Why?" Kaletor snapped. "Why would you betray me?"

"Because the Empire is weak. Discontent hounds every street corner and pervades every home. Corruption blackens every heart. Luxury and excess undermine Spartan morality. Can't you see it? The entire system is broken. This war has made it clear. Why else would so many people rise up against us?"

"I don't care why people rebel. All that matters is that we crush them when they do. As long as I lead the army, the Empire is invincible."

"It can't last. Soon enough, every Greek, every Persian, every Egyptian, every Thracian, everyone who isn't Spartan will come for us."

"And when they do, I will kill them all."

Hullis's eyes went wide. "You're mad. You can't defeat the whole world."

Kaletor barked a laugh. "And why not?"

At that moment, distant voices sounded from deep within the fort.

Hullis looked to the back wall and the hall's interior door. "What's happening?"

Kaletor was all too willing to answer that question. "The men are being roused. Soon we will seal the gates so no one can escape. Then I will unleash all three Phalanxes on the city until every Lycurgan is dead. Sparta is about to bleed, and your cult is about to end."

Hullis looked back at him, an expression of wild shock on his face. "What? You can't attack Sparta."

"Yes I can," Kaletor said, relishing the fear in the traitor's eyes. "You and your Lycurgan friends are a plague on us all, a disease that must be cut out. Once the people of Sparta suffer the pain of random, unfair slaughter, they will expose every single Lycurgan when I ask them to. Because if they don't, more and more will die.

"But you can save many lives, right here and now," Kaletor went on, glaring down at his general. "Give me the names of all your leaders. I want to know who else in the aristocracy is Lycurgan. You give me that, and I will limit the bloodshed. You give me that, and their deaths will be quick."

The reaction that came was unexpected. Hullis slowly shook his head, a grin spreading across his lips, before loosing a laugh of glee.

"This is your plan?" he boomed when he cut the laugh short. "You think killing me or anyone else will accomplish anything? You've always been a violent, mindless brute, Kaletor. You're a fool of the highest order—"

"*Names*," Kaletor bellowed, slamming a fist to the table. "Give me the names."

"Why would I?" Hullis spat. "You have nothing to threaten me with. But that's all you know, isn't it? You only know how to threaten and terrorize and kill. But no matter how many people you slaughter or control, there will always be more to oppose you, Kaletor. That's the problem with violence, and that's what you don't understand. The more you use it, the more it comes back at you. It's a hydra that you cannot stop."

Kaletor felt his jaw bunch as the urge to kill burned through him.

"See," Hullis said, pointing up at him. "You want to kill me right now. Even though you need me to talk, you want to kill me. You are a slave, Kaletor, a slave to your anger. And no slave can rule the world."

Kaletor lashed out with the torch, swinging it horizontally just over Hullis's face. "*I am no slave*," he shouted, spittle flying from his mouth. "I control every Phalanx of the Empire. Even the emperor now answers to me. I am the most powerful man in the world, and you were my righthand. You were one of the few I trusted. We've been friends since we were young—"

"Friends?" Hullis cried before loosing a mocking laugh. "You really have gone mad. I was nothing more than a pawn to you, a pawn to be used and discarded like everyone else. How could we be friends? You don't care about anyone but yourself.

"I often wondered, as we followed your orders to destroy city after city, slaughtering thousands of innocent people, if you still believed you were the hero, if you still believed you were like Achilles or Leonidas. It seemed impossible as the reek of burning flesh filled my nose and the terrified wails of children pierced my soul. But you're such a mindless brute, so perhaps you managed it. Perhaps you managed to believe you were the hero you once aspired to become. But you're not, Kaletor. No matter how badly you want to be, you're not the hero. You're a monster. You're not Leonidas. You're Xerxes."

It was all Kaletor could do to hold himself back and keep his arms from shaking. "The names, Hullis. Give me the names."

"Everything you touch burns and dies. Everybody hates or fears you. You are the bane of all that is good—"

"Enough! Give me the names, you bastard!"

"You will never win," Hullis went on, his tone sharp and dripping venom. "No matter how many people you kill or how much power you think you have, it will never be enough. You'll always want more. And you will suffer every day of your life, just as you have suffered these past years. Yes, I've noticed your pain. You're terrible at hiding it. You've suffered ever since Vaseus ran away from you—"

Kaletor roared, raised the torch high, and swung. The flaming end cracked Hullis's nose. He swung again, then again and again, roaring louder and louder as he did. The flames caught in Hullis's hair.

Before long, the traitor went limp.

After a final blow, Kaletor staggered back, his throat hoarse and raw. His chest heaved as he drew in ragged breaths, keeping his glare fixed on Hullis's bloody face and burning hair.

He was your friend, Kaletor. Once, he was your friend.

Staring at Hullis's motionless body, he bellowed, "You're the reason I'm like this, Vaseus! You were the only light in my world. I needed you, but you abandoned me. Now, there's only *darkness!*"

FIFTY

When that War Season came, Chalrog attacked the other Clans as he always did—without honour and without mercy. During one battle, he carved through the enemy alongside his fellow warriors. But this time, some of the Superiors around him melted away, leaving him exposed. The enemy Superiors closed in. Chalrog fought them off for a time, but even he, the greatest warrior alive, couldn't win a battle alone.

When fatigue finally slowed him, Chalrog fell.

The Spoken Tales

Dusk had fallen, and the scout report was that the enemy had pitched their camp. Knowing this might have brought Jarka some manner of peace.

But it didn't. Unease had become constant, an undercurrent of unrest as permanent as the forest they moved through. It came from not knowing whether or not the other units had made it through another day. No amount of scouting or shared intelligence seemed able to remedy this feeling of blindness.

It feels like I'm sending more and more yagars to their deaths. It feels so wrong. What would Mother and Father think? What would Jazith think?

He released a heavy sigh and dropped his gaze from the orange sky visible through the canopy. As he had been doing more and more, he was sitting slightly removed from his unit, most of whom were lounging within a small copse of white birches.

Whereas before their quiet chatter was a distant background to his thoughts, Jarka now listened more closely.

". . . have a mate?" a middle-aged female named Anith was saying from her cross-legged position.

Vaseus, who had taken up her customary position at the center of everyone, translated the question into human words.

The man named Thedin, a balding farmer of stocky build, nodded and replied, Vaseus translating again.

"Why is that so hard to believe?"

With a smile on her face, Anith answered. "You're just so ugly. You must ply her with wine before she'll go to bed with you."

Both yagars and humans laughed together at the expense of the aging man. He grew red in the face and gave no response.

"Don't mind her," a young male named Yathox piped up once the laughter subsided. "She's as cold as the frozen North Lands."

As the good-natured banter continued, Jarka focused his attention on Vaseus. A smile played on her lips, and her green eyes were bright and alive. Her unbound golden hair glided across her shoulders and grazed her cheeks as she turned to look in every direction, translating in a lively voice, laughing easily and often. She was in her element.

Despite the darkness that hounded him, seeing her so happy made him smile.

The relaxed banter continued as warm dusk deepened towards cool night. Eventually, everyone's jubilant mood started to lighten his.

He was considering joining in when he heard something. He rotated his ears back and looked in the direction of the sound, muscles tensing with a sharp inhale.

But then he saw who it was. Settling back down, he watched Kika, a young female from Tavyka's unit, pick her way between the brush and tree of the forest. Her attention was on the lively group in the copse of birches, oblivious that Jarka was not among them.

"Never assume, young one."

Her body visibly jerked in surprise as her eyes darted to locate him. She shook her head then, a relieved grin exposing the tips of her fangs.

"You scared me," she said as she approached.

"You must always be vigilant," he said, extending an arm to invite her to sit with him. "Keep your eyes wide, your ears alert, and inhale through your nose. Allow your senses to help you."

She lay her spear down and sat beside him. "Is that what you do? Is that why no one can ever see you before you see them?"

He gave her a small smile. "I've been taught by the best. What word do you bring this time?"

Seeming to suddenly realize who she was speaking to, she sat up a little straighter as she spoke again. "We just heard that two of our units suffered heavy losses today. They banded together and attacked, burning one of the enemy's supply wagons. But before they could get away, the Spartans closed in."

Jarka's heart sank into his gut. "How many?"

"We're not sure. At least thirty, maybe more."

He looked away, fingers digging into his thighs. "Do they not understand? Move in small units, never in large groups. Why don't they *listen*?"

Several birds flew off from among the branches above, probably spooked by his hissing words.

He drew in deep breaths, trying to calm his flaring reaction. His gaze went to Vaseus. She was looking right at him, all traces of merriment missing from her face.

"Are the other four units in position?" he asked, looking back to Kika.

"Yes, Warlord," the young scout replied evenly. "When we heard they were in position, Tavyka sent me to tell you."

"And they all know to only attack on my signal?"

"Yes. On your signal, we strike and withdraw. Don't let them rest easy."

"Exactly. Wear them down bit by bit."

She hesitated then, the uncertainty plain in the vertical slits of her dark eyes. "Will this really work? Can we win fighting this way?"

It was as if she knew his mind. In the look she gave him, he saw reflected his own desire for certainty, the unflappable certainty that had once been his.

But he wasn't certain. He didn't know if what they were doing would work. And no matter how badly he wanted to, he wouldn't lie in order to give her something he lacked.

"Thank you for the information, Kika," he said, rising to his feet. "And good luck tonight. Be sure to eat something before you head back."

He set off then, leaving both Kika and his unit behind. He moved at a brisk pace and maintained it until the fading sound of their voices ceased altogether.

"What news?"

He had heard her coming, but only now did he look her way. "Nothing much," he replied, starting to pace between a huge moss-covered log and a pair of towering pines.

Vaseus clambered over the log and dropped into the confined area. "What's going on?"

He pivoted away to face the pines, releasing a sigh and letting his shoulders sag. "Two more units again today. Thirty or more this time."

"At least it wasn't three hundred."

"Maybe it needs to be," he said, coming back around to face her. "Because it feels like we're losing. Every day they push deeper into our lands, burning Small Villages as they go. If this keeps up, they'll destroy our homes all the way to the North Lands, and then where will the young and old go? We won't be able to evacuate them forever."

"I know it's hard to bear," she said, taking a step towards him, "but it's going to work. You'll see. It just takes some time."

"My people are suffering, Vaseus. *My* people. They look to me for strength and victory. But I'm failing them."

Her eyes were gentle as she moved to within arm's reach. "I know, my love. I really do. But you need to trust me. This will work in the end. We just need to give it more time—"

"I don't see how time will make any difference. There are still too many of them. How can time reduce their numbers?"

"As I've said, it's a gradual process. We move or destroy food stores, we ambush them over and over, we draw them further away from the Empire so that it gets more difficult for them to resupply. Eventually it builds, it all adds up. They will lose spirit and run out of supplies. Once they are weak and exposed, then we destroy them."

"But in the meantime, they push us further away from Sparta," Jarka said, crossing his arms over his chest. "I thought we were supposed to destroy the Empire, not flee further and further north."

"Have you already forgotten the battle? You can't just force this to happen. There are no shortcuts. We need to defeat Spartan armies, and we know that fighting them head-on doesn't work. I'm only trying to help—"

"Are you? I'm starting to doubt that. My sister is still over a thousand miles away, imprisoned and alone. Your people remain oppressed, subject to violence, pain, and death. Yet all we do is retreat north, losing just as many as we kill. Are you sure you're here to help? Because it doesn't always feel like it."

"What are you saying? Why else would I advise this course?"

"Maybe you're one of them. Maybe you're an agent of the Empire, sent here to bring the yagars together to make it easier to destroy us and conquer our lands."

Even as the words left his mouth, he wished they hadn't.

She stepped back as if he had struck a hammer blow to her chest. The fire in her eyes dimmed to a depth of anguish beyond description. She seemed to collapse in on herself, down into something small and vulnerable.

"Vaseus, I . . ." he started, but trailed off as she turned to walk away.

Her movements were slow and stiff. She didn't cry and she didn't speak. She made no sound.

She made no sound at all.

He stared after her, wanting to call her back. But nothing came out. It felt like his throat had squeezed shut.

He considered rushing to apologize and take it all back. But his legs were heavy, as if they were filled with stones, and it felt like his feet were rooted to the ground.

Every impulse was the wrong one. Every possible action felt feeble. He had sliced open a wound that he could not close.

And so, he remained there, frozen in place, struggling even to breathe.

FIFTY-ONE

To stand triumphant over your defeated enemy is the pinnacle of a Spartan's life. To die
on the battlefield in service to Sparta is its
most glorious end.

Thrasilaus of Thebes

Kaletor stood in the middle of the street with arms crossed, watching
his Spartiates breaking down the doors of every building in sight.
Several bodies were strewn across the black stones, casualties of the
night. It was impossible to know if they were innocent civilians or Lycurgans.

He looked at the corpses. Whether they were innocent or not made no
difference. Either way, they had fulfilled their purpose.

He started tapping a finger to his bicep as his mind drifted back to the
previous night. After killing Hullis, he had rushed to join his men in the
slaughter. As instructed, they had struck at random. To start, they charged into
quiet homes to cut down families. As panic and confusion flushed hundreds
into the streets, the Phalanxes rushed through the city, cutting down all in their
path. Almost none offered resistance. It had been like killing pigs, and it had
gone on all night.

He had lost himself in the carnage, forgetting the betrayal that had gouged
deep troughs through him. Now, in the cool light of morning, reality was all
too vivid.

He was itching for more action. There was no telling when Vaseus would
return to torment him.

He was idly picking at some dried blood caked on his hand when a scream split the air. From a simple, one-story structure of ancient, grey brick, four Spartiates emerged, dragging two women and a small boy. They threw the trio into the street, eliciting more cries of pain or terror.

Kaletor wasted no time. "What were you doing?" he barked as he moved to stand over them. "Why were you hiding?"

They huddled together on the ground, the women hugging each other to form a protective shell around the child.

The older of the two looked up at him with tearful eyes. "What do you want? I don't understand. Why are you doing this—"

"*Answer the question!*"

They all shrank away and cried out in fear.

"Our—our husbands," the same one sputtered, "told us to hide. We heard the screams. They—they didn't know what was happening. They thought the ci-city was under attack. They went to fight."

"And where are they now?"

"I—I don't know. They didn't come back."

Kaletor straightened and stepped back, hands going to his hips. They were just more useless peasants, which was all they were finding. Still, the Lycurgan presence could have dug deep fingers into the city. Even the poorest woman might know something.

Looking to the Spartiates who had dragged the peasants out, he said, "Take the boy."

The women wailed as the dirt-stained pair were pulled away from each other. The boy tried to run, but one of the Spartiates snagged his collar and corralled him close.

"Please," the older one cried from her knees, reaching out toward Kaletor. "Don't hurt my son. We've done nothing wrong. Please leave him—"

"Stop your mewling," he snapped, looming over her, hands balling into fists. "I have much to do, so don't waste my time. If you and your sister give me the names of every person you know to be Lycurgan, the boy will live. It's that simple. Do you understand?"

The mother blinked rapidly, the creased furrows of her brow deepening. "Wait, what? Lycurgans? Why? What do they have to do with anything—"

"They are a plague on our great city, a rotting sickness that I'm cutting out like bad meat. That is why my Phalanxes attacked last night. That is why every gate is sealed shut. That is why we are hunting down every living man, woman, and child. Every single Lycurgan will be found and executed.

"Now, tell me the names of every man you know to be Lycurgan. Tell me now or your son dies."

The mother shook her head as more tears streamed down her cheeks. "But sir, I don't know any Lycurgans. Please. If I did, I would tell you, I would tell you straight away."

Kaletor glared down at her for a long moment, eyes boring into hers. "Liar." He looked to the Spartiate holding the boy. "Kill him."

The woman screamed and twisted away.

His jaw bunching, Kaletor bent down to snag a fistful of her hair and yanked her head back. "Give me a name!"

"I don't know any!"

"Your husband's one of them, isn't he? *Isn't he?*"

"No—"

"Nikanor!"

Kaletor held up his free hand to stay the Spartiate's knife, looking to the sister at the same time. "Who?"

"Nikanor," the other woman repeated from where she sat on the ground. "He's a blacksmith that lives near here."

Kaletor released the mother and strode over to the younger one. "How do you know he's one of them?"

Though she shrank away at his approach, her reply was steady. "I've heard his opinions over the years. He's a blockheaded fool without a shred of subtlety."

"What about his friends? His family?"

"I don't know for sure, Champion. He doesn't have much of either. If they are, they are much quieter about it."

"Anyone else? I want them all, including those you suspect."

"No, sir, that's it. Everyone else we know are good, solid Spartans."

He gave her a long, hard look, probing for deceit. But she appeared true, even though he was hoping for any excuse to throw them all in jail.

Releasing a heavy breath, he turned and walked away, calling out, "Leave them."

With the sound of the mother crying out her relief as she embraced her brat, Kaletor spied a runner approaching from further up the street. He checked on his men, who were continuing to search every building, though most were empty.

Once he was in the midst of the methodical procession, he stopped in the middle of the street and waited with arms folded over his chest.

The runner, a young man of no more than eighteen years, arrived in a rush. "Greetings, Commander—"

"Deliver your message, boy. And be quick."

The youth blanched, his laboured breath hitched and rattling. "I bring word from the 17th kohort of the 4th Phalanx, sir. We've encountered resistance within the southern district. Many Lycurgans have barricaded themselves in shops and houses, while others have attacked the gate to try to get out. We've suffered some losses—"

"And what?" Kaletor snapped, arms straightening at his sides. "You want reinforcements?"

"N-n-no, sir. Just keeping you informed, sir. Any new orders?"

"Just kill them all, boy. Make sure you kill them all."

The youth nodded vigourously. "Yes, Commander. Very good. I'll tell them."

While the messenger scurried back the way he had come, Kaletor sensed someone else approach from the other direction. He came about to see that it was another runner.

"What now?" he growled.

This one was older and bearded, his voice low and sullen. "I bring word from Captain Zagris, Commander. We've finished sweeping the northern parts of the city and progressed into the eastern district. Not much there. Mostly just the poor and ignorant. They don't know anything about Lycurgans."

Kaletor's jaw bunched as he dug his fingernails into the heels of his palms. "Useless. They're all useless."

"Agreed, sir. Orders?"

For a moment, he seethed in silence, teeth clenched tight.

But then, suddenly, an idea burned through his mind, and a grin came to his lips. "Yes. Enforce the following policy: every family must give up the name of at least one Lycurgan. Those that give three or more names will receive twenty drachmae. Those who fail to provide a name will be arrested on the charge of treason. I will then judge who is loyal to Sparta and who is not."

If the bearded runner was alarmed, he hid it well. Giving a sharp nod, he said, "Very good, Commander."

He turned away and was about to take off when another idea surfaced in Kaletor's mind.

"One more thing," he said, bringing the runner back around. "Anyone I deem guilty of not disclosing what they know will watch their eldest child, grandchild, or youngest relative burned alive in the arena. Make sure they all understand that."

Once more, the runner accepted the order without reacting. "Very well, sir. Anything else?"

"Dismissed."

This time, Kaletor didn't linger to watch the man depart. He turned around, found a group of four of his men exiting a nearby house, and moved towards them.

"Spartiates," he called, drawing their attention. "I have a task for you."

They received the same orders he had just given the bearded runner. He assigned each one a different part of the city to spread the word to, then sent them on their way.

As they ran off and disappeared into the city, Kaletor nodded to himself. *Now we will purge Sparta of every last Lycurgan traitor. Many will die, just as it should be. This is how I save the Empire. Aren't you proud, Vaseus?*

FIFTY-TWO

No one's quite sure what her true name was. To us, she is Selka. It's widely believed that no single yagar has ever seen more of the world than she did. The legend says that in the beginning, she led a conventional and ordinary life. When she came of age, she was a skilled warrior, well on her way to becoming a Superior of the Western Waterfalls Clan. But this all changed when, one day, she left. No one knows why. She just left.

The Spoken Tales

Jarka ran on beneath the towering trees of the forest, accompanied by his human and yagar warriors. Just ahead, visible as flashes of red and bits of gold, their prey fled, a group of about forty Spartans trying to rejoin what remained of their main force.

The chase continued in relative silence. There were only the sounds of pounding feet on the grassy forest floor and the occasional snapping of a twig.

He focused on keeping his breathing level and maintaining his pace, careful to keep the enemy in sight. He didn't feel the need to check on his unit—they knew what to do.

At last, the Spartans reached the shoreline of a small lake. Through the spaces between tree trunks and branches, Jarka saw them looking this way and that, casting about for an escape route.

Gathering his voice, he shouted, "Now!"

His yagars loosed a blast of ferocious roars, and his humans bellowed out their war cries. Jarka picked out Vaseus's voice among the commotion somewhere to his right, sending a pang coursing through his chest. With a roar of his own, he sped into an all-out sprint, regripping his spear tightly in hand.

The sudden uproar had the desired effect. Panic seized the Spartans and they bolted onto the small trail that hugged the shoreline. Some pushed others down as they scrambled to escape.

Charging headlong, Jarka came upon a man who had just pushed himself up from his belly. His spear scythed through the red cloak, then he ran on, feet slapping off the cool mud.

Another trailing Spartan veered into the lake, apparently hoping the water might save him. He didn't get far before he tripped and crashed into the shallows. Jarka rushed in and cut the human down.

Then he was running again, pursuing the disorganized enemy.

At that moment, the other unit lying in wait sprang into action. Yagars and humans, twenty-two in all, came flying around the shoreline from where they had been waiting at the lake's eastern end. Loosing ferocious roars and excited whoops, they charged straight at the fleeing enemy. The leading Spartans had time only to fall to their knees and die on the spot.

The survivors in the middle froze in place as they realized that there was no escape.

One at the rear turned, loosed a wild howl, and charged with sword raised high. Jarka threw his spear, and the human fell.

In a rush, his unit was there, swords and spears flashing. Some of the remaining Spartans fought back, but they all fought alone. Jarka retrieved his weapon, and fighting in tandem with Anith and Orzon, helped cut down four more. His unit carved through the remainder, and soon even the few trying to swim away were dispatched.

Suddenly, everything was still, and it was over.

Pulling in deep breaths, Jarka looked around at the fallen. To his relief, he saw only Spartans. His gaze then found Vaseus, who was standing at the water's edge. When their eyes met, she looked away.

"That went well."

Jarka let his gaze linger on her before coming around to reply. "Just like we planned. Any losses?"

Tavyka glanced back over a shoulder to the yagars and humans milling about near the lake's edge. "Not today," she said after a moment, bringing her attention forward, her silver-blue eyes keen and alert. "You?"

"Not today."

The former undefeated Warlord nodded. "These ones were even more panicked than the last group."

"That's because the bravest die first," Kika chimed in, moving to join them. "It seems there's nothing but cowards and weaklings left."

"I never thought I'd say it, but this way of fighting seems to be working," Tavyka said. "They've become easy to scare, easy to trap, easy to kill."

Jarka only just kept himself from looking back, knowing how vindicated Vaseus must have felt hearing that.

"But they aren't defeated yet," he said. "They still number in the thousands."

"For now," Kika said, grinning wide enough to expose her single remaining fang. "They can't hold out much longer. We carve them down more and more every day. Soon most of them will be dead, and those still alive will be running for their mothers."

"Yes, my friend," he said with a nod. "Soon enough."

"So what's our next move?" Tavyka asked. "The last thing I heard was that Pythax's unit was nearly done preparing their ambush."

"Yes," Jarka replied, "at the Small Village to the east. I've sent Relyk, Bex, and Alarix to join their units with his. The Spartans will reach the village tomorrow or the next day. If all goes well, they'll believe it's deserted and enter. Once they do, we attack from every side."

Kika barked a laugh. "Yes! They will fall by the hundreds. This will be the end of them, I know it. The few that survive will flee south in a headlong rush. At last they will break."

"What about us?" Tavyka asked. "And all our other units?"

"Tonight, we rest," Jarka answered, rolling his shoulders to relax the tightness in his back. "In the morning we strike the rear of their column as they march. As for our other units, I've already sent word asking them to continue harassing the enemy. I know of fourteen units nearby that are keeping at it, striking from the safety of the trees, hitting at night. The Spartans do not have a moment to rest. We're wearing them down, so our task is simple—keep at it."

Tavyka nodded. "Very good, Warlord. We will set up camp for the night and be ready to move at dawn."

As the white-furred and grey-spotted female walked back to her waiting unit, Kika said, "Listening to her could make you think that we're losing this war."

Jarka knew why. *She still resents me for tarnishing her perfection. I can see it in her eyes.*

Aloud, he said, "Gather everyone together and find a good spot to camp. Somewhere in sight of the lake, if you can."

Kika gave a short response, but Jarka barely heard it. Thinking of Tavyka had triggered a memory, and in that instant, he remembered days gone by. Before long, his mind turned to those early days and nights with Relyk, Imzen, and Vaseus in particular.

He hadn't fully realized it at the time, but there had been joy then, playfulness and fun too. Their journey had been straightforward. Together, the four of them had overcome every obstacle, and nothing had felt so rewarding.

As the thoughts came, he looked to her, but she had already turned away, moving with the others towards the dense forest. He watched her until the mixture of red, yellow, and green foliage concealed her from view.

"Not so simple anymore, bee," he muttered to himself. "Not anymore."

After a long moment, he shook himself and set off to follow.

FIFTY-THREE

To brave men, the prizes that war offers are
liberty and fame.

Lycurgus of Sparta

Sitting still had become something of a problem. Within moments of taking his seat, Kaletor had stood to pace from one side of the spectator's box to the other, prowling back and forth like a wild mountain cat. Staying still brought on too many thoughts, which led to too many imaginings of what could happen.

Yes, it was better to keep moving.

"Are you sure about this?" said Ockos, his voice thin and wispy in the cool, night air. "How do we really know these people are protecting Lycurgans?"

Kaletor's jaw bunched as he glanced to where the emperor sat next to his yagar daughter. The old man was buried within dark, heavy blankets. Only his head and the ivory diadem atop it were visible.

"Like I've told you before, whether they're guilty or not isn't important. We must end the Lycurgans, and this is the only way to do it."

Though all sixteen Spartiates standing behind the three chairs were holding torches, the wavering yellow light did little to pierce the night's darkness. Both Ockos's and Sola's expressions were shrouded in shadow.

"So you say," Ockos croaked, "but I'm not so sure. Even if this needs to happen, must it happen here, in this way, in front of the entire city?"

"That's the whole point," Kaletor snarled, hands flexing into and out of fists as he put more effort into his strides. "I know you've been safe in the palace this whole time, but the Lycurgan threat is still very real. Their attacks on my men continue. We hunt them night and day, yet they refuse to give in. That is why we must do this. This is the statement that will bring us victory. Once the people see this, once they witness this horror, anyone still supporting the Lycurgan's will stop, and their resistance will crumble. They will not be able to hold out without the protection of their friends."

As he finished, he looked to the crowd that filled the surrounding seats of the Kolosaio. His hoplites and Spartiates stood vigil on every staircase, the light of their torches revealing row upon row of shadowy figures. There was almost total silence; only the occasional voice rose up from that sullen void.

Though much of the crowd was hidden in swaths of darkness, Kaletor could sense their ominous mood. The city had become heavy, burdened by the same shock and grief experienced by any conquered people.

It was likely that they blamed him for their suffering. But they didn't understand. He seemed to be the only one who knew what had to be done. Only he knew that this was for the greater good.

His brooding didn't last long, for it was interrupted by more of the old man's crooning.

"It just doesn't feel right. I don't think the people will like this. They aren't used to so much darkness and despair. What if this turns them against us? What if they think they might be next?"

"They won't turn. But even if they did, it wouldn't matter. They are no more than a disorderly mob, no match for my Phalanxes. They would pose no more threat to me than an army of ants."

"It's not just the mob of Sparta that I'm worried about," Ockos pressed on, shifting his weight as if he too could no longer endure sitting still. "What happens when word spreads across the Empire? I needn't remind you how recent the widespread rebellion was stamped out. What if those remaining dissidents conjure up renewed hatred toward Spartans? This could serve as a rallying cry to turn even more people against us. And we still haven't heard from Belisar whether or not he completely defeated the rebels that joined with the yagars. What if they come back? It could be the spark that ignites an even greater revolt—"

"Enough!" Kaletor barked, wheeling on the emperor. "Enough of your ramblings and wild imaginings. You've become a frightened old man filled with delusions of doom and defeat. The rebels are crushed. *I* defeated them. *I* killed thousands upon thousands to restore order to the Empire. The only threat that remains are these *damn Lycurgans*."

The last of his words cut like scythes through the dark arena. Though Ockos had shrunk into the high back of his chair, his shaky response was not long in coming.

"But what if this doesn't stop the Lycurgans from fighting on? How long will you keep the city sealed? How many more people will you arrest? How many more children—"

"*As many as are needed!*"

With this bellow, Kaletor was suddenly standing face to face with Sola, who had jumped up to stop his advance on the emperor. He glared up into the vertical slits at the center of her eyes, fingers itching for a spear.

"He's right, Father," she said, her voice calm and her gaze steady. "You speak of things that may never happen. Enough."

From behind her, Ockos released a defeated sigh. "Fine."

Sola stayed where she was a moment longer before returning to her seat. When she did, Kaletor saw that all of his men had drawn their swords and pressed in, poised to fight.

Dropping his gaze to Ockos, he said, "Do not forget who holds the real power here, old man."

The emperor's nostrils flared, and Sola visibly bristled, but they both kept their mouths shut. No matter how much they hated him, they knew that they could do nothing about it.

A shrill, piercing scream split the night air. Kaletor let his glare linger on his puppet emperor, baring his teeth in a silent snarl. Then he turned away and looked to the oval ring below.

One end was filled by thirty-four men and women, all those he had found guilty of treason. They were bound by chains that linked them together through the collars fastened around their necks. On each end, the chain was staked into the ground.

They had been there for quite some time, docile, watched closely by thirty-four hoplites standing directly behind them. But now their time had come.

It started with that lone scream. Then there was a chaos. Loud wailing, crying, and uncontrollable sobbing filled the still, night air. They all strained at their bonds and reached out towards the opposite end of the ring.

Crossing his arms, Kaletor shifted his gaze to watch the children being dragged into the ring from one of the access gates. All across the sand stood oil-slicked pyres, each one a snarled bundle of twigs and branches. A lone stake rose up in the middle of each bundle, like tiny towers. There were twenty-two in all.

The silent crowd looked on as each child was led to one of the pyres.

Some of the guilty went manic then, thrashing in their chains, flailing their limbs like crazed beasts. The hoplites moved in, smashing their shields into their charge to quell the surging movement.

Some of the older children tried to run towards their relatives. They were beaten down. The wretched wails of the young mingled with the desolate pleas and screams of the old.

None of it mattered. Before long, every child was forced onto a pyre and bound to its stake.

Seeing that all was ready, Kaletor turned back to those who shared his box.

He moved to stand directly before Ockos and Sola, and over the continuous screaming and wailing, said, "Listen. Listen. This is what comes to those who defy me."

Without waiting for their reaction, he moved to the nearest Spartiate, took his torch, and returned to the front rail.

For a moment, he hesitated. But before he allowed himself a chance to reconsider, he waved the torch back and forth above his head.

Those hoplites bearing torches within the confines of the oval ring moved towards the pyres.

The guilty understood, and their screams intensified to another level. They thrashed in their chains even more frantically than before. The children's cries rose to an earsplitting volume.

Through it all, the hoplites closed in.

One pyre was lit first. Then another. Then another. Before long, they were all ablaze.

There was pure terror then. Screaming and crying, the children strained to get away, eyes fixed on the flames reaching for their feet. The adults wailed, screamed, cried, and shouted.

Kaletor looked to the crowd. They were deathly silent. He knew the horror they all felt, knew the evil they all saw.

They couldn't see what he could see. They didn't know what he knew.

"This is wrong, Kaletor. This is so wrong. You have truly become a monster."

He had been expecting Vaseus's voice to sound in his head, and so was neither alarmed nor disturbed. Looking back to the arena floor, he watched as the flames reached the children's legs.

With the screams of pain and anguish filling everything, he gave his response. "You still don't understand, Vaseus. I will win. Even if it means everyone must die."

FIFTY-FOUR

Incredibly, Selka didn't just leave her home—
she left the Forever Forest altogether. She
ventured into human lands, into the unknown
regions of the west. It's said she always evaded
the humans she came across, and that they
weren't nearly as numerous as the humans to
the south. Still, some tried to attack or capture
her, but her skills and speed allowed her to
escape time and time again.

The Spoken Tales

Jarka rammed his spear into the Spartan's belly. The man groaned as he collapsed to the ground.

He pulled his weapon free, looking for the next one to attack, but then relaxed. His unit and several others had already swarmed the handful of hoplites that had stopped to delay the pursuit. Their red cloaks and golden shields were now as still as their owners.

"*Wait,*" Jarka hollered at those who had already resumed the chase. "Regroup. Catch a breath."

"No, let's keep at it," a nearby human protested, pointing his sword down the road. "There's still more, and they're close."

"He's right," a tall, muscular male said, the roll of his shoulders producing an audible crack of his neck. "They're probably just over that next hill."

Jarka kept his gaze forward to confirm that all the humans and yagars ahead of him had stopped.

"We have the numbers," he replied, "so we can afford to rest. They cannot. The more tired they are, the easier they will fall."

"Can it get any easier than this?"

Boisterous laughter came from everyone strung out along the road.

Jarka laughed along with them, then said, "Rest up and take a drink. We move again on my word."

Some dropped to a knee, others remained standing. Everywhere yagars and humans chatted and laughed together, some in pairs, others in small groups. It was clear that friendships had been forged, not only in his own unit, but in others as well. Those that remained quiet appeared content.

The simmering hatred that had once been directed toward the opposite race was replaced by mutual respect. Combat had brought them together, and a string of one success after another had everyone in high spirits.

They had run the small number of surviving Spartans out of yagar lands some days ago. Now they were chasing them back into their Empire. More units were collecting in the southernmost parts of the Forever Forest to join the pursuit. Soon, every yagar and human warrior would come together to form a single army once again.

As he looked on the happy group all around him, Jarka smiled wide. Where once they were divided, now they were united.

Perhaps we can win after all.

He moved among them, meeting the gaze of most, nodding and sharing the occasional word. Yet even as he did, a sliver of darkness remained, like a splinter in his mind.

He kept searching, but, as usual, he could not find her.

Day after day, Vaseus remained a ghost. When he did happen to spot her, she was not alone, so he could not tell her that she had been right about everything. If they could just speak in private, he could tell her that and apologize. But she wouldn't let him, and so his torment continued.

Still, there was much more at stake than his life and what he wanted. Much more.

Jazith needs me to stay focused. We are her only hope. I must see this through. I must save her, no matter what.

This recurring thought pulled him away from the dark sliver and into action. "Move out!"

Having given the order, he started running again, running with hundreds of yagars and humans as they passed through the enemy's lands. As they ran, he resolved to mend all that was broken.

*   *   *

By evening, they had covered eight or nine more miles and pitched camp around an abandoned farmhouse on a low hill. On the eastern horizon, a tiny village was visible, nestled at the foot of a solitary mountain. Otherwise, the surrounding landscape was flat and unoccupied. Vast swaths of dying grasslands stretched out in every direction. Far to the south was a long range of mountains beyond which, apparently, lay the former kingdom of humans called Makedonians.

As the light of another autumn day faded, Jarka peered to those distant lands, his legs stretched out long before him. Somewhere out there were the few remaining Spartans. They were tired and desperate, ripe for total defeat. This was why Jarka's call to halt for the day had caused some displeasure. Many wanted to hunt down and finish off those who had caused them so much pain. He didn't blame them.

But some were bound to escape on their horses. He was less concerned with that and more concerned with allowing the trailing units to catch up. When word reached Sparta of their army's defeat, another one would surely march out to meet them. Another battle was inevitable. When it came, he knew they would need every warrior they had.

From among the multitude of yagars and humans sitting at their fires all around him, one conversation suddenly snagged his attention.

". . . killed ten more today," a male exclaimed. "At least."

"And yet not one of them was as impressive as my last," a female replied. "It was when that last group of the day stood and blocked the road by that little bridge. I saw that Lagedin was in trouble, on the verge of being run through. I rushed in, took one of them out quick, and without slowing, swept out a leg straight into another one's shield, fouling up the sword destined for Lagedin's chest. Before the Spartan made another move, I finished it with the thrust of my spear."

"It was a thing of beauty," a human, presumably Lagedin, said. "She saved my life."

The first speaker, the male, said, "Too bad. Now we all have to keep putting up with your horrid stench!"

Belting laughter erupted in response, drowning out Lagedin's protesting.

Jarka chuckled to himself. Like everyone else, their spirits were high, and the mood in camp was light. Talk was boisterous and laughter constant. Everything sang like the alive music of a mountain stream. The delicious smells of wood smoke and roasting meat delighted the nostrils.

Very few had fallen during the course of the day, despite several more last stands made by small bands of Spartans. No one had cause, it seemed, for discontent.

With all of this floating through his mind, Jarka suddenly spotted Vaseus striding between the rows of fires twenty steps away from where he sat. Seeing that she moved alone, he pushed himself up and set off.

Her golden hair was tied at the back of her head, a few loose strands hanging down to touch her brow. She wore her usual pine-green, long-sleeved shirt and leggings, their tight fit revealing how the shape of her body—

He shook himself to break the seductive spell she cast on him. *It's not the time for that*, he berated himself, though he still found his gaze drawn to her smooth, flowing movements.

He followed as she weaved her way through the camp, doing his best to appear inconspicuous.

She continued at a steady pace and eventually came to the abandoned farmhouse. The area around it was clear of tents and persons, and the noise grew faint. Without slowing, she entered the crumbling structure through one of the gaps in the stone walls.

Jarka checked over a shoulder. Seeing that no one was watching, he went in after her.

Standing beneath a wide crossbeam with her arms folded, she watched him approach. "You look surprised. You're not as stealthy as you once were."

"Apparently not," he replied, moving across the brittle bed of straw covering the floor until six paces separated them. "You know me better than most."

"You sure about that? I thought I was a Spartan agent sent to lure the yagars into a catastrophic defeat. I thought I was your enemy."

The acid in her words burned hot through his chest.

"I was in a dark place," he managed, trying to recall everything he had been waiting days to say. "Things were bleak. I looked around and saw suffering, and I needed something to blame—"

"So you blamed me," she cut in, her eyes wide and fierce. "Do you know how much that hurt? I thought you trusted me, just as I trusted you. Do you have any idea what it's like to have someone you trust completely turn on you like that?"

"No," he admitted, "I don't. But I know it would hurt. I blamed you because it was easier than blaming myself. I couldn't accept that I was the cause of all the death and pain around me. So I blamed you instead. But it was wrong. I was wrong. I was to blame for all the suffering that came to my people. You had nothing to do with it. And I have no excuse for hurting you like that. You didn't deserve it."

As he spoke, her stance remained closed, and her expression hard. "You're unbelievable. After everything we've been through, to accuse me of being one of them . . ."

She trailed off, closing her eyes and shaking her head. "Just looking at you makes me angry."

"And yet you led me here to talk. Whether you believe it or not, you want to hear what I have to say. You were right and I was wrong, about all of it. I'm sorry for what I said, bee. Really sorry.

"Can we put it behind us?" he finished, taking a small step towards her.

At that moment, the ferocity in her eyes slackened, and it seemed like she would accept his advance.

But then a scowl curled her lip and she moved to the side. "It's not that easy, Jarka," she said, pacing away, then turning back. "One apology doesn't make it all better. It doesn't heal the wound you caused."

"I know. I'm so sorry. You were right, I couldn't have done any of it without you. Your courage and self-sacrifice are greater than anyone I know. Without you on my side, I won't succeed."

She growled, her arms going stiff at her sides. "All your words do is drive the knife in deeper. You accused me of *being your enemy*. I trusted you completely, but you proved that you don't trust me. That's not something you can fix."

"But I do trust you," he said, his chest feeling tight. "I've always trusted you. I spoke from a dark place, and I said something I didn't mean. I need your help, bee, now more than ever. I love you—"

"*Stop*," she snapped, tears brimming in her eyes. "Just stop, okay? I can't do this. We can't do this anymore. We've been fooling ourselves for long enough. The world will never accept us. Yagars and humans are enemies. It's been that way for all time. I was naïve to think we could change that."

He took a step towards her, wanting desperately to wrap her in his arms and ease her pain. "But you are, bee. You *are* changing that. Where once there was hatred and division, now there's friendship, cooperation, trust, and even love. *You* did that. You brought our people together. You showed them the way."

"It won't last. It can't. They're just using each other because it suits their needs. Once the war is over, things will go back to normal. We'll all go back to our own homes and our own lives."

He took another step towards her, nearly close enough to reach out and touch her folded arms. "I know you, bee. I know you don't really believe that."

He reached out, but she stepped beyond his hand and broke their locked gaze.

"It's better that we stop this now. There's too much at stake. We both need to do our part to ensure we win this war. That's all that matters."

Her words cut clear, and in that instant, he realized what was happening.

Suddenly, his throat was dry and tight. His stomach lurched and his knees nearly buckled.

"Don't do this," he said, his voice choked. "Please don't."

She released a ragged breath. "Goodbye, Jarka. We won't meet in private again."

She wiped at the tears in her eyes, turned, and walked away.
As he watched her go, it felt like someone had plunged a blade into his heart.

FIFTY-FIVE

Danger gleams like sunshine to a brave man's
eyes.

Euripides of Athens

The acrid tang of sweat permeated everything, mixing with the stale
dust and humid air. It was a festering pool of human suffering beneath
the low ceiling. Through the rank stench Kaletor passed, striding
quickly to speak with the Lycurgan claiming he would come to terms.

The flickering torches held by his escort of four Spartiates bathed the prison
in pale, yellow light as they proceeded. Every cell was filled with Lycurgans,
each one wearing only a threadbare tunic. Most were heavily bearded and
reeked of unwashed filth, their skin smeared with grime and dirt. Here and
there came the soft whimpers of women and children.

Passing through the labyrinth of dark, narrow halls, Kaletor peered through
the rusty iron bars at these enemies of the Empire. Most were huddled at the
rear of their cell, languishing like rats on the stone floor. A few stood close to
the front, looking back with fury in their eyes.

It didn't matter how they appeared. The mere sight of them stirred Kaletor's
lust to kill.

"This one, Commander," one of his men said, coming to a stop and
pointing to a cell that was at the very rear of the prison.

Without hesitation, Kaletor went right up to the iron bars. "Which one of
you is Salagus?"

From the eight figures sitting with their backs to the three walls of their cell,
one stood and moved from the shadows into the light. The torches revealed a

lean man wearing the same threadbare tunic as the rest of them. His head was shaved bald, and his mouth was encircled by a neatly trimmed goatee.

"I am Salagus," he declared. "You are Kaletor?"

"You claimed to be the Lycurgan's leader when you were arrested," Kaletor said, "and that you and your fellow traitors wanted to turn yourselves in. Tell me why."

The forty-something-year-old nodded and crossed his arms. "Because we want it to end. The thirty-three men that surrendered with me are the last surviving Lycurgans in the city. We submit to defeat. You have won, Champion."

"But why give in now, after holding out for all this time?" Kaletor asked, stepping close enough to smell the rusted iron. "Tell me why, Lycurgan. Tell me why."

The man's bright blue eyes flared, and his face darkened to a look of contempt.

After a moment, he uncrossed his arms and looked away. "We surrendered because of you. All of our friends and allies have turned their backs on us. You killed innocent children, and you would have killed more if we continued to resist. But now it has to stop. Every Lycurgan is either dead or in prison. You don't need to terrorize the people anymore."

The strain in his voice made it plain that this Salagus was used to getting his way. He no doubt had grown accustomed to being in a position of authority and power. Knowing this brought a grin to Kaletor's lips as he watched the traitor squirm.

"Now that we have . . . been defeated," the so-called leader went on, glaring back once more, "I would ask that the few of us still alive be released, allowed to leave Sparta and go wherever we choose."

"Is that so?" Kaletor scoffed. "The leader of the Cult of Lycurgus seeks mercy and favourable terms. But you're in no position to be making demands."

"It is not a demand. It is a request, and only fair given our cooperation."

Kaletor slapped a hand to the iron bars and barked a laugh. "You make it sound like you surrendered willingly. But you only surrendered because I *made* you surrender. And now you want mercy? You killed my men. You think you're going to just walk free? Did you actually think that's how this was going to go?"

"We are Spartan, the same as you. We deserve fair treatment—"

"Not *one* Lycurgan will go free," Kaletor snarled. "Not one. You are all traitors. You are all condemned to death or slavery. I didn't shut the city's gates, torture hundreds of people, burn children alive, and sweep the entire city hunting you bastards down just to let you go once you gave in. I did all that to crush you into oblivion. I did all that to wipe the Lycurgans out. And now that you're all dead or captured, I can finally finish this."

He paused then, breathing hard, savouring the ghastly dread that had spread across the fool's face.

Adopting a savage grin, he continued. "I want you to know what's going to happen to your followers. Every man of fighting age or strength will be publicly executed in the Kolosaio. The rest will be sold into slavery. Every family will be split apart, scattered to the farthest reaches of the Empire. Mothers will never see their children again. Brothers will never see their sisters again. Wives will never see their husbands again."

By the time he finished, Salagus was quivering. Whether it was due to rage or despair was difficult to tell. Regardless, it was clear he suffered.

Kaletor's grin widened. "Something to say? Do you think I'm being unfair? Perhaps I should just kill you all and be done with it—"

"*No!*"

The single, bellowed word echoed loudly off the cold stone walls.

As it faded, Salagus released a shaky exhale and let his head hang. "Please," he said, his tone soft and quiet. "That won't be necessary."

Kaletor snorted a laugh. "That's what I thought. Enjoy your final night, traitor."

With one last, long look at his defeated enemy, he turned and left. Accompanied by his men, he retraced his steps back through the bowels of the prison.

Eventually, they rose from the cold depths and stepped out into the street. A steady rain had begun, but this had not dissuaded Sola from waiting at the top of the stairs.

"What are you doing here?" he said, noting how the rivulets of water were running down her black-and-yellow fur as if running down a leaf.

"I bring word from the emperor," she replied, apparently as indifferent to formality as he was.

"I don't have time for his delusions today."

"It's about the people. Many have come to him to voice their complaints. He fears that if something isn't done, there will be mob violence."

Kaletor was already on his way by, but now whirled to face the yagar. "What complaints?" he snapped, hands clenching into fists.

"The main one is lack of food," she answered, her voice steady yet still able to cut through the pattering rain. "Trade couldn't get into the city, so the shipments of corn and grain stopped coming—"

"I already sent word that all trade is to resume."

"Even so, sufficient quantities of food will not arrive for many days. If the starving poor get desperate enough, there will be rioting."

"No matter. My Phalanxes will cut them down if they do."

"That's not all," the yagar went on, her golden eyes steady in their intent regard. "Corpses remain littered across the city. The rotting flesh has turned putrid, and the people complain that the foul odour is on every street. They also say that your men are using threats and even violence to take their money and food. They're afraid every time they leave their houses—"

"Afraid?" Kaletor snarled, his head jerking to one side in a quick spasm. "*Now* they're afraid? What about when Lycurgans roamed free? I eliminate a fanatic cult of dangerous, violent criminals, and this is the thanks I get? The ungrateful swine!"

"They say the city has become a joyless, lifeless place. They want things to go back to the way they were."

"Really?" he said, breath flowing hot. "A lifeless place? I should set my Phalanxes on them again. Then they'll know what a lifeless place is."

Instead of responding, Sola's gaze shifted from him to the street beyond.

"Now what?" he snarled, half-turning to glance over a shoulder.

A lone horseman was riding at the gallop down the middle of the street, the clattering of hooves audible through the constant patter of rain. The horse's white coat was drenched and splattered with thick globs of mud.

Its rider wore the red-plumed helmet of a ranking officer. Like his mount, he too was filthy. The muck was caked heavy to his cloak and armour.

Kaletor came round, crossing his arms over his chest. "What kind of fool rides through the city in this?"

The rider kept his speed up until he was within ten paces, then yanked hard on the reins. The horse tossed its head as it clattered to a halt, snorting great plumes of air. The man dismounted in a rush, and the way he moved tipped Kaletor off to who it was.

"Ackadus. What are you doing here—"

"The yagars are coming," the teenager said, his voice strained, each word clipped. "Thousands of them. We need to order every Phalanx in the Empire back to Greece—"

"The yagars?" Kaletor cut in. "What are you talking about? Belisar sent word that you had nearly destroyed them."

"He thought we had. But he was wrong. Please, we have to hurry. They will be here soon—"

"Enough, boy. Where is Belisar? Where are my Phalanxes? I want to speak with someone whose mind is not broken—"

"Are you not hearing me?" Ackadus shrieked, his eyes wild. "Belisar is dead. The Phalanxes are gone. We won the first battle, then pursued them into the Forever Forest. But then it all went wrong. They ambushed us day and night, constantly picking us off a few at a time. There was nothing we could do. Those of us that survived have been retreating for weeks. We thought that if we made it back to Makedonia, we could regroup. But they ran us down."

He paused to drag a muddy hand down his face. "Everyone died. There were too many, and not just yagars. Thousands of rebels have joined them. It didn't matter what we did. There were too many. They just kept coming. By the time Belisar ordered us to make a last stand, we were outnumbered at least eight to one. It was a massacre."

A chill that had nothing to do with the rain snaked up Kaletor's spine.

He must be insane. It can't be. I would have heard something before now.

But even as this thought came, another immediately followed. *I sealed the gates. If word came, it didn't get through.*

For the briefest of moments, he didn't know what to do or say.

Fortunately, the moment didn't last long.

"So while your companions stood and died, you ran away. You're a coward and a disgrace to every Spartan that's ever lived. You always were weak, Ackadus. But even I thought you were better than this."

"Weak?" the prince snapped, jerking his hand away from his face. "I'm weak? You have no idea the hell I've been through. You have no idea what it's like to be on the run and hunted like a dog. You've never faced a horde of yagars moving faster than anything should be able to move."

All of a sudden he went quiet, and the fire in his eyes died. "But you'll see," he said slowly, his voice small and cracked. "You'll understand soon enough."

Kaletor had balled his fists, ready to attack. But for some reason, attacking the teenager felt pointless and insignificant. He grit his teeth as he stood there, hating his powerlessness.

"What do they want?" Sola asked into the ensuing silence.

Ackadus looked to her briefly, then shrugged and glanced away. "I don't know. Justice? Revenge? Whatever it is, they want to kill us all."

FIFTY-SIX

Over a year later, she arrived in the North Lands. This is where Selka's legend began to take root. It started with the stories she told about her adventures in the west. The yagars of the North Lands were amazed, especially the youngsters. Word started to spread as fast as a fleet-footed deer. The legend had begun.

The Spoken Tales

The constant hum of voices in camp drifted in through the canvas walls of the tent. The smells of horse and smoke that reached his nostrils were faint.

All of it was a distant background to Jarka as he paced around the large oak table and its eighteen straight-backed chairs. Soon everyone would arrive, and the war council he had called would begin. There was much to discuss and important decisions to be made.

Before all that, he had hoped that this time alone would relax his mind and restore his energy. Instead, his thoughts had run rampant, hot and unstoppable as a charging bull.

It wasn't new. Whenever he wasn't preoccupied with one of the many tasks required of him, his mind would cut straight to Vaseus. The harsh pain that had engulfed him during the first few days had eased, but only just. It still felt as if someone had slashed open his heart.

I never imagined it would ever come to this. How could I accuse her of being one of them? I still can't believe I said that. How could I be so stupid?

The slap of canvas forced him out of his mind. He stopped pacing and faced the entrance, attempting to settle into his practiced role of the confident leader.

Tavyka and Relyk entered. The sunlight filtering in at their backs appeared to illuminate the ex-Warlord's white fur.

"Welcome, my friends," Jarka said, moving to greet them with the army's new embrace of gripping each other's forearm. "How fare your units?"

"Very well," Tavyka answered, stepping by to sit at the table. "They love success, humans and yagars alike, and there's been plenty of it these past weeks."

"Will everyone be here?" Relyk asked, the strain in his eyes as plain as the sun in the sky.

Jarka gave his friend a reassuring smile. "I believe so."

A moment later, the dark-skinned human leader Masos arrived with three of his so-called captains. They were followed closely by Alarix, the ex-Warlord with black fur and six circlets of white stones spaced evenly down his left arm, and Pythax, the ex-Warlord of the Shaded Meadow Clan.

As the flow of persons continued, Jarka welcomed each in turn, smiling and laughing as he did. He felt the tightness in his shoulders gradually melt away. It was a welcome relief.

By the time the flow eased, the tent was filled to bursting. Seeing that all but one chair around the table was occupied, Jarka scanned their faces to see if she had arrived.

She hadn't. He looked to the entrance, keeping his gaze there for a long moment. But no one else entered.

He released a quiet sigh, then turned away and moved to stand at the head of the table.

The noisy chatter gradually tapered off when he raised his hands.

"Thank you all for coming," he said once quiet reigned. "For anyone who does not already know, I have invited every Second and their Third, as well as some Elders and the human leaders, to attend this war council. This way you all will know what's discussed and decided. To avoid confusion, only those seated at the table will speak. Understood?"

He looked around the tent, seeing that most standing around the table were nodding.

"Again, thank you for coming. Let us begin."

"What about Vaseus?"

It was Masos who asked, his dark hair a long, thick mess. "Shouldn't we wait for her?"

"She is speaking with the leaders of Corinth," Jarka replied, trying to ignore the flutter in his stomach. "And as we know, discussions with potential allies can take a long time.

"Which leads us to the first point we should address," he continued quickly.

"What's the latest word on uprisings across the Empire?"

"Details are scarce," Masos declared. "But from what we can gather, the rebellion has been rekindled. We just heard that the people of Byzantium and the regions surrounding their city have defeated the Spartans stationed there and declared their independence. Also, we have reason to believe that the people of Segestica, Sarmizegetusa, and Bylazora have joined our cause, as well as parts of Egypt and Phoenicia, including Leonida and Jerusalem."

"How can you know this?" Pythax asked.

"We don't, at least not for sure," Masos admitted. "But it stands to reason. Some of these people must have risen up. Otherwise, the Phalanxes stationed there would have been recalled to intercept us. The only explanation for their absence is that they're preoccupied."

"I don't like it," Alarix growled, the fur of his neck bristling. "There could be thousands of Spartans bearing down on us from the north, or sailing across the sea and hitting us from the east. We need to know that our flank is secure before we advance on Sparta itself."

"I don't think that's necessary," Relyk chimed in. "Look at how many towns and cities in Makedonia and Greece have already joined us. And that's just the ones we've come into contact with. I never would have believed it, but Vaseus was right—these humans see us as some kind of liberators."

The mention of her name sucked the air from Jarka's lungs. There was a lull then, as if they were all waiting for him to comment.

Setting his hands to the table, he swallowed and said, "It's true. Their support is what's allowed us to come this far south so quickly. If Corinth, Argos, and Mycenae do the same, we need not worry about our flank. If any Phalanxes arrive from distant lands, their movement across Greece will be contested."

"Only Argos and Mycenae remain."

Everyone looked to the tent's screened entrance. Somehow Jarka had known it was her even before she spoke. His throat constricted as she stepped into view.

"You won them over?" Masos asked, his dark eyes wide. "Corinth is with us?"

Her gaze shifted to meet Jarka's in the briefest of glances before she looked to the others at the table, a small smile coming to her lips. "Yes. Six hundred barrels of grain, four hundred casks of water, and four hundred hoplites will join our march on Sparta. The Isthmus of Corinth is open."

Whoops and hollers erupted in answer, accompanied by raucous applause and fists pounding the table. Jarka forced a smile to materialize and clapped with the rest, doing his best not to stare.

"What did you say to convince them to give us so much?" Loriz, an Elder from his former Clan, asked once Vaseus took her seat and the commotion died down.

"Does it matter?" Tavyka said, her hulking frame making Vaseus, who had sat beside her, appear even smaller than usual. "The way is open and we can continue our march. Those supplies and warriors will make us stronger. That's all that matters."

"Which brings us to the main purpose of this war council," Jarka said, standing a little taller as he forced his gaze away from Vaseus to sweep across the table. "Deciding how to take Sparta and win this war."

The gravity of the statement was not lost on anyone, for a long and heavy silence ensued.

He looked from one face to the next, waiting for someone to speak. He was not surprised when that someone was Masos.

"Once we pass through the Isthmus, we should take the road called Southern Laconia. It weaves through the Arcadian mountains and then straight to Sparta. It's the quickest way, and speed is our greatest weapon now."

"Won't they be expecting that?" Alarix protested.

"Probably, but if we're quick enough, we can surround the city without a fight."

"That sounds a lot like putting your hand into the gaping maw of an angry mother bear," Tavyka said, "and daring her to bite down."

"Taking Sparta will be difficult," Masos came back, "but we have the numbers on our side. The direct route is our best chance."

"The blatant, brutish attack in combat is obvious and foolish," Relyk said. "Every yagar is taught this lesson."

"We're not talking about a Challenge," Masos snapped. "We're talking about taking a city. The direct assault can work if you have the numbers."

"And what happens if the Spartans meet us outside their walls?" Vaseus questioned. "Did numbers matter the last time we attacked the Phalanxes? Can numbers defeat a wall of shields and spears?"

"What other choice do we have?" Pythax asked.

"Approach the city from two sides," Vaseus replied, her eyes fierce as she looked at everyone but Jarka. "Force them to fight on more than one front. The phalanx formation is invincible in a head-on fight. But it's rigid. It doesn't do well when attacked from the side or rear. Come at them from more than one direction. That's how we use our numbers to our advantage. That's how we win."

"And that's impossible," Masos said. "The only way to Sparta from the north is on the Southern Laconia."

"There is another way," Vaseus countered. "I lived in Sparta for fifteen years. I know the lands around the city. To the west of the Southern Laconia is a path that leads to a pass through the Taygetus mountains. I know that road."

"What if that pass is being watched?" Alarix asked, interlacing his fingers together atop the table. "Surely the Spartans know about it as well."

Vaseus shook her head, strands of her golden hair playing across her face. "They won't be watching it. The terrain is too narrow and too broken for the Phalanxes to deploy properly. If they fought us there, we would win. They know this, and that's why they won't fight us there."

This time there was no immediate questioning, and silence reigned.

Despite the turmoil inside him, Jarka smiled to himself. Her plan was always the right one. It had taken him a long time to learn this, but now that he had, he looked back on his past certainty with amusement.

Does that mean she's right about us too?

The thought caused his smile to drift away.

"I can live with that," Masos boomed, breaking the silence. "As long as we move out tomorrow."

The others around the table nodded in agreement.

"The element of surprise is key to success in battle," Tavyka said. "This gains us that."

"And yet it's only the first step," Alarix added. "What happens when we arrive on these two fronts? I doubt the Spartans will allow us to do as we please."

"I've heard the city's walls have never been breached," Pythax said. "What do we do if they're holed up behind their walls?"

"Starve them out," Masos rumbled. "Surround the city and lay siege until they run out of food."

"That would take months," Vaseus came in. "By now they will have stockpiled huge quantities of food."

"We can't afford to take that long," Relyk said. "Phalanxes from across their Empire will surely return if given enough time."

"That's why we're going to take the city by force."

As was happening more and more, everyone's attention went to Vaseus. Jarka watched it all unfold, struggling to suppress the part of him that wanted to hold her.

"But how?" Masos asked.

For the first time since sitting down, Vaseus looked directly at Jarka. In that frozen moment, there was something there, something subtle. But then it was gone, for she looked away and gave her answer.

"It's my understanding that Kaletor, the man in command of the Empire's Phalanxes, is in Sparta. If that's so, I believe I can draw him and his men out to fight."

"Commander Kaletor?" Masos said, his brow furrowed. "He's in the city?"

"Who is this Kaletor?" Tavyka asked, bristling as if ready to spring into action.

"You haven't heard of Commander Kaletor?" Masos asked. "They say he singlehandedly took Athens when his army's assault was on the verge of disaster. He's been leading his Phalanxes across the Empire, crushing every city and town that rebelled against Spartan rule. He's had thousands upon thousands of prisoners put to the sword, including women and children. He is ruthless, merciless, and feared by all. Some say he cannot be defeated."

"But I knew him before all that," Vaseus said, her eyes intent. "I knew him when he was young. We used to play as children. We spent all our time together. A long time ago, he was my closest and dearest friend."

"I don't understand," Alarix said. "How does that help us?"

"I will provoke him," she answered. "I know things about him that he won't want anyone else to know. When we speak, I will send him into a rage. He has become proud and hateful, and he won't be able to control himself. He will bring all his men out and attack us."

"That could work," Masos commented. "His anger is well known."

Vaseus was nodding as she said, "All we have to do is present him a target and damage his pride. That's all it will take."

"But how will you get close enough to speak to him? They'll kill you the moment you approach the walls."

The words had come out before Jarka could stop them. Luckily, the table didn't seem to notice the personal nature that was there, just beneath the surface.

Her answer was swift. "I will approach alone. When he sees me, he won't be able to help himself. He will talk to me. I know he will."

Jarka's breath stuck in his throat. *No. Out of the question!*

He wanted to say it. Needed to. They could kill her and nothing could stop them. But he knew that to say this would surely draw suspicion, so he bit it back.

"Sounds good to me," Relyk picked up. "All those in favour, raise your hand."

Everyone did.

Jarka heard himself declaring that they would march tomorrow and that the council was concluded, but only just. In his mind's eye, he saw her standing in front of the walls of a city. High above, hundreds of men had arrows in their bows, each one poised to be released. And when they flew, he could not save her.

He could not save her.

FIFTY-SEVEN

Here is courage, mankind's finest possession;
here is the noblest prize that a young man can
endeavour to win.

Tyrtaeus of Sparta

Kaletor could feel a vein throbbing in the left side of his neck as he glared at Heliodorus, the young captain of the 9th. "How many, damn you?"

"Last we counted, the 9th numbered four thousand, six hundred and thirty-eight strong."

"When was that count?"

The straw-haired man kept his eyes high and away as he answered. "About two weeks ago, sir."

"That's not good enough. Count again and bring me the total tomorrow."

"Yes, Commander."

"Now get out of my sight."

Heliodorus saluted then hurried down the long, stone staircase leading to ground level.

Kaletor looked left and right along the length of the rampart, checking on the actions of both hoplite and slave as they went about preparing the wall. Some were carrying bundles of arrows to stack against the four-foot-high parapet. Some were repairing gaps in the stones or replacing old ones. Still others were carrying buckets of oil to dump into the two huge, iron cauldrons.

Seeing that nothing was being done slowly or incorrectly, he stepped close to the parapet to gaze upon the land stretching out from Sparta's northern wall.

The dim light of the fading sun revealed quiet emptiness throughout the sweeping grasslands and bronze fields of wheat. The Southern Laconia marched straight north from the gate, as lifeless as the Taygetus and Parnon mountain ranges running parallel to the road on either side.

Soon, the land would look very different. A horde of traitors and savages was coming.

He set his hands atop the rough stone blocks of the parapet, his jaw clenched tight. *I've come too far to fail now. You think to take this city, but I won't allow it. I will kill every single one of you.*

"Commander."

The voice brought him around. Coming up the stairs was Ackadus, followed closely by Sola. Seeing them elicited a moment of longing for the days when Hullis was his primary aide.

Releasing a low growl, he stepped away from the parapet and met them in the middle of the wall. "Finally. Report."

"It's not good," Ackadus said, his blonde hair again cut to short bristles, and his face clean-shaven. "Corinth was not as loyal as we thought. They did not oppose the enemy at the Isthmus. It's likely they too have joined the rebellion."

Kaletor barked out a string of curses.

"Unbelievable," he snarled when he finished, wiping the back of his hand across his mouth. "Even our oldest allies abandon us. They're all spineless, two-faced cowards!"

"Only Argos and Mycenae stand in the way," Ackadus said, "and they likely won't resist either. If the enemy moves fast, they'll be here in five days—"

"Do not tell me what I already know, fool. What else?"

"The emperor is even more concerned about the mob," Sola chimed in, her golden eyes intent. "They remain on the brink of violence. If anyone finds out how close this invading army is, there could be panic. He thinks that having the Lycurgans languishing in prison is only worsening the situation—"

"Don't talk to me about the mob or Lycurgans," Kaletor spat, the vein in his neck throbbing hotter than before. "They don't matter now. All that matters is defeating the enemy, and to do that, I need every hoplite we have.

"Tell me about the other Phalanxes. What do we know?"

Ackadus rubbed his small, pointed chin with forefinger and thumb as he replied. "The 3rd and 13th are tied up, fighting rebels in Halicarnassus and Rhodes."

Kaletor released a growl. "What about the 6th? Are they sailing across the Aegean?"

"No word from them yet. There's a rumour that they were wiped out, but we don't know if that's true."

"What about Egypt?"

"Several garrisons, including those in Thebes and Leonida, have been slaughtered or expelled. Most of the province has risen in revolt. Last we heard from the 12th was that they were trying to restore order, though they are severely outnumbered."

"What about the 5th and 15th?"

"Still no word. It's likely they're also busy fighting."

Kaletor barked a curse, pounding a fist into the other palm. "Are you saying that none of our Phalanxes are free to reinforce us?"

The teenager nodded. "Yes. Even if some of the Phalanxes aren't busy fighting, they're so far away that they won't be here for weeks. We're on our own."

Hot sweat had prickled to life under Kaletor's arms, in his hair, and on his neck. He longed to strike something. Instead, he barked a wordless roar at the sky.

"How many Elites, hoplites, and Spartiates do we have in the city?" he snapped, bringing his eyes down to glare straight at Ackadus.

"The 16th is nearly at full strength, but the 8th and 9th are down several kohorts. With the Elites, that gives us about thirteen thousand strong."

"It's not enough," the fool went on. "We could never get a good count, but I believe the yagars number at least that many. Hundreds, maybe thousands more rebels within Greece have surely joined their ranks. We cannot win this fight. We must leave the city and retreat. We need time to join forces with the other Phalanxes—"

"*Flee?*" Kaletor raged, the explosive urge to throw the emperor's welp from the rampart firing through every muscle. "Abandon Sparta? You're not only a coward—you're a madman as well. You don't deserve to bear those arms."

"I'm not a coward!" Ackadus shrieked, his face turning red in an instant. "I did what I had to, which is what we need to do now. If we stay here, we will all die!"

"Spartans do not run, boy. If Leonidas were here, he would cut you down on the spot. Invaders approach, hellbent on destroying Sparta. We will defend her to the last man. I don't care what it takes. They will not take from me all that I have gained."

As he finished, he stepped in close to Ackadus, daring him to retort. The useless brat didn't back down, and their glares locked horns.

During the violent silence, Sola moved to stand at their shoulders. "Enough of this. If we're on our own, what must we do to save the city? How do we win this fight?"

Kaletor waited until Ackadus conceded by turning and stepping away.

"Easy," he then said, glancing at the yagar. "We kill them all."

"How?"

"By marching out and cutting them down."

"March out?" Ackadus snapped, wheeling back around. "Why? We're out-numbered. They would outflank us—"

"I've been leading Phalanxes into battle for a decade, boy," Kaletor growled back, "and not once have I been outflanked. A bunch of yagars and farmers can't outmaneuver me."

"You underestimate them," Ackadus argued. "They've learned since the first time we fought them. They know that attacking the phalanx straight on doesn't work. But they know nothing about taking a walled city by force. Let them come to the walls and we'll rain arrows down on their heads. They cannot take the city if we fight from the walls."

Kaletor shook his head, fingers digging into the base of his hands. "I do not need walls to protect me. Besides, that would take too long. Whether it's in three days or three months, the only way to win is to get in close and cut them down."

Once again, he and Ackadus were glaring at each other. But it seemed the brat was learning, for his only response was to release a haughty snort.

Sola, who had remained standing motionless and silent at their sides, now said, "What you suggest is the riskier of the two options. I don't think the emperor would approve."

"The emperor doesn't know how to win battles," Kaletor said, shifting his gaze up to the yagar's broad face. "I do."

She stared down at him, the breeze sifting through her fur. "Then how do you plan on winning this one?"

He held her eye for a moment longer before moving to the parapet. "We will block the road where it is closest to the mountains," he said, pointing to where the feet of the Taygetus and Parnon mountain ranges encroached nearer to the road. "And we'll deploy right up against the slopes of the Taygetus. They won't have room to get around on our left. Our line will extend from there, stretching solid across the plain to the Parnon. They will have room to do only one thing—attack head-on."

The yagar moved to stand beside him, eyes scanning the land around the road.

"Do we have enough hoplites to cover that much distance?" she eventually asked.

"Yes. With ranks six deep."

"What if they don't take the road?" Ackadus asked as he moved to stand on Kaletor's opposite side. "What if they come through the Taygetus pass?"

Kaletor released a dismissive snort. "How? They don't know the way."

"But some Greeks do. They could lead them through the mountains."

"The yagars have no knowledge of strategy or tactics. Even if some Greeks suggest the mountain pass, the savages won't listen. They'll come straight for the city."

"But what if they—"

"I've had enough of your cowardly doubts, boy," Kaletor snapped, baring his teeth in a vicious snarl. "Get out of my sight before I throw you from the wall."

The prince stayed his ground. "Your plan could fail. You could be leading Sparta to annihilation."

"I never fail," Kaletor growled, looking back to the land beyond the city. "Don't you know that yet?"

FIFTY-EIGHT

Selka continued on alone, heading east until she left yagar lands behind once again. Here the humans were even less numerous. Wide open spaces of untouched wilderness stretched to every horizon. Even animals were scarce.

The Spoken Tales

With an army at his back, Jarka laid eyes on the city that had built an empire. It was huge, sprawling across much of the wide valley. Two towering mountain ranges ran past it on either side, stretching far into the distance.

As he looked on the city's high, stone walls, his mind turned to the original reason he had come here. Somewhere within those distant walls, Jazith was imprisoned.

She has to be. I'm coming, Jaz. I'm going to get you out of there.

"What's that?" Relyk, who was walking at his side, said. "Something on the road."

Jarka shifted his gaze, squinting against the late morning sun. He soon saw what his friend referred to. Just visible on the horizon of undulating hilltops was a glint of flashing gold.

At first, it was barely visible. But then, as they continued up a gentle rise in the road, it became clear what it was.

"Enemy spotted," he barked. "Sound the halt."

As Relyk turned to shout for the column to stop, Jarka looked around at their surroundings. Spotting a grassy hill just ahead and to one side of the road, he ran over to ascend to higher ground.

When he gained the top, what he saw punched the air from his lungs. A mile or so away was an unbroken wall of golden shields, red cloaks, and upraised spears that stretched from the foot of the mountains on the right, over the road, to a steep-sided hill near the mountains on the left. It was impossible to know exactly how many there were, but it was clear that several thousand Spartans stood between them and the city.

He heard someone follow him up the hill, and when they spoke, he knew it to be Tavyka. "I guess we don't need to lure them out."

Jarka continued scanning the distant line. He couldn't find any weak spots, though it was difficult to tell how deep their ranks were. The front line itself was several hundred across.

Two more ascended the hill to join them.

"Zeus's beard," Masos boomed. "That looks like at least three Phalanxes."

"I thought they were supposed to be much closer to their walls," Relyk said.

"They are," Masos replied, moving to stand on Jarka's left. "At least that's what I'd do. But sometimes Spartans do strange things."

Tavyka released a low growl. "Why didn't you say so before? Our whole strategy is based on them seeing our two forces and panicking—"

"That doesn't matter now," Jarka interrupted. "We must decide what to do, and quickly."

There was a brief stretch of silence then, the trio around him undoubtedly considering possible solutions.

Tavyka was the first to reach one. "They want us to spread our front line as wide as theirs. We shouldn't comply. I say we keep our front shorter and bulk up our middle. That way we can punch a hole through the heart of their center. Once we break through, we can wheel around behind and hit them on two sides."

"A direct, head-on attack won't work," Relyk disputed. "We can't break through their wall of shields." He stepped forward, pointing to the right side of the Spartan line. "Look where they're standing. See how the foot of the mountain juts in towards the road? That's the only thing protecting their flank. If their line moves forward or back, that barrier is gone, and we can get around behind them."

"They'll know that," Tavyka countered. "They won't budge unless we force them to."

"That's why we need to draw them forward," Relyk explained, motioning with both hands to illustrate the imagined movement as he spoke. "We line up in plain view, move to within two hundred feet, then hold. Either they take the bait and come to us, or we stay in a stalemate and shout curses at each other from a distance."

"That's it?" Masos questioned. "We just stand there and hope they attack?"

"No," Jarka chimed in, eyeing the valley, the enemy, and the mountains on either side as a plan took form. "Not for long anyway. We form up and march close, as Relyk suggests. But if they stay where they are, which they probably will, we charge, push them back, and get around behind their flank."

"I don't think that's a good idea," Masos said. "A third of our army is somewhere in the mountain pass. Shouldn't we wait for them to arrive? They'll be able to come down behind the Spartans' line."

"Do you see them?" Jarka said, motioning towards the dark green that was the tree-covered slopes and the tall, white-capped peaks reaching towards the blue sky. "Because I don't. They could still be days away."

"But that was the plan," Masos argued. "Come at them on two fronts."

Yes, Jarka thought, looking to the western mountains that marched alongside the valley and past the city. *I remember. Vaseus's plan.*

"Plans change," he declared. "We have a chance to end this here and now, and I'm not letting it slip away. I want our line as long as theirs with three units in reserve. Relyk, find Alarix and tell him to lead the right. Tavyka, you lead the center, and Masos, you take the left."

As he finished, he looked to all three of them. Tavyka nodded, her silver-blue eyes afire. Relyk also nodded, though he appeared more sober.

There was a slant in Masos's return gaze as he said, "Since when did you become so reckless?"

Jarka held the human's eye for a moment before replying. "How do you think I made it this far?"

To that, Masos just shook his head and turned away.

"Go, all of you. I want the army lined up before the sun reaches its peak. Fight well, my friends."

"Fight well, Warlord," Tavyka and Relyk echoed.

As the trio returned to the waiting column, Jarka looked back to the Spartan line, a huge mass of men, spears, and iron. His gaze then shifted to the city beyond them. With any luck, his sister was somewhere within those stone walls.

I'm coming, Jazith.

*   *   *

Kaletor shifted in the saddle. "Why are they so slow?" he snarled to no one in particular.

His personal guard of five hundred Spartiates mounted beside and behind him remained silent, the occasional snort or forceful exhale from one of the horses the only sounds.

Eventually, though, one among the mounted men supplied his opinion. "They know we won't come to them. They know the phalanx too well. They know its greatest strength and greatest weakness."

Not for the first time, he questioned the wisdom of having Ackadus so near at hand. He grit his teeth and reminded himself that it was to stoke his fury.

"You've said that before," he spat, feeling the stifling heat of his helmet and armour more acutely than ever. "I didn't want an answer."

"Then why did you ask—"

"Because I hate waiting!" he bellowed, twisting in the saddle to glare at the witless fool.

The teenage prince appeared to shrink deeper into his shiny golden armour. He quickly faced forward, his expression veiled by his helmet.

"It would appear," he said, his voice quieter, "that you won't have to wait much longer."

"What?" Kaletor snarled as he looked back to the enemy army.

They had been slowly moving into some sort of battle formation a mile or so to the north. Now, however, they had started to advance.

"Finally," he growled, checking on his own line. Stretching far to the left was the 16th. He had bolstered their numbers by reinforcing them with Elites. Their gold cloaks comprised the back two rows. Most of the hoplites were hardened veterans, and there were many Spartiates among the ranks, making it the strongest Phalanx he had. He had put them there because more so than anywhere else, the left had to hold.

In the center was the 8th, behind which waited Kaletor and his personal guard. Some more Elites were scattered throughout this Phalanx. Kaletor hoped that having them among the ranks would inspire the hoplites to fight harder than they ever had before.

Further down the line was the 9th, the Phalanx that had suffered the most casualties while fighting the Lycurgans. Despite this, Kaletor had not reinforced them with any Elites. He knew that the right could afford to give ground if it had to. Since the enemy knew the Achilles heel of the phalanx, they would hit the left much harder than the right in an attempt to get around that side.

As far as he could tell from sitting atop his horse, the shield wall was solid all the way down the line. Every man was in his place and ready to fight. His preparations were complete.

Satisfied, he looked back to the enemy. They came on at a fast walk, a sea of yellow and black. Most carried only a spear and wore no armour. Men were scattered amongst the yagars, appearing small and insignificant next to the savages. Their front matched the length of the three Phalanxes, but it was impossible to tell how deep their ranks were.

As they left the low hills and came onto the flat plain, Kaletor saw how disorganized their front ranks were.

"They aren't even lined up into proper rows," he said aloud. He turned back to Ackadus. "How did you let this rabble destroy your Phalanxes?"

The teenager kept looking straight ahead as he replied. "You'll see soon enough."

Kaletor barked a laugh and turned back to the disorderly mob. As he scanned the mass of approaching yagars, another question came to him. "Do they even have a commander?"

"I don't know," the prince answered, his tone flat. "We never saw one."

Kaletor laughed harder this time.

Watching the savages and traitors break into a charging run, he said, "They've never faced a *real* army before. They've never faced me."

Yagars all across the line sprinted headlong at the Phalanxes. They closed the distance incredibly fast, leaving the men far behind. Neither side loosed wild shouts or bellowed war cries. There was only the thunderous pounding of thousands of footfalls.

Watching the charging yagars about to smash into his wall of shields and spears, Kaletor felt the hairs stand up on the back of his neck. He leaned forward in the saddle, hands squeezing into fists, wishing he were there, in the front line, shield locked and spear held firm. He had stayed back to be able to move quickly to the critical point of the battle. But now that he knew they were going to win, he just wanted to fight.

Blood pumping hot, Kaletor watched thousands of yagars slam full tilt into his invincible army.

From where he stood with Relyk atop a shallow hill two hundred yards behind the front line, Jarka watched the colossal impact. Many warriors leapt high as they arrived, sailing bodily into and over the wall of iron. There were mighty roars, pained screams, the clash and clamour of spears hitting shields. All of it fused into a cacophony of chaos.

Following that first contact, the huge mass of yagars and humans pressed in behind the front line. The fighting became a dense confusion of tightly packed bodies. It was almost impossible to follow.

Jarka gripped and regripped his spear as he paced back and forth across the hill's apex. "This is wrong," he growled. "We should be fighting with them."

"I know," Relyk said. "I feel it too. But you know why we're back here. If the right doesn't get around soon, we need to send the units in reserve to support."

Despite knowing this, Jarka had never felt so useless. Every bone and muscle in his body demanded that he sprint into the fray and fight alongside his fellow warriors. The sounds of battle pulled at him like a pool of water pulls at one dying of thirst.

But all he could do was pace and look on from a distance, his eyes wide and ears rotated forward. He squeezed his spear tighter still.

The battle progressed painfully slow. He scanned from one side of their line to the other, willing his friends to smash through the Spartans. Wherever he looked, he saw hard fighting and death.

Through the dense mass of bodies, he could make out a few yagars leaping high and driving their spears down over top of the enemy's shields. The rest was mostly obscured, a melding of yellow and black and gold and red.

"Look there," Relyk suddenly cried out.

Jarka snapped his attention over. "Where?"

"In the center," Relyk said, pointing to the very heart of the battle. "I think it's Tavyka's own unit. They've broken through the shield wall."

Following where Relyk was pointing, Jarka looked to the center and saw it. A small wedge of warriors, both yagars and humans, had forced their way into the otherwise unbroken shield wall. Several yagars had white fur.

"Yes!" he shouted, jabbing a fist skyward. "Exploit it. Follow them in. Flood into that gap!"

Many indeed saw the opening and rushed into the wedge. The sheer number of bodies in the break pushed the Spartans back.

But soon, their forward momentum slowed, then stopped altogether. The middle ranks of Spartans had formed a semicircle of locked shields and jutting spears, which bogged things down. They stiffened, and the wedge of yagar and human warriors was pressed in on itself, denying them room to maneuver.

"Help them there!" Jarka bellowed. But no one could hear him.

Snarling, he took off down the hill—

Relyk snagged his upper arm. "It's too late!"

He twisted to get free. "Let go! They need help!"

"It's too late, Jarka!"

He twisted again and got loose. As he took off, he looked to the beleaguered unit. The Spartans had squeezed them in and were nearly finished cutting them all down.

Jarka stopped, a pained snarl clawing its way up from deep in his throat as he watched so many warriors fall.

"Remember what has to happen above all else," Relyk said. "The right has to get around and hit them in the flank."

Jarka kept his focus on the horror in the center. The wedge collapsed, disappearing within the shield wall.

He ground his teeth hard and swept his gaze down the line to either side, needing to see other breakthroughs. But everywhere he looked, the wall of shields remained intact.

He released a rattling breath. "What have I done?"

"They've got spirit," Kaletor said, his wrists crossed over the saddle horn, "I'll give them that. Not too smart though."

Ackadus, who had been quiet since the battle started, remained silent.

Kaletor snorted a laugh as he checked on his left wing. As expected, the fighting was fiercest there. The 16th was up to it, still holding their position firm. Hundreds of the enemy had fallen at the foot of the mountains, victims of those veteran hoplites and Spartiates. The enemy kept up the attack, but the Phalanx had sustained few casualties and showed no sign of breaking.

The sight brought a grin to Kaletor's lips. Victory was coming, despite the temporary breakdown in the heart of his center. He shifted his attention there, satisfied to see that the 8th once more held the line.

The fighting here was close at hand. The cries of the stricken and the clash of arms continued as men and yagars fought on. He couldn't explain how that cluster of yagars had plunged so deeply into the phalanx formation. He had never seen such a thing before. It was undeniable how fast, powerful, and skilled these savages were.

And yet, despite all their ferocity, they were no match for his Phalanxes.

The battle stretched on and on, a stalemate all down the line. Bit by bit, they were wearing down, just like every other army that faced the phalanx wall. Kaletor could see it.

"They can't keep this up much longer," he growled, his grin wide as he glanced at the descending sun. "Perhaps we should ride around their left wing and send them into a panic."

"I wouldn't," Ackadus answered. "They aren't broken yet."

"Then we can break them ourselves," Kaletor said, rotating in his saddle to face the sour welp. "I won't sit and do nothing this entire battle. I want to fight these savages. I want to see what they're made of. Maybe I can find their commander and kill him myself—"

"The Taygetus mountains, Commander! Look to the mountains!"

The jarring yell had come from one of his men.

Kaletor furrowed his brow as he came about and looked to the western mountain range. What he saw filled his mouth with ash.

An army of yagars was swarming down the mountainside. Some had already emerged into the valley, with an untold number streaming down the slopes that were obscured by towering pines. They were already making straight for the 16th, which was oblivious to the impending attack. Soon the yagars would arrive and smash into the Phalanxes unprotected flank.

His roar was so ferocious it sliced blades through his throat. "Impossible. That's *impossible!*"

He jerked on the reins, yanking his mount's head to one side. He looked back to the ongoing battle in front of him, searching for an answer he knew he would not find. All three Phalanxes were fully engaged, fighting all the way down the line.

Nothing. He could do nothing.

"Sound the retreat," Ackadus hissed. "We need to get back to the city and save as many men as we can—"

"No!" Kaletor howled, jerking the reins viciously to the other side to force his horse around. "On your commander, men! Charge with me! Charge for Sparta!"

With that, he dug his heels hard into his mount's sides. Head tossing, the stallion took off. A thunderous roll boomed as his men exploded into action and rode after him.

His mount tossed its head and tried to rear up. Kaletor dug his heels in even harder to keep it charging ahead.

"Kaletor!" Ackadus called, his voice barely audible over the pounding hooves. "There's too many! We can't win this! We must pull back to the city—"

"Coward!" Kaletor bellowed, twisting to call back over a shoulder. "I'd rather die—"

His horse bucked, its hind legs kicking back. As he looked forward, its head came up and slammed a hammer blow straight to his chest. The air in his lungs was forced out and his body went stiff.

When his horse bucked again, it threw him from the saddle, and the ground rushed up to meet him. All at once there was a slamming impact, shocking pain, enveloping blackness.

He had known the darkest of depths. But now, as he watched thousands of warriors emerging from the mountains, he soared.

Thank you, Vaseus. You've saved us all.

"Everyone's hanging on," Relyk cried, riding the same high.

Pulling his gaze from their approaching reinforcements, Jarka looked down the line. The battle raged on. Neither side had given ground, and most seemed unaware of what was coming. Only a small group of horsemen behind the phalanx appeared to know, and they were riding up the road towards the city.

"Can we go yet?"

Jarka glanced over to Relyk. His friend was grinning and bouncing on the balls of his feet.

"What happened to holding back to make sure the right gets around?" he asked with a grin of his own.

"As soon as we hit them from behind, it's over. We're about to send these bastards running. Shouldn't we help send them on their way?"

Before answering, Jarka glanced back to the yagars and humans charging straight for the unsuspecting Spartans. Although he couldn't see her, within that multitude of bodies was the woman who had left him.

You are greater than any of us, bee. I know now that nothing can stand in your way.

Turning back to his oldest friend, he clapped a hand to his shoulder. "You go. This is your moment of triumph as much as anyone's. You deserve to be part of it."

Relyk's wide grin slackened a little. "You're not coming?"

"I'll stay back. I want to make sure we hold all the way down the line."

"You sure?"

Jarka huffed a gentle, easy laugh. "Go on. Get going."

Relyk brought a hand up to rest on Jarka's arm. "Don't get killed."

With that he took off, accelerating down the hill to sprint towards the right wing.

A spike of shouts and screams drew Jarka's focus back to the battle. Vaseus's force had slammed into the back of the enemy's line. Hundreds of yagars swarmed in. The Spartans were helpless, unable to turn or counter.

Those that survived the initial impact were forced deeper in, squeezed together from both front and back. Some tried to fight on, but without their shield wall, they were no match.

No mercy was given as the vice tightened, and beneath the two-sided attack, the Spartan left disappeared.

With the opposition they had fought for over an hour gone, the right wing merged with the reinforcements, and together they swept around to attack the center.

As they neared, the remaining Spartans saw them coming, and panic struck. Those who could turned and ran, discarding their spears and shields as they fled. The warriors who had been fighting joined with those coming down from the mountain, and together they chased the enemy towards their city.

From where he stood atop the hill, Jarka watched it all unfold. Victory was theirs, and there was one to thank above all others.

As humans and yagars streamed towards the city, tears welled in his eyes.

"Thank you, my love. Thank you for everything."

FIFTY-NINE

Rise up, warriors; take your stand at one
another's sides, your feet set wide and rooted
like oaks in the ground. Then bide your time,
biting your lip, for you were born from the
blood of Herakles, unbeatable by mortal men,
and the god of gods has never turned his back
on you.

Tyrtaeus of Sparta

The moment Kaletor opened his eyes, it felt like fire was coursing through his chest. He grit his teeth and craned his neck to look. Blood-soaked bandages encased his bare torso. It was only a glimpse before daggers stabbed through his head.

A snarl burst from his throat as he squeezed his eyes shut and let his head fall back to the pillow.

It was a long time before the mind-splitting pain slackened at all. When at last it did, memory of what had happened came rushing in.

The reinforcements from the mountains. I led the charge, but my horse threw me. The yagars were going to overrun us. They should have killed me. Why didn't they kill me?

"Talos!" he bellowed, forcing his head back up. He noticed the familiar surroundings of his bedroom and that sunlight streamed in through the window before the pain forced him to lie flat.

As if his ears were stuffed with cloth, he distantly heard someone enter. Pushing through the throbbing in his skull, he managed to open his eyes and stiffen his neck.

There was his slave, as old and bald and bronze as ever, his face devoid of any expression.

"Tell me," Kaletor growled, "what . . . happened? How did I . . . get here?"

Talos stopped at the foot of the bed. "After you were thrown from your horse, you were out cold," he explained. "One of your men draped you over a horse and rode you back to the city. We weren't sure if you would survive—"

"Who . . . led them . . . away from the battle?"

His slave blinked. "Prince Ackadus."

He bellowed a roar, but as he did, fire seared across his forehead. The roar devolved into a strangled shriek, and he collapsed flat.

He stayed still, gulping great lungfuls of air.

As it finally eased, he growled, "I'm going to . . . kill him. Where is that coward?"

"I'm not sure, Master. If I had to guess, I'd say he's at the palace."

Sucking in each breath through clenched teeth, Kaletor braced his arms and back and pushed himself up to a sitting position. Fire burned through his chest, blood pulsed in his head, and black dots blotted his vision. He paused there, blinking and breathing harsh.

"Help me up."

"You've been in bed for four days, Master. Your wounds are not yet healed—"

"Help me up, slave!"

Talos hesitated a moment longer before moving to do as he was told. Kaletor took hold of the Athenian's weathered arm, planted his other hand on the bed, and pushed. When his legs took his weight, he cried out and would have crashed to the floor if not for his slave's support.

There he stayed, his breath hissing loud and harsh. He clenched his jaw tight.

Eventually, he rasped, "Take me to the nearest horse."

The next twenty minutes were a haze of pain, staggering steps, stumbling falls, and the fiery rage that drove him through it all.

Leaning heavy on Talos, he finally reached the stables, crawled onto a horse, and rode through the city. Everything was blurred and he hardly noticed any of the buildings or people he passed.

Finally, he arrived at the emperor's fortress. Dismounting as heavy as a heap of clothes falling to the floor, he staggered to the closed, guarded gate.

Straightening out of his bowed walk, he growled, "Take me to Ackadus."

The Elites must have known who he was, for they cooperated without hesitation. As he followed the pair who escorted him, Kaletor could feel blood trickling down his left temple and from several spots across his chest. He grit his teeth and clenched his fists to push through.

They proceeded into the palace, and eventually came to the throne room.

Stepping through the towering double doors, he saw Ackadus and Sola standing at the base of the spire of marble. Ockos was at the top, seated upon the throne of molten gold.

Looking to Ackadus, he walked straight towards them. "Ackadus," he shouted, hands balling into fists. "We're still alive. Why are we still alive?"

Whatever they had been discussing fell away, and all three looked at him.

"You're awake," Ackadus said, the disappointment in his tone obvious. He moved away from Sola, his red cloak sweeping just above the floor. "We thought you might—"

"I ordered the attack," Kaletor spat, continuing straight for him. "But we didn't attack, did we?"

"I saved your life. If it wasn't for me, we all would have died—"

"Only cowards fear death. You don't deserve to call yourself a Spartan!"

He rushed Ackadus, lashing out a fist for his face. The teenager stepped aside, and the momentum of his swing sent Kaletor sprawling. His chest seared anew when he hit the floor, pulling a roar up from his belly.

By the time he twisted around and got to his knees, Sola had arrived. She stooped down and wrapped him in a bear hug, pinning his arms to his sides.

"Enough, Champion. We're all on the same side—"

"Release me, savage," Kaletor snarled.

He fought to break free, but she was strong, and his body was too weak.

"Release me!"

Instead of doing as he demanded, she squeezed him tighter. The fur of her arms and chest felt like thousands of tiny slivers digging into his skin.

Her whiskers stabbed his left ear as she leaned in close. "Your beloved Sparta is on the brink of destruction. Either we save it together or it all ends. What's more important—punishing Ackadus, or saving the Empire?"

As she finished, she let him go and stepped clear.

Freed from her crushing embrace, air flooded Kaletor's lungs, burning harsh through his chest. He doubled over, gasping and sputtering.

"The force that came down from the mountains hit the 16th from behind," Ackadus said without waiting for him to recover. "The entire Phalanx fell where they stood in mere minutes. With the shield wall broken, the 8th and 9th were rolled up like a scroll. Those who could retreated to the city. Many were cut down along the way."

"Cowards," Kaletor snarled, wiping at the blood and sweat that had collected on his brow with the back of a hand. "They deserved to die. Just as you do."

"We would all be dead if it weren't for me," the prince spat, his lip curling, "and Sparta would have fallen—"

"She still will if we don't act wisely," Ockos came in, his voice sounding like thin reeds in the wind. "The city is surrounded. Nothing and no one can get out. Soon we'll be running low on food, that is if the yagars don't break in first."

"As I said, Father, we need to get out now. All we have to do is make it to Egypt. We have two Phalanxes there, and we can send word for more to join us—"

"Impossible," Ockos said. "The entire city is surrounded. Surrender is our best option now."

"We could distract them. If we attack from the north gate, they'll be drawn there. Once the way is clear, we can ride south and disappear—"

"*Enough!*"

The word exploded out with such force that it helped pull Kaletor from his knees to his feet. A rush of blood swam in his head, but he snarled it away.

Glaring up at the emperor on his high throne, he barked, "No one is surrendering. No one is running away. You are all cowards without honour. But you, Ockos, are the Emperor of Sparta. For you to be a coward is the greatest crime of all. I should kill you here and now—"

"That's *enough* out of you," Ockos shrieked, stabbing a bony finger down at him. "You are wounded and outnumbered. One word from me and you die."

"Killing each other," Sola said, her calm tone so quiet in comparison, "will solve nothing."

"But this is all his fault," Ockos hissed, his dark eyes wide as he pointed even more emphatically at Kaletor. "He led the Phalanxes out to be destroyed. He led nearly all of my Elites to their deaths. He said the enemy wouldn't come over the mountains, but they did!"

"He's right," Ackadus seconded, taking a step towards Kaletor, crouching at the knee as if readying himself. "You caused all of this. And now what? You want us all to die in some suicidal last stand?"

"You think you can kill me, boy?" Kaletor snarled, wheeling on the teenage brat. "Come over here and I'll choke the life out of you—"

"No one is killing anyone," Sola cut in, moving to stand between them.

"But he's gone mad—"

"He has the loyalty of the army," she said, now standing face-to-face with Kaletor. "We need him if we're going to survive this."

Kaletor thought to attack, but deep down, he knew his body would fail him. It was a fight he could not win.

Baring his teeth in a snarl, he turned away and looked back to the emperor. "Listen to your savage. I am your only hope."

Due to his spewing outburst, Ockos's diadem of gold-flecked ivory was listing on his scalp, like a ship about to capsize. He didn't seem to notice as he nestled back into his high-backed throne, his sunken eyes darkening. "What do you propose we do?"

"What we always do. Fight."

"We'll lose," Ackadus growled. "Guaranteed."

Kaletor directed his glare at the arrogant fool.

Eventually, he looked to Sola. "What's the current situation?"

"As our emperor said, we are besieged," the towering yagar replied. "The enemy has the city completely surrounded. Their main camp is to the northeast, and they always maintain a battle-ready line just beyond bowshot."

"Is every gate into the city barricaded and guarded?"

"Yes, ever since the survivors made it back."

"Have they attacked the walls?"

She shook her head, the vertical slits of her pupils steady. "Not yet. They appear content to wait."

"Because they know they've won," Ackadus grumbled.

Kaletor ignored him. "How many?"

"It's hard to tell for sure," Sola answered. "They're constantly moving. Our best guess is thirteen thousand."

"At least," the teenager spat, coming around to involve himself. "Assuming that's right, we're outnumbered four to one. If it comes to a fight, we can't win."

"We don't have to," Kaletor snapped, a splinter of sharpness stabbing across his forehead. "We just have to keep them out until other Phalanxes arrive."

"How long will that take?" Ockos called down, his voice shrill. "Weeks? Months? They could attack today, overrun our defenses, and kill us all. We should surrender now, before it's too late."

"Or at least open up peace negotiations," Ackadus said. "They might want something we can give them. There's a chance—"

"We *fight*," Kaletor snarled, glaring at both cowards in turn. "That's it. You two may have forgotten what it means to be Spartan, but I have not."

Leaving no space for any retort, he looked back to Sola and said, "How many men bearing arms do we have?"

"Just under three thousand."

The figure lanced his mind like the thrust of a sword. *Three thousand. Just days ago, I had over twelve.*

He balled his hands into fists. "That's not good enough. Find every man and boy in the city, put a spear or bow in their hands, and add them to our defenses."

"Peasants?" Ackadus protested once more. "You would entrust our protection to the mob? They'll run the moment the fighting starts—"

"There's nowhere *to* run," Kaletor fired back, baring his teeth at the infuriating welp. "Even they know that. They know that death will come if they do not fight."

"Even if they do fight," Ockos said, looking like a spindly puppet without strings as he leaned forward on his throne, "it won't make a difference. When those yagars attack, what then? There's too many of them. Even you cannot win this."

"You know *nothing*, Ockos. I have never been defeated. I will keep them out until more Phalanxes arrive. That's the end of it."

The emperor shook his head, his diadem listing even further. "No, Commander. You will fail. And when you do, we will all die. Under your watch, Sparta will fall."

Kaletor looked from the weak, scared old man to his useless son. As he glared into their eyes, he silently vowed to kill them both the next chance he got.

He met Sola's steady gaze briefly before turning away. "Take me to the wall. I need to see what we're up against."

He had expected some kind of objection, but none came.

Before they left, he stole a final glance back. Both were watching him, Ackadus from the foot of the stairs, Ockos from where he teetered on his throne.

Soon, Kaletor thought, *I will look down on your corpses.*

SIXTY

Before long, she returned, this time to the Forever Forest. It was then that the legend really took off. She told stories of her travels to everyone she met. Those who heard from her told others, and the word kept spreading. She visited one Clan after another until she had seen them all. Eventually, everyone knew about the adventures of Selka.

The Spoken Tales

Jarka ascended the ladder. The rungs were crude, many of them slanted and unevenly spaced. He kept his focus on the climb.

Eventually, he passed through the hole in the center of the tower's platform, stepped off the ladder, and moved to the railing. He peered across the no-man's-land to the city that held his sister.

From the height of the tower, he could see the walkway that was the top of the city's walls. As always, it was lined with men, silent sentinels playing their part in the stalemate. Facing them was an unbroken ring of yagars and humans, thousands of warriors doing their part to keep the enemy trapped. Voices of those in camp drifted up from directly below, as did twisting plumes of sparks and smoke. The heady scent of burning wood filled his every inhale.

He crossed his arms as he took in the scene. He wondered if anyone knew his true purpose for climbing to the top of their hastily built tower. In camp there was always something to be seen to, always another discussion to be had or complaint to be dealt with. All of it was necessary, for nothing could be left to chance. And although everything was going as well as it could, he was spent. He wanted more than ever to rescue Jazith, end this war, and return home.

His gaze drifted up, settling on a few lazy clouds sailing across the warm, blue sky. He released a heavy sigh as he looked at them.

Free and clear, not a single care or worry. I was like that once. Will I ever be again?

"How's the view?"

Jarka glanced over a shoulder in time to see Vaseus step off the ladder. "I didn't hear you coming up," he said, looking back to the city.

The boards creaked underfoot as she moved to stand beside him. "The grain and cattle have just arrived from Athens, and more supplies from Corinth and Mycenae won't be far behind. We can stay out here for weeks, even months if we have to."

"Yes. Everything is going well."

"And yet you don't sound very thrilled."

"I am."

"You look tired."

"I'm fine."

"What's wrong—"

"Why are you up here, Vaseus?" he interrupted, turning to face her. His tone was clipped, though he hadn't meant it to be.

She took a deep breath and tucked some loose strands of blonde hair behind her ears. "I've been meaning to talk to you."

"We have talked."

"I mean alone."

He blinked once. "Why?"

She ran her slender hands down the front of her form-fitting, pine-green tunic, a gesture she performed when she was uneasy. "Because of something that happened during the battle."

The breeze stiffened, pushing through Jarka's fur. He kept his gaze fixed on her bright green eyes and said, "Go on."

Her hands settled just above her hips. "When we were still up in the mountains, we saw that the fighting had already begun. In that first glance, I knew that we were taking the worst of it. As I looked down, the thought that struck me was like a sword plunging straight through my back. I thought 'Jarka's down there. He might be dead.'"

Her voice wavered then, and tears brimmed in her eyes. "I've never ran so fast in my life," she pushed on, a stifled kind of laugh spilling out with the words. "It's never been more clear to me how much I care about you. I would have killed hundreds of them if they hadn't fled. When it was over, all I was left with was not knowing whether you were alive or dead. I've never been more afraid in my entire life."

Again, she faltered, huffing a choppy sigh as she looked down at her feet.

The urge to wrap her in his arms came on strong, but he stayed silent and didn't move.

She pulled in a few steadying breaths before bringing her gaze back up. "I was so afraid that I'd lost you. It was clear to me then that I never should have ended it. I thought I was doing the right thing. I thought I could sacrifice what I wanted for the greater good. But I was wrong. I know it's not fair of me to say this, but I want you back, Jarka. I don't ever want to lose you."

The tears that had pooled in her eyes spilled out and ran down her cheeks.

As she wiped at them, Jarka faced forward, bending at the waist to set his forearms to the wooden railing that encircled the platform. "You want me back," he said softly.

In the corner of his eye, he saw her move closer. He interlaced his fingers as a battle raged in his mind. On one side there was his responsibility to every yagar, including his sister. On the other was his desire to be with Vaseus. In between the two sides arose a question.

Does it have to be one or the other? Can I be with Vaseus and still lead us to victory?

That was it. That was the vital question.

In answer, something his father had once said sounded clear in his mind. *"The greatest warriors aren't just the strongest or most talented. The greatest warriors are the ones who can focus completely on the task at hand."*

Keeping his gaze on the high stone walls and the army facing them, he forced his voice to work. "I'm sorry, bee. I can't. You were right. This is bigger than either of us now. There's too much at stake. I need to stay focused on defeating the Spartans, and so do you. We had our time, but that time is up."

While he spoke, his throat tightened and his mouth became dry. Now, in the silent gulf gaping between, it was difficult to breathe.

The silence stretched on, a silence poisoned with pain. Jarka couldn't bring himself to look at her. He didn't want to see how deep his words had cut.

Finally, after what seemed an eternity, she spoke. "So. You've finally learned."

Her tone was wry yet devoid of anguish.

He swallowed and glanced over. "Only because I had a patient teacher."

The hint of a smile played at her lips, and she breathed a muted chuckle. As he looked into her clear, green eyes, he felt something between them that went beyond words. It was clear that nothing else had to be said.

A bit of space opened up, the tightness eased, and the question he needed to ask came. "I have to believe that my sister is in there. Where will they be holding her?"

Vaseus brought a hand up and ran her fingers through her hair. "The dungeons beneath the arena. I can lead you there. But first we need to get inside the city."

He shook his head. "No. Vaseus—"

"It's okay. You're right. We need to stay focused and do what we have to do. This is what *I* have to do."

Protests rose in his mind as she returned to the ladder. He tried to conjure up the right words to stop her. But he knew she wouldn't listen.

"There has to be another way," he said anyway. "It's too dangerous."

She swung herself onto the ladder and met his eye. "I started this. It's only right that I finish it."

Without another word, she was gone. For a frozen moment he didn't move, paralyzed by the possible actions he might take.

"Vaseus!" he eventually called out.

She didn't respond.

He turned to the rail and shouted, "We attack the city! Prepare for battle!"

SIXTY-ONE

The drums of war, march to their beat. Sharpen
your spear. Carry your shield. Hold your nerve.
Kill your enemy.

Thrasilaus of Thebes

His head pounding and chest throbbing, Kaletor surmounted the sharp climb and joined Sola at the wall's parapet. Ignoring the furtive glances of the hoplites to either side of them, he set his hands to the rough-hewn stone and looked upon the enemy's army.

A long line of yagars and humans stretched all the way across the road, reaching around and out of sight to either side of the city. Those that were lined up directly in front of their camp stretched across the valley beyond the length of the entire northern wall.

He hadn't believed they numbered thirteen thousand. If they did indeed surround the entire city, they likely numbered even more than that.

He released a rattling growl to disguise how short of breath he was. "I've faced worse odds."

Sola, standing on his left, said, "Ackadus was right. There are at least four of them for every one of us."

Meaning victory is almost impossible.

This thought snapped through his mind before he could stop it. Another followed right after.

Even I cannot win this. If we fight, we will be defeated.

"They have no way of scaling or breaking through the walls," he snarled, more to himself than to Sola, "which means their only way in is through the gate. In that chokepoint, numbers count for nothing. The phalanx wall will stop their assault. All we have to do is draw them in and make them fight the way we want them to."

"How?"

"By opening the gate."

"Are you mad?" Sola said, turning to face him directly. "You can't do that. There's too many of them. We will be overrun."

"Leonidas and his three hundred faced down over two hundred thousand Persians using the same strategy. It will work."

"But they were fighting Persians. We are fighting yagars."

"It doesn't matter," Kaletor growled up at her. "Only worms cower behind walls. We are Spartans."

Her perpetually neutral expression was gone, replaced by narrowed eyes and a subtle quiver of her whiskers. "What happened to waiting it out until help arrives?"

He barked a mocking laugh. "That was a lie to keep Ockos out of the way."

Dismissing the glare coming from the vertical slits in her eyes, he returned his gaze to the scene beyond the wall. The moment he did, he saw movement within the enemy's camp.

"They're massing," he said, watching as hundreds of them moved between the tents and headed for the camp's entrance. "Why?"

Sola's response was delayed. Eventually, she said, "I don't know."

"Have they done this before?"

"No."

The yagars and men within the camp were coalescing into a column at its heart. He had seen enough.

Stepping back to the inner edge of the rampart, he looked down to the gatehouse below and hollered, "The enemy is preparing to attack! Sound the alarm!"

The hoplites below bolted into action. A moment later, the horns blared two long notes.

Kaletor wheeled back around, bellowing left and right, "Archers at the ready! Hoplites and Spartiates form single rowed phalanx!"

Everything turned to frenzied movement. Many ran across the rampart, their footfalls pattering like hard rain on stone. There were harsh shouts and barked orders as the Spartiates, hoplites, archers, and even peasants moved to their positions.

As the defense organized around him, Kaletor stood with Sola at the parapet and watched the enemy's movements. The swelling column marched from the camp, moving forward at a steady walk. Before long, there were at least six thousand of them approaching the city.

"Someone approaches," Sola said, pointing out to the road.

Kaletor looked to where she pointed. Sure enough, well out in front of the massed army, a solitary man was walking briskly along the road.

Kaletor squinted to make out details. The rebel was slight and short. He wore no armour, and his blonde hair flowed free in the breeze.

"Who is this fool?" he said.

Realizing that the rebel was within bowshot, he called out, "Archers!"

"Wait," Sola snarled over the drawing back of bowstrings on either side. "She is alone and unarmed. She comes to talk, not fight."

"She?" Kaletor said, leaning forward with hands atop the stone to look more closely.

The yagar was right—it was a woman. There was something familiar about her. He narrowed his eyes, trying to see what she looked like.

It can't be—

"Kaletor!" the woman called out, stopping about eighty feet from the wall. "I know you're up there, Commander. I wish to have words with you."

That voice. He knew that voice. But it wasn't possible. She couldn't be standing there on the road, calling out to him. He had to be dreaming.

He rubbed at his eyes. But when he looked again, she was still there.

"Do we fire, sir?" someone nearby asked.

Kaletor shook himself. "No. Only fire on my signal."

While the man relayed this order to his fellow archers, Kaletor moved into one of the gaps between the massive stone blocks that topped the wall. He was about to say one thing, but remembering that so many of his men were listening, said something else.

"Are you the one leading this pathetic rabble?"

"If you want to save your people, listen carefully," Vaseus answered in that clear, crisp tone of hers. "Sparta is finished. Your Empire is collapsing and will soon be no more. It's time for the emperor to relinquish his throne. Open the gates, lay down your weapons, and we can discuss the terms of your surrender."

"You never did understand us," Kaletor hollered back. "Spartans aren't like other men. We do not fear death and we do not surrender. That's why we always win."

Even from a distance, it was clear she was more beautiful than on that last day they had seen each other. He could feel old, long-dead feelings stirring in him like a brewing storm. He grit his teeth and pushed them back.

"That's your father talking," she called out. "But you're not like him, are you? Have you forgotten the promises you made to me when we were young? You were going to be so much better than him."

"Do not speak of my father," Kaletor barked. "He died a hero, fighting traitors like you and your friends. You will not stain his name with your dishonour."

Vaseus crossed her arms under her breasts. "Dishonour? I wouldn't speak of dishonour, Commander. I've heard about the things you've done. You've ordered your men to murder thousands of innocent people. You've killed women and children. How, Kaletor? How could you—"

"*None of them were innocent,*" Kaletor bellowed, leaning forward at the hip with both hands on the stone. "Not one. Any man who turns against Sparta has condemned his women and children. Treachery spreads like a plague. It seeps into the very blood of anyone it touches. Your so-called innocents were already infected. All I did was cut out the festering sore."

She shook her head as if deeply disappointed. "Have you forgotten everything we dreamed of together? We wanted to make the world a better place—"

"I have!"

"You haven't! You were supposed to protect people, not execute them. Don't you remember the promise you made me?"

"I remember that you *left,*" Kaletor bellowed, his neck taut. "You ran away and never came back."

"You promised that you would do the right thing. No matter what. We were supposed to be better than our parents."

"I am better. My father was a mere captain. I'm the commander of every Phalanx in the Empire, and I'm heir to the throne."

"You may have more power than him, but you're not better. The boy I knew was better. The boy I knew sacrificed himself to protect me. Tell me, Kaletor—what happened to that boy? Who do you protect now?"

Before he could stop it, his mind snapped back to that day. The desperation he had known swelled fresh, the desperation to spare her from his father's wrath.

"*Go! Run!*"

His plea rang in his head, and he saw the terror in Vaseus's eyes before she fled. Then came his father's fists, pounding into him—

"Go!" he roared, a roar that ripped through his throat. "Run!"

She hesitated, arms uncrossing and returning to her sides. Her demeanour softened as she said, "Kaletor—"

"*Archers.*"

The bows came up, a subtle song of wood being tensed.

Vaseus wheeled and sprinted back up the road.

Glaring at her, he bellowed, "Fire!"

The bowstrings twanged and hundreds of arrows arced high. The slender black missiles sped away from the wall, seemed to hang in the air, then dipped and plummeted toward the ground.

In that instant, he knew a choking ache.

Then the cluster fell.

Most bounced and clattered off the stones of the road just behind Vaseus's heels. As he watched her run, the ache dissipated.

He clenched his jaw and balled his hands into fists. "Hoplites and Spartiates to the gate!" he shouted left and right. "All hoplites and Spartiates to the gate! We fight!"

He whipped around, but as he did, fire seared across his chest. A throttled growl escaped before he clamped it down. He pressed a hand to his bandaged chest and stepped back.

"You can't do this," Sola growled, moving close to block him from going any further. "We won't hold."

Kaletor glared up at her, releasing a ragged exhale. "Sparta will win or die."

SIXTY-TWO

The power beneath the fur
The might within the spear
The will inside the mind
The honour to respect it all

The Spoken Tales, a poem

"Remember," Jarka said to the group that had joined him at the front of the column, "stick to Tavyka's plan. We carve a hole into their formation, but this time, our human friends will prevent the Spartans from reforming."

"As long as they know how to aim," Alarix added.

"I selected the best we have," Masos countered. "As long as they can gain the walls, they will not fail."

"Are you sure you're up for this?" Tavyka asked him. "This fight will be hard. Probably too hard for a human to survive."

Masos grunted. "Is that concern I hear?"

She barked a laugh. "You wish."

"I trust the rest of the army knows that they only need to keep the Spartans occupied," Pythax chimed in. "At least until we punch a hole in the shield wall. I'd hate to see any of ours fall while trying to break through."

"Did word spread in time?" Relyk asked.

"Yes, everyone should know the plan," Jarka replied. "I told—"

His words died on his lips when he saw hundreds of black arrows fly from the walls. They arced high, then dove towards the ground.

He looked for Vaseus and saw that she was running.

Snarling, he took off.

"Jarka! Wait!"

He disregarded Relyk's plea. As he sprinted, the arrows came down all around her.

Behind him, someone bellowed, "With your Warlord! Charge!"

A rising explosion of roars and shouts erupted in answer.

He hardly noticed. His feet pounded on the stone road as he eyed the top of the wall for another volley. It didn't come. He ran straight for Vaseus, and as he did, all he knew was the distance that separated them.

Finally, the distance was gone. "Are you hit?"

She shook her head as she bent over, setting her hands to her knees. "No."

The instant he knew she was unharmed, his singular, narrowed focus expanded. His heart was slamming into his chest wall as hard as a beating drum. He felt the ground shake, and he heard the pounding charge of thousands at his back.

"Did it work?" he asked, stealing a glance over his shoulder. The army would overtake them in seconds.

"Yes," she said between breaths. "Go."

"What about—"

"I'll be fine. Go!"

He looked back again. The front line was twenty yards away.

"Don't get yourself killed," he said to her.

She met his gaze. "I won't. Now go!"

He nodded once, then hefted his spear and sprinted toward the city.

*   *   *

"Fire!" Kaletor barked down the rampart. "Fire at will!"

Archers to either side did as he commanded, nocking arrows, drawing them back, and releasing them to speed down at the incoming horde. Many yagars were struck and fell, but the charging mob was unstoppable.

Like a tidal wave of black and yellow, the huge savages surged right up to the base of the wall all the way down the line. The front ranks swarmed in toward the open gate.

There, bristling out from the gatehouse like the top of a mushroom, waited a wall of Spartiates and hoplites, packed tight together with shields overlapping and spears jutting out.

"Brace!" Kaletor bellowed down from directly above them.

The yagars slammed bodily into the phalanx at an all-out sprint. Their speed and sheer numbers hit the wall of iron, the impact of it forcing his men back. The onrushing tide kept coming, a successive hammering, like four blacksmiths smashing hammers into a sword one after the other.

More from behind the front poured in, their bodies slamming into those ahead of them, their numbers feeding a crushing forward push.

The phalanx was forced further and further back, squeezing them in towards the narrow pass of the gateway. The power of the horde's charge was unrelenting.

"Push, Spartans!" Kaletor howled down. "Push!"

Gradually, the momentum of the charge waned. The vast mob of yagars continued to press in, but they could no longer run.

Freed from that initial pressure, the phalanx stiffened. Still solid within the shield wall, the men started lancing out with their spears. The yagars tried to avoid them by spinning away, but they were too close together. They tried to attack, but their spears were foiled by the wall of iron shields and armour. There was nothing they could do but die.

Watching it unfold from above, Kaletor grinned wide. "That's it, my Spartans. Hold them there. Kill them all!"

Neither side was giving ground. His plan was working.

Satisfied that his men would hold, he turned away and hurried to the stairs. He pressed a hand to his bandaged, throbbing chest as he descended, taking them two at a time.

After Jarka finished cutting down another one, he felt a hard tap on his shoulder. He shuffled back and Alarix stepped past, roaring as he attacked.

Standing removed from the fight, Jarka felt a sting from the gash in his left shoulder. The initial impact had been all power, and he had fought desperately to survive. His breathing was harsh as he watched the battle continue. The clash of arms, the shouts of men, and the roars of yagars dominated everything.

Looking back to their own ranks, he bellowed, "Scale the walls!"

Keeping an eye on the Spartans in front of him, he watched for the ladders. He didn't have to wait long. One after another the ladders went up, and their human counterparts started climbing. Many were hit by arrows and tumbled to the ground. But more took their place.

Jarka shifted his attention to the fight at hand. He watched Alarix spin away from a thrusting spear. Tavyka stepped in and took the Spartan down. Beside her, Relyk fended off three attacks, ducking under one before deflecting away the other two. He then countered with a quick thrust. But the shield wall denied him, and a spear cut across his forearm. He roared and attacked again. This time his powerful blow knocked a Spartan to the ground.

Pythax rushed forward to finish the kill. A neighbouring Spartan thrust his spear at the ex-Warlord. Pythax blocked it and fought on.

To his left, Tavyka killed another, and Alarix went for the gap. But the second line of Spartans was ready, and two spears jabbed out. He deflected one, but the other got through. He snarled and twisted away, face contorted in pain. Another Spartan attacked, intent on a killing blow. Despite the wound, Alarix batted it away. He stepped back, blocking another attack.

Masos rushed forward to help, bellowing as he joined the fray. Jarka moved to do the same—

But pulled up when Tavyka shifted over to protect the human's exposed side. She foiled one attack, then another. Given the space, Masos managed to take a Spartan down.

Tavyka stepped aside to avoid another thrusting spear. She roared as she countered with an overhead strike. The Spartan raised his shield to block, but too slow. Yet even as he fell, the gap in the line was immediately filled by another.

Next to her, Pythax staggered with a wound in his thigh. Jarka surged forward, deflecting away a spear that had been destined for the ex-Warlord's chest. Relyk also moved to help, plunging his spear into the Spartan's side. Jarka rushed in to exploit the gap, but it was a feint. He stopped up and drove his spear past a shield in the wall. The stone leaf head felled another one.

Relyk timed his next attack perfectly, and the gap widened. Tavyka also cut another down, and suddenly, they had the momentum. Jarka felt a thrill fire through him as he took two steps forward and drove his spear out. It struck the Spartan who was moving to shore up the gap and knocked him flat. Another one saw and jabbed his spear at Jarka's belly. He batted it wide, and at the same moment, Tavyka arrived to cut the man down.

Jarka went for the next with a side swing. The Spartan ducked under it and added his shield to the shield wall. Jarka flowed into an overhead swing. When this was blocked, he transitioned to a quick strike at the one facing Relyk. Unsuspecting, the human fell.

They were starting to carve a hole into the phalanx. But before they could drive deeper, they needed archer support.

Fighting together, they kept up the attack. Tavyka rotated back to allow Alarix forward. Soon, Pythax moved in to give Relyk a break. Tavyka then came ahead again so Masos could rest. While the battle raged on every side, bit by bit, they cut their way into the enemy line, always moving in tandem with each other.

Jarka's arms were tiring when he stepped back and Relyk took his place. He felt the burn in his lungs as he looked to the walls. It was difficult to tell, but it seemed like some of the arrows were being shot straight down into the Spartan ranks.

He kept watching. Sure enough, a few were falling amongst the enemy.

"We have archer support," he hollered to everyone. "Keep at it."

Alarix and Tavyka were fighting together as if sharing one mind. She blocked an attack, and at the same time, Alarix drove his spear into the Spartan. The man's neighbour suddenly rushed forward and cut his spear across Tavyka's shoulder. She roared and dispatched her attacker. The sequence left a gaping hole in the enemy line, which the pair moved to exploit.

Beside them, Relyk and Pythax lent support. Relyk blocked two attacks, then countered. His spear found its mark. Pythax plunged forward, smashing bodily into two overlapping shields. The force of the impact staggered the Spartans. While Relyk took out one, Pythax took out the other.

Just beyond the battle line, arrows hit the Spartans from above, and the shield wall was slower in reforming.

Seeing all this, Jarka realized the moment had come.

"Yagars," he bellowed, glancing left and right and raising a balled fist. "On your Warlord! Attack!"

Many nearby warriors roared in answer, and like a rushing tide, they surged forward.

Looking back to the melee, Jarka saw Pythax take a spear to the chest.

"No!" he yelled, rushing forward.

Pythax fell to his knees. Another Spartan drove his spear out—

Masos arrived in time to block it, but the move left him exposed. From within the shield wall, a spear was thrust into his gut.

Jarka roared as he attacked. His spear got past a shield and punched through armour. Before he could pull it back, another Spartan jabbed his weapon out. The iron leaf head cut across Jarka's forearm.

As he snarled from the pain and twisted away, a wave of yagars arrived. They slammed into the disordered shield wall, breaking it apart further.

Freed of the immediate need to fight, Jarka looked to Pythax. The ex-Warlord was on his side, and his eyes were blank. Masos lay nearby. He too wasn't moving.

Jarka roared, gripped his spear tight, and rushed back into the fray.

The driving wedge was doing its work, pushing into the phalanx and preventing the shield wall from reforming. Amongst the press of bodies, Jarka spotted Relyk and Tavyka. He weaved his way towards them.

Tavyka was fending off a trio of Spartans. Jarka attacked the one on her left, leaping to drive his spear over the man's shield. The next one fell with an arrow in his back, and Tavyka cut down the third.

With that resistance gone, they continued forward. Tavyka roared and thrust her spear out high. When the Spartan raised his shield to block, Jarka rammed his spear into the man's gut. Then he spun behind her, coming around to whip his spear into another one's side. She took two quick steps and kicked a Spartan in the chest. The man crashed into those behind him.

They pressed on with many others fighting alongside them, carving deeper into the enemy formation. Without their solid shield wall, the Spartans were collapsing.

One of them faced Jarka squarely, his shield and spear ready. Jarka rushed in and drove his spear out. The human brought his shield up, deflecting the attack high. A counter came back, a straight thrust at the chest. Jarka sidestepped it, which allowed Tavyka an opening to take the man down. Another Spartan charged forward, intent on smashing into her with his shield. Jarka rushed around and drove his spear into the human.

Alongside everyone else, they fought on, forcing the Spartans back.

"Reform the line," Kaletor bellowed. "Lock shields, you fools! Hold them! Stop them!"

The small gap in the center was widening as more yagars flooded in. From where he stood directly beneath the wall at the rear of the formation, Kaletor could only watch as the phalanx began to come apart. Panic had infected some hoplites, and it was already spreading.

His voice was raw from shouting, but the fire burning through him didn't care. His hands were balled into iron fists, fingernails buried in the base of his palms.

"Fight harder! Do not back away! Get your shields in line and hold fast! Do not let them set foot in our city!"

The wedge of yagars pushed deeper into the breach, forcing his men out to either side. The phalanx was coming apart. Without the unbroken wall of shields locked together, every hoplite and Spartiate was forced to fight as an individual. Instead of always fighting what was straight ahead, they had to shift left or right to meet an oncoming attack.

Wherever Kaletor looked, he saw yagars overwhelming his men. They were faster, stronger, and bigger. They were too much.

"We need to fall back," Sola, who was standing beside him, called over the raging battle.

"Retreat?" he snapped without looking away from the fight. "No. We can't let them get into the city!"

"We can't hold them here. We don't have a choice—"

A wordless roar ripped up his throat and exploded out. Directly before him, the hoplites not yet engaged were gradually backing up.

Teeth gnashing, he tightened his grip on his spear and started forward—

Sola's fingers dug hard into his shoulder. "Don't be a fool," she growled. "We must retreat."

"Release me," he barked, twisting to break free.

The moment he did, it felt like shards of iron stabbed through his chest.

The snarl that came out was vicious.

He writhed and twisted again. The jerking movement broke the yagar's hold, but at a cost. His legs buckled and he collapsed to his knees.

He remained there, head hanging towards the cobbles as he sucked in ragged breaths.

As soon as the pain started to ease, he surged back to his feet.

"Order everyone back," Sola pleaded at his side. "Do it now before they all flee in panic."

Through the tears springing into his eyes, Kaletor saw what she saw. All semblance of the phalanx was gone. Those still standing were backing up faster and faster. The yagars were relentless as they pushed and pushed toward the opening of the gate.

It was undeniable—the disease of panic could seize every remaining hoplite and Spartiate at any moment. Defeat was unavoidable.

Kaletor snarled and moved to charge ahead—

But just as he took a step, a thought pierced his mind. *The Empire still lives. Phalanxes remain. I can go south, sail east, and return with ten thousand men. I can still win.*

This quick flash of possibility kept him rooted in place. For a moment, he was in limbo, caught between the chance of future victory and the need to fight.

Then, another idea. *And if I am to die, I will take Ockos and his brat with me.*

The beginnings of a plan came to him, and he had his course.

"Fall back! Back into the city!"

The survivors needed no further convincing. The rearmost ranks turned and rushed through the narrow corridor that ran under the wall, calling out to others to fall back.

Kaletor held one final glare at the mob of yagars making their way toward the gate. He grit his teeth in a snarl before looking to his approaching men, each one a pathetic excuse of a Spartan.

"Follow me," he barked before forcibly turning himself away from the unfinished fight. As he did, he met Sola's gaze.

"Where to?" she asked.

"The palace."

Jarka rushed ahead, moving along with the continuous forward momentum all around him. A Spartan was backpedalling away, spear and shield up.

He jabbed his spear high without slowing. The Spartan jerked his shield up to block. With the stone leaf head skittering off the golden disc, Jarka stepped in close and lashed out with a left hook. His fist cracked into the man's cheekbone, and the force of the blow threw the Spartan off balance. He followed with a quick spear thrust to the ribs.

Shouts and roars echoed through the stony passage as more and more

Spartans fell in the narrow gateway.

Jarka cut down another, then another. The advance was steady now. Without their shield wall, the Spartans were no match.

Through the constant commotion came shouts from just within the city.

Soon, the Spartans were giving ground even easier than before.

Seeing they were ripe for panic, Jarka bellowed, "Rush them!"

A great roar of exuberance went up as all those around him surged ahead. The few Spartans still standing their ground were overwhelmed.

With that last bit of resistance gone, the attack became a sprint. Immersed within the tide of yagars and humans, Jarka sped through the rest of the narrow corridor until he found himself beyond the wall.

Directly ahead was a wide street lined on either side by small, cramped buildings. The red and gold Spartans were running between them into the depths of the city.

"After them!" he called over the pounding footfalls and excited whoops and hollers. "Don't let them get away!"

He peeled off from the onrushing tide, stepping out to stand a few paces beside that dense stream of bodies. There he waited, watching the continuous flow of yagars and humans running past. Their eyes were wide and fierce with the relieved joy of survival and success.

Among their multitudes, he spotted the one he was searching for. "Vaseus!"

She heard him and cast her gaze around. When she found him, she veered through the moving column. As she approached, he decided to tell her about Masos and Pythax later.

"We did it," she exclaimed, slowing to a halt. "Now we need to find the emperor—"

"My sister," Jarka interrupted. "Lead me to her."

Her brows drove down towards the bridge of her nose. "Now?"

"Yes."

"But we need to secure the city first. We should wait until it's safe."

"I'm here to set her free. I won't wait."

"It's too dangerous."

"Only if we were alone. But we won't be."

Without giving her time to object, he stepped close to the bypassing column and called out for volunteers to assist their Warlord. Seeing who asked, several yagars peeled away from the onrushing column.

Jarka waited a few moments, then made the request again. This time a few humans were among those who pulled up to join them.

Moving among the newly formed group of thirty or so, he called out, "My friends. I go to free all yagars imprisoned here. Would you care to join me?"

They answered with a rising roar.

He returned to Vaseus. "Better?"

She shook her head. "When did you get so stubborn?"

He felt the tips of his fangs expose as he smiled. "You taught me well."

Lungs screaming, chest a searing inferno, and head pounding, Kaletor ran on with Sola leading the way. Buildings on either side of the streets were no more than a passing blur. The sounds of pounding feet and the cries of the stricken were dull and distant. He didn't know how far behind they were, but there was no doubt that the yagars were cutting his men down in the streets.

They came to an intersection. As Sola veered left, he pulled up and turned around.

"Twenty more, form a line," he bellowed through gasping breaths to the nearest hoplites and Spartiates. "Let ours through, then form phalanx and hold them here!"

It was the fourth or fifth time he had given such an order. And, for the fourth or fifth time, his men obeyed without hesitation, even though they must have known it was a death sentence.

As they faced about, he looked back up the street. In that brief glimpse, he saw the mob of yagars, a black and yellow mass of bodies choking the street full. The reds and golds of his men were dwindling as the enemy continued their relentless pursuit.

Gritting his teeth in a snarl, he turned away and ran after Sola.

They came to another intersection and turned right. As they rounded the corner, the topmost parts of the palace were visible in the distance.

With the shouts and howls and bellows of friend and foe alike echoing behind him, Kaletor willed his weakening legs to carry him on.

He had to reach the palace. It was all that mattered now.

SIXTY-THREE

After visiting every Clan, Selka was still intent on seeing even more. This time she travelled south. She was never seen or heard from again.

Some think her luck ran out and that she was finally captured or killed by humans. Others believe she went on exploring, avoiding the humans at every turn, for the rest of her days. We may never know for sure what happened to her. But one thing is certain—her legend will live on.

The Spoken Tales

The only Spartans Jarka saw as they ran were a few curious youngsters peering out from within the closed shutters of their homes. Like the pain of his wounds, he ignored them as Vaseus led them down street after street.

Soon, they had left the noise of the battle far behind. They turned another corner, and suddenly, they were approaching a massive building that towered high above the others. Vaseus led them across the open space of smooth, white marble that surrounded it, passing by several tall statues.

Once they were within the building's shadow, she stopped before a large gate of black iron pikes.

"We need to break this chain," she said, pointing at the metal links wrapped tight around the gate's center.

While a female came forward with a hatchet, Jarka moved to stand beside Vaseus. "So this is the arena?" he asked, peering into the shadowy space of bare marble directly beyond the gate.

"It's called the Kolosaio," she answered, standing close enough that he could hear her laboured breathing. "This is where they force yagars to fight in front of thousands of spectators."

"Like our Challenges?"

"Not exactly."

The female's hatchet came down and broke the chain.

As it clattered to the marble, Jarka said, "What do you mean?"

Vaseus pushed the gate open, the metal hinges creaking. Then she glanced over, her expression grim. "Here they fight to the death."

She ran in without another word, forcing him to put aside his questions and run after her.

The arena was dark and shrouded in shadow, but it was clear that they were progressing around an outer ring. To the left towered tall, thick columns of white stone, all of them spaced evenly apart. In between each one stretched a wall of black bricks. To the right was much the same, except for yawning doorways that opened to stairs leading both up and down.

They ran until Vaseus turned to one of the inner doorways and took the stairs down. With their thirty or so volunteers at their back, Jarka followed her down.

The air cooled and the darkness deepened as they descended. They passed by two more openings before reaching the bottom stair. There wasn't much light in what had to be the very bowels of the arena.

Vaseus pressed on, leading them down a long, low hallway. There was no paint or columns anymore, just rough stone underfoot and crumbling brick walls.

At the end of the hall, she turned left onto a downward-sloping ramp. A little ways further was a small door. She turned the metal handle and walked through.

Jarka ducked low and hurried in after her, but had to stop up to avoid running into her back. Stretching ahead on either side was a labyrinth of iron bars, broken up only by narrow rows to walk between them.

Two things were immediately obvious. The first was that it was a dungeon with a vast series of prison cells. The second was that every single one was empty.

"They should all be here," Vaseus said, hands going to her hips. "When I lived in Sparta, this is where they kept your people."

Jarka slipped past her and went to the nearest cell. Like all the others in view, the iron-barred door was ajar and protruding out into the hall. He stepped to the threshold of the cell, peered inside, and sniffed. The air smelled stale. There was nothing but a bit of dry straw on the hard stone floor, much of it bunched into a back corner. The space within the cell wouldn't allow for three full strides in any direction. As he looked, he squeezed his spear in a death grip.

"No one's been down here for weeks. Maybe even months." He turned to face Vaseus. "Where are they?"

She shook her head. "I don't know. This is where yagar prisoners were always held."

"They must be somewhere else. Who would know where they were moved to?"

She wiped the back of a hand across her brow, then brought it up to smooth down her golden hair.

After a moment, she said, "The emperor. The emperor must know."

Jarka moved to stand with her. "Then let's go ask him."

*   *   *

Kaletor scrambled up the stairs, finally gaining the top and final landing. "Get those doors open," he rasped at Sola.

As she ran across the platform, he turned his back to the palace, gasping for air as he looked down to the street below. The men he had ordered to hold the bottom step were gone, swallowed up by the relentless horde. Yagars were rushing up the wide staircase of white marble, cutting down more Spartans as they went. Of all the Spartiates, only a handful of his personal guard remained.

"Hurry!" he hollered down at his remaining men before turning away.

On watery legs and with a hand pressed to his chest, he followed Sola and staggered through the open doors. Inside the huge entrance hall were Ockos, Ackadus, and some members of their court, all standing along the back wall.

Seeing this, Kaletor stopped up and said to Sola, "We need to barricade ourselves in."

She snapped her golden eyes to him. "But we'll be trapped—"

"Not if we escape out the back before the yagars get around behind the palace. While they try to break in, we'll have time to get away."

She must have realized the truth of what he said. Without another word, she rushed over to a low bench beside the yawning doors and picked it up.

He shifted his attention to the Spartiates and hoplites who had ascended the stairs and were rushing across the platform towards him. "Seal the door!" he bellowed at those nearby.

He moved beyond the doorway, allowing his remaining Spartiates and a few hoplites to run inside.

"Turn and face!" he shouted to the rest as they approached. "Form phalanx and hold them off until the doors are sealed!"

A couple disregarded the order and ran inside, but the rest slowed and came together, facing out and overlapping their shields. Those still coming saw the forming phalanx and hurried to add their shields to the formation.

A solid line formed about twenty-five paces in front of the palace doors, and none too soon. Several yagars had also gained the top stair and were already sprinting across the platform. Watching them cut down those hoplites too tired or slow to make it to the line, Kaletor grit his teeth and moved to fight with the phalanx.

But even as he took a step, he remembered that only he could save the Empire.

He bared his teeth in a vicious snarl and called out, "Fight for your lives, men! Fight for Sparta!"

With their answering roars ringing and the yagars charging towards imminent impact, Kaletor turned away and rushed back into the palace. Couches, four-foot-high marble pedestals, large paintings, and shields were all choking the doorway.

Once he clambered his way through it all, Kaletor said, "Seal the doors. No one else gets in."

Hoplites hurried across the entrance hall, bringing more items to pile at the door.

Knowing it wouldn't hold for long, Kaletor pointed to his Spartiates. "You five with me."

"What are you doing?"

Kaletor ignored Sola's question. With the five men behind him, he crossed the room and made straight for the emperor. "It's time to go," he growled, his voice echoing up into the high ceiling.

"Where?" Ockos said, standing as if he were nailed to the wall. "There's too many of them and there's nowhere else to go."

"No," Kaletor said, maintaining a brisk pace. "There isn't."

As he finished, he came within four paces and rushed forward. Ockos's eyes bulged. Ackadus moved to intervene. Kaletor drew his arm back, his spear levelled—

Something struck his elbow and sent his thrust high, causing the leaf head to smash into the wall a few inches above Ockos's head.

Kaletor twisted right, glimpsing Sola just as her fist slammed into his temple.

*　　*　　*

"Let's burn it down."

At first, Jarka didn't react to Tavyka's suggestion. He and Vaseus had just climbed the stairs to be told that the surviving Spartans had barricaded themselves inside the palace.

Now standing before the sealed doors and surrounded by hundreds, he asked, "Is the emperor in there?"

"We're not sure," Relyk supplied, standing with them despite a wound in his side and a few on his arms.

"I'm with Tavyka," Alarix chimed in, moving to push against the huge doors. "We've tried to break through, but it won't budge. Better to burn the whole thing down, then search for the emperor's bones."

"It's not that simple."

Jarka glanced over to Vaseus standing at his side. Her shoulders were clenched and her hair was tossed. Still, as she stood among them, her air of confidence was unaffected.

Tavyka asked, "What do you mean?"

"The emperor has yagars imprisoned somewhere in the city," Jarka answered. "We need him to tell us where before he dies. We need to get inside."

Alarix asked the obvious question. "How?"

Jarka looked to the doors, scanning up and down.

After a moment, he said, "We need axes, and something to use as a ram."

Kaletor opened his eyes and there was pain. He squeezed them back shut and brought both hands to his head. A thousand daggers stabbed his temples and forehead. He was sprawled flat on his back, and with teeth clenched, he writhed on the floor.

Eventually, mercifully, it subsided. He relaxed his tensed muscles as he lay there, motionless, chest heaving as he breathed deep.

Gradually, his head became lighter. When he felt it was possible, he eased his eyes open once more.

Three Spartiates were standing around him. Kaletor tilted his head to look at their faces. All wore their helmets and were unknown to him.

"Are you alright, Commander?" the one on the left asked.

Kaletor rolled to his side, put his hands on the floor, and pushed himself into a sitting position. "What happened?"

"The yagar blindsided you. We took her down as fast as we could."

He shifted his gaze away from the men to look around the room. Sola was lying beside him, completely still and face down on the floor. Further away stood four Spartiates and five hoplites, arrayed in a loose line facing the back wall with shields and spears raised. Huddled together were those they guarded, the silken-robed members of the court. At the center was Ockos, his eyes red and cheeks stained with tears.

Reaching a hand out, Kaletor growled, "Get me up."

Fire seared across his chest as a Spartiate pulled him to his feet. He grit his teeth as he looked to the palace's front entrance. Three more Spartiates stood behind the pile of furniture, paintings, and columns that were heaped against the tall doors. He heard nothing coming from the other side.

"How long have we been here?"

"No more than a few minutes, sir."

He closed his eyes. *That's too long. The entire palace will be surrounded.*

"What's your grand plan now, Champion?"

Kaletor knew exactly who called out that sarcastic question. He stepped over Sola's body and strode towards the back wall.

"Don't test me, Ackadus," he snapped, passing through a gap between two Spartiates to stand before the group.

The pompous brat was next to his father, his mouth bleeding and a swell bulging around his left eye. "This was always how it was going to end," he scoffed, his pointed chin jutting out. "Sparta is conquered, and the Empire is no more. This is all because of you—"

"Silence," Ockos shrieked, the word coming out as a ragged sound that echoed across the room. "Or do you too want to die?"

Kaletor met the teenager's glare, daring him to react. The prince shook his head and looked away.

"We need to surrender," Ockos said. "Before they break in and kill us all."

Kaletor clenched his hands into fists, about to shout at the old fool—

But stopped when something started pounding into the doors. He looked over, a curling snarl tugging his upper lip.

Then, as abruptly as it started, the pounding ceased, and a voice called out. "Are you in there, Kaletor? It's Vaseus. Let's talk."

For a moment, he didn't move or react. He glanced back to Ackadus and Ockos.

"If they try anything," he said to his men, "kill them."

He turned away and crossed the room, setting a hand to his chest as he approached the barricaded doors. The throbbing lessened some at the touch.

"It's over, Kaletor," she called out from the other side. "You can't win. Open the doors and lay down your weapons. No one else has to die."

"We are Spartans, *traitor*," he growled back, teeth gnashing. "Spartans never surrender. Or have you forgotten that?"

"You have already proved your honour and courage. It's time for this to end."

He was about to shout back, but suddenly, something hit him like the point of a driving sword. It was that word she used, the word honour. He recalled hearing that it held the highest esteem in the yagar's warrior culture.

And then, there it was—an idea, and maybe, a path to victory.

"I will open the doors on one condition."

She took a moment to answer. "What condition?"

"That your leader faces me in single combat."

"Why?"

"To end this honourably. If I win, your entire army must leave the Empire and never return."

"And if he wins?"

"The emperor will order every Phalanx to disband and every garrison to leave their post. The Empire will be no more. That's what you want, isn't it?"

This time, the silence that followed was much longer. He could hear muffled voices, Vaseus's as well as another's. They spoke in the yagar tongue.

Eventually, the foreign words ended. On the other side of the door, there was the soft brush of footsteps, followed closely by Vaseus's answer. "We accept your terms."

Gritting his teeth in a silent snarl, he said under his breath, "Perhaps now I will finally have a real challenge."

"Keep close together," Jarka called over the scrapes and bangs sounding on the other side of the doors. "But don't bunch up. Make rows three or four wide, then go in one row after another."

Rank upon rank faced him, ready to file through the entrance. Tavyka, Alarix, and Relyk would follow directly behind him, as they should. If it weren't for them, Pythax and Masos, the army never would have broken into the city.

He nodded to them. Despite their wounds, they met his gaze with stern and determined expressions.

"You don't have to do this," Vaseus said at his side.

Before turning, he said, "Remember, do not attack. Watch, stay ready, but do not attack."

With everyone around him nodding their understanding, he faced forward. He let his gaze linger on the tall doors.

Finally, he glanced down to meet her piercing green eyes. "Did you say something, bee?"

Her smile was gentle as she moved to stand closer beside him. "I can force them to come to terms. They have no choice but to accept what we ask for."

"It almost sounds like you think I won't win."

Just as he finished, the doors swung open, the heavy wood groaning on hinges. The gaping entrance was empty, and beyond it stretched a massive room with marble floors. The depths of it were shrouded in shadow.

Jarka leaned over towards her. "Just follow my lead."

She chuckled as they walked inside. Once they crossed the threshold, the Spartans came into view. Their familiar shield wall was formed along the back wall, a single line of ironclad men.

In front of their protruding spears stood one man. His arms hung loose at his sides, a spear in one hand and a shield in the other. Neither he nor the warriors behind him moved or made a sound.

"So that's him," Jarka said, feeling the tension trickle off him as they moved cautiously into the room. "Kaletor."

"Yes. The one responsible for the deaths of thousands."

As the space between them lessened, Jarka saw that the human's short black hair was slick with sweat, and his grey eyes were pits of smouldering rage.

Suddenly, he barked out a few words. Jarka stopped and glanced to Vaseus. "What did he say?"

"That that's close enough," she supplied.

He looked over a shoulder to those behind them.

"Hold here," he called out, his voice ringing off the high, vaulted ceiling. His warriors spread out to either side without going beyond where he and Vaseus stood.

Satisfied, Jarka faced forward, focusing on his opponent once more. "I suppose he looks strong. For a human."

"Don't underestimate him," Vaseus said. "He's been immersed in a world of violence all his life. It's widely believed that he's faster and stronger than any other Spartan."

"Sounds like we have one or two things in common."

Sensing her gaze on him, he glanced over. Seeing that she had that worry knit in her brow, he flashed her a smile. "Am I wrong?"

She released a soft chuckle and shook her head. "Come on. Let's go talk to him first."

He nodded once. "Yes. Let's."

Watching the pair move away from the horde that stretched across the room, Kaletor strode to meet them. The closer they got, the more convinced he was that the yagar was unremarkable. He sported a few wounds and was no bigger than most others. He moved slowly, appearing almost docile. But most telling of all was the casual air about him. His eyes, which were dark brown with amber rings in the middles, were soft and full of light. His face was unburdened, almost careless. There was no threat about him whatsoever.

Kaletor narrowed his eyes as they came together, studying the yagar more intently. His yellow and black fur was full and thick, revealing that he was in his prime. Small, blackened antlers encased his left shoulder. His spear was simple, nothing but a stick of unadorned wood ending with an uneven, stone leaf head.

No matter where he looked, he saw nothing that marked this savage out as impressive.

They stopped ten paces short. "This is Jarka," Vaseus said, "Warlord of all ten yagar Clans. He has agreed to fight—"

"Then why are you talking? Kaletor growled. "Step aside before I cut you down as well."

"Just hold on," she said, holding out her arms. "First we need answers. Where is the emperor?"

"Can't you see him? He's cowering back there with his useless son."

While she craned her neck to look, Kaletor shifted his attention back to the so-called Warlord. Their eyes locked, and again Kaletor saw only amusement there. He tightened his grip on his spear and shield. The itch to attack was barely containable, as if there were a living beast inside him begging to be unleashed.

"One more thing," Vaseus said into the charged silence. "The emperor's female yagars are normally imprisoned in the Kolosaio's dungeons. Where are they?"

At first, Kaletor thought to withhold the answer. But the need to fight was so great that he didn't care if they got what they wanted.

"They're locked up in the dungeon beneath the palace."

Vaseus looked to Jarka and translated the answer. The yagar simply nodded, his amused expression unchanging.

"Enough talk," Kaletor growled, bending at the knee as he brought his spear and shield to bear. "Now we fight."

Apparently satisfied, Vaseus turned aside to go, but then stopped when the yagar spoke in his garbled language.

"What now?" Kaletor snarled.

Vaseus turned back to translate. "He asks if you will be fighting to kill."

Kaletor could almost feel his blood boil. "Of course!"

Again, Vaseus translated. The yagar's response was to smile, revealing the tips of his fangs. He then dropped into some sort of loose fighting stance.

Kaletor needed no other invitation.

"Vaseus," Jarka barked as the raging Spartan suddenly charged. He sprang forward to intercept the spear. On the move, he met the driving thrust with his own spear and deflected it high. His momentum took him straight at Kaletor's shield. The Spartan planted firm and rammed the golden oval out with all his weight. Jarka twisted to sidestep. The shield slammed into the left side of his torso and sent him spinning. He only stayed upright by going with it, stuttering his steps as he twirled.

Coming out of the spin, he kept moving, trying to gain space. Six hurried steps, then a hard pivot. Kaletor was right on him with surprising speed. Jarka whipped his spear out, batting Kaletor's jabbing attack aside while sliding right. Kaletor followed up with a driving, downward strike. Jarka moved with it, sweeping his spear up to deflect the attack wide. In that same motion, Kaletor rushed in to ram his shield forward. Jarka pushed off his left leg to get clear.

The end of this sequence finally allowed him an opening. He swung his spear out horizontal at Kaletor's head. The Spartan ducked under. Jarka moved with the power of the swing, coming around with an even stronger strike. The leaf head slammed into the top edge of Kaletor's shield with a brief burst of sparks. Somehow, the human absorbed it with a snarl and countered with a low driving thrust. Jarka brought his spear down in time to knock the attack away. He countered with a quick jab at Kaletor's right side. Again, the Spartan was fast enough to bring his shield across in time.

The dance went on, wood snapping off wood, stone clanging off iron, as they traded blow for blow. Jarka flowed with it as he countered, attacked, blocked, and moved. There was only the Spartan, his spear and his shield.

It seemed impossible, but he couldn't overwhelm Kaletor with speed or power. Somehow, the human was staying with him.

Jarka deflected a rising thrust up and over, dipped a shoulder low, and wrapped his free arm around the middle of Kaletor's spear. Then he twisted hard, yanking the weapon from the Spartan's grip. Letting it fall to the floor, he swung his spear across. Kaletor got under it, barking a growl as he did. But the move left him exposed. Jarka snapped out a sharp kick that hit Kaletor square in the chest. The Spartan staggered back, gasping for air.

Jarka rushed forward and lanced his spear straight out. Kaletor brought his shield to bear, absorbing the blow with his shoulder behind the disc. Jarka transitioned into a sidewinding swing. Again, the shield was there. Jarka drove right. Kaletor extended to block, but it was a feint. Jarka's spear didn't hit, giving him the chance to snap it back around for the Spartan's exposed right side—

Only to be foiled by the sword Kaletor pulled loose from the scabbard at his hip.

That sequence should have ended it. The block was so impossible that Jarka knew a moment of shocked disbelief.

In that brief instant, the upper hand he had gained disappeared. Kaletor stepped back, pulled his shield tight to his body, and crouched into a ready stance.

Standing slightly removed from the human, Jarka released a harsh exhale.

Well, that was impressive.

Kaletor released a ragged bellow and charged. Jarka jabbed his spear straight at him. The Spartan took it on his shield, stepped, and slashed his sword out. Jarka backpedalled and swung his spear high. When Kaletor deflected this away with his shield, Jarka followed up with two jabs. Again, the Spartan blocked. Jarka tried a feint, but Kaletor didn't bite, using the opening to step in and thrust his sword point straight out. Jarka spun away to get clear. He whipped his spear around, aiming high. Kaletor ducked under—

A thrown spear sailed less than an inch above the Spartan's head and plunged into Jarka. He groaned, his weapon falling from his hand. He looked down and saw that the spear was buried in his chest.

He brought his hands up to take hold of it—

Kaletor watched the yagar fall to the floor, then looked back over his shoulder. Sola had risen enough to get one forearm under her. In the moment that his eyes met hers, she slumped back down and didn't move.

Somebody cried out, a lone sound of pain echoing through the chamber. Kaletor turned back. Vaseus had rushed to the fallen yagar and was kneeling at his side. Tears streamed down her face as she pulled him onto his back.

"Jarka," she cried, "wake up. Open your eyes, Jarka. *Open your eyes!*"

As he looked on, Kaletor's mind started to churn. *That spear was meant for me. I should be dead. But this could work. I can make this work.*

"The fight is over," he said over Vaseus's crying, "and I have won. That means your entire army must leave Sparta and never return."

Vaseus didn't seem to hear him. She was crouched over the yagar, her face close to his, weeping and carrying on.

Kaletor turned to the horde of yagars filling half the room.

"Go on," he barked, advancing towards them and waving them away. "You must leave. Understand? Get out."

They all stood there, motionless, some looking at him, others at their Warlord. They appeared dumbstruck.

"I have won," he barked. "Which means you all must leave. That was the—"

"No!"

Kaletor turned back to Vaseus, who had risen and was advancing on him.

"We're not going anywhere!" she shrieked, her eyes wild and her cheeks wet.

"But that was the deal," he growled, facing her down. "If I won, you must go—"

"But you *didn't* win, did you? You had help, which violates the rules of single combat."

"I didn't want help. I survived, he didn't. Victory is mine—"

"No!"

She turned to the horde and shouted something in their foreign tongue. In response, they all levelled their spears and started advancing.

"Vaseus," he snarled, dropping into a crouch and bringing his shield to bear. "Tell them to stand down."

"Goodbye, Kaletor," she spat. "The Empire dies with you."

"*No!*"

He pivoted hard and jabbed his sword at her face. She dipped under it, drew her sword, and swung up on a diagonal arc. He deflected it off his shield and countered with a high swing. She went under again. He brought his sword over his head and swung straight down. She swung her sword so that it intercepted and deflected his wide. He stepped right and lashed out—

Piercing coldness sliced into his side. He howled and arced back, eyes finding his assailant. A white-furred yagar held on to the other end of the spear that was in his ribs. Its fellow savages flowed around them.

Kaletor ground his teeth, bellowed, and rotated around to attack—

But a blade plunged into his belly before he could.

A deep groan hissed through his lips. Snarling, he turned back around. Vaseus held her sword in both hands as she glared at him, her teeth clenched and breath gusting. Fresh tears fell from her fierce eyes.

Kaletor felt his strength escaping. His legs buckled, and looking her straight in the eye, he sank to his knees. He felt the spear being yanked from his body. As he howled, Vaseus pulled the sword from his gut.

He collapsed back, blood spewing from his mouth when he hit the floor. He heard Vaseus speak, but he didn't understand what she said.

Heat poured from his body. Black dots peppered his vision. He clenched his jaw, trying to fight it off.

But it was too hard. He couldn't stop the darkness.

Jarka heard something. He didn't know what. He was coming out of sleep, although it felt deeper than usual, and it was infused with warmth. It took a long time, but slowly, he came out of it.

He opened his heavy eyes. He was on his back. He couldn't move, which was fine. He didn't want to. Sleep remained very near, and its pull was pleasant.

He let his eyes close—

"Jarka!"

The shout was jarring, and he reopened his eyes. There was Relyk, his face close.

"Hello, old friend," he said, the words coming slowly. "I seem . . . to have fallen."

Relyk didn't reply. There was fear or worry plain in his eyes.

"It's okay," Jarka said with a soft smile. "You hear me? It's . . . okay."

With tears brimming in his eyes, Relyk nodded.

Vaseus appeared on Jarka's other side, opposite Relyk. Her cheeks were wet, and her eyes were puffy.

"Hello, bee," he said. "How are . . . you doing?"

She reached up to set a hand to his cheek. "You know me. I'm fine."

He breathed out a gentle laugh. "Yes. I know you."

A wave of sleep came, and his eyes closed on their own—

"Jarka," Vaseus cried.

Her voice pulled him back, and he opened his eyes.

"We know where your sister is," she said. "Just hold on. We've sent a group to find her. She'll be here soon."

"Jazith," he said, his smile returning. "My dear sister."

Memories of her came into his mind. He closed his eyes again, and it was soothing as he let the world slip away—

"Jarka!"

At first, he had no desire to reply. But eventually, slowly, he reopened his eyes.

"You have to stay awake," Vaseus implored. "Don't you let go. Don't give up on us."

Instead of responding, he looked to Relyk. "She sure is . . . stubborn."

His friend nodded. "That she is."

"You better . . . keep an eye . . . on her. Don't let her get . . . into too much trouble."

"Don't you worry. I'll watch out for her."

It was getting more difficult to stay awake. Fighting through it, he held Relyk's gaze for a long moment.

Eventually, he looked back to Vaseus. "Tell me," he said to her, "aren't you glad that . . . you followed my lead?"

She laughed, even as tears spilled onto her cheeks. She reached a hand up to cup his face. "Yes, my love," she said, her voice soft. "You helped me save the world. You were the only one who could."

He looked into her eyes, her perfect, green eyes, and smiled. She met his gaze, and despite her tears, smiled back.

Thank you for your love, Vaseus. Thank you so much.

He didn't say it out loud. He knew he didn't have to.

Movement behind her drew his attention. A group of yagars had entered the room, and one among them caught his eye.

Jazith!

He tried to say her name, but nothing came out. It didn't matter though. He saw her, and he knew peace.

The darkness closed in. He allowed it to come.

Vaseus stood and staggered away, bringing a hand up to cover her mouth. Most yagars had knelt or sat down all around Jarka, their collective attention fixed on him. A few wept, but most looked on in silence.

She wanted to run. She wanted to leave it all behind.

She stumbled as she tried to get away—

A wail split the air, a wretched sound of absolute pain. The anguish in that sound ripped violently into Vaseus. Her legs gave and she fell to the floor.

The yagar who could only be Jazith wailed again, and this time, something snapped inside Vaseus. She felt it all, tearing through her, ripping her apart. There was nowhere to run. There was no escape.

All at once, the pain exploded within her, and she screamed. She squeezed her eyes shut as the scream ended, her chest seized up so tight she couldn't breathe. She curled into a ball, her fingers contorting.

When the next breath finally came, she sobbed uncontrollably. Her entire body shook as she wept, tears flooding from her eyes.

As the agony consumed her, she brought her arms over her head to cover her face. Her chest heaved and her lungs burned.

There was no end to it. And there was no escape.

SIXTY-FOUR

Some fear the end of things, and rightfully so.
But if nothing ended, nothing new could begin.

Eurydemos of Corinth

Why am I not dead?

It was the question that had gone through his mind over and over since he had woken up the day before.

Without warning, fire seared through his torso. He wrapped his arms around himself, growling and spitting as he rode it out.

Finally, the pain subsided some, and he sprawled flat across the floor. He looked down at his bandaged belly. Not for the first time, he considered ripping through it so he could bleed to death.

"Kaletor."

He recognized that voice. He turned his head to see Vaseus standing on the other side of the bars, illuminated by the orange torchlight.

"You," he rasped, rolling onto his side. "What have you done? Why am I still alive?"

Her gaze was steady as she looked at him. "I had your wounds stitched closed before you could bleed out on the floor. It sounds like you haven't yet figured out why."

He clenched his teeth tight and managed to stand, despite the agony that cut straight through him. "Don't play with me, Vaseus," he snarled. "Just tell me why."

"It's quite simple—revenge. I want you to suffer for what you've done. I want you to rot in prison and experience a living nightmare before you die."

"You can't keep me locked up here forever," he said, holding his sides as he gingerly stepped towards her. "All of Sparta worships me. Someone will break me out the first chance they get."

She shook her head. "No, Kaletor. You're never leaving this cell. No one's coming for you."

"You're wrong. The people will rise up—"

"I should have known you would turn out like this," she interrupted. "Even then, I could see the darkness in you, and the violence. But I never imagined my best friend could ever be capable of doing such horrible things."

Kaletor blinked, unsure how to reply. His wounds were already starting to throb, and he felt lightheaded.

"What did you expect?" he eventually growled. "You left and never came back. You didn't care what was going to happen to me."

"Of course I did. I wanted to come back for you. But I was young and afraid. After what happened, I didn't know if you'd even come with me."

"You left me behind," he growled, stepping right up to the iron bars. "Don't play the fool. You knew exactly what would happen to me if I stayed in Sparta, and you still walked away. You did nothing."

She stood her ground and looked him straight in the eye. "For a long time, I felt guilty about leaving you. But at some point, I realized I wasn't responsible for your life. You turned into a monster, Kaletor. Nothing I could have done would have changed that."

"Enough. Where are my men? And where's Ockos?"

"Your men are dead and the emperor has surrendered. Finally, you will pay for everything you've done."

Nausea was pooling in his belly, and he had broken out in a cold sweat. "Vaseus—"

"Ockos formally agreed to all of our terms," she cut in. "Every Spartan garrison across the Empire has been ordered to leave their post. The Phalanxes are being disarmed and disbanded. All government officials are being dismissed. The emperor relinquished his throne and no one is taking his place. From now on, Sparta will be ruled by us—"

"No!" Kaletor bellowed, his head swimming. "You're lying. Ockos would never agree to such terms."

"Whether you believe it or not changes nothing. Your precious Empire is no more. All your fame is nothing more than smoke on the wind. Your triumphs are dust. You have no power anymore, and everything you ever did was for nothing—"

He roared and punched at her face. His knuckles bounced off the iron bars, and his stitched wounds spit sparks through his torso. The pain was excruciating, and he fell to his knees.

Vaseus hadn't flinched. She stood there, looking down at him for a long time. She seemed to be drinking in his suffering. Her eyes were filled with anger and hate.

Eventually, and without another word, she turned on her heels and walked away.

Kaletor was holding onto his sides as he gasped for each breath. Watching her go, he gathered his voice and bellowed, "Vaseus! Vaseus! *Vaseus!*"

She didn't answer or turn back. Before long, she disappeared.

Consumed by the pain and rage, he roared again.

"I'll make you pay for this, Vaseus. One day, I'll *make you pay!*"

* * *

Vaseus stepped outside and saw Relyk across the street. As he approached, she looked up. The sky was clear blue, and the sun was warm on her skin.

"So, what now?"

She brought her gaze back down. When their eyes met, she knew exactly what he meant.

What do we do without him? How do we make this work?

The answer came swiftly. *I don't know. I miss you, my love. So much.*

It was a moment before she could get the words out, words she hoped would somehow keep her going.

"Now, we free everyone."

ABOUT THE AUTHOR

Hamilton Baker is a small-town librarian, and this is his debut novel. His short story BLOOD AND HONOUR was selected to be published in the 2016 edition of *Shoreline,* a compilation of Canadian literature from Polar Expressions Publishing.

Hamilton is a lifelong ancient history nerd (with a tattoo to prove it), and has travelled to both Italy and Greece to walk the paths of his characters. He lives in Ontario along the shores of Lake Huron and spends his summers bicycling around town with his wife and playing soccer with his friends.

CONNECT WITH ME

Thank you so much for reading IRON SCARS!

If you enjoyed it and have time, I would sincerely appreciate a short review or rating on Amazon, Goodreads, or other retailer sites. This is my debut novel, so reviews and ratings can go a long way in helping others discover the book who may also enjoy it.

To connect with me and learn more about the world of IRON SCARS, please visit these sites:

Website : https://www.authorhamiltonbaker.com
Facebook : https://www.facebook.com/authorhamiltonbaker
Instagram : https://www.instagram.com/authorhamiltonbaker
Amazon : https://www.amazon.com/author/hamiltonbaker
Goodreads : https://www.goodreads.com/book/show/1986057 50-iron-scars

Stay tuned for what might come next . . .